Praise f

...ERIES

'**Fu** ... m about a you ... ead Ayisha Ma

... nny Colgan

'Fu

... McFarlane

'A ... rtant book. **Ge**

... Jnexpected ... Mr Chopra

'Th ... erefore, you are

... Y Magazine

'Th ... us romantic is **s** ... d will reso- nat

... d Magazine

'A l ... r . . . It's an ent ... ntemporary lov

... s Magazine

‘**Laugh-out-loud funny from the off**, this witty, unapologetic, honest, fun and feisty tale fully deserves the buzz it’s been getting. We can’t wait for the inevitable film to follow.’

Heat Magazine

‘Fans of *Bridget Jones* certainly won’t be disappointed, since Malik achieves **the perfect balance of romance and humour**.’

The Independent

‘**Move over Bridget Jones** – there’s a new heroine charting her romantic disasters – this time minus the Chardonnay . . . refreshing and funny.’

Sunday Mirror

‘**Feisty, funny and relatable** it’s the feminist romantic comedy you’ve been waiting for.’

Elle Magazine

‘**Best of the New Books** . . . for fans of *Bridget Jones’s Diary*.’

Grazia

‘**Must-read** . . . Liven up your daily commute or boost your bed-time routine with [this] page-turner.’

Marie Claire

‘Most refreshing of all, Sofia doesn’t need to undergo some sort of wild identity crisis before she gets her happy ending . . . [a] **sharp, funny but ultimately very normal portrayal of life as a British Muslim**.’

The National

The OTHER HALF of HAPPINESS

Ayisha is a British Muslim, lifelong Londoner, and lover of books. She read English Literature and went on to complete an MA in Creative Writing (though told most of her family it was an MA in English Literature – Creative Writing is not a subject, after all.) She has spent various spells teaching, photocopying, volunteering, editing and being a publicist.

Also by Ayisha Malik

Sofia Khan is Not Obliged

The OTHER HALF of HAPPINESS

Ayisha Malik

ZAFFRE

First published in Great Britain in 2017 by
ZAFFRE PUBLISHING
80–81 Wimpole St, London W1G 9RE
www.zaffrebooks.co.uk

A CIP catalogue record for this book is available from the British Library.

ISBN: 978–1–785–76073–0

Also available as an ebook

1 3 5 7 9 10 8 6 4 2

Typeset by IDSUK (Data Connection) Ltd
Printed and bound by Clays Ltd, St Ives Plc

Zaffre Publishing is an imprint of Bonnier Zaffre, a Bonnier Publishing company
www.bonnierzaffre.co.uk
www.bonnierpublishing.co.uk

For my sister, Nadia, whose dreams for me have always been bigger than my own.

DECEMBER 2012

'All's Well That Ends Well' by Yes, I'm Muslim, Please Get Over It

On www.[illegible].co.uk

Reader, I married him. But there was no band of Punjabis, jacked up on [illegible]. We had one imam and two witnesses [illegible] and [illegible] Karachi, saying [illegible] (blessed by the [illegible] enter into marriage [illegible]).

We [illegible] leading to the mosque [illegible] at me [illegible] my parents [illegible] his eyes flickered towards [illegible] to be husband. I gave him the most pathetic [illegible] and [illegible] at me [illegible] and understand [illegible] distinguish between [illegible].

[illegible] side of his face in [illegible]

[illegible] turned to speak [illegible]

[illegible] toward my voice. Look at [illegible] necessary beads and tension.

[illegible] at the imam. Especially when he smiles [illegible] I was confident [illegible] of circumstance and experience," said [illegible] if he wasn't

'All's Well That Ends Well' by Yes, I'm Muslim, Please Get Over It

On www.sofiasblog.co.uk

Reader, I married him. But there was no band of Punjabis, jacked up on lassi. We had one imam and two witnesses listen to me and Conall in Tooba Mosque, Karachi, saying 'I do' three times (because by the third time you might've changed your mind).

We padded down the white marble floors leading to the mosque's entrance and took off our shoes. Imam frowned at me, asking where my parents were, as his eyes flickered towards my Irish soon-to-be-husband. I gave him the most pathetic look possible and said in Urdu, Conall squinting at me to try and understand, 'Islam doesn't distinguish between colours.'

'*Sofe* . . .' whispered Conall from the side of his mouth. 'Whatever you're saying . . .'

'He's a hypocrite,' I said as the imam turned to speak to our witnesses.

Witness One shot me a look. I lowered my voice. 'Look at him – holding on to his rosary beads and racism.'

Conall smiled at the imam. Generally, when he smiles he means it and maybe the authenticity of it was confusing.

'We're a product of circumstance and experience,' said Conall to me. (He'd be a philosopher if he wasn't a documentary photographer.) 'That's why I'm so understanding when you can't tell the difference between things like the brake and accelerator,' he added.

'Everything's the wrong way round here.'

The imam cleared his throat before he asked me: 'He is Muslim, haina?'

For a moment I wanted to lie and say no – just to annoy him – but that would've been un-Muslim of me.

'Yes. He is.'

Imam asked Conall in English: 'You tell people? "*I am Muslim. I believe*"?' He furrowed his dark brows. I resisted the urge to sing 'In a Thing Called Love'.

'Sorry?' said Conall.

'You believe what we believe?' Imam leaned forward. 'Hmmm?'

I rolled my eyes. Conall gave me a sideward glance.

'Imam-sahib,' I said, 'even I don't believe *everything* you believe. Let's just say he believes enough.'

Imam looked at both (Pakistani) witnesses. 'Nowadays girls answer for their husbands.'

I yawned. Conall nudged me.

'He's not my husband yet, so if you could hurry this along.'

'Beta, these things shouldn't be rushed. You must think if the person you are marrying will bring you closer to Allah.' He looked at Conall again.

But I'd already waited *so* long. Yes, my family wasn't here, and yes, I hadn't told anyone, but being in my thirties should have some benefit: like making my own decisions.

'Beta,' said Imam, his tone softening. Conall by this time was speaking to our witnesses. 'We know in Islam there is no black, white, green, blue. This would be wrong. But people aren't as forgiving as Allah. There is a reason they say you should marry what you know. Do you *know* him?'

I wish I could say I took a Conall-like moment here: absorbing the weight of these words because they might shape my future. What I wanted to say was that I'd listened in the morning to a London-based sheikh on YouTube talking about the importance of interracial marriages in promoting unity. But I wasn't in London any more. I was in Karachi.

'Marriage is a gamble,' said Imam, which wasn't the most appropriate metaphor given we were in a mosque. 'But at least with a Pakistani, you will understand how to play the hand you are given.'

'Imam-sahib, I'm not here to play anything,' I said. 'I'm here to marry the man Allah has chosen for me.'

Sofia Khan is author of *Lessons in Heartbreak and Laughter,* Ignite Press, to be published in April, 2013. Follow her on Twitter @SofiaAuthor.

JANUARY 2013

The Lie of the Land

Tuesday 1 January

10 a.m. Oh my *actual* God. There's a man in my bed! A real-life *man.* I prodded Conall to make sure he wasn't a figment of my overactive imagination. Then, sitting up in bed, I pinched myself in case I was dreaming – because these things can happen, and better to find out sooner rather than later. That's when I caught a glimpse of my red pants flung over the fan on the ceiling, right next to my red hijab. (Doesn't matter that I'm living in Karachi squalor; colour coordination is very important.) Would it be inappropriate to Instagram that?

Note to self: Must not become person who pretends their life is perfect via the medium of social media.

I really *did* get on a plane four months ago with Conall to come to Karachi, and last month I really *did* marry him.

To Suj, Foz, Hannah: What should I *do* with him?

From Hannah: Lucky for you I'm up for morning prayers to tell you that if he's asleep I wouldn't do anything. Unless you want to be charged with assault.

Hannah always makes very good points.

From Suj: Jump him! Early start to gym. Sofe, get some exercise in too. Haha xxxx

From Foz: For God's sake. Wake him up. Doesn't he know you need to make up for lost time? If I wasn't on a break from men I'd elope with one of the hot South Americans here. Can't believe you got married without us. Though at least you don't have to worry about table settings xx

As do Suj and Foz.

'The pinging from your phone's going to be the end of me,' said Conall, putting his arm round me and drawing me closer.

He opened his eyes. I imagine the blurry ceiling was materialising as he squinted at the fan.

'Christ – are those your pants?'

'You really should stop taking the Lord's name in vain,' I said.

He looked at me, amused, as he brushed the hair away from my eyes. 'Old habits.'

There are times, as a practising Muslim woman, you have to take stock of your life – having a man in your bed for the first time would be one of them. No one really prepares you for it: having to weave this much happiness with this much fear of what could go wrong. If I hadn't married Conall ASAP, then A) the film *The 40-Year-Old Virgin* would be plaguing my every still-unmarried day and B) maybe I'd have booked the next plane home and sat in my room for the rest of my life, swiping left or right on Tinder instead of having to *feel* all these things.

From Suj: BTW Han, see you tonight. Foz, bring a hottie back with you. Everyone being in different countries is a joke. When the hell are you both coming home? xxxxxx

I felt a sudden pang and shook Conall's arm.

'Hmm?'

'Suj and Hannah are meeting tonight.'

'Mm,' he replied.

'I wonder where they're going.'

Silence. If home is where the heart is then why does mine constantly flit towards London happenings?

'Do you think they've made a booking? Han will have done. I'll message Suj to make sure she's not late.'

'OK.'

I waited for a little more input.

'You don't care, do you?'

'About Hannah and Suj's dinner plans?' he replied.

'You could *pretend* to be interested,' I said.

He opened his eyes and pulled me closer. 'Were you this annoying before we got married?'

'No. I saved this part especially.'

Billy, our adopted cat, popped her ginger-and-white head out of the bathroom door and meandered over. I took a biscuit out of the drawer for her. Does Conall actually find me annoying? I'd probably find me annoying if I were married to me. I looked round the room with its flaking paint and grimy curtains – the lonely desk in the corner, which is meant to be a work area but instead only reminds me that I have no work. If I've decided to live in this cesspit, it must be love. More's the pity. Anyway, I did my Isktikhara before marrying him – that foolproof prayer which, once you've decided to do something, makes your path easy if it's good for you, and difficult if it's bad for you. That moment, when we sat in the mosque, there was nothing but ease. (Apart from the imam's negativity, of course.

But negativity is not a sign. I think.) And it wasn't just because one day I might be asked to take part in a documentary about *real-life* forty-year-old virgins.

'Do you think Mum's forgiven me?'

'Since yesterday?' he asked, eyes closed again.

'What other ways can I say sorry? Maybe a card?'

Her face swims in front of me every time I think about it. She'd waited thirty years for me to get married and then I went and did it without her, not six months after Dad died. I'm such a brown disappointment. Waves of guilt slosh around my stomach: the natural conclusion to an unnatural wedding.

'She'll come round,' said Conall.

I could only imagine Dad's disappointment if he were alive: the peering over the glasses; the shaking of the head. It made me want to slink back under my covers. I looked up to tell Dad I was sorry, except it didn't seem appropriate when I caught sight of my knickers. Plus, they only served as a reminder that it wasn't an *I'd-change-things-if-I-could* sorry. My guilt swelled into the size of a hernia.

'You're a grown-up, Sofe. Well, most of the time –'

I hit Conall with my pillow but looked at his face, which manages to be, by turns, both grumpy and kind.

'Just when I think you're a bit brown you go and say something so *white*,' I said.

'I didn't know being a grown-up was race-dependent,' he replied.

'Look at me, Conall,' I said, pointing to my face. 'I'm a Paki – oh, bloody hell,' I added as he shot me an unimpressed look. '*Pakistani*.'

'No, please, carry on perpetuating racial slurs.'

Typical – as if the guilt hernia wasn't bloated enough.

'The point is, there are certain things a Pakistani daughter shouldn't do – one of them is to marry outside her race. Fucked up royally there, didn't I?'

'What are the rules on Pakistani daughters swearing?' he asked.

'*Secondly*, if she does decide to jump racial ships, then to at least do it in *front* of the community. That way they can gossip about it at her wedding, behind her back, like normal people.'

He put his hand behind his head and stared at the ceiling. Did he regret it? Was he wondering how to use my hijab to strangle me? Or even strangle himself? Was he having converter's remorse?

'No point dwelling on it,' he replied.

'Yes, thanks. That hadn't occurred to me.'

He turned towards me. 'Go back to sleep, Sofe,' he replied, pulling the covers over me. 'I love you when you're asleep.'

I laughed as Billy nibbled at the biscuit. The beeping of car horns, as usual, hadn't stopped all night, and were now accompanied by the bleating of sheep – all lined up, naturally, outside our block of flats.

'It's like *Dante's Inferno* meets *Animal Farm*,' I said.

I miss the small things: hot water; being able to scroll through Twitter without gasping for Wi-Fi. A cockroach skirmished in the corner. *Vom*. It says something about my personal growth that I didn't actually vom. I picked up my slipper to kill it when Conall grabbed my arm and pulled me back under the covers.

'Be useful for once and keep me warm,' he said, sliding his hand on to my bum. 'Aren't you cold without your pants?'

'What do you mean, "for once"?' I said, wrapping my arm around his. 'I've opened your eyes to a new way of life. Before me you were all sullen and now look . . .' I sighed. '*Before Sofia*. You can call it BS. As in, that's what life used to be.'

Although, when I open my eyes, I'm not sure I haven't converted to *his* way of life. His breath tickled the back of my neck as he laughed.

'Shut the fuck up.'

I enveloped the blanket around us to block out the Karachi cold – and my negative thoughts – when there was a knock on the door.

'Come in,' said Conall, which begs the question: doesn't he think a person should get dressed before you let someone into your bedroom?

The door creaked open and there she was, peering into the room with her darty eyes and long limbs, already kitted out for the day. How I've ended up sharing a house with this woman, along with a documentary film crew, in the middle of the worst parts of Karachi, rather than the huge, marble-floored, multi-storeyed houses that my dad's side of the family live in I'll never know. Well, I do know: Conall. I looked at Hamida, who lowered her gaze. She's readiness personified. I wonder whether this is one of the reasons she was so unperturbed when her husband – who we're never allowed to mention – left her.

'Oh, sorry. Con, I thought you'd be ready.'

I hate it when she calls him Con.

'We can talk later,' she said.

She glanced up at my hijab and knickers. I told myself to be reasonable. You can't dislike a person when they've not technically done anything wrong. It must be the unnatural pressures of being married and living as if in a commune: not the way her gaze flickers between me and Conall, the odd time I catch her staring at me or the way she never laughs at *anything* I say. I thought Conall was tough to break.

'No, it's fine,' said Conall, pinching my bum as he got out of bed.

I smiled at her. Hammy didn't return the favour. She glanced at the ceiling once more before they left the room to talk about their film documentary. I lay in bed and stared at the ceiling too. *Purpose*. That's the thing. Although I'd envy them both a little more if their purpose didn't include filming in a slum. This was depressing because the idea of coming here with Conall for some charitable reason was great in theory, but not quite so fulfilling in practice. This is why you should never attach yourself to another person's purpose. As a thirty-one-year-old, relatively independent, emotionally self-sufficient woman, I should've been wise enough to know this.

'But that,' I said, picking up Billy, 'is what makes this love malarkey so tricky.'

I put her back down and looked at my phone. Wi-Fi had gone again.

'Why does nothing work here?' I said, shaking the phone.

'Talking to yourself again?' Conall was standing over me, hands on his hips.

'Lamenting. To Billy,' I replied.

He looked around for Billy, who'd disappeared. Much like my sanity.

'Most couples have a few good years before lamenting,' he said, sitting next to me.

I tugged on his black beard, flecked with more grey than a few months ago. Is this life's doing or mine? I do love his beard, and not just because it sets off the unusual blue of his eyes (although it's a pleasing by-product) but because it's homage to his Muslim-ness.

Note to self: Give money to charity as thanks for fact that I get to sleep with my next-door neighbour, turned friend, turned Muslim husband.

Then he gave me this look. A serious one. Well, a sexy serious look, so I wasn't sure whether he wanted to have a shag or give me a lecture.

'*I'm ready*,' came Hammy's voice.

'Think of the shitty Wi-Fi as a social media detox,' he said.

'Hmm,' I replied, thinking about this. 'Maybe then I could blog about it?'

'You do know that there are people who live without proper food?'

Of course he's right. That's the problem when you haven't been to Afghanistan or Sudan and God knows where else – wanting things like hot water and electricity sounds unreasonable. Turns out a person can suffer from all kinds of dependencies.

'Yes. *Obviously*,' I said. 'Heating might be useful, though. Sleeping in twelve items of clothing is boring.'

'Oh, really?' He slipped his hand back round my waist when there was another knock at the door.

'*How long will you be?*' called Hamida.

'He's coming!' I shouted, giving Conall a semi-remorseful smile for my loudness.

'God, you have a big mouth,' he said.

'Isn't that why you married me?'

He leaned in and considered me for a moment. 'It was the only way to get you to sleep with me.'

I laughed. Stupid sod. 'Here, have a biscuit.'

I took one out of the drawer and it would've been the perfect time to put my hands down his pants when we heard: '*Feroza will be waiting for us*.'

Taking a deep breath, I looked at him. 'We could still go and live with Chachi,' I said. 'Just for a bit more privacy. And, you know, electricity.'

'I'm not living in comfort while the rest of the team have to stay here,' he said as he began searching for his 35 mm lens.

'How do you cope with such an excess of morality?' I asked.

He looked up and stared at me.

'Don't worry, I get it. *The team*. Speaking of,' I added, trying not to get distracted by his bare chest. 'Better go before team leader has a coronary.'

Bit inconvenient to have sex right now anyway. Why did no one warn me about having to shower (including washing your cascade of hair) *every* time you have a shag? Obviously I *knew* the Muslim rules, but try spontaneity when you live in a hovel where the water's always cold. He looked down at me and rubbed the back of his neck.

'When we get home we need to have a talk,' he said.

There was that serious look again. My heart skipped a beat. Nothing good ever comes from someone saying those words. Was it regret? Was it finally here?

'About what?'

'Just . . . things.' He gulped down his glass of water.

'FYI – you should never make someone wait a whole day to find out what "*Things*" means.' I used air quotes because they annoy him.

'You could do with a bit of patience,' he said. 'And I know you're trying to annoy me,' he added, pointing his finger at me.

I laughed. 'I hope your water's not boiled and you get the runs.'

'Might be worth it seeing as you'd have to nurse me better,' he said. He stared at me for a while and the fluttering of mad creatures in my stomach prevented a smart retort.

'Weren't you looking for something?' I asked.

He paused. 'Right. Yes. What was it?"

'Your lens. In the drawer,' I told him.

Why wasn't I repulsed at the idea of looking after him, runs and all? What has happened to me?

'*Conall . . .*' came Hammy's voice, which I think I had the capacity to throttle, so at least not all my natural instincts were dead.

'Before you go, mind if you hand me my hijab and pants?' I said, looking up at the fan.

He stood on the bed and picked the items off the fan.

'Your highness,' he said, handing them over and kissing me. The long type of kiss. The kind that – forget home – makes me forget my hijab and pants.

I'll stop complaining about where we're living. It's not that bad. Well, it *is*, but then being in an adult relationship is also about compromise: weighing up the pros and cons, and if Conall got fed up with all my moaning and told me to leg it, that would definitely be a con.

'Thanks, husband,' I said, smiling.

Just then, Billy sprang up on the desk and deposited a dead mouse on the table.

God, I'm a Londoner, get me out of here.

1.40 p.m. My God! Was cleaning the flat when out of nowhere I heard a huge crash, so violent it seemed as if the walls were shaking. Jawad, the servant, rushed into the room a few seconds later.

'What was that?' I said.

'Wait here,' he replied.

I couldn't just wait! I ran up to the rooftop. Plumes of smoke rose from not too far away. The noise of sirens blared as people flooded out of their homes. A bombing. I turned round as the door flung open and Jawad was standing there.

'Baji, I told you to stay there. Conall-sahib has told me to look after you when he's not here.'

'Where is he?'

I went to run down the stairs but Jawad stopped me as he got his phone out and called him. It took several rings before someone answered. I closed my eyes in relief as Jawad handed the phone to me.

'I'm OK, Sofe. I'm OK.'

2.55 p.m.

> **From Katie:** Are you all right?? Let us know you're safe. Love you xxx

2.56 p.m.

> **From Hannah:** Your penchant for dramatics just because you're now a writer is ridiculous. All limbs intact? Xx

2.57 p.m.

> **From Suj:** Toffeeeeee! Come home! Twenty-eight people dead. So sad. My old man says the world's ending. Thanks, Dad. Miss you. FaceTime later xxxxxxx

3.25 p.m. 'Oh, thank God,' said Maria as I picked up her Skype call. '*Mum, she's OK*.'

'Would she have forgiven me if I were dead?' I asked, closing the bedroom door behind me. Everyone was sitting in the living room with their head in their hands.

'*Don't* go out,' she said. 'Tell Conall to stay indoors too. Foreigners get kidnapped all the time.'

'Hai hai!' came Mum's voice before her frowning face came into view. 'Forty years ago your baba moved to London for a better life and you're back where he started. Conall's mama, baba don't say anything? But they are *goray*. White people don't think of these things like us.'

'*Mum*,' I said, tears surfacing.

Despite her racism (and tendency towards run-on sentences) all I wanted was to hug her. It's this place. Everything feels on the verge of collapse and I'm made for sturdier foundations. Mum looked at me, her eyes softening. Then she seemed to remember what I'd done and disappeared as swiftly as she'd emerged.

'Sorry,' said Maars.

She lifted my nephew up to the screen who made a wild attempt to grab her iPad. 'Say hello to Khala, Adam. Doesn't she look like someone who's having a lot of sex, despite all the bombs?'

'*Maars*,' I said, feeling smug and mortified in equal measure.

'Don't be such a prude.'

'When will Mum start speaking to me?' I asked.

'Right now she's just crying about the Karachi madness. Says she doesn't want you to end up a widow like her,' said Maars.

'Oh God – she needs to stop watching Bollywood.'

Although the fact that she didn't want Conall dead was a good sign. The thought of Conall and co. driving back at the time the bomb went off punctured my denial that we were safe. Anxiety enveloped my stomach.

'Sofe, you *eloped*. And Mum's not been feeling well. Has this cough she can't seem to shift.'

'What's wrong with her? Has she been to the doctor? It's not pneumonia, is it? Or TB?'

What if something happened to her while we were estranged? How would I live with myself? I had to take a deep breath. It's not how short life is sometimes, but how shocking its end can be.

'Calm down. She's fine. It's *people*. Coming over and filling her head with ideas,' she added. 'Running away –'

'I didn't *run* –'

'Getting married, without telling anyone –'

'It was spur of the moment –'

'Not coming back to see us . . .'

Did these grievances come from Mum or Maars? The guilt hernia was ready to explode.

'It was all very quick.' She leaned into the screen, her eyes looking bigger than usual. 'I mean, how well do you actually know him?'

'It's *Conall*.'

She raised her eyebrows. 'Yeah, but who's his family?'

'I didn't realise we were living in a Regency novel.'

'You can tell a lot about a person from their family,' she said.

'I hope not,' I replied as she stuck her finger up at me.

She handed Adam a rusk and added: 'You never just marry one person. You marry their whole family.'

Pffft. No one knows this better than Conall. Poor man. But to be honest, I've tried not to think about his parents. Mum's silence manages to speak a thousand run-on sentences about how she sees our marriage, but has Conall even told his mum and dad? Has his brother, Sean, told them? Sean, who seems to have an absolutely fine relationship with the parents. Every time I bring the subject up with Conall he starts brooding around the house. Something about the rigidity of his movement, the shadow that passes over his face prevents me from pushing the matter. (This, I realise, reflects poorly on my sense of personal resolve.)

'Maybe . . .' Maars began. 'I don't know. Maybe you and Conall should come home? You've been away long enough. Then there's Mum.'

God, I missed London, but I tried not to think about leaving here because Conall won't want to go until the project's finished.

'Well?' said Maars. Before she could say anything else the screen went black as the electricity went out, leaving us – literally and metaphorically – in the dark.

Wednesday 2 January

5.25 a.m. Conall and I didn't sleep very well. By the time I did nod off he pulled me out of bed for morning prayers, practically carrying me to the bathroom to make pre-prayer ablutions. I think it was the first time that he prayed extra while I crawled back into bed.

I'd told him last night what Mum said about me becoming a widow.

He grabbed my hands and pulled me into his lap. 'Complicated woman, your mother. Considering.'

I put my arms round him. 'Not many people can understand voluntary madness.'

I wanted to add: *why haven't your parents called you to ask if you're OK*? Billy sat watching both of us.

'People live in this city, safe enough, every day,' he said.

'Because they don't have a choice. Not because they're making a documentary about slums, building shelters, saving the world,' I said. 'Yes, I know, well done on all the philanthropy but there are plenty of homeless people in London.'

He looked at me. 'I'm not leaving until the job's done. This is important.'

For a moment I wanted to say: *more important than your wife*, and had to resist the urge to get up and throw a biscuit at him. That would've looked a bit stupid, though. It's my own fault really. His obsession with being useful to people is one of the reasons I'm here. No one can say idealism isn't catching. Ever since my chat with Maars, though, I just wish it could be catching in London.

'Don't you miss home?' I asked.

'No,' he said. And then he shifted me on to the bed and looked at me so seriously that home became a misty thought against the solid lines of Conall. 'Not with you around.'

I closed my eyes again, vaguely remembering that he'd wanted to talk about something yesterday, before I fell asleep with the image of him sitting on the prayer mat, looking into the distance.

Friday 4 January

12.20 p.m. Outside the netted windows I saw two guards with Kalashnikovs, pacing the street. People call London frantic but at least it's frantic without the fanatics. Well, mostly. Conall and co. went back to the slums like the heroes that they are. As if my fears of him being shot, kidnapped, run over or mauled by a dog aren't rampant enough.

Psychology #101: the death of a parent leads to the conviction in a domino effect of death. Keep having dreams of Mum sailing away in a ship. I'll just do some reading, a lot of praying and not wonder about the fact that the highlight of my day is going to be a Skype meeting with my publisher/ex-colleagues.

3.55 p.m. I paced round the spacious, mangy flat. Couldn't concentrate as I kept thinking about the bombing, Mum, and what Dad would think about my elopement if he were alive. Then there's the whole thing about how long we'll be here. When we first arrived the idea of an unknown return date felt exciting. I was being spontaneous, which is all the rage nowadays. But what comes after spontaneity? When I'm in the house alone, while everyone's out saving the world, I wonder what my life outside of Conall means. Billy meandered over as I wiped the glass table, ready to bleach the floors, as Foz Skyped.

'Oh my God, was there a bomb?' she exclaimed. 'When, where, how? What day is it, by the way?'

As her face came into focus I noticed the beach, spanning out behind her, and the sea that seemed to go on forever.

'Why am I in a hole and you're on a beach?'

She smiled as she adjusted her floppy hat and took a sip from an iced tea. 'I'm on my balcony. Like the view?'

'I'll see your beach and raise you a cat and doodh-patthi. Like it?' I asked, showing her Billy and my mug of milky tea.

'No, it's awful. Just wanted to make sure you're OK. You're mostly at home, aren't you?'

'Like a regular nineteen-fifties housewife,' I replied.

'What do you *do* all day?' she asked.

I tried to think of ways to make reading and cleaning sound interesting but noticed the hint of a frown behind her huge sunglasses.

'Oh shit, I have to go,' she said. 'I have a surfing lesson.'

'Bankers don't surf,' I told her.

'*Ex*-banker, darling. Well, on-a-break banker.'

She blew me a kiss and told me not to leave the house unless the building was burning.

5.30 p.m. 'Hello? Sofia, ca– you he– me?'

Brammers' pixie-like face blurred as I held my iPad outside the bedroom window.

'Gosh, is that sheep I can hear?' she asked.

I perched on the sill, gripping the iPad in case it fell into a mass of sheep's poo. 'Yes.'

Brammers' face froze as her finger made its way towards her head. There are certain things I didn't realise I'd miss when I left London but my ex-boss's habit of sniffing her scalp after she'd scratched it wasn't one.

'How . . . interesting. Is this Conall's choice or yours?'

Apparently, there's something about a white man converting, getting a beard and going to Pakistan for a long period of time that doesn't sit well with people.

'Ah! Sakeeb and Katie are here.'

Sakeeb? Who's Sakeeb? Does she mean *Sakib*? In which case, is there another brown person in publishing? Brammers swivelled her screen as Katie's face came into view.

'Sweetu!' I exclaimed. 'Come closer! Let me see your face.'

I took in the narrow features, grey eyes and choppy blonde hair. I almost cried with happiness as Katie smiled back before giving me her 'let's be professionals' look.

Conall says that my enthusiasm for my friends can border on hysterical, but all that tells me is what an emotionally reticent sod he is. As Katie shifted away from the screen the first view I got was of someone's crotch, which is always a little alarming. His face then appeared.

'Sofia,' he said.

'Hi – you're Sakib?'

He smiled, showing a perfect set of white teeth, looking oddly fluorescent against his yellow tie.

'It's good to meet you. Of sorts. Finally,' he said.

'Do you pronounce your name Sakeeb or Sakib?' asked Brammers.

'Either way, doesn't matter,' he replied.

'Sakib,' I said. 'Sakeeb isn't a name.'

'Oh, I'm so sorry,' said Brammers, putting her hand to her chest. 'You should've said.'

He looked embarrassed. Was he a brown apologist? Have I spent too much time with Conall? Although this was a turn-up for the books that Conall would like: a meeting with an equal ratio of brown to white.

'Sakib's here to build our list of diverse authors,' said Brammers. 'He's of Indian descent *and* Muslim. Like you,' she added.

'I'm Pakistani,' I said.

'Ah, yes. Of course.'

Katie looked down at her notepad.

Sakib adjusted his tie as he said: 'We're all very excited about the book coming out. Obviously Katie's doing the pub—'

'– *Dhaniya! Das rupee ki gatthi, dhaniya!*'

God Almighty. As if sheep weren't bad enough I had vegetable-stall man selling coriander for ten rupees a bunch. Worst thing was we actually needed some.

'Could you hold on – two seconds?'

I ran out, bought some coriander for ten times its value – because the guy was old and I was trying to show gratitude via charity (a lot easier to give money than wheel the cart around for him). I rushed past the six transvestites who'd come singing and dancing on to our street.

'Sorry,' I said, unmuting Skype. 'Go on.'

'And we feel that it's an excellent opportunity to –' Brammers stopped short. '*What* is that noise?'

'Transvestites,' I explained. 'Singing outside my window.'

'Right,' said Brammers.

Sakib rested his ankle on his knee, tapping his pen on Brammers' desk.

'I'll get straight to the point, Sofia. We've been brainstorming ideas with editorial and Katie,' he said.

Katie avoided my gaze. Whenever she's involved in ideas it usually spells inconvenience.

'Your set-up is quite unique,' interjected Brammers. 'String of unsuccessful dates with Muslim men, an engagement, a break-up, falling in love with your Irish next-door neighbour, him converting and you now being married and living in Karachi.'

Another cockroach scurried into the bathroom.

'Quite a story,' said Sakib. Was that judgement in his tone? 'Here's the thing: we want you to write a guide to marriage,' he said.

Hain?

Sakib looked at Brammers and Katie. 'Not quite the reaction we were hoping for.'

'I'm not a professional married person,' I said.

I mean, I barely know anything about it myself.

'*Muslim* marriage,' said Brammers. 'Cultural conflicts, fish out of water – that type of thing.'

'The religious aspect,' added Sakib. 'I think readers will be fascinated about Conall. There are so many negative stereotypes about converts to Islam –'

'Just this morning the front page in the papers was about a group of British Muslims flying to Syria,' added Brammers. 'Three were converts.'

'It's all very *personal*, isn't it?' I said.

'No more personal than the dating book you've written,' he replied.

Typical to have past mistakes thrown in your face. The point is that I didn't really think that one through. I've decided to consider things more now that I'm older, wiser, etc.

'Although,' he added, 'I was slightly concerned at the portrayal of Muslim men in your book.' He smiled. 'We're not all like that.'

I paused. 'When a good one comes along, I'll make sure to write a book about him.'

Brammers gave Sakib a weak smile. Something, somewhere, began leaking into my mind. It felt like a ridiculous idea, but was it?

'I don't think my husband would like it.'

They paused.

'A continuation of your story would be something readers will be interested in.' Sakib looked at Brammers again. 'I really think it'll work.'

It wasn't the same reluctance I'd felt when I'd been asked to write the first book. This wasn't – *oh my God, how the hell am I meant to do that* panic. Thoughts of Conall's reaction dissipated, giving way to possibility. Because you can take possibilities for granted until you get stuck in a place that doesn't seem to offer any. I looked at Katie.

'I think it'd be aces,' she said.

Sakib cleared his throat. I let the suggestion penetrate my Karachi-fogged brain. It wasn't the worst idea, and right now, it felt like the only idea in which I could do something other than wait for my philanthropic husband to come home. Maybe this would bring some meaning? I was already thinking about the opening gambit: the mortifying prospect of having sex for the first time in your thirties.

'Sofia?'

'Sorry?' I said, looking up at Sakib, Brammers and Katie.

'I understand you're busy there,' he said.

Ha! Yeah, watching bleach dry.

'But how about coming to London?' he added. 'The book's coming out in April. It'd be good to sit down and brainstorm ideas for the second book.'

Katie was beaming.

'Come back to London. Now?'

Her beam quickly changed to eye-rolling.

'If your husband doesn't mind.'

My heart somersaulted at the mention of London. Was it a sign? Perhaps I could persuade Conall now that there's an actual reason to go back home? This could be divine intervention.

'Unless it's not what you want,' added Sakib.

I could beg Mum's forgiveness in person. She couldn't ignore me then.

'No,' I said. 'It is something I want.'

Now all I have to do is convince my husband.

8.10 p.m. Which is no mean feat when said husband comes home, exclaiming, 'Why's no one fixed those feckin' wires?'

He slammed the front door, walking in without Hammy and co. I was on my hands and knees, scrubbing the floor with bleach.

'Chri— Sorry. Just leave the floor alone.'

I sat up. 'Hello to you too, apple of my eye.'

He collapsed on the sofa, putting his arm over his face as I went and sat next to him. He sniffed.

'I thought you might like to smell bleach after a day of smelling dung,' I said. I lifted his arm and puckered my lips. 'Go on, gi's a kiss.'

He laughed and flattened his palm on my face. Then he put his arm round me. We sat in silence for a while, each lost in our respective thoughts. How might I say: *Oh, I'm going to write a book about our marriage, and let's go to London?* He was still looking into the distance when he said: 'Tell me something . . . Islamic.' He really is very odd sometimes.

'Like?'

'Anything,' he said, taking my hand and resting his head on the back of the sofa. 'Tell me about repentance. I've heard it's good for you.'

The nice thing is how well my hand fits into his.

'Extremely,' I replied. 'As an ex-Catholic you should know all about it.'

He'd closed his eyes. 'There are a lot of things I didn't pay attention to when I was younger.' He opened them again. 'Oddly, I think AA's the first place I began to really feel that God-connection.'

Sometimes he makes me want to just protect him from all the badness in the world, which is ridiculous because he's a grown man; but you can't help how you feel.

'Plus, I married you for your perspective on things like life,' he added.

I nudged him. You don't need to be married for long to pick up on irony. 'Well, my soul feels very cleansed afterwards.'

He turned his head towards me. 'Your mucky soul?'

'I know. Imagine. Anyway, you already know not to worry. You've converted so all past sins are forgiven. Lucky bastard.'

'All sounds too easy to be true,' he said.

His face looked as foreign to me in that moment as this setting. Then Hammy and the crew flooded in.

'Come on, yaar,' she said to a crew member. 'Things aren't going to change by sitting on your prayer mat and asking Allah for it.'

Must remember that kindness is the best virtue.

'Why don't we just get the mullahs to run the country? Women will walk around in niqabs and get beaten for opening their mouths,' she added.

How offensive would it be to smash a plate over her head? There's something about her accent that makes me violent. Each word is pumped with drawling arrogance. *Oh my Gooood. How cuuuuuute. What are you talking about, yaaaaar.* Conall says that I sound elitist, which is ridiculous because you can't be elitist when you're from Tooting.

'Oh,' she said, spotting us.

She was wearing an oversized jumper with a pair of Timberlands and a knitted scarf, her hair up in a scruffy bun, and still managed to look attractive. Me? Well, I smelled of bleach.

'What do you think, Sofe?' Conall asked.

I paused, not sure to which part he was referring.

'Sofia wants the mullahs to take over?' said Hammy.

'She'd sooner put a gun to their head. But she won't believe for a second that anything's stronger than prayer,' he added.

Hammy leaned against the glass table, taking off her scarf.

'Well, yes,' I said. 'As long as you get off your arse and also *do* something.'

I live with cockroaches, not fairies. Just then Jawad came in, wearing purple earmuffs, which momentarily distracted me. I wanted to take a picture to send to the girls.

'Chai?' he asked us.

The lights flickered and we all looked up before they went out again.

'Oh, don't worry,' I said to Jawad. 'I'll make my own tea.'

Hammy grinned. 'Jawad, she's from London. They do things themselves there.'

'Baji,' he said, turning to me. 'I am here to serve you.' He looked straight at me, and to be honest I was a little unnerved by the intensity of his gaze. 'And your husband.'

My eyes flickered between Jawad and Hammy. I was so bored with feeling this way: out of place even with Conall around.

'Can we talk?' I said to him.

He nodded as we made our way into our room.

'Baji,' Jawad called out.

I turned back and he was holding out my phone. Hammy was on the sofa, flicking through her notebook.

'Oh,' I said. 'Thanks.'

He bowed low before he walked past me, out of the room.

'He's . . . helpful.' I said to Hammy.

Without looking up, she said: 'These servants . . . they love the smell of foreign money.'

Why couldn't Conall have heard that?

8.50 p.m.

From Katie: Sweetu! Have you told Conall? Crazy busy here. My world's falling apart without you. Obvs. Love you xxx

11.25 p.m. When I went into the room Conall had gone into the shower. He came out in his towel and stood in front of the electric heater, which was a bit diverting. Taking a deep breath, he rubbed his eyes.

'So,' he began. My heart was thudding rather faster than usual. 'We –'

'Let's go back to London,' I interrupted.

'What?'

I began blabbering about the meeting and the book, and that it would only be for a few months.

'Sofe, slow down,' he said.

I closed my mouth and tried to read his expression, which, as usual, was unreadable. It took a few moments before he spoke.

'I didn't realise you wanted to go back.'

Which wasn't very intuitive of him. He was so still that if I didn't know better I'd say he'd fallen asleep. He clenched his jaw. I went into the bathroom, keeping the door open, to wash off the smell of bleach. Best way to cut tension is with movement.

'We weren't meant to stay forever,' I said.

I scrubbed the skin off my hands as my face-wash fell into the sink, because people can't even seem to fix a shelf properly around here.

'I didn't think we'd be here this long,' I added, walking back into the room.

'It's not exactly an overnight project,' he replied.

In the haze of getting on the plane and eloping we didn't quite discuss a timeline. I hadn't thought we needed to. Happiness felt infinite – practicalities were unwanted parameters.

'How much longer do you expect we'll stay?' I asked. 'Let's use a measure of days. For the sake of clarity.'

'Sofe, I don't know. How long's a piece of string? You knew this when you came.'

I sat down on our bed. 'No, actually, I didn't.'

He leaned his hand against the wall and looked at the ground. Conall's a ground-looker – and it's got nothing to do with lowering-your-gaze-modesty.

'We didn't really talk that bit through, I guess,' he said, coming to sit next to me.

'No, too busy getting hitched,' I responded. 'It's just that I don't do anything here all day. It's, I don't know – depressing.'

He looked so serious I had to add, 'I didn't say *you're* depressing.'

'You know we can't go.'

Whyyyyyy? I tried to think of reasons we absolutely *had* to go but these tended to be more Sofia-specific than Conall-specific.

'But,' I began, 'don't you think that if we went back to London you could get some crappy wedding photography jobs and make money to, you know, help the cause?'

I looked so desperate that if anything was a cause, it was probably me. He paused; looked at me; scratched his beard. He was thinking about it! Finally, I'd made a good point!

'It'd be helpful, right? For the project?'

'Your concern for it is touching, Sofe.'

'And us,' I added.

He clasped his hands and stared at the ground again.

'Listen, it'll only be for a few months,' I said. 'I'd do my book stuff and then we'd come back and you could finish what you've started.'

It was perfect. I'd get my London fix and we'd come back with me ready to live the remaining Karachi days without wanting to kill myself.

'Hmmm,' he said thoughtfully.

I put my arms round him, making a mental note to appreciate my husband more. Also, love the way he smells.

'What's this book about exactly?' he asked, taking my hand.

Oh dear. I sat back, thinking of how to form the words carefully so they didn't sound worse than they were. *You know, this and that. Marriage. Our marriage.*

'Sofe?' he said, with that tone of warning he seems to use so often when saying my name.

So I told him.

'Are you kidding?' He let go of my hand. 'A book about *our* marriage.'

'General Muslim marriage. It'll be funny. I mean, if I didn't laugh, I'd cry,' I said, looking round the room.

He didn't even pretend to acknowledge my grievance, which was rather poor form.

'No,' he said.

'Excuse me?'

'It's not happening.'

'That's funny because I've already agreed it is,' I replied.

He stood up. 'Without asking me?'

'*Asking* you?'

'Talking to me.'

'Think of the money,' I said. 'And, you know, he's brown.'

'What?'

'My editor. I mean, he's *British*, but, you know, Indian.' I thought the diversity of it would give Conall cause for positivity.

'I couldn't give a fuck.'

Apparently not.

He opened the dresser drawer, took out his comb, then slammed it shut again. 'This is the problem with society,' he said. 'Lives are exhibitions. Everyone wants to be feckin' seen. Meanwhile the world's falling apart.'

He threw the comb on the dresser table. 'Why you'd want to do it is beyond me.'

We both stood feet apart; my heart seemed to be pumping in my throat.

'You didn't seem to have such a problem with the first book,' I said.

'That was your life then.'

'It's my life *now*,' I retorted.

He paused. 'Funny. I thought it was our life.'

'This doesn't feel like *our* life,' I replied, spreading my arms out. I grabbed my pyjamas and took them to the bathroom to get changed.

'I've seen you naked. I don't know why you still get changed in there.'

'And anyway,' I said, coming out in my PJs, 'we need to be practical. We've *no* discernible income. This money's for both of us.'

'Every time you say things like *discernible* I know you're pissed off.' He paused. 'But I'd never do something you disagreed with.'

'So let's go to London. I disagree with being here.'

Silence. It was too late. His face was obstinate. Which goes well with his personality so I should give him points for consistency.

'You know, your principles are all very nice but they won't keep a roof over our head.'

'We're not going anywhere,' he said.

We? Just because he was getting his boxers in a twist, who said my knickers should put up with it? Couples don't have to do everything together, surely? And why should all my decisions be based on what Conall can and can't do?

'What's stopping *me*?' I said.

He clenched his jaw. 'You want to go?' he said.

'Yes.'

'To write this book about our personal lives? Without me?'

No. I wanted us to go to London *together*.

'What's the other option?' I wanted to ask what was the harm in being personal, anyway? To explain that I can't *not* do this. Because I don't want to just be his wife. I want to *do* something.

'Well, who am I to stop you then.'

My heart felt like it'd lodged itself in my throat. This was not how the conversation was meant to go. 'OK,' I said, my voice wavering on account of the lodged heart. I got into bed. 'I guess that settles that.'

The pauses seemed to be getting longer and longer. 'I don't like this, Sofe,' he said.

I waited for him to come into bed because if there's one thing that's a bore it's arguing with Conall.

'And I don't like that you put the toilet roll on the wrong side of the toilet seat. Or are never too far from a potential bomb exploding. But everything's a compromise, right?'

'I told you, Sofe,' he said, walking towards the bedroom door. 'I don't like it.' With which he left the room, closing the door quietly behind him.

Sunday 6 January

10.10 p.m. I went to the rooftop to get some air. As I opened the door I saw Conall and Hamida, standing side by side, engaged in some kind of serious conversation. The door creaked and they turned round. Hammy put her hand on his arm and walked past without looking my way. The only thought that came to mind was: *I'm leaving my husband alone with this woman.*

Note for book: An unforeseen consequence of taking the emotional plunge into marriage can be neurosis.

'What was that about?' I asked as he turned to look back into the night. Dark skies to match his dark thoughts.

'Nothing,' he replied.

The cold air emanating from his mouth looked like smoke. God, I could've done with a fag. I suspect he felt the same, but since Dad's death I'm being sensible.

'Looked very serious for "nothing",' I replied, wrapping my shawl around me. I waited for his answer. Resolve in the face of chronic silence isn't easy.

'She doesn't find it easy. Being alone,' he finally said, looking at me.

Aside from his look of disappointment, which made my insides curdle (if such a thing's possible), it didn't sit very well that Conall didn't share everything with me. It's perfectly reasonable, obviously, but that logic wasn't helpful. I tried to reason with my internal commotion: you can't be territorial over someone's confidence.

'I still don't get why her husband's in Dubai and she's here,' I said, scratching the concrete wall.

I noticed his eyebrows contract.

'That's not fair. I'm going for a few months, not permanently,' I said. 'Anyway, what was their problem?'

He paused. 'Differences.'

'Tricky thing, those,' I said.

We could barely see a few feet beyond the foggy night-sky, which felt like an all too suitable metaphor.

'I'm booking my flight for the end of the month,' I said.

He nodded.

'I'll get to beg Mum's forgiveness in person,' I added.

I noticed the hint of a scoff, so subtle it could've been an intake of breath. Sometimes his reasonableness was very hard to argue with, but right then I wished he could understand how my guilt was practically an ulcer.

'I don't know what's so hard to understand,' I said. 'Just because you only speak to your parents at Christmas.'

As soon as the words came out I stopped. Conall jammed his hands into his jean pockets. He does this sometimes with such reluctant force I wonder whether it's to physically stop himself from hitting something or someone. What could possibly be so bad that he doesn't even like them mentioned? And as his wife, how much of his personal history is mine to be known?

'You know what I mean,' I said.

He stepped towards me. I'd never quite realised how much bigger than me he was, how imposing his figure could be. He didn't move and I could barely get any words out. He didn't have to say anything – his look said it all: *don't mention them again.*

How do things so quickly spiral into unknown territory?

Later that evening when we were in our room he got the prayer mat and laid it on the ground. I caught a glimpse of his tense face – a concentration of something like fury.

As he began to pray, into my head came the voice of the imam who'd married us: *'How well do you* know *him?'*

Note for book: Whatever you do – if writing a guide to marriage, don't end up penning your very own marital misery memoir.

Thursday 10 January

11.15 a.m. My God, Mum's discovered Facebook! She's sent me a Friend Request, which given that she's not talking to me in real life is something. Is she going through my profile, reading all my congratulation messages, seething at each emoji?

3.40 p.m. 'You're coming back to London?' said Hannah, her image blurring on FaceTime.

'Yes!' I said, finally able to be excited with someone.

When I told Maars she thought it was great until I mentioned I'd be coming back alone. The most ridiculous part is when she told Mum – yes, the woman who hasn't spoken to me since I got married – Mum said: 'She is already arguing with her husband! This girl never keeps quiet.'

Which was rich, considering.

'That's quite alternative,' said Hannah, who wanted a detailed description of my conversation with Conall, how he reacted and how I felt about leaving him behind with Hammy. 'The two of them living in the same place,' she added. 'All kinds of tensions can rise.'

'Yes, thanks, Han.'

A lump of anxiety wedged itself in my throat. I'd spent the past week trying to forget about their tête-à-tête, but every time I see them together I look out for indicators of more confidences shared, secret glances, that kind of thing. As well as the usual praying five times a day, I've given myself a mantra, along the lines of *stop being such an irrational arsehole.* (Although is it irrational??)

'It certainly says something about your relationship with Conall,' she said.

'What?'

'I'm not quite sure. Although you clearly trust him, which is good. But still – months without him . . .'

'It's really not that big a deal. Wouldn't you do the same if you were here with Omar?'

She paused, scrunching up her nose in thought. 'Definitely not. I don't think anyone I know would.'

Oh. 'Am I mad?' I asked.

'No . . . I mean, not really. It just took me long enough to find him. I'm not fed up with him yet,' she said.

'I'm not fed up with Conall,' I replied. 'But apart from wanting to be home, wouldn't you want to be *doing* something?' I paused. 'I suppose you doctors are always doing something. Between your career, Suj's glamorous modelling lifestyle, and Foz's journey of self-discovery, it's a wonder I've not swapped you all for less ambitious friends. Not to mention Conall's *raison d'être.*'

'You have ambitions.'

I raised my eyebrows. 'Writing a few books to pay some bills and because you have nothing better to do isn't the same as ambition.

And yes, I'm very grateful for the opportunities, but it just doesn't feel like *mine*. You know?'

'Sofe, the key to happiness is to stop wanting it all. One of the many things Omar and I discovered when we spoke about the future.'

'The future?' I asked.

'Yes.'

'Oh.' I paused. 'What exactly about the future?'

'The usual: what we both wanted, the fact that I'm barren.' A shadow seemed to pass over her face. I wanted to reach into the phone and hug her. 'Making sure we were on the same page. I didn't need to marry a man who'd then leave me because I can't have children. The point is, if you're getting married the halal way – without the years of dating and living together – then you have to have The Conversation. Several, actually – about how you'll both live together.'

I'm pretty sure Han had a lever-arch file of questions for Omar before they got married.

'It's not sexy, but it'd be irresponsible otherwise,' she added.

'Yeah, but serial killers never say they're serial killers.'

'Delicately observed, Sofe.'

I laughed. God, I missed the girls.

'For example, how many kids does he want? Where will you live? I know, it's boring – but that's what you do as a couple – work it out. You guys did that, right?' she asked.

I suddenly felt like I was in an exam only I'd revised the wrong stuff. Billy was sleeping in the corner of the window. She had the right idea.

'Sort of.'

I couldn't quite recall what the conversations were. I remember Conall asking whether I was sure.

'Yes, of course,' I'd replied.

'You want to be here? With me?'

Here, there, *anywhere*.

'Because we can wait,' he'd said.

But I didn't want to wait – I was seizing moments. If Dad's death had taught me anything it was the importance of doing that. I'd already made a string of mistakes in the past – I didn't want waiting around for Conall to be another one.

'You didn't, did you?' said Hannah.

'Well . . .'

'*Sofe*. You're always telling us not to rush into things. Trust you to go and get carried away.'

'Excuse me. I'm still very much in command of my actions and feelings.'

She laughed. 'Yeah, all right, love.'

Suddenly I wondered where my head had been the past few months.

'It's fine. You always have been single-minded,' she said.

I wasn't sure whether she meant that I was focused, or that I've always had the mind of a single person. I had to go because I heard Conall and co. come home early for lunch.

'I'll see *you* in a few weeks,' she said, blowing me a kiss and signing off.

It does make me think: what other things have I not thought through?

Monday 14 January

6.55 p.m.

From: Sakib Awaan
To: Sofia Khan
Subject: London

Hi Sofia,
Delighted you'll be in London at the end of the month.
I'm looking forward to working with you.
Best wishes,
Sakib

At least one man in my life is happy about it.

Not that he's a man in my life. Obviously.

1 a.m. Couldn't sleep. I stared at Conall like some lovelorn woman, then stopped in order to maintain my sense of self. I got out of bed to go to the rooftop. There's something beautiful about Karachi at night – the distant sounds, the misty air, the people you can see, if you look hard enough, getting ready to sleep. Except when I got up there I wasn't alone. A silhouette turned round as the door creaked open.

'Oh. Sorry,' I said.

Hammy was having a fag, wearing a glove on one hand. I was going to turn round, but then there aren't many chances I get with her alone. Perhaps I could begin to understand why Conall likes her.

'Mind if I stay?' I asked.

She shrugged. Her enthusiasm is one of the many things that endear her to me. I stood next to her, leaning my elbows on the wall as Hammy took a drag of her cigarette. I inhaled the nicotine. We were both silent as she seemed to be deep in her own thoughts. She must've caught me looking at her.

'You know, the good thing about being married is you don't have to answer any more questions about marriage,' she said.

No, I'll have others to answer when I get to London. People are never short of questions. No wonder death is inevitable – everyone's exhausted from the Life Inquisition.

'Nosy relatives?' I asked.

She gave a slight nod.

'Don't worry,' I said. 'The marriage question is the lifeline of ninety-nine per cent of Pakistan's population.'

Quiet.

She looked at me for a while.

'When I first met Con—'

Breathe.

'– in Afghanistan he'd ask me all these questions about Islam and I was like, *dude, I'm not the person to ask*. I left my home because of all that bullshit. I thought he was one of those gora types, you know; who leave their country to find themselves and end up finding God.'

She looked at me, her eyes flickering towards my hijab. 'But he really converted for you,' she added.

I wanted to say that Conall doesn't do anything he doesn't want – something perhaps we both have in common. Anyway, in the end it can't have *all* been for me. There was the seed of something there and I just watered it. I'm very useful like that.

'That's something,' she said.

I don't mean to sound self-involved but why was no one talking about my compromise? I could already hear Mum: *women always make the sacrifices*. Not Hammy, though. She let her husband leave. Though God knows what the reason was. Just then we heard a bang. Hamida and I both started, looking round to see where it came from.

'Was that . . .?'

She nodded. 'We'll find out where it came from tomorrow.'

My heart was thudding. 'This place,' I said, shaking my head, thinking about its bombs and guns that go bang in the night. 'Don't you feel unsafe?'

She gave a wry smile. 'Everyone scares too easily. You're just seeing the worst side of it. You don't like it enough to give it a chance.'

It wasn't that I didn't like it; it just wasn't home.

'London isn't perfect,' she said. 'And trust me, the way things are going, one day there'll be chaos there as well. Especially for you hijabi types.'

I thought about this, taking in the air that smelled like mud, just after it's rained. Perhaps she was right. The thing with chaos is, it doesn't just burst on to the scene – it can creep. Maybe, one day in the distant future, chaos would creep into London too.

'There's always comfort in the chaos you're familiar with,' I replied.

She looked at me. 'Unless you're Con, huh? He loves the unfamiliar. Crazy guy,' she added rather too fondly.

I didn't need someone to tell me what Conall is and isn't familiar with. Why did she even spend time thinking about that? Or was that what they talked about?

'Don't you miss your husband?' I asked.

She threw her cigarette on the ground, the last embers flickering as she turned to me. I thought she was going to leave, but she just put her hands in her pockets.

'He was my best friend,' she said after a while.

'Oh,' I said.

I'd assumed hers was some kind of arranged, loveless marriage.

'Then you must really miss him,' I added.

She picked up the cigarette butt and flung it out into the open air. 'You just can't help who you fall in love with.'

She looked at me with such intensity my insides shifted. Then, without another word, she turned round and walked out of the door.

Sunday 20 January

10.50 p.m. Bit difficult to get your husband to start speaking to you when he doesn't come home before midnight. He says he's doing night-time photography. *Sure*. If you're pissed off with someone, then be sensible and shout at each other until you're both over it.

Spoke to Suj about coming back without Conall.

She paused before saying: 'Fuck it.'

Every day that he comes home late, I'm inclined to agree with her. 'How's Charles?' I asked.

'You know what, Toffee? *Fine*. We've both had a few photo shoots together and it's been all right. I quite like him. Weird, isn't it?'

Suj's always been modest with her proclamations of love.

'All these years we spent having man-drama and now look,' she added.

'This must be everyone's happily ever after,' I said, wondering why I didn't feel very jubilant. 'Your dad's OK about him then?' I asked.

'Oh, please. Charles is black. But as long as I'm OK with it, the old man's going to have to learn.'

Note for book: Stick to your guns, but also know the limits of what you can change.

Tuesday 29 January

12.45 a.m. I'm leaving in *two* days. TWO. And he's still coming home late. I've been occupying myself with writing but today when he came home just an hour ago, I wanted to throw my laptop at him. I didn't. Obviously. If he doesn't realise what an arsey thing that is to do, why should I be the one to tell him? He dropped his bags on the floor, balancing a tray in one hand complete with a sandwich and tea. I pretended to concentrate on the screen.

'You're working late,' he said.

'Makes two of us,' I mumbled.

He handed me a mug of tea.

I looked up at him. 'Oh, thanks.'

'Hungry?' he asked, offering me the other half of his peanut butter sandwich.

I turned round and looked at what I guess was a peace offering; the weirdly yellow bread that only made me miss home more.

'You know that's not bread,' I said, going to sit on the bed with him.

'Perhaps you'd like me to go bake you some. Straight out of the Aga,' he replied.

'Yes, thank you. Wholemeal, if you will.'

'I can think of a few ways to use that Aga,' he said, leaning forward, the flicker of a smile.

It's his face. I could be a lot more resolute if I didn't look at it so much. Unfortunately, it's also become one of those things I like to look at. (In a strictly non-psycho way. Obviously.) Was leaving a mistake? Had to keep reminding myself that it's temporary. Yet there's something about packed suitcases that feels permanent. He reached into his bag, getting out a book and a package.

'What's this?' I asked, picking up the book, which was in Urdu.

'It's for Jawad. He's quite the philosophical guy, you know. I got him this book on Sufism. Thought it'd interest him.'

'You like Sufism?'

He paused. 'I don't like the way people can use it socially as a more acceptable version of Islam, but there's something there, don't you think? The idea of purifying the inner self?'

To be honest, I'd stopped listening to him because I was too busy thinking about how kind he can be and finding it all rather attractive.

'Hmm? Yes, I suppose so.'

Then he handed me the package. I looked in it and there was a bundle of pants.

'You lose yours all the time,' he said.

I laughed as he rolled up his sleeves, exposing his tattoos as he leaned against the bed. I wonder what they'll look like when he's old and wrinkled.

'Could've got me flowers,' I said.

'I knew you'd appreciate pants more.'

Unfortunately, he was right. My insides churned – I needed an antacid. Why couldn't he come with me? Someone knocked at the door and Hammy peered in. Who else?

'Sorry, I know it's late.' She glanced at my hijab-less head. 'Conall, the material guy for the shelters called. Phone him in the morning, huh?'

He nodded. 'Sure. You OK?' he asked.

I found myself bristling. *Asking how she feels is not a crime against humanity, Sofia. Even if it feels like a crime against you.*

She gave a martyred nod and then left the room. What was he thinking as he looked at the ground?

'Fancy a shag before I leave?' I said.

'Always the romantic, Sofe.'

He took my mug and plate from me, putting them on the side-table before holding my face in his hands. 'You know I love y—'

'Don't say that!' I exclaimed putting my hand over his mouth. 'Not, like, seriously.'

'What are you on?' he managed to mumble through my hand before he moved it away.

'The more you say a thing the less true it becomes,' I explained.

He laughed as he looked at me. 'This a tried and tested theory?'

'Just trust me,' I said.

'What am I going to do for entertainment when you're not here?'

What am I going to do without Conall to pull me into his arms?

'You'll be too busy crying yourself to sleep, I should hope.' *And you'd better not go finding a replacement*, I wanted to add.

'You know I do, though, don't you?' he said.

I nodded, leaning in to kiss him. The bristly beard used to feel weird, but I rather like it now. 'I suppose I do too. You, I mean. Not myself. Obviously.'

'Obviously,' he replied.

Conall managed to get to sleep but I lay in bed, looking at his face: the one that launched a thousand feelings.

Maybe you never can quite have it all, but there are moments in life – like now – when I think maybe I do.

FEBRUARY

Where the Heart is

Friday 1 February

2.10 p.m. 'Is this your first time to London?'

Moustachioed uncle (because when you're brown, every elder is an uncle or auntie) next to me on the plane didn't take feigned sleep, earplugs or book-reading as signs to leave me alone. I took a deep breath and almost choked on his cologne. At least it overrode the smell from the toilet.

'It's home,' I replied, turning a page of *The Hitchhiker's Guide to the Galaxy*.

'How many brothers and sisters do you have? What do your parents do? Where do you live?' he continued in Urdu.

It was all I could do to stop myself from shoving my book down his throat. I kept looking out of the window, thinking of Conall.

'Sorry, Beta. I'm asking a lot of questions,' he said. 'But you remind me very much of someone I know.'

'I live with my husband,' I said in answer to his last question.

I twisted the gold band on my finger, remembering the story behind it when Conall gave it to me.

Uncle Mouch looked round the stuffy plane. 'Where is he?'

It wouldn't be the first time someone would ask me this question. 'In Karachi.'

'Ah,' he said. 'Visas take long now. My nephew's been waiting two years for his wife. The laws are very strict. Canada's better now.'

'My husband's not Pakistani,' I explained.

Uncle Mouch furrowed his brows. 'Oh.'

I sighed and told him I'd momentarily forgotten which husband I was talking about – my fourth husband *is* Pakistani.

'This is your fourth marriage?' he asked, leaning forward.

Having four husbands was a lot more fun than explaining the truth. 'Yep. And probably not my last.'

He leaned back in his seat. '*Beta*,' he began (presumably calling me *daughter* was going to take the sting out of the lecture he planned to give). 'In Islam divorce is very serious. A hijabi should know this, no?' He looked at my scarf. It wasn't just a head covering, but a useful indicator of who I must be.

'Well,' I replied. 'Having a boyfriend's haram so I thought I'd make the most out of marriage.'

I always wondered whether I was a miserable cow just because I needed to get laid, but turns out that had nothing to do with it.

The plane had barely touched the ground when everyone got out of their seats, opening overhead lockers and shuffling around. I watched the grey skies and the spatter of rain on the window before switching my phone on and checking for messages.

From Conall: Message me when you've landed.

From Maria: Tahir and Auntie Reena will be there to pick you up. So glad you're home. Xx

Before the crowds began to exit Uncle Mouch turned round and said: 'Your husband's like a garment for you, as you are for him, Beta.' He shuffled out of the seat, his stomach pressed against it as someone pushed past him.

'You know we women – we like changing our garments all the time.'

He paused before he smiled. 'You really do remind me of someone I know.'

Poor her.

From Suj: Toffeeeeeee! You're BACK! Call me when you land. Let me know how it goes with the old dear. Love youuuuuu xxxx

I smiled as I received messages from Katie and Hannah too. By the time I'd looked up Uncle Mouch had gone. Conall's fine with Hammy. What does it say if I can't trust my husband with another woman for a few months?

Men and women in luminescent waistcoats stood by as I was poised to run into the arms of Heathrow Airport. As I went through security it didn't look like Heathrow's arms were quite so open, but that didn't matter.

To Conall: I'm home xxx

9.50 p.m. Oh my God, I must have chronic case of delayed reaction. Zooming down the motorway I realised that it was the first time I'd be seeing Mum since I got married . . . she'll know I'm no longer a virgin! In fact, Auntie Reena and my brother-in-law, Tahir, also knew! Horror! I mean, not as horrific as *still* being a virgin, but even so.

I got out of the car, looking up at the house, and felt a surge of joy. Then I looked at Conall's house next door – the one his brother

Sean's renting since we're in Pakistan. I guess it's mine too now. Isn't it weird the things that you end up sharing, just because you now share a bed? The front door opened and out came Maria, flinging her arms round me. She'd grown out her hair which was rather a lighter shade of brown than her Pakistani heritage suggested possible.

'Thank God you're home,' she said. 'Did you take the M25?'

'Yeah,' replied Tahir.

'I told you, you should've come through Kingston.'

'Beta, there was so much traffic,' said Auntie Reena. 'I told him too, but he wouldn't listen.'

Tahir got my suitcase out of the car. 'No, she didn't,' he whispered, watching Auntie Reena go into the house. 'She was too busy changing the station to bloody Sunrise Radio.'

Maars laughed and told him she'd make him some tea.

'What's Mum's mood like?' I asked Maars.

'Like you eloped?' She put her arm round me as we walked through the front gate. 'Sorry, love.'

'Where's Adam?' I asked, dying to see my nephew.

Also, children have a way of calming tense waters, but he was asleep. I held my head high and walked into the living room.

'Oh, she is here,' said Mum, sitting on the brown leather sofa.

'Hi, Mum.'

She bobbed her head like one of those dogs in car windows.

'"*Hi, Mum*" she says.'

Mum looked at Auntie Reena, as if saying *hi* was the most outrageous thing I'd done.

'Your baba's churning in his grave.'

'Turning, Mum,' I replied.

'Haan, what do I know? I'm just your mother. I only pushed you out of my *phudi*—'

Tahir choked on his own saliva.

'*Mum,*' exclaimed Maars.

'I'll er . . . I'll make that tea,' said Tahir, tripping on the step on his way to the kitchen.

'Did you have to mention vaginas in front of my husband?' whispered Maars to Mum.

'Where does *he* think he came from, hmm? His father's pe—?'

'*Mum!*'

'*Mehnaz!*'

Maars and Auntie Reena spoke in unison. Dishes clattered in the kitchen.

'Thirty-two hours' labour I had with you. *Thirty-two*. My best years I spent raising you. Now what do I have to hear from people? *Her baba died and she ran away with a white man*.'

I looked her in the eye. I'd give her time to rant about the sacrifices she'd made and how disappointing I was, but her disappointment in my choice of husband wasn't going to be race-dependent.

'Maybe you and Dad should've thought of that before you moved to a country full of white people,' I said.

Maars cleared her throat. Auntie Reena looked at the coffee table, though that was possibly because she wanted the chocolate cake that was on it.

'Le! Listen to her. You think I am so backward? That I have a problem because he is *white*? You will have such pretty children. If he was black –'

'Don't spoil it, Mum,' interrupted Maars.

Mum stood up to her full five foot one inch. 'I'll deal with anyone who says something about your husband because he's white. As if Pakistani men are so great.'

Auntie Reena shook her head. More clanging in the kitchen.

'But, Soffoo, all my life I only thought of you and Maria and you didn't think of your mama once, making such a big decision?'

I looked at the ground, shamed into silence.

'No,' she said, turning to Auntie Reena. 'Not even a phone call to say: *Mama, I am sorry I'm an unthoughtful daughter but I think I will marry the gora neighbour because, like my baba, you should have a heart attack too*.'

'I'm sorry, Mum,' I said.

She stepped towards me. 'You know, your aunties and uncles always said we gave you too much freedom. And we both said, to hell with them, our daughters won't be trapped in a house just because they're girls. But so much freedom you took that you forgot the people that gave it to you?'

Turns out freedom isn't a birthright but a gift wrapped up in consequences. Her look of rage morphed into hurt as she walked past me and up the stairs into her room.

'Well,' said Maars, taking a deep breath. 'That went well.'

I need a fag.

Saturday 2 February

9.15 a.m. Woke up in state of confusion in my childhood bed, forgetting about the past year, thinking I was single again. Had me breaking out in a sweat. For some reason Auntie Reena stayed the night. I heard her clattering around in the kitchen with Mum. Picked up phone to Skype Conall but he didn't answer.

Going into what used to be Mum and Dad's bedroom I sat on the bed. I thought about the smell of cigarettes that'd waft in when he entered a room; his white stubble when he came back from the hospital after his first heart attack; the white sheet they covered him with when we found out he'd never come back at all.

His absence felt easier to reconcile in Pakistan. But this house; it's crowded with the empty spaces he's left behind.

11.55 a.m. I tiptoed down the stairs – like any self-respecting thirty-one-year-old – and Mum and Auntie Reena were drinking tea. Called Maars to ask why Auntie was here rather than with her husband.

'Tahir! *Tahir!* He's crying!' Maars shouted on the other end of the phone. I pulled my mobile away from my ear. 'Sorry,' she continued. 'Mum says they're having problems.'

'Why? They're *old*.'

'So?' she said.

'They've been married *forever*.'

'Exactly. Oh, for God's sake. I'm coming! Have to go. He can't find the steriliser.'

When I went into the room and said hello, there was silence. I was going to break Mum down. I'd make her forgive me.

'House is looking good, Mum,' I said.

She raised her eyebrows. 'Don't you see how much painting it needs? But you never see things.'

Right.

'Beta, when's your husband coming?' asked Auntie Reena.

I watched Mum, who'd picked up her iPad and was flicking through FB.

'Oh, he's not,' I replied.

Hurumph. From Mum.

'Haw, Beta, you left him, just like that?' said Auntie Reena.

'No, I just wanted to come home and see everyone.'

She leaned forward. 'But . . . without your husband?'

I tried to explain that he has important work to do there and that I have important things to do here. Although, considering Conall was helping to save lives while I was just scribbling words, perhaps that was stretching it.

'He is OK with this?' she asked.

I kept looking at Mum, who seemed to be typing something. If you decide to elope, you need to ensure no one knows that only months into your marriage, your husband is pissed off with you for A) leaving the country and B) the book you've been asked to write.

'He's really glad,' I said.

'Glad?' she repeated. 'Beta, men should never be glad when their wife's away.'

'Well, not *glad*,' I said. 'He's unhappy too.'

Auntie put her flower-patterned teacup down. 'Beta, men should never be unhappy when their wife's away.'

Honestly, juggling all these versions of life is very tricky.

Note for book: There is an abyss in the line between glad and unhappy; make sure you don't fall into it.

Mum got up and told Auntie Reena that they needed to go to Homebase to look for tiles for the kitchen. Because when in turmoil, re-tile the kitchen floors.

4.10 p.m. Called Katie but she's in Devon with her family. Hannah had guests round and Suj was with Charles. Foz is still gallivanting around South America. Tried to call Conall but couldn't get through. Couldn't even go to see Sean since he was on holiday in South Africa.

What's the point in being home when no one is home with me?

4.35 p.m.

To: Sakib Awaan
From: Sofia Khan
Subject: Meeting

Hi Sakib,
Hope you're not checking emails on a Saturday but just so you know, I'm in the country now. Happy to set up a meeting when you are.
Best,
Sofia

To: Sofia Khan
From: Sakib Awaan
Subject: Re: Meeting

Welcome home. I don't believe in weekends. I hope you don't think you'll be getting any. I'm a tough editor. It's the brown in me.
Next Thursday at 2 p.m.?

To: Sakib Awaan
From: Sofia Khan
Subject: Re: Meeting

I believe that life should be a weekend. Going against the brown grain is what I live for.
Thursday at 2 p.m. it is.

To: Sofia Khan
From: Sakib Awaan
Subject: Re: Meeting

We'll have to beat that out of you. Or bribe you. Katie tells me you like biscuits?
Great, see you then. Look forward to it.

He does sound rather cool, doesn't he? I wonder what else Katie's told him.

7.50 p.m. Managed to get through to Conall today.

'Hi.'

'Hi.'

Pause.

'How are you?' he asked.

'Good. You?'

'Fine.'

Pause.

'How's your mum?'

'Pissed. And not the drunk kind.'

'Christ help us if she was.'

I looked round my bedroom – funny how quickly something can begin to feel like a distant past, even when it's right there.

'Not sure how I'm meant to get her to forgive me.'

'You're creative, you'll think of something.'

He didn't seem to get how depressing it was. I heard laughter in the background.

'You're up late,' I said.

'Just sitting with everyone.'

I could hear Mum and Auntie watching Zee TV downstairs. None of the girls have got back to me and Maars didn't come over because Adam wasn't feeling well. I wanted to tell Conall that I missed him, but it felt like some kind of weakness. Especially since it didn't seem the feeling was mutual. He had everyone, apparently, and I had Zee TV.

'Listen, my battery's low. Generator's still not fixed.'

'Why's your phone never charged?'

'Because it doesn't have quite the same energy as my wife,' he replied.

I laughed.

He paused. 'You know I'm thinking about your pants.'

Lifting the covers, I got into bed. 'They're thinking about you too.'

Another pause. I turned over to what should've been his side of the bed and said, 'I bloody miss you . . .

'Hello? Conall?'

I looked at my phone and the call had been lost. Typical. After a while Auntie Reena came into my room and sat with me, telling me about the tiles she and Mum had picked out.

It'll be a sorry state of affairs if I travel all the way back to London just to have Auntie Reena as my best friend.

11.30 p.m. Ha! Just found old stash of cigarettes under my mattress and hugged them! I'm obviously still a conscientious objector to fags, but nothing will drive you to smoke more than listening to your mum and aunt go on about sodding kitchen tiles.

1.05 a.m. Mum was sitting in the pale glow of the lamp when I went downstairs.

'Couldn't sleep,' I said as she looked at me.

Nothing.

'I'm going to make tea. Do you want some?'

I took her silence as a yes.

When I sat down, handing her the cup, she said: 'Maria tells me your new book is about marriage.'

I cringed at the idea that she might think I assume I'm some kind of expert. I nodded.

'What have you written so far?' she asked.

'Not much.'

She sipped her tea.

'Your baba always wanted things his way,' she said. 'That's where you get it. I was told that to be a good wife I had to listen to him, so I did. One year passed, two years turned into five, and sometimes when I'd be giving you and Maria food or fixing his shirt buttons, I thought: *he doesn't see how much I hold back my happiness for his.* So, when I began to open my mouth, he was shocked.' She looked at me. 'You wouldn't remember these times. You think he was happy? Arguing and shouting. Uff. You began to understand things by then. But see how slowly he began to respect what I said? To ask me for advice until I became the only one he listened to so I always got *my* way. Except for last year.' She looked over at the picture of her and Dad on their wedding day. 'He used to say to me: *Mehnaz, I hope I die before you, because I don't think I could live without you* . . . See? Your baba . . . he got his way in the end.'

A tear dropped into my teacup.

'Life with him wasn't easy.' She looked into her cup. 'But sometimes, life without him feels very hard.'

Monday 4 February

11.50 a.m. Was sitting in Mum and Dad's room again, while Mum and Auntie Reena had gone to take advantage of the spinach that's on offer in Lidl. Kept thinking about what Mum said yesterday. Didn't even realise when Maars walked into the room with Adam until she handed him to me. He grabbed my face with his hands, blowing bubbles of spit through his chubby cheeks. (Chubby cheeks are the best. Unless they're yours, obviously.)

'She'll come round,' said Maars. 'It's just people have been saying that it wouldn't have happened if Dad was still alive. I think it feels like a personal failure.'

'But it's *not*,' I said. Why did I make her feel like she'd failed?

'You're telling me that you wouldn't have thought about it a little more if Dad were alive?'

'The end result would've been the same,' I said.

Maars held on to one of Adam's hands. 'The thing is, you know Mum loves having stuff to do and now Dad's gone she's at a bit of a loss. Why do you think I come over all the time with fatty here?' she said, looking at Adam.

'Dad was quite high maintenance, wasn't he?'

I never realised how much Mum liked maintaining him.

'Anyway,' continued Maars, taking Adam back. 'She's just rattier than usual and now she has Auntie Reena to rant with.'

'Misery has enough company here then.'

Had to remind myself that I was here to see my friends too – although God knows where they were – and to start work on the second book. Focus.

'Come on. Sitting here is depressing,' said Maria, standing up.

'What Mum needs is a plan,' I replied.

'Just be careful, Sofe.'

'Of what?'

She kissed Adam on the cheek and said: 'That you don't start seeing Conall through other people's eyes.'

8.50 p.m. Oh God. Why is it that it's precisely the wrong shit that comes out of my mouth that then comes into being? Between Adam crying and Mum and Auntie Reena organising the pot plants, the house was driving me crazy so I went out to have a fag. They say things aren't nearly as great as you remember them to be, but I'm sorry, fags are.

When I came back in (went upstairs, washed my hands, stuck a chewing gum in my mouth, sprayed myself with perfume – like old times) Mum was sitting with an odd kind of agitation. Maria looked wide-eyed and excitable as if she'd just had a spliff. Auntie Reena smiled very widely. Too wide for it to mean anything good.

'Beta, sit down with us,' she said.

I did so, looking at the three faces then at Adam, wondering whether I should be wishing to be him right now.

'What's going on?' I said.

'Don't sound so worried, Sofe,' said Maars, smiling at me in encouragement.

'What?' I asked.

'We're throwing you a wedding,' blurted out Maars as she clapped Adam's hands together.

Hain?? Auntie Reena began shuttling out words.

'People don't know you are married and we must have a wedding otherwise what will they say? Your Auntie Bilkees talked and talked about what you did and, hai hai, she ate my head.' Auntie Reena grabbed hold of her head as I held on to mine. 'Look, here's the guest list.'

She waved three pages of A4 paper at me. 'Only three hundred people. How many will come from the groom's side? He's gora na – probably not many.'

I tried to gain control of the thousand threads of thought that were shooting out of my head. 'He's also Irish.'

'But he's gora?' repeated Auntie Reena.

I tried to explain that weddings were rather a big affair in Ireland too. Conall and I were both cultural anomalies.

'Irish and white aren't the same thing,' I replied, distracted. How was this happening? Why can I not go one year without looking at a wedding list?

'Better to put down sixty,' said Mum.

'The thing is,' I ventured, 'I don't think a wedding's necessary.' I gave a weak smile, beginning to appreciate, on a whole new level, what my dad had been up against.

'Hmph,' said Mum, putting the guest list (who the hell was the Saqlain family and why were there eleven of them??) on the coffee table and looking away from me.

'Listen, Beta –'

'No, Reena,' interrupted Mum. 'We can only ask our children to give us happiness,' she said. 'We can't expect it.'

Mum the martyr was so much worse than Mum the despot.

'It doesn't have to be *huge*,' said Maria, looking at me in warning.

'Well,' I began, 'three hundred people isn't really *small*.'

'But –' began Maria.

'Nahin, nahin,' said Mum. 'Doesn't matter. I'm just a mother. What do I matter?'

I took a deep breath, caught between the sadness of the mother I witnessed last night and the potential wrath of my husband. 'It's just that Conall's not here,' I said. 'We can't have a wedding without a groom.'

'Le, so you tell him to come,' said Mum. 'He can't do that much for his wife? Why would he want to stop our enjoyment?'

Our enjoyment?

'And waisay, Soffoo, as a wife you must learn to stand up and say what you want,' said Mum as Auntie Reena nodded. 'Men take advantage.'

It was the first time Mum had addressed me without sneering, so I didn't point out that the same could be said about wedding-crazed mothers. People go on about financial debt, but no one tells you about the debt of life. Interest charged at infinite APR. I needed another fag.

'Just *one* event,' said Maars, eyes so wide I thought her eyeballs would fall out.

'Le, where's the fun without a mehndi as well?' replied Mum.

'Yeah, you're right – two events,' Maars concurred.

'O-ho! We forgot the Bahaduris,' said Auntie Reena, adding seven more names to the list.

I felt the thread of my sanity slowly unravelling.

'Oh, my beta,' said Mum, getting up and then bundling me in her arms. 'I knew you'd be a good girl.'

'But –'

She took my face in her hands and looked at me with that motherly affection that escapes her now and again. That kind of look can dent the sturdiest of souls.

'Maybe we should book you a facial, haina?' she added.

Then again . . .

Before I knew it the three of them had sprung off their seats, Maars handing Adam to me while they investigated how much decor was in the shed from Maars' wedding. I followed them out, Adam wriggling on my hip.

'But isn't it a useless expense?' I said to three arses sticking out of the shed.

'What?' asked Maars, turning round and holding up bunting.

I wanted to cry. 'Mum, we could give the money to people who need it,' I added.

'Le, Soffoo, giving to charity is good, but everything should be in moderation,' said Mum as she got out what looked like ten metres of fairy lights.

Note for book: When it comes to weddings, human rights can't trump the rights of fairy lights.

This is it, isn't it? This is the beginning of the end.

Tuesday 5 February

11.40 a.m. 'Where were you last night?' I asked as Conall picked up the phone.

'Hello?' he said.

'Conall?'

'Yeah, Sofe. Hang on. No! *Seedha*.'

'What's straight?' I asked. 'Doesn't matter. I tried calling last night.'

'Sorry, got caught up with editing photos and fell asleep.'

'*What* is that noise?' I asked.

'New shelters. Feckin' no one taking proper directions.'

'Right. Listen, I need to speak to you.'

'OK, hang on.'

More noise and shouting.

'Sorry. You OK?'

'Yeah, fine. Well, not really.'

'What's wrong?' he said.

'No, nothing's wrong, it's just –'

'Can you tell them I said to the right. That's *left*. Sorry, Sofe, go on – what is it?'

'The thing is, you see . . .'

Oh God, how was I meant to tell him without sounding feeble?

'Well, you know, Mum's forgiven me,' I said.

'That's grand, Sofe. I told you she'd come round. Is that it?'

There was nothing for it, really, was there? 'She's throwing us a wedding. March thirtieth. Don't suppose you're available?'

Pause. 'What?'

'A wedding. For us.' Pause. '*Surprise!*'

'I . . . *what?*'

I explained last night's scenario to him, but he didn't seem to feel quite the sense of obligation that I'd felt.

'We never wanted a wedding,' he said.

'*Very* good point. But it's just an event, isn't it? Plus, we'll get presents.'

'I don't give a shit about presents. I didn't think you did either.'

'It's not as if I'd say no to them. I mean, something other than pants wouldn't go amiss.'

Silence.

'Hello?' I said.

'Sofe,' he said, his tone softening. 'I can't come to London for a wedding.'

'It's *our* wedding. Plus, we could get the whole civic ceremony out of the way too.'

He paused. 'Make it more difficult for you to ever leave me.'

Why on earth would *I* ever leave *him*? Permanently, I mean.

'But I can't just up and leave everything here.'

Yes. He was right, though I couldn't help but think that it'd be nice for him to just abandon logic and principle and do something I ask.

I didn't even feel angry. Just deflated. The dissonance of logic and hope can do that to a person. 'I know, but God, Conall, weren't you even thinking about the book launch and being here for that?'

Silence.

'Will you stop going quiet?' I said.

'I know. I'm sorry, but what do you want me to do?'

Pause.

'Hello?' he said.

'Nothing, I guess,' I replied.

'Sofe, you know –'

Just then Auntie Reena's head peeped through my bedroom door. 'Sorry, Beta, you don't mind, na?'

She came and sat on the edge of my bed, even though she could see the phone in my hand.

'Sofe?'

'I have to call you back.'

I tried to muster a smile for Auntie Reena.

'Beta . . .' She looked agitated as Bollywood music played downstairs.

'What's wrong?'

'What will people say at your wedding when your uncle isn't there?'

'Hmm?'

'Your uncle is very selfish,' she replied.

'That can't be true,' I said, thinking that it was probably exactly true. Does Conall feel I only think about myself? *Do* I only think of myself?

'Men change,' she said. 'They forget everything – that you've been their wife, maid, looked after their mother while having to forget your own one in Pakistan. You know how our men are. Beta, what you did was not very good to your mama, but sometimes I'm very glad you married a gora. They're different. O-ho, you know Sonia? Auntie Mishaal's daughter? She married a gora and she tells me how he makes her chai and dinner and asks how she is. As if their lives are both – what do they say? Equal.'

It wasn't *all* Pakistani men but the scales were certainly tipped in the non-progressive direction.

'Your mama said that Conall will find out what he has to deal with now he's married you but, Beta, we both know you're a good girl.'

She patted my leg and smiled while I thought of the vote of confidence my mum had in me.

'But when men are away from their wife . . . well. You know it is their nature to look at other women.'

I wondered – had Uncle gone and had an affair?? Why is a new lease on someone's life so often detrimental to another's? Something pinched at my insides as I thought of Hamida and Conall, together every day, coming back to the same house every night. What was I thinking, leaving him like that?

'Your mama has been better to me than anyone. But other people? They think I am shameless for leaving him. What do they know how he has made living with him impossible?'

She looked at her hands that glittered with gold rings.

'Tell people that,' I said.

'I would rather people judge me than feel sorry for me.'

Judgement is so much more bearable than pity.

'Oh –' she leaned towards the door, listening to the noises from the TV – 'It sounds like the daughter-in-law is about to poison her mother-in-law.'

Just as she was about to leave, she turned round. 'I will be at your wedding, even if my husband is not.'

The same could be said for me.

Note for book: If you're going to have an important conversation with your husband, make sure you're in the same country. If you're going to have a wedding, make sure there's a groom.

12.45 p.m. 'This is madness! You're in the country and I haven't seen you,' exclaimed Katie on the phone. 'Devon was the dream. How's being back home? Has your mum forgiven you? Ugh, this rain, Sweetu. Insane.'

Sometimes it's nice speaking to Katie because she often does the speaking for you.

'Meeting on Thursday,' she continued. 'You'll love Sakib. Sometimes I wish you'd married him. In fact, I kind of wish I'd married him. Though I love Conall. Obvs.'

'And your husband, remember.'

'Yes, that too. Anyway, how are you?'

'Well, my mum's decided to throw me a wedding.' I couldn't quite bring myself to add that my husband wouldn't be coming to it.

'Oh.' Pause. 'That's good, no? You love weddings.'

'*No*, I don't.'

'No, you don't. I thought maybe Karachi had changed you.' Katie then asked if I could talk my mum out of it, just as I heard Maars being instructed to climb a ladder to put up the fairy lights. 'Won't Conall like a bit of a song and dance? Tom's going to be so excited when I tell him.'

'No, he's not really the singing, dancing type,' I replied.

'That's a shame. But I guess you can't have it all.'

Thursday 7 February

11.20 a.m. 'See here,' said Mum, showing me her Facebook profile on her iPad. 'I can create an event and people will RSPCA there.'

'RSVP, Mum,' I said. 'Although, having seen the guest list, calling the RSPCA wouldn't be such a bad idea.'

'Hmm?' She seemed to flush as her eyes scanned the screen.

'What?' I asked.

'Nothing,' she replied, suppressing a giggle. 'Acha, am I looking fairer?'

'Yeah. People will think you're Conall's mum.'

Why did I mention his mum? Serves me right for trying to be clever. I pretended to pay great attention to the gold-sequinned favour boxes.

'Oh, haan, give me her number so I can speak to her for an invite. It doesn't looks nice na otherwise. And when is Conall coming?'

'Oh, not until next month,' I replied, waves of panic crashing around inside me.

Luckily, Mum seemed distracted so I ran up to my room only to see I'd missed a call from him.

To Conall: Just getting ready for meeting. Call you later. Are you coming to our wedding now? Xx

11.35 a.m.

To Foz; Suj; Hannah: Hello, friends of mine who haven't come to see me. Where the fuck are you? Well, I know where you are, Foz. Just thought I'd let you know I'm having a wedding 30th March. Maybe I'll see you then. Loving you very begrudgingly. Xxx

1.40 p.m. So weird coming into my old workplace. First of all, there was the Tube journey, which was a bit of a counter-culture shock. I kept smiling at people – *I'm back!* No one seemed to care. Then I entered the best part, the grey professional bubble with its concrete walls and mechanical smiles. Thought of Conall and his defiance of social expectation by following his passion. Funny how the thing you love about someone can also be the thing that means they're on the other side of the world. My problem's obviously a lack of passion – something that *makes* me want to wake up in the morning and get out of bed. Tonight I'll make a list of things I'm passionate about.

Ooh, look. Fresh muffins!

1.50 p.m. 'Gosh, look at you,' said finger-sniffing Brammers as we sat in the conference room.

God knows what that meant. I smiled.

'How are your kids?' I asked.

'Feral.' With which she got out her phone and started showing me pictures of them. 'I must follow you on Instagram.'

We spent so long searching for each other on social media that by the time we were ready to actually talk, Katie was walking in with Sakib. I flung my arms round her until Brammers began clearing her throat.

'We go way back,' I explained to Sakib, shaking his hand as we sat down.

I noticed a wedding ring. (Old habits and all that.)

'I've heard about it. Several times,' he said, smiling at Katie.

Brammers looked bored. The first thing I noticed was just how *brown* Sakib was. It always stands out more in publishing offices. I must blind people with my hijabi brownness. They gave me the contracts to sign for book two when he handed me a book.

'Your proof.'

It was *my* book! I stared at its hot pink border, the dark turquoise with block, gold lettering: *Lessons in Heartbreak and Laughter.* And there was my name: Sofia Khan.

'You should be really proud,' said Sakib. 'I mean it.'

I did feel proud. Prouder than I'd thought I would.

Katie got her notebook out and went through the list of things she'd pitched and lined up for me. 'There's lots more we can do. Festivals, features . . . there's already been so much interest with the whole Muslim marries Irish convert angle.'

'Maybe you and Conall can do a joint event?' suggested Sakib. 'I've heard he's handsome. Women will like him.'

I had PR fatigue. Plus, why couldn't I do something that was just me? Didn't sound very marriage-spirited, though.

'Conall's not the publicity type,' I said, looking at Katie.

Not the publicity type, wedding type, or living-in-one-place type, which begs the question – what type is he? Restless type – that's what. If I only knew him on paper, I'd have put the paper in the shredder. Aside from that, I could imagine him, sitting in conversation, irritated by the mundane questions. I picked up a biscuit.

'It'd be a good tie-in for the second book,' said Sakib.

'He's very busy,' I said. 'In Karachi.'

Sakib paused. 'Right.' He poured some coffee and passed me the cup. 'He'll be coming for your launch, though?'

Katie looked at me. Sakib leaned forward, the office light catching the glint of his gold watch.

'Oh, he'll be here for the wedding, anyway,' said Katie.

Argh!

'I thought you were already married?' he asked.

'I am. It's my mum. You know, the parental celebratory rights,' I replied.

He smiled and raised his eyebrows. 'Oh yes, I know about *that*.'

Brammers put two cubes of sugar in her coffee.

'How about pitching a strong feminist stance?' Katie interjected.

'I'll be shot for saying this,' said Sakib, 'but I always thought women preferred romance to feminism.'

Brammers shook her head while he wasn't looking, as if it was just the typical thing a man would say.

I took another biscuit, thinking about Conall. Romance versus feminism. 'Whoever said you can't have both?'

3.45 p.m. Just as I was walking out of the building Sakib caught up with me.

'You know, I just wanted to say . . .'

He paused, looking very shiny – like a new doll – even on such a grey day. I liked his black, thick-rimmed glasses.

'Yes?'

'I hope I don't sound patronising . . .' He cleared his throat. 'It's just that, I feel very proud.'

I looked round to see what exactly he might be proud of. 'OK . . .' I said.

'Of you.'

It made me blush. I've never been very good with the candour of compliments. 'Oh.'

'I mean, this is brown-to-brown speaking,' he added conspiratorially, and then looked immediately embarrassed. 'Sorry, I –'

'No, it's fine . . . Thank you.'

It was kind of patronising, but he meant well. And it was weird – the camaraderie in colour. It almost felt un-PC.

'Good. Great.' He stuck his thumbs up at me.

Buffoon in me ended up doing the same to him.

'We'll speak soon,' he said.

'Yes. Soon.'

I sat in St James's Park, a little lifted, which goes to show how fickle feelings can be. I'd been dreaming of a decent cappuccino for months but now I had one and it was too strong. As I watched passers-by the lift began to deflate. When was contentment going to kick in? The bench was still wet from the rain and I thought I was getting a cold. I attempted to get excited at the prospect of book publication but something didn't quite feel right. It turns out that thoughts are no more significant sitting in a park in London than they are sitting in a flat in Karachi.

My finger hovered over Conall's number. It was ridiculous to hesitate over calling your own husband.

'Hi,' I said as he picked up the phone.

Pause.

'Hey.'

Forget about the last conversation, Sofia. Think about now.

'Guess what I'm holding?' I said.

'Well, I'm not there so I hope it's not what I think it is.'

I laughed. What was I talking about, Conall on paper? He's more than ink and parchment.

'My *book*.'

'Ah. How does it feel?'

Love his voice.

'Better than I thought.'

He paused. 'That's grand. You deserve it.'

I watched the overcast skies that looked ready to chuck it down with rain again.

'I never liked that saying. People don't get what they deserve generally, do they?'

Mum didn't deserve to lose her husband. Auntie deserved one who appreciated her. Murderers don't deserve freedom. But if we all began thinking about what we deserve and what life gives us, well: that way bitterness lies.

'You get what you get and that's the way it's meant to be,' I added.

'Some might ask what the point is then,' he replied.

'Well, dear husband, that's where believing in God comes in handy. Bigger picture and all that.'

'I'm not sure how I feel when you start making sense, Sofe.'

'Shut up.' I turned the book over in my hand, smiling. 'Have you changed your mind yet?'

'Sofe . . . '

'It's really not that complicated,' I said.

Lightning flashed and I got a chill in my bones.

'Listen, Hamida thinks –'

Thunder roared as I got up when I realised he'd said Hammy's name. 'Hamida?' I asked.

'There's too much to do here. I'm sorry. I should be there, I know. I just can't.'

I know that tone. My own husband won't be at my wedding. How exactly was I going to face this? What was I going to tell everyone?

'Feels like you've been away for a long time,' he said. 'My moral compass is all over the place.'

I ran down the stairs of Green Park Station as the rain began beating down on the ground. 'Maybe you should consider letting it guide you back home.'

7.50 p.m.

> **From Foz:** Darling! What do you mean you're having a wedding? It's so soon! Can't believe I'll miss your pissed-off face on stage! Xxxxx

Will anyone I want actually be there? Must remain calm. I have to get Mum to cancel. How can there be a groom-less wedding?

10.45 p.m. Mum and Auntie Reena had gone to the cinema when the doorbell rang. I opened the door and it was Suj and Hannah!

'Did someone get married?' said Hannah, walking into the house.

I leaped into Suj's arms as she lifted me off the ground and consequently almost broke her back.

'You guys are shits for not abandoning everything and coming to see me sooner.'

'I think my husband's co-dependent,' said Hannah.

'Your husband needs more friends,' said Suj.

'It's so weird. I'm like, I need to see my girls and he's all, but I'd planned an evening for us,' said Hannah.

Ugh. 'Isn't that annoying?' I asked.

'Totally. But it's better than him ignoring me,' she said. 'He doesn't understand. When you get married in your thirties you've formed all these close female friendships and the man ends up being a bonus. Men don't bond in the same way.'

This is what I'd missed: Hannah's analysis of life. She looked at the fairy lights wrapped around the bannisters.

'Toffee, I can't believe you're having a wedding,' Suj exclaimed.

There was the panic again.

'But before that, do you have any Sudocrem?' she pointed at a minute pimple on her temple.

'She hasn't shut up about it the entire journey,' said Han. 'Here: we brought pizza.'

Hannah went into the kitchen to get plates out while Suj looked at her pimple in the mirror. 'I have a photo shoot tomorrow,' she said.

'That pimple's not going to ruin your modelling career.'

She turned round. 'Let me look at you, Toffee. You look amazing.'

Which was so untrue but so *Suj*.

We sat and ate, catching up on the past six months. I don't mean to be sentimental here but you can't really underestimate the comfort of friends.

'Foz messaged this morning. She's in Peru,' said Suj. 'Lucky cow.'

'So, when's Conall coming?' asked Hannah.

I picked at the mushroom on the pizza. 'Not sure, exactly.'

'Man with a cause,' she said. 'Is he actually quite practising? Praying regularly?'

'Underlines verses from the Qur'an and all sorts,' I replied.

'Fascinating, isn't it?' she said.

'Fucking great,' added Suj, looking into her hand-mirror. Despite being Sikh, she feels very strongly about other people being Muslim.

'He's not started dictating to you, has he?' asked Han. 'Why are your jeans so tight, why's your forearm showing?'

Suj looked up from her mirror.

'*No*,' I said. 'He's not a fundo.'

'I think I'd find it quite hot if Charles told me my jeans were too tight,' said Suj.

'You'd throw a plate at him,' I said, cutting a piece of pizza for her.

'Maybe I would.'

'She'd run him over with a bulldozer!' said Han. 'What's Conall's brother like?' she then asked. 'Is he a liberal? Liberals don't mind converts.'

I told them he's away – speaking of, having been away myself I'd forgotten how many questions Hannah asks.

'Who cares what anyone thinks,' said Suj. 'It's about fucking time you were happy.'

Love Suj.

'What about his parents?' said Hannah. 'They're Catholic, right?'

'Bloody hell, get the Pope on the line,' said Suj.

I shrugged. 'He doesn't really speak to them.'

This time Suj put her mirror away. 'He doesn't speak to his parents?'

I closed the empty pizza box and opened another. What was I meant to say? *Tried asking my husband about it but he doesn't talk about them.* That doesn't sound like winning behaviour. They had to get to know Conall before they could judge him. Just then I heard the keys in the front door and Mum and Auntie Reena came in.

'Ah, Betas. You make sure you are ready for the wedding,' said Mum to them. 'Suj, you must do Soffoo's make-up and, Hannah, you are in charge of making sure no one takes the centrepieces.

'So shame Fozia won't be here. I don't understand what all this *finding yourself* is. If you don't know where you are, then what have you been doing in your life?'

It wasn't worth explaining Foz's need to stay in South America longer than necessary due to her break-up. On a less selfish note, it was probably best for her since Kam was always trying to claw his way back into her life. The further she was from him the better. Before anyone could respond, Mum had turned her back and was already checking Facebook.

'Love how your mum just gets on with things,' said Suj as we all hovered at the door.

I was inclined to check what exactly she was getting on with, but I had enough on my plate.

'It's great being married and still living with your mum,' I said.

Note for book: When married to someone, standard state should be of cohabitation.

'You can't have the hot convert husband and a sane mum,' said Hannah. 'Life isn't that kind.'

'Don't listen to her, Toffee.' Suj grabbed my arms. 'Life should only ever be kind to you.' With which she pushed Hannah out of the house.

I spent the rest of the night wedged between Mum and Auntie Reena, looking online at chocolate fountains.

To Foz: I really miss you xxxx

Friday 22 February

11.20 a.m. Argh! Have spent morning teetering on the edge of bedroom window (having a fag) and hysteria. Tried to speak to

Mum about postponing wedding but she's already sent save the date e-invites! Combo of lack of personal space, looming wedding without an actual groom, need to buy a dress (apparently that's important), Mum badgering me about Conall's parents and Auntie Reena keeping me up, talking about her life's regrets, is driving me to excessive nicotine intake. Not good for head, heart or lungs. Everyone keeps asking when Conall will be here. Must breathe. Mum's addiction to Facebook doesn't help. She's constantly giggling, tapping at the screen. Shouldn't she be knitting or something?

I noticed a taxi pull up outside and saw Sean climb out of the car. That was when Mum mentioned that he'd come over one day after Conall and I'd got married and she never really spoke to him after that.

'*Mum*, he must think we're so rude,' I said.

'And I think it's very rude you got married without telling your mama,' she replied, swiping something on her iPad.

What if Sean thinks Mum's racist? And not the casual, *but-some-of-my-best-friends-are-black* type racist. I mean the proper *you're-no-longer-my-daughter-and-I-want-nothing-to-do-with-you* type racist.

It was time to pay my new bro-in-law a visit. Especially since it seemed he'd be the only Irish representative at the wedding.

Must remember am paying my dues to Mum and then the debt will be paid. Though am beginning to feel like Greece in this continent of filial duty.

1.20 p.m. 'Hi,' I said as Sean opened the door.

He frowned at me at first, but recognition seemed to dawn as he broke into a smile. 'Look who it is. My new sister-in-law.'

'Should I come back later? You must be jet-lagged.'

He waved his hand and summoned me into the house.

I've decided I like Sean (more than his brother right now, actually). They look incredibly similar except that Sean is (very) clean-shaven, an easier version of Conall: the way he'll walk up to you with a big smile and shake your hand so hard it might fall off. Or how he'll just let the cigarette hang from the corner of his mouth (while you're trying not to lust after it – the cigarette, that is).

'This certainly cries out bachelor,' I said as we walked into the living room.

It was so different now with its black leather sofa and HD TV mounted on the wall – all glass tables and fluffy rugs. I noticed photos of Sean and Conall as kids. Another one of what I assumed to be his parents; his dad looking unimpressed and his mum giving a tight smile; and a dog, lolling his tongue out. Conall never had pictures of his parents when he was living here.

'And that's *exactly* what I was going for,' replied Sean, looking pleased. 'Sit. Drink?'

'No, I just wanted to say hi.' And er, sorry about my mum, who's rude, but not racist.

He sat down. 'So, he finally did it. He actually got married.'

I waited for the expression: to *you*. But if it happened then I missed it.

'This should be good for him,' he said.

Which was an odd thing to say, but I nodded because it was important to be agreeable. Then I told him about the wedding.

'But Conall won't be there?' he said.

I shook my head.

'He's not coming to his own wedding?'

'No.'

'Sorry, I don't understand,' he said.

Yes, Sean, welcome to the Crackpot Family. I told him that brown weddings tend to be less about the bride and groom bound to each other for eternity and more about three hundred guests, bound to the promise of biryani.

'Oh,' he said, looking confused. As well he might. 'Well, I get big weddings . . . I'll be there. 'Course.'

Just then his phone rang and he picked up. 'Speak of the devil.' He looked over at me. 'Your wife's hanging out with me and where the feck are you? Mm? No.' He turned away. 'What?' He glanced back at me. 'Right. I see. Sure. Sure. Why didn't you . . . fine.'

He turned round again and gave me this look I couldn't quite understand.

'Right. Sure . . .' Sean handed the phone over to me. 'I'll just get my bags upstairs,' he said, walking out of the room.

'I'll send a video message for the day,' said Conall.

'Yeah. That's just as good.'

I looked at the dinner table: the place I used to sit and write, Conall coming in and out, bringing me coffee and tea, giving me life advice. Why couldn't he be here again? Even if it was just to hug me. Maybe I'll write a chapter on 'The Comfort of Arms'. As in a person's arms – not weapons. Obviously.

'You decided on this wedding without me. Trust me, I get it, what with your mum and all. But don't blame me for not being there. You love logic, Sofe. Where is it now?'

Turns out I err on the side of too much hope.

Sunday 24 February

7.10 p.m. 'Where are you going?' I asked Mum, who was hovering at my door, dressed in her Sunday best.

I was trying to write. Chapter title: *Great Expectations* . . .

'How do I look? she asked, touching her hair tied back in a chignon.

'Very nice.'

She paused. 'You're writing?'

I nodded.

'It isn't easy always, haina, Beta?'

'Writing or marriage?'

'O-ho, marriage.'

The jewels around her neck sparkled. Dad bought her that necklace on one of her birthdays. We were poor for so long that when we finally had money Dad's presents got increasingly extravagant. Maybe it was easier to be married when you had to focus on important things like putting food in your children's mouths. Except now we have rather too much food, but I don't think asking for poverty is particularly sensible.

'First year is always hardest,' she said.

What exactly did Mum know about me and Conall? Whenever I think she doesn't understand something it turns out it's not that she doesn't get it; she just doesn't get bogged down by it.

'Acha, I'm going. Your auntie's downstairs. Be nice to her.'

'Obviously, Mum.'

She went to leave and then turned round. 'Marriage can be hard, but I think it is worth it.'

Thursday 28 February

9.15 a.m. It's life's irony that I'm the one getting married in under four weeks and Mum's the one who's walking around with a face mask on. The knots in my stomach multiply each passing day. It's not just that Conall won't be here – it's what people will think his absence means. What does it mean? How much longer can I leave it to explain to Mum what's going on?

'Uff, I don't know when your Auntie Reena will go home,' said Mum, lowering her voice as she checked whether the rice was done.

'I thought you liked her being here,' I said, noticing her flushed face.

'She is going around like her life has ended because she has left her shit husband. Her hair all grey now. How many times I told her about discounted hair dye in Boots.'

Mum grabbed a rag and began to wipe down the coffee table. 'Your baba left us all, Soffoo. Thirty-five years and gone.' She looked at the dirty cloth and threw it in the bin. 'But at least he died. Reena's husband behaved so badly she is now left high and fly.'

'Dry, Mum.'

'But you know: men don't wait like women do,' she said. 'And the biggest thing I realised, watching Reena with her long face?'

'What?'

She stood up, inspecting her face mask in the mirror. 'I'm not dead yet.'

12.05 p.m. 'Acha, do you think I should wear my orange suit with red embroidery or red suit with orange embroidery?'

So, Mum, funny thing: my husband's not coming to the wedding.

'Soffoo?'

'Hmm?'

'O-ho, Maria! Should I wear my orange suit with red embroidery or red suit with orange embroidery?'

'Red with orange. Who's this person coming for lunch?' asked Maars, walking into the kitchen. 'One second.' Her phone rang as she spoke to her mother-in-law, calling about Adam.

'Sorry, the woman looks after him *once* and she thinks she's the fairy godmother.'

'Maria, you should be grateful she's looking after him at all so you can enjoy your lunch here. You children don't know sacrifices grandmothers make.'

'Don't know why you're defending her. It's not as if you like her,' said Maars.

'Haan, she is very miserable. But still, don't we mothers deserve our own life?'

'Yeah. Of course,' said Maars, as if it was the most obvious thing. Which it was.

'He's from Karachi,' said Mum.

'Who?' I asked.

'The guest.' Mum tasted the lassi and added more sugar. 'An old family friend. He found me on Facebook. Technology is amazing, haina? I remember how I used to write letters and waited and waited for replies. Now just one click and you find someone from forty years ago.'

Maria and I looked at each other as Mum turned to us.

'You both behave yourselves tonight, hmm? He's from a very good family and doesn't need to hear what *bakwas* you both talk.'

I wanted to highlight for the record that we weren't the only ones capable of talking *crap*.

Went up to get changed and Maars came into my room. 'Is it me or is Mum acting weird?'

I looked at my phone to see if I had a missed call from Conall, but they've become increasingly infrequent.

'I don't know.'

Was he with Hamida? What were they talking about? I had to tell Maars; the anxiety was driving me mad. Just then her phone rang and it was Tahir.

'With Sofe, waiting for this guest.' She rolled her eyes at me.

'What do we talk about?' she said. 'Yes, Tahir, we all sit and bitch about our husbands. OK, I'll call you when we're done. Yeah. Love you too. He's so paro,' she added when she put the phone down, looking more fond of him than I'd ever seen her. Just then Auntie Reena came into the room. She stood there, looking sullen.

'What's wrong?' asked Maars.

'Nothing, Beta. What could be wrong with me? I don't complain.'

'Come on, let's go and watch some Zee TV,' said Maars, putting her arm round her and leading her out of my room.

Auntie Reena wasn't doing a very good job of showing that life gets less complicated with age.

6.50 p.m. Oh my *actual* God above, below, all around me. First, *why* can't I just shut up and give simple answers to simple questions, when I know things always come back and bite me on my restless rotund arse? Second, what the hell just happened??

The doorbell rang and I went to open it. I looked at the man's face and thought: *he looks familiar.* The receding hairline, the stout and strong frame, the friendly smile, the moustache . . . *oh my God.*

'Uncle Mouch!'

'Ji?'

Uncle-fucking-mouch! From the plane. The one I told I'd been married four times! What was he doing ringing our doorbell??

'Salamalaikum,' I said, smiling so hard I thought my jaw might break, praying he wouldn't recognise me.

He looked at me for a moment, a question in his mind appearing, and then the slow dawn of realisation.

'Oh.'

Just then he looked over my shoulder – his face changing from surprise to relief.

'Mehnaz,' he said.

He looked back at me.

'Wasim,' said Mum.

Who's Wasim? This is Uncle Mouch. Mum came forward, practically pushing me out of the way as he handed her a bunch of twelve red roses, which I felt was inappropriate, as flowers go.

She looked at the roses as he watched her.

'The ones you left,' he said.

Hain? He came in, looking around and complimenting Mum on the house, saying hello to Maars and Auntie Reena.

'Sit, sit,' Mum said, giving the roses to Maars. 'Put these in the nice vase, Beta. This is my younger daughter, Sofia, and Maria is the eldest.'

He cleared his throat as I tried to avoid his gaze.

'Haan, I've met your youngest daughter,' he replied.

Mum's warning not to talk crap came about thirty years too late. I felt the colour rise to my cheek. In my defence, he was being *very* nosy.

He explained our journey on the plane, thankfully skipping the part about the four husbands.

'It was an interesting talk,' he said.

I needed a fag. I went to the kitchen, pretending to go and help Maars.

'Sofe . . . what did you do?' she said, as soon as she saw my face.

I told her about the plane journey.

'You bloody idiot,' she said, looking up from arranging the roses. 'Mum's going to kill you.'

I patted my dress as if I'd find a packet of fags. Maars grabbed my arm as we went back in the room and sat down.

'Just try not to speak,' she whispered.

'Betas, your mama looks the same as she did forty years ago.'

Mum blushed. Uncle Mouch's moustache really was very black. He started talking about his wife, who apparently died a few years ago. He looked up and said: 'God's will. So many years you spend with one person it is like losing half yourself.'

Mum nodded. Though I'm not quite sure Mum could be any more whole than she already was.

'And where is your husband?' he asked Auntie Reena.

Cue: awkward moment. She looked at all of us as the colour rose to her cheeks, which were stuffed with paan masala.

'He's no longer with us,' said Mum.

'Ah, I'm very sorry,' he said.

'Has Mum just killed Uncle off?' I muttered to Maars.

'Yep.'

'And I was very sorry to hear about Shakil,' he said.

Tears glistened in Maars' eyes and for a second I thought Dad might come bounding down the stairs, his voice booming from the passage, asking Mum where he'd put his glasses, and what this strange man was doing here.

'Betas,' he added, looking at Maars and me. 'Your mother and I were great friends before she got married. Always the life of the party. Even now she is.'

Auntie Reena shifted in her seat and Mum wasn't lifting her gaze from the ground. Had the mention of Dad made her cry?

'I know your baba only passed away last year. He was a good man. But you children have open minds.'

His gaze rested on me. What the hell was he talking about?

'Love is a thing that never dies. Even forty years later.'

He looked at Mum. I looked at Maars. Maars looked alarmed. What the hell was going on?? Then he reached out and put his hand on top of Mum's.

Why was he touching her? She lifted her gaze and looked at him, but why wasn't she taking her hand away and throwing him out of the house??

'Oh my God,' whispered Maars.

'Hai, Allah,' I said Auntie Reena.

I tried to see the expression in Mum's eyes, thinking I'd find grief at the mention of her dead husband, but I didn't find that at all. It was the opposite of grief.

Uncle Mouch looked at us, leaning towards Mum. 'Betas . . .'

My heart was thudding, a dark thought entering my confused mind. *No, surely not.* But there was his hand, still on top of hers.

'I am marrying your mother.'

MARCH

The Married and the Martyred

AYISHA MALIK

Muslim Marriage Book

Qabool hai: literally translated to mean, I do. Except we Muslims say it three times – for purposes of clarity. The question is always the same: do you take this man/woman, son-of/daughter-of to be your husband/wife. The woman's asked if she accepts the money the groom has promised – which she can use for a good old shopping spree, or, if things go badly and end in divorce, use to celebrate release from clutches of the husband that she once loved.

'No vows?' I hear you ask. It's all implicit, isn't it – honesty, fidelity, sickness, health, etc. But sometimes it's helpful to think about what you're really saying 'I do' to. What curveballs can married life throw? Is anyone truly ready for the consequence of two separate histories converging, and prepared for the past that can sometimes crawl its way into the present?

Friday 1 March

10.45 a.m. 'But what about Dad?' I'd exclaimed when that Mouchman had left the house.

Mum got up and made her way to the kitchen. 'Unless your baba comes out from his grave, Soffoo, I'm not married any more.'

Maars rubbed her temples.

'How well do you even know him?' I said.

'My daughter who ran away with a gora is asking her mother this – very good.'

It was awful. My mother was actually right.

'I was married for *thirty-five* years. You know how long thirty-five years is? Thirty of them we spent arguing.'

It felt about the same ratio as me and Conall. This didn't feel like a good omen. Mum got a bunch of grapes, put them on a plate and handed them to us. 'They're washed. Eat them.'

'You always say you don't need anyone,' Maars said, quieter than usual.

'He isn't anyone.'

'But . . . but you're our mum,' I said.

It sounded far less ridiculous in my mind than it did out loud, but she was – she was our *mum*.

'I am nothing else?' she replied, looking at both of us.

She's been living with the 'mother' label, 'wife' label, with all kinds of labels her whole life, and I never realised – not in any conscious way – that she is more than a label.

'Mehnaz, you should think what people will say,' said Auntie Reena, who'd opened her eighth packet of paan masala.

'My whole life I've been told what to do. I was told who to marry and where to live and I damn care now. People always do what they want . . .' She looked at me. 'Now it is my turn.'

Maars and I sat in a café. She touched her head, as if she was in pain. Adam grinned, sitting on her lap without a care in this upside-down world.

'It's just –'

'I know. It's only been nine months.'

It's not that I have anything against old people finding happiness, it's just that I didn't realise my mum was in *need* of happiness. So soon. Maars lifted her coffee, not quite bringing it to her mouth, her eyes still fixed on some faraway place. 'He'd better not be a shit.' She looked at me. 'We have to give him points for marrying the mother of a woman he thinks has had four husbands.'

'Thanks.'

'We'll have to be adults about this.'

'Yes.' My reflex to start throwing things around was probably not what Maars had in mind.

'Yes,' Maars said.

'Have you told Tahir?'

She nodded.

'What did he say?'

'He was shocked, wasn't he? But then just said it's probably a good thing. Have you told Conall?' she asked.

That familiar feeling of wrenched insides came back as I shook my head.

'When *is* he coming? The wedding's round the corner.'

I gulped my coffee and bile down. 'He'll be here soon.'

Oh my God, Mum's going to have a date at my wedding and I'm not!

10.50 a.m. Ugh! Awful thought swept through mind . . . Mum's going to have *sex*! Wish I could pluck brain out from my head and never have to use it ever again.

I'm having a fag.

10.52 a.m. Maybe old people don't have sex?

10.53 a.m. Just googled and apparently not only do they have sex, but STD rates in older adults are rising. Uncle Mouch might look harmless and polite, but so did Auntie Reena's husband.

Item #356 in life: drop into conversation that future stepfather should be tested for STDs.

Monday 4 March

9.35 a.m.

From: Sakib Awaan
To: Sofia Khan
Subject: How's it Going?

Hi Sofia,

Just checking in to see how the book's going? Let me know if there's anything you have for me to read.

Best wishes,

Sakib

How's the book going? *How's the book going?* How can I think of the MARRIAGE book when my own mother is getting married??

9.39 a.m.

From: Sofia Khan
To: Sakib Awaan
Subject: Re: How's it Going?

It is going A-OK. Brilliantly, even. Wedding is taking over, though. You know brown people love a literal song and dance.

MY MOTHER IS GETTING MARRIED.

But otherwise everything is great.

9.41 a.m.

From: Sakib Awaan

Only too familiar with it. I'm known for my Bollywood dance moves, in case you need to hire professional dancers.

An image of Sakib, lifting his perfectly ironed Savile Row trousers at the sound of Bollywood music made me actually laugh out loud.

9.45 a.m.

From: Sofia Khan

That sounds entertaining and horrifying in equal measure.

9.49 a.m.

From: Sakib Awaan

It truly is. But the number of weddings I go to I feel it should've been the obvious career choice.
Good luck,
Sakib

Friday 8 March

10.10 a.m. Mum's engagement will just take a while to get used to. I can be an adult about it. Like Maars.

12.45 p.m. Went to Dad's grave and sat on the ground, staring at his gravestone. It's fine and well being adult but it's only been nine months. How can someone move on so quickly?

Have been trying to organise dinner with Suj and Han but something or another keeps coming up. Decided to call Suj.

'Toffee! Sorry, I've been meaning to call you but . . . guess what?'

'What?' I asked, getting up from Dad's grave.

'I'm moving in with Charles!'

'Fudge! Shut up. That's great.'

'My old man nearly had a heart attack,' she said, as I turned back and had one more look at Dad's grave.

'Is he speaking to you?' I asked.

'He is, but it wasn't easy,' said Suj. 'Who else does he have? Oh balls, Sofe, have to go but see you before the wedding, OK? Do you need me to do anything?'

I wasn't quite able to tell her Mum was getting married.

'I'll send you pictures of the flat,' she said. 'It's *so* nice.'

'OK . . . oh, hang on, Hannah's calling,' I said, checking my phone.

'OK, love you! Don't tell Han, I'm calling her tonight.'

'Where have you been?' I said, answering Han's call.

'Omar and I are going to adopt.'

'Oh,' I said. 'Bloody hell. That's not the answer I was expecting.'

She told me about the past few months and how they'd been talking about it. 'We want a family, you know,' she said. 'And I can't have my own so . . . well, it feels like the right thing.'

'Han, that's . . . that's incredible.'

She seemed to breathe a sigh of relief. 'I messaged Foz this morning but haven't heard from her.'

'No,' I said. 'I don't know where the hell she is.'

'Are you OK?'

'Oh yeah, I'm fine. Great. We should celebrate your news,' I said.

'What about you?' said Han. 'You going to pop them out soon, or give it a few years? It gets harder after your thirties – mid-thirties, I'd say. But still, you wouldn't want to risk it.'

Babies?? I'm barely managing to keep myself together let alone babies.

Then she asked if I'd spoken to Conall about it, and how does he feel, and what's his opinion and *oh my God*. These were my best friends but suddenly they felt so new. Maybe they were. Hannah was donning a new layer of adoption and Suj was fitting into her new role as long-term-moved-in-girlfriend.

Note for book: In the relay race of life, don't be surprised if you begin falling further and further behind, because the thing about races is that everyone is too focused on the finish line.

To Foz: Our friends' lives are changing and you're somewhere taking surfing lessons. Can you find your way back home, please? Thanks. Love you xxx

The thing is, when I think of the finish line, the only person I can see waiting there is Conall.

Ugh. What a sap.

Saturday 16 March

10.40 a.m. 'Soffoo, wedding is in two weeks and you haven't told me how many people are coming from Ireland for the wedding. What day is Conall arriving?'

Mum was scrubbing the windows in her bedroom with Fairy Liquid. Every time I look at her she seems a different creature altogether – a spring in her step that has me exhausted just watching her. I need to buy another pack of fags. How much longer can I keep the secret? People can be dim, but they're going to notice if the groom's not at the wedding. Momentarily considered borrowing Katie's husband, Tom, or better yet, Sean, to sit on stage with me, but don't think Conall would be mad about the idea.

'I'll call his mum again and find out,' I replied.

Mum turned round, taking her yellow rubber gloves off. 'Very weird family who keeps forgetting to call you back,' she said, but I was blinded by a flash of multicoloured light.

'What is *that*?'

She broke out into a huge smile, thrusting her hand in my face. 'My engagement ring.'

'Oh my bloody hell. Is he loaded?'

'Hain?'

'Rich?'

'Of course. He was colonel in the army. See your ring, Soffoo?'

She eyed my gold band, looking like the grief-stricken widow she should be, but grief-stricken for the wrong reasons.

'I like it,' I said.

Can't believe I was comparing engagement rings with own mother. Especially when own mother feels sorry for mine.

'Do you really like it, or because you have to like it?'

I looked at it and remembered when Conall got it out of his pocket. We were sitting on the outside step of the Karachi flat – people staring at us, the unlikely pair, me not giving a damn and Conall looking so at home I should've known he'd want to stay as long as possible.

'See this?' he said, holding it up to me. 'The man who sold it to me –'

Man? What man?

'Don't worry, I got it checked and it's real. Jesus. Anyway, I met him in Bangladesh – remember when I was there for a week? He told me it was his mother's who'd fled India in 1971. She was leaving with her family – her husband was fighting in the war – and realised she'd forgotten her wedding band. She went back for it when she heard an explosion. She lost her whole family.' He paused.

God, he was grim sometimes. I thought about my own family, muttering a prayer for their safety. This story didn't feel like a particularly good omen.

'But this ring,' he said, turning it around in his hands. 'It saved her.'

I watched him stare at the ring with such intensity anyone would've thought it belonged to his own mother. These are the people with extra goodness – that kind of excess empathy is hard to find.

'You really are a sucker for a story,' I said.

'Shut up and give me your hand.'

He put the ring on and I have no idea why tears surfaced my eyes.

'Good,' he said. 'You need something to show you're married.' He looked at me. 'Plus, I'd like to think of you as a woman who will always survive. Despite adversity.'

It's funny, because you never can be sure how a person sees you.

'We didn't know we were getting married when you went to Bangladesh,' I said.

'No,' he said. 'But the ring was always going to be yours.'

I'd twisted it around my finger, an unusual cocktail of emotions swelling in my chest. 'You know that if there was a war I'd be the first to go,' I said.

He took my hand and replied: 'Killed by your own people, probably.'

I nodded. 'Or just can't be arsed to move.'

'Still,' he said, looking at me, 'you'd probably save a person or two along the way.'

I came out of my reverie and noticed Mum staring at me as I rubbed the ring on my finger.

'I really like it, Mum,' I replied.

She was looking at her own by this time, though. 'See how it shines?'

That's when I noticed she was no longer wearing Dad's ring. A sinkhole seemed to give way in my heart. Her happiness shouldn't be hard to see, but it was, and I don't know how much of a bad daughter that made me.

'I'm just going to do some work,' I said, knowing the only place I'd be going was Dad's grave.

I ran down the stairs, grabbed my jacket and opened the door when I started. There he was, flesh and sturdy bones.

'Conall?'

I couldn't believe it. I dropped my jacket and jumped into his arms, taking in the scent of musk, plane and Pakistan. He came home!

'What are you . . . ? You didn't . . . Why didn't you tell me?' I looked at his lovely face and I'm not ashamed to say, perhaps I was a little dog-like, kissing it. I guess that's what happens when you realise how much you miss a person. His arms tightened round my waist.

'Thought I owed you a surprise,' he said.

Everything was going to be OK. Those weeks of worry were needless and irrational. He was here and we'd be OK.

'Soffoo! Who is it?' came Mum's voice from upstairs.

I looked up at him again when a figure caught my eye. There she was, standing behind the gate, suitcase by her side; the oh-so-familiar figure of Hamida.

'Hai hai, you are wasting the heating,' came Mum's voice as she thudded down the stairs.

I stepped to the side.

'Hi,' said Conall.

Mum's face hardened, her lips pursed, Fairy Liquid and rubber gloves squeezed to her chest. Just then I heard a car pulling up and engine turning off.

'What's going on?' came Maars' voice as she got out of the car.

She looked at Hammy as Tahir unstrapped Adam from his car seat.

'You are here,' said Mum to Conall.

I heard banging at a window and saw Maars telling Auntie Reena to get out.

'Maybe we should go in,' I suggested, but Mum didn't look like she had any plans to move.

Conall clenched his jaw and put his hand on his chest. 'Mrs Khan – I'm sorry. Really.'

'Well! Would you look who it is.'

I angled past Mum to see Sean striding past Hammy, towards Conall, bringing him into a hug.

'You came,' he exclaimed.

'Why wouldn't he come?' said Mum.

'Inside, anyone?' I said.

'Who's your friend?' asked Sean, looking at Hammy.

'Oh, this is Hamida,' replied Conall.

'Oh, *you're* Hamida!' Sean was already shaking her hand. 'I've heard plenty about you.'

'Who's Hamida?' asked Mum.

'She works with Conall,' I explained.

I looked at Maars, who mouthed: *Why is she here?* I don't know! Why were there so many people here??

'Beta, don't mind me, you drop me back home,' said Auntie Reena.

'Hai Allah, she's started,' mumbled Mum.

'It's kind of cold out here,' added Tahir, holding Adam.

'Yes, please let's go inside before the neighbours start complaining.'

'Maybe I should go to my friend's,' suggested Hammy.

'No, wait,' answered Conall, looking back at Mum. 'It was all Sofe's idea, you know,' he said.

'Excuse me?' I said.

'Don't listen to her,' he added to Mum, pointing at me. 'She tricks you with her words.' He paused. 'But I am sorry. If it caused you pain.'

'You should think before acting so you don't need to say sorry,' she replied.

His jaw tightened again and I thought, *please don't let this be the time you start talking about your principles and how we're adults and blah blah bleugh*.

'You're right,' he replied.

He did that every so often: reminded me of the reasons I married him. Putting up with my mad mother was right up there. I wanted to kiss him. That was before I looked at Hammy again.

'Mum, *what* is that on your finger?' exclaimed Maars.

Mum waved her hand in the air, forgetting that my husband was in front of her, asking for forgiveness.

'It's bigger than yours, haina?'

I saw Tahir lean in and ask Maars something. Mum looked back at Conall, observing his unkempt beard.

'Chalo,' she said, moving to one side. 'Come indoors.'

3.50 p.m. There was a lot of throat clearing. Now and again Mum stared at her ring. Auntie Reena's paan-munching speeded up whenever she witnessed it.

'Your mum's getting married?' whispered Conall. 'Think you should've mentioned that to me?'

I've tried to tuck Mum's OAP love story into the folds of my unused mind, but flashing engagement rings make it hard to forget. Sean slapped his hands together, smiling at the room, just to fill the silence.

'Listen,' Conall continued to whisper to me. 'About Hamida – I'm sorry but –'

'You had a good flight then?' asked Tahir for the third time.

Conall and Hamida nodded. *What was she doing here?* I kept glancing at Mum, who gave Auntie Reena unimpressed looks every time she considered Hamida.

'So, this is my nephew,' said Conall, walking up to Adam and picking him up. He threw him in the air as Adam's drool fell to the floor. I've not had much pause to consider my ovaries but I wondered why they seemed to be throbbing at this sight.

'Maybe we should go to Sean's and unpack?' said Conall, looking at me. 'Sofe, you want to bring your stuff. You don't mind, do you?' he asked Sean.

'No, it's fine,' he said.

'Soffoo,' said Mum urgently. 'Come in the kitchen.'

I followed her and she said: 'Le, listen to this. You can't stay in the same house as your husband . . . sharing a bedroom . . .' *Cringe.* She cleared her throat. 'It doesn't looks nice.'

'Mum, we're *married.*' *LET ME BE WITH MY HUSBAND.*

'You think people care?' she continued. 'No, no,' she said, looking at my stomach. 'Are you pregnant?'

'What? *No.*'

'Good, because how people will talk otherwise.'

'What's going on?' said Maars as she joined us.

'Mum says I can't stay with Conall.'

'Oh God,' said Maars.

'Is everything OK?' It was Conall. 'You're all talking kind of loudly.'

'You understand these things, don't you, Conall?' asked Mum.

'We'll talk about this later,' I said to Mum.

'Soffoo, what would your baba think, hmm?'

'Now you care what Baba would think,' I murmured.

'Hain?'

'Nothing.'

Mum stared at me. 'Do you think it will look nice for your widowed mama to explain why you are sleeping together before the wedding?'

Silence. Conall looked at the ground, jamming his hands in his pockets. What was I meant to do?

'Listen,' he said, looking at me, 'why don't you come over when you're ready?' With which he nodded to Mum and left the house.

4.15 p.m.

From Suj: Toffee! Do you like my new patio furniture? Is it too dark? The lighter one wasn't as nice. Was well expensive – can you tell or does it look like any old shit? xxxxxx

I wished patio furniture could be the peak of my concern.

6.45 p.m.

From Hannah: My God, who'd have thought adoption would be so complicated? Kid needs a home and loving parents, I can provide both, just give me one. Sorry have been crap. Do you need wedding help? Heard from Foz? Yours, Frazzled. Xx

10.30 p.m. *It's only two weeks.* That's the argument I keep hearing. I told Mum I was going to Sean's and expected more illogical arguing when she said: 'If you think I haven't heard enough gossip, then do what you want. Anyway, your Wasim Uncle and I are going for dinner.'

My mum had a date. With her *fiancé*. Why wasn't she concerned about the gossip *she'd* have to listen to?

'People can say what they want about me – I damn care – but I won't hear anything about my daughter.'

'Waisay, who is Hamida? You think it is proper for a girl to live with two men? What would her mama and baba say?'

'Soffoo,' said Auntie Reena to me. 'No matter how nice men might seem, they are very weak when it comes to temptation. That's why you should have a baby soon. Men don't leave their children as easily.'

Well, nothing like that sentiment to anaesthetise the old ovaries.

Before I went to Sean's I sneaked into the alleyway at the back of the house and had a fag.

He let me in and I walked into the living room where Conall was sitting. Hamida was in her room.

'My moralising brother and sister-in-law, finally together,' said Sean.

Sean bowed his head and took my hand. 'Now, I've hidden the alcohol, so we're good to go.'

'Is Conall telling you what you can and can't have in your house?' I said.

'Technically, it's my house,' replied Conall.

I looked at him to see if he was mad about what had happened with Mum. It's always hard to tell when he's being genuinely patient or just hiding being pissed off very well.

'You could do without the alcohol. Not to mention the pork and women,' added Conall.

'Right, well, hungry?' Sean asked.

'Always with the sanctimony,' I said to Conall.

'It's not sanctimony,' he replied. 'It's experience.'

Sean cleared his throat. '*Caponana d'estate* and *ditalini rigati* something or another – that's with sun-dried tomatoes. But first a good old Caesar salad.'

We sat at the table as Sean went into the kitchen. 'Dinner's ready,' he called out to Hamida.

Bloody Hammy.

'Listen, Mum just needs a bit of time to get her head around things. And thank you,' I said. 'For coming.' I hesitated. 'But what's Hamida doing here?'

Before he could answer Sean returned with drinks as Hammy followed him.

'This is an impressive last-minute spread,' I said. Hammy was *not* going to deter me from acting like a normal person, rather than a jealous lunatic wife. Had to remember, he was *here*. That meant something.

'Sofia – you married the wrong brother. This guy throws a pile of shit together and calls it food. Me? I take love and care,' said Sean.

'Don't pay a bit of attention to what comes out of his mouth,' said Conall, looking tired. 'You bankers have all the money without an ounce of the morality.'

Sean threw his hands in the air. 'Guilty.' He picked up his fork and looked at us. 'Well,' he said, looking at Hamida. 'Don't these two look very . . . *Muslim*.'

Conall shook his head, the hint of a smile showing. 'Shut the fuck up.'

I caught Sean staring at Conall for a moment – a stare that didn't quite go with his easy nature.

'You've gone and increased your chances of wearing an orange jumpsuit, though,' he said.

'We all know he thrives on a challenge,' said Hamida.

'She's got you down,' replied Sean.

'We got stopped at immigration for four hours,' she said. 'He loved every minute.'

Conall's fork scraped against the plate.

'All those stamps in your passport's going to land you in prison one of these days,' said Sean.

There was that look again – a question mixed with caution.

Conall clenched his jaw as he wiped his mouth with a napkin. 'Let it.'

'So, you're the one keeping him out of trouble when he's in Karachi?' Sean said, looking at Hamida. 'When Sofe's not around, of course.'

'Only because he does the same for me,' she replied.

When Conall looked up and gave her such a kind smile, I thought I might throw my fork at someone. They held each other's gaze a fraction longer than necessary. Something was happening. I felt it with a certainty I hadn't before and another sort of panic came over me.

Sean considered her for a moment. 'You don't wear a scarf.'

'So?' She picked up her drink, smiling. 'Do you think all Pakistanis are the same?'

'I've got a feeling none of them are quite like you.'

'OK,' said Conall. 'Keep your one-liners for your dates.'

Sean threw his napkin on the table. 'My brother. He's no fun at all. Life just sapped it out of him.'

Conall stopped for a moment, still looking at his plate.

Sean paused. 'Better clear this up.'

Hammy went to help him and I took the chance to say sorry to Conall again. Why wasn't he looking at me??

'It's fine,' he said, reaching out for a drink. 'Me here, you next door – it'll be like old times.'

'Not with that tone it won't.'

He took a deep breath.

'Who's handling the oh-so-important project now that both of you are here?' I asked.

'She insisted on coming, Sofe. I couldn't say no.'

'Why are you OK with me not living with you?' I asked.

'Why are you looking for an argument? Because if we wanted to do that I could ask how that book about our marriage is going.'

I looked at the table. Why does he think I always want to argue? And why has he only been in the country for a few hours before it feels like we are.

'It's not *specifically* about our marriage,' I mumbled.

'Listen, I put up with a load of shit from you, Sofe.' He paused, his voice softening. 'But so do you from me. So I'm here.'

I wanted to ask whether this meant he was OK about the book now, but I didn't want to spoil the moment. 'Hamida made me see that.'

I gripped my glass.

'I probably should've warned you that she was coming, but I wanted to surprise you. Plus, she's been through a lot.' He leaned into me. 'If it's one thing you can do it's cheer a person up.'

In the case of Hammy, I think he was being rather optimistic, but when someone puts such faith in your abilities, I suppose you have to give it a try.

To Foz: Where the hell are you? Haven't heard from you in ages. All OK here, but something doesn't feel right. You and your bloody *Eat, Pray, Love* journey. Still love you. Xxxxx But answer your damn messages.

Sunday 17 March

6.15 p.m. Mum told Hammy to come to my dress fitting because the more time she spends here the less time she's with Conall and Sean. I was grateful on the inside but obviously pretended to roll my eyes at Mum's suspicious nature.

Maria watched Hammy take a seat in the TV room as she came into the house.

'Why don't you like her?' whispered Maars, while everyone was bustling round her.

'She's fine,' I replied.

Maria picked Adam up and said, 'Your khala's a little liar, isn't she? Yes, she *iiiis* – yes, she *is* a little liar.'

'You must look for something nice for the wedding too na,' Mum said to Hammy, looking at her skinny jeans and sweatshirt. 'You are very tall, you will look nice in a sari.'

Mum then began asking her about her parents as the tailor stuck more pins in my gold and coral dress, my arms sticking out as if I were about to be crucified.

'What does your baba do?' she asked.

'He's a general. In the army.'

Mum abandoned filling the favour boxes.

'Oh,' she said, giving me a look that suggested this was the first thing I should've told her. 'Beta, you should've brought your parents to the wedding.'

'Well, I don't really speak to them,' she replied.

She looked Mum straight in the eye. It was exactly like her not to flinch. Am I a flincher? Should I be less flinch-y?

Is this what Conall and Hammy have in common? Apart from being non-flinchy, does he tell her things about his family that he can't tell me?

'Acha? Why not?' Mum asked as boldly as Hammy had answered.

Hammy gave a wry smile. 'Let's just say they don't like my lifestyle choices.'

I mean, to be fair, which Pakistani parent would? What with her getting gritty when she clearly comes from money. But then I married a white guy so I could hardly talk.

'Ooh, pakoras,' I exclaimed as Auntie Reena came in with tea and snacks.

I stepped forward, not realising the length of material wrapped around me as my foot got caught and I went lunging forward, knocking the tray out of Auntie Reena's hands and hitting the floor, face first. The cups of chai fell all over the flooring, and my body was punctured by several pins as a shower of pakoras fell upon me.

'Fuck,' I said.

'Haw hai!' exclaimed Mum.

Hamida looked at me in disgust. Even in the midst of my chai-stained wedding outfit I thought: does she wonder why Conall married me? I tried to sit up as I removed a pakora from my cleavage. Sometimes I really do wonder the same.

7.35 p.m.

> **From Foz:** What do you mean something doesn't feel right? All OK here. Miss you XX

11.45 p.m. So, Hamida was with Conall while I sat with nothing but pakoras for company. I checked that Mum and Auntie Reena were asleep. I think Mum believes I've become a sex-starved maniac. But, I mean, what's the point in being married if you can't shag at will? Or, you know, just *hold* a person.

When Conall opened the door he looked at me for a moment, then leaned forward.

'Christ, is that a . . . pakora?'

'Bastard.'

I walked past him and into the living room where Sean and Hammy were sitting, watching television.

'Hey, sit,' said Sean.

Hammy just looked at me, as if bored by my very presence.

'It's fine,' I replied, walking into the kitchen for a bit of privacy.

'You muppet,' said Conall. 'Is the pakora why you have a face as long as your internal monologues? We all fall from grace now and then, Sofe.'

I leaned against the counter, not paying much attention to what he was saying.

'Bit shit being in different houses, isn't it?'

He nodded. Then he opened the kitchen cupboard and got out a jar of peanut butter.

'I fucking love you,' I said as he handed me a spoon.

'You're easily pleased.'

'It's what the peanut butter represents, Conall.'

I sat on the counter and opened the jar. 'Ooo, it has bits. I love me some bits,' I said.

Conall's eyes travelled from the spoon to me. I put the jar down and hooked my fingers into the waist of his jeans, pulling him closer. He was just leaning in when a flash of light came from next door. Next thing I saw was Mum, head full of rollers, arms folded, glaring at me. Conall blew out a puff of air and rubbed the back of his neck.

'Nuts for another day, I guess,' I said. 'Sorry.'

Not as sorry as I was for myself, though. As I walked past the living room, catching sight of Hammy, I said a quick prayer under my breath.

'For protection from bad things,' I explained to him.

'Yeah, I need that,' he replied. 'Protection from the wedding.'

Note for book: If possible, try to ensure there's an ocean between you and the in-laws. Short of that, a different postcode will do.

Monday 18 March

9.35 p.m. Went out to write and came home as Suj and Han were coming over. Was brought face-to-face with a man called Malcolm, wearing a white beret.

'Malcolm, man,' Mum said, 'you have to get the house painted before the wedding.'

Mum thinks he's her Jamaican brother from another mother. Getting engaged has put a tune in the unstoppable song of Mum.

Malcolm broke into a pearly white smile, asking if it was my wedding or hers as we both look like sisters. If only you knew, Malc, if only you knew. Mum giggled as she added: 'And you will put the new TV in my bedroom, man?'

I really wished Mum would stop speaking like that, even if Malcolm didn't seem to mind.

'When I'm married it'll be nice to watch TV in bed, na?' she said to me.

Oh God.

'Acha, Soffoo, Malcolm will give me an estimate for breaking this wall down so we can live in one big house!'

My God.

'What? A hole-in-the-wall?' I replied, aghast at the idea.

She nodded very passionately when the doorbell rang.

'Seen that brother of mine anywhere?' asked Sean as he walked into the living room.

'He said he was going to the mosque,' I replied, looking over at Mum to put a stop to her ludicrous wall-smashing plan.

'Oh.'

'You see the garden?' said Mum, walking into the kitchen with Malcolm. 'All back of house needs painting too.'

'So, he goes to the mosque a lot, does he?'

'Hmm? Yes, I suppose.'

'Right. Not that I have a problem with it,' he said. 'Just that . . .'

'What?'

'Nothing. Forget it.' He looked around the house.

Mum rushed into the room, leaving Malcolm in the garden. 'He's doing the painting so cheap,' she exclaimed. 'Sean, come, sit. Have tea.'

'No, thanks. I'd better go.' Sean looked restless.

'Are you OK?' I asked.

'Yeah, grand. I'll go then.'

As he left, Suj and Hannah came through the door.

'Hi,' he said, doing a double-take at Suj. As do most people, to be fair.

They both paused, looking at each other.

'Bye, Sean,' I said.

'He's quite fit, isn't he?' said Suj as she and Han walked into the house.

'Girls!' exclaimed Mum. 'Where have you been?'

'Oh my God, Auntie,' exclaimed Suj, grabbing my mum's hand and looking at her ring.

Mum gave her the whole *he's a colonel* spiel.

'It's very brave what your mum's doing,' said Han as we went in the kitchen to make tea.

I glanced at Mum giggling as Suj held the ring to the light. 'Hmm.'

'Too many women would care about people,' she said. 'Look at her; a big eff-you to anyone who judges her.'

Hannah looked as proud of Mum as I probably should be. I switched the kettle on, getting mugs out of the cupboards. 'I suppose so.'

Suj shot me a look as soon as Mum told her about the hole-in-the-wall idea. Hannah took the teabag that was dangling from my hand. 'He's not replacing your dad.'

'Malcolm?'

'Tst, Uncle Wasim.'

I thought about it for a moment. 'No. He's having his cake,' I said. 'All those years of struggling and finally coming to a point where they were at least content . . . I don't know. Mum and Dad lived the grit. This is fluff. I suppose it doesn't seem fair that Uncle Mouch is getting to live Mum's comfort days with her.'

'Fair on who?' she asked.

'Acha, Soffoo . . .' Mum cleared her throat as we sat in the living room. 'Has Conall done his soonthay?'

I spurted out my tea. Oh my *actual* God. Cannot believe my mum asked me whether my husband has had a *circumcision*.

Suj looked like she'd been sucker-punched. 'What? Like, have it . . .' She made scissor signs with her hands.

Why, why, *whyyyyyyy*??

'*I don't know*,' I said to Mum.

'Haw, haven't you seen it?'

'No! I mean, *yes*, but . . .'

Please someone save me! Maria and Auntie Reena walked in as Mum filled them in on the topic *du jour*. Maars handed Adam to Hannah and left the room. A few seconds later, laughter erupted from upstairs.

'Hannah, you are religious. He should have a circumcision, haina?' said Mum.

'Because, Beta,' joined in Auntie, 'when someone says they are Muslim, doesn't mean they will be Muslim, na?'

Apparently all that stands between being Muslim or not is foreskin. *Vom*. Ironic thing is if Conall started talking about spirituality they'd kick him out of the room.

'I'm not sure I have the scholarly qualifications for this particular . . . matter,' replied Han.

'That's gotta hurt,' said Suj.

'Wait,' said Mum, getting her iPad out.

For a minute I thought she was going to ask Sheikh Google.

'See, Soffoo. Why ask you something when I can organise it myself?'

Had she already booked an appointment for Conall??

'Well, Adam,' I heard Han murmur, 'isn't this uncomfortable?'

'Do they even do that for adults?' said Suj.

'See, technology?' said Mum. 'Who did I find on Facebook, Sof-foo, but your *mother-in-law*.'

Oh no. Oh no, no, no.

'*Mum . . .*'

I got a hot flush.

' . . . *What* did you say?'

'I told her that she must come to the wedding.'

Oh God.

'You shouldn't have done this, Mum. I told you I'd handle it.'

'The wedding's in twelve days and you weren't telling me anything.'

What would Conall say? What would he *do*?

'He doesn't speak to them, Mum.'

She paused. 'Le, what do you mean? He doesn't speak to his parents and he's walking around without a circumcision?'

'You never told me about his parents,' said Maars, walking back into the room.

I'd lost track of what I know, what I've told people and what everyone is supposed to know. My brain was beginning to sizzle.

'If a man is like this with his own parents, then who are in-laws to him?'

'Small, small things people get upset about,' said Auntie Reena, opening a packet of paan masala.

No one knew about the darkness that comes over his face whenever his parents are mentioned. I felt sick.

'I have to go,' I said, getting up as Suj, Han and Maars all looked at me.

'Where? Your Auntie and Uncle Scot will be here soon.'

That's what I needed; more family members.

'But –'

'O-ho, sit, sit. We have so much to discuss for the wedding,' said Mum. 'Once the painting is done and Conall has his circumcision, everything will be perfect.'

Tuesday 19 March

8.20 a.m. Woke up early to go and speak to Conall. Everyone was awake. I said I was popping out to the shops and Auntie Scot said, 'Acha? What shops are open this early?'

Bloody aunties.

6.55 p.m. It was bad. It was so, *so* bad. Was embroiled in being tasked with putting more fairy lights up and fetching medication for Uncle Scot and God knows what else. Sneaked over next door under pretence of needing to get milk. It was ages before Hammy answered. I walked in, asking where Conall was.

'Taking a shower.'

I went upstairs and she followed me.

Them living under one roof isn't what matters right now.

'Oh, hey,' said Conall.

He looked at both of us, then stood around in a towel as if it was acceptable to be half naked in front of someone *who's not your wife.*

'I need to speak with you,' I said.

'I'll just be in my room,' said Hammy.

I followed him into the bedroom. *Why* did I have to tell him something that would ruin everything? Just when he didn't seem angry at me, when he'd done everything I wanted by coming to London and not minding every time Mum gets a new notion in her head.

'Listen,' I began.

He walked towards me and kissed me so suddenly I went with it – because, well, you know.

'No, wait, I need to tell you something.'

'Mhmm.'

He's just so *broad*. I was figuring out how I'd tell him about our respective mothers when he'd already unzipped my jeans and taken my top off. There was banging at the wall. I forgot how nice he smells as we lay on the bed, his towel on the floor next to my knickers. What did I need to tell him again? Another bang.

I put my hand on his chest, heart racing, and looked at him. 'What is that?'

'Who gives a fuck?' he said, pinning my wrists down.

I concurred when the hammering continued, muffled voices coming from next door.

'Oh,' I said. 'It's Mum.'

'*What?*' he said, stopping for a moment to look at me.

'Mum's getting a flat screen.'

'Sofe –'

This just reminded me of her hole-in-the-wall idea.

'Sorry, carry on.'

The hammering was replaced with drilling, but it didn't matter because, God, I'd missed the weight of him on top of me. The drill sped up to a screech as if it was about to burst through the wall.

'O-ho!' we heard Mum exclaim. 'Look what you've done, man.'

I put my hand on my head and looked at his face.

'You've got to be kidding me,' he said.

Have I mentioned I love that face? I remembered what I had to tell him.

The drilling stopped as I noticed that it had drilled a tiny hole through the wall, cracks appearing along the paint.

'*Conall*,' she called out. 'Are you there?'

He stopped, bowing his head and closing his eyes. There was muffled noise from the other side.

'Where is that Soffoo? Who is going to fix this, man?'

'Don't worry, Mrs Khan. I'll call my brother.'

I put my hand on Conall's face as we stared at each other, him shaking his head.

'*Conall?*' came Mum's voice again, this time so close it was as if she was in the room. Was she peering through the new peephole?

We both got up and started putting our clothes on, listening to Mum argue with Malcolm in the house of perpetual renovation.

'Sofe,' he whispered, putting on his T-shirt. 'Your ma's nice and all, but please tell me this won't be the rest of our life?'

I laughed but also thought: isn't it nice to know there's a future waiting for you with the person you like the most in it? Then I remembered what I'd come to tell Conall in the first place.

'Christ,' he said, picking up pieces of concrete that had fallen on the floor and putting them in the bin.

'I need to tell you something,' I said.

'That we need to move?' he replied, inspecting the cracks.

'Your parents are coming to the wedding.'

His expression changed in an instant.

'I'm sorry,' I said, explaining what happened. As the words came out his stillness became increasingly worrying. 'It's a chance for reconciliation,' I added when he didn't speak.

Mum was still shouting at Malcolm.

'Your ma had no business inviting them.'

He stared at me before he left the room, slamming the door behind him. I went downstairs.

'She felt it was rude not to,' I replied.

I mean, it *is* rude.

'This could be good,' I said. 'I mean, what if your parents think I've *brainwashed* you and that's why you're not speaking to them?'

I could see the *Daily Mail* headlines: *Convert to Islam Severs Family Ties upon Demands of Scarf-wearing Wife.* And didn't he know how lucky he was to have both parents? What I wouldn't do to hear the sound of my dad's thunderous voice, even if it was to shout at me for eloping. Conall stared at me, his chest rising and falling, his fists clenched.

'That's not the reason,' he said.

'Then what?' I asked, lowering my voice as I remembered Hammy in her room.

He got two mugs out of the cupboard, switching on the kettle. We waited for it to boil in silence. Just as I was about to say something he opened the cupboard.

'What the fuck?' he said, taking out a bottle of vodka. He slammed it on the counter. 'I told him about this shit.'

'Keep your voice down.'

'Doesn't he know what this stuff can do to you?'

I wasn't sure if Conall was speaking as a Muslim or an alcoholic. Keys rattled through the door as Sean walked in and bounded up the stairs, saying, 'What a minger. Tinder pics looked nothing like her.'

Conall took the bottle and followed him up there. After a few minutes his raised voice travelled down the stairs – something about Sean being disrespectful. Then I heard Sean say: 'That's rich.'

Just then Conall's phone beeped. I looked round the kitchen and saw it on top of the microwave.

From Hamida: Con, what's going on? What was that banging? And keep your voice down. Do you need to talk?

Talk?? Talk about what? I held the phone in my hand. My finger lingered over the message as I resisted the urge to swipe and read their previous exchange. There are many things I don't want to be in life; being *that* wife, is one of them. I put the phone down.

Conall: 'I want this shit out of here.'

Sean: 'Christ, calm down.'

I went and stood at the bottom of the stairs.

Sean: 'I know, but fuck – this isn't the time.'

Conall: 'I need to pray.'

'What? You do a lot of that, but it's not doing much for you, bro.'

Silence.

In a lowered voice I heard Sean say: 'Do you really believe all this? I mean, are you actually Muslim? Or is it just because . . .'

My heart lurched somewhere in my stomach. Then I heard a bang – as if someone had hit a wall or table. I ran up a few steps and saw the two of them through the bannister. Conall was leaning into Sean as I heard him say, 'Of course it's because of her. *You* of all people should understand.'

The door to Hamida's room was ajar. Going back into the living room, I tried to calm the thudding of my heart. He came back downstairs.

'Go home, Sofe.'

'I –'

'Just go.'

'I'm sorry,' I said.

He looked at me and gave a short nod.

'It just –'

'It's fine,' he said, rubbing his hand over his face. 'I'll deal with it.'

'Are you su—'

'*Sofe*. It's *fine*.' He walked up to me. 'Once this wedding's over we'll talk. I promise. I'm booking a weekend away – just you and me.'

Why couldn't he explain it now? What was going to happen? Was he going to leave me on account of my interfering family? Before I could ask, there was banging at the door and when I opened it Mum exclaimed, 'Hain? What are you doing here? How long does it take to get milk?'

She gave me a look – one that told me she knew milk was not the reason I'd left the house. 'Your Auntie Scot has something to say about everything. And I still have to tell them I'm engaged.'

She looked over my shoulder at Conall, disapproval written all over her face. 'When the wedding's over, you both can spend all the time you want together.' Mum's features seemed to soften as she watched him. 'Acha, before the wedding, make sure you trim your beard a little. You don't want to look like a fundamentalist.'

Friday 22 March

10.15 a.m.

From Conall: Just picked Ma up from airport. We'll be over at seven.

To Conall: Are you nervous? I'm nervous. Can you warn your mum that my family tend to be slow-burners?

Of a person's energy.

It's been calm. Strangely so. Conall seems to be carrying on as normal but I can tell there's something wrong by the distant look he has. I tried getting him to talk about what was on his mind but we've not had a minute alone. Mum's invited everyone for dinner in honour of my in-laws. Conall clenched his jaw (as per), but then just said they'd be there. Have asked family to remember to speak English though I'm pretty sure no one heard. They were too busy listening to Auntie Reena shouting at her husband over the phone.

'Your poor Auntie Reena,' said Mum, flinging water into the dough mix in the Kenwood. 'But she doesn't remember that this is a wedding house – no one wants to listen about her divorce.'

'Is she really getting divorced?' I said.

Felt bad for Auntie and had to pray two nafls to God just to make sure my marriage wouldn't have the same conclusion.

'Haan,' said Mum. 'Now I have to worry about her giving me the evil eye because she keeps asking what will happen to her when I get married. And Malcolm's brother still hasn't come to fix my wall.'

'Speaking of, Mum – you're not knocking down the wall,' I said.

'Haw, bu—'

'No, Mum. Just no.'

She went back to her Kenwood, looking unimpressed with my assertiveness. The only other saving grace tonight is that at least Uncle Mouch isn't coming because Mum hasn't told the rest of the family yet – maybe there'll be a miracle and she won't have to.

Sorry, God, for that thought.

But not that sorry.

10.45 a.m. I've locked myself in the bathroom because it's the only place I can get any privacy from Auntie Reena, who wants her bikini line waxed. Ugh.

> **From: Sakib, Awaan**
> **To: Sofia Khan**
> **Subject: Error**
>
> Hi Sofia,
> I'm really sorry but we were putting the contracts through and realised you missed signing a page. Any chance you can come into the office today to expedite things?
> Sakib.

Yes, of course! I've all the time in the world! Honestly.

11.15 a.m. Argh! There was no hiding from Auntie Reena's bikini line and so when my phone rang Maars picked it up. It was Sakib and she told him to come over tonight to get the contracts signed. If I could give my family a lesson in anything, it would be barriers.

1.30 p.m. 'You look like you're about to throw up,' said Maars, coming into my room when I finished praying.

'I think I might.'

'Don't be nervous.'

I explained that tonight's assortment of people doesn't inspire confidence.

'Mum started talking to me about her wedding dates,' she said.

'Don't make it *worse*,' I told her.

'After Ramadan. Here. His kids will fly over. Hopefully your wall will be fixed by then.'

'Oh God.'

'Then another event in Karachi.'

I kneeled on my bed, burying my head in my pillow.

'You know,' continued Maars, 'Tahir asked that if he died first would I get married so soon after. I was like, *yeah. Already have someone on standby*.'

She walked over to my dressing table and started trying on different lipsticks. 'Of course I wouldn't,' she added.

'No,' I replied.

She shrugged. 'Maybe when I'm sixty I'll think differently.'

12.35 a.m. My God. I need a paracetemol and a fag.

'Hello,' I said as I opened the door to my mother-in-law.

I didn't realise she'd be so *small*: her brown shoulder-length hair set in curls, slightly rugged skin and small freckled nose. Conall introduced us as Sean stood, holding a bunch of flowers. I stepped forward, not sure whether to shake her hand or give her a hug. Her eyes hovered over the fairy lights and bunting.

'Hello,' she replied, smiling.

I leaned forward, putting my arms round her in an awkward one-sided hug; she patted me on the back. When I stepped back she stared at me. Was she thinking: *This: this is the girl he converted for?*

Sean came in, handing me the flowers, whispering, 'I'm sorry but I had to have a drink. I mean . . .' he glanced at Conall and his mum, walking into the living room.

'Welcome. Come, come,' exclaimed Mum, glancing at Conall's mother's bare legs. 'But where is your husband?'

Sean looked at his brother, then at his mum before she answered, 'He couldn't leave work at such short notice.'

'Oh. I see.'

I held my breath, wondering what the verbal landmine that is my mum might add.

'Well, I'm very happy you came,' she said. For a moment, I did love her for her sheer sense of hospitality.

'Thank you,' said Conall's mum – who I'm told to call Mary. 'Certainly was nice of you to invite me,' she added, glancing at Conall.

'Ah, Hamida, Beta, you are also here. Good.'

Hammy came in, handing some sweetmeats to Mum, which was thoughtful of her. I'm sure the fact that Conall was there to witness her thoughtfulness had nothing to do with it.

'Everyone,' said Mum. 'This is Conall's mama.'

Everyone went quiet and looked at her, standing at the door.

'Hello,' she said, her face flushed.

Sean smiled. Auntie Reena stood up and hugged Mary for at least thirty seconds. Mary's arms seemed as reluctant to go round Auntie's as they did mine.

'In our culture,' said Auntie Reena, 'the mother of the groom is *most* important person.'

Mary looked up at Conall whose face, of course, I couldn't read, though Lord knows I try.

'That's very nice,' she replied.

'Mehnaz – flowers,' said Auntie Reena.

Mum was standing, at the ready, with a festoon of chrysanthemums and marigolds and placed them around Mary's neck.

'Oh, well . . .' she said, looking down.

Mum then got out two more and put them around Conall and Sean. Maars hid her face behind Adam, lowering her head as they all stared at the garlands around their necks.

'It's tradition, mate,' said Tahir, helpfully, to Sean.

Uncle Scot got up and shook Conall's hand, insisting that he was like a father to me, which was the first I'd heard of it.

'We are very happy about this marriage,' he said, speaking rather louder than necessary. 'Some people would mind but we are forward-thinkers. What is white and what is brown?' He looked at Mary. 'We are all the same in the eyes of God.'

Mary gave a tight smile. 'Indeed.'

As we all went into the conservatory Mum scoffed and whispered to me: 'He wasn't even going to come to the wedding. Auntie Reena spent two hours on the phone to persuade him.'

Great.

Mary, Conall and Sean sat in a row, on the sofa, in all their wreathed glory.

Silence.

Uncle Scot cleared his throat. 'Do you like spicy food, Mary?'

'It's got a bit of a kick for me,' she replied.

'Sorry?' said Uncle.

'Too much kick,' she repeated.

He leaned forward, squinting. 'Hmm?'

'It's too much for her, Uncle,' I said.

'I *love* it,' said Sean. 'I made some dhal the other day. Killer.'

'Kill who?' asked Auntie Scot.

'No, *killer*,' I explained. 'As in it was good.'

'Oh.'

Silence.

Hamida and Conall exchanged a look.

'You know,' began Sean, 'our ma doesn't leave Kilkee let alone Ireland much. First time you've flown for what? Twenty years?'

'I love my home,' she replied, speaking slower, her voice raised. 'London's a frantic place.'

'We can't live without London,' said Mum, a few decibels louder than Mary. 'You must. Come see. Your children more.'

'My boys know where I live,' she replied.

'Conall,' continued Mum, 'you only get one mama in your life. You should look after her.'

Conall looked down, eyes fixed on some orange petals that had fallen to the floor.

'Well, I can look after myself. But a bit of company never harmed anyone,' replied Mary.

There was a five-second delay between Mary finishing her sentence and Mum, Auntie Reena and the Scots smiling.

Every time I looked at Conall, I kept trying to decipher what he was thinking. He seemed to be friendly enough with everyone, but then he'd look distracted and I noticed Hamida staring at him.

'Have you heard Indian music?' Uncle Scot asked Mary.

The woman's not left Ireland in twenty years, but yes, it's her favourite pastime.

'We show you.'

Oh God. Uncle Scot switched on the CD player. 'This isn't like the modern music now. No . . . just listen . . .'

Uncle Scot closed his eyes. Mary leaned forward, a show of polite concentration. Sean shuffled in his seat.

'Oh, Soffoo, go upstairs and get the CDs next to my drawer,' said Mum.

Lord have mercy.

I stood in Mum's room, CDs in my hand, thinking of Dad. 'If you were here, Baba,' I whispered, 'I'd probably ask you for a cigarette and I don't think you'd say no.'

As I came back down the stairs I noticed a figure standing outside the house. I opened the door and it was Sakib, leaning against the wall. He turned round.

'I rang the doorbell but no answer.'

'Oh, I'm so sorry.'

He smiled. 'I could hear the music. Sorry, I see there's a party going on.'

'In-laws,' I said meaningfully. 'You didn't have to come over, really.'

'I only live in Clapham – not far. Anyway, your sister insisted.'

Of course she did. I handed him the CDs while I signed the contracts so he could leave as quickly as humanly possible.

'This is a good one,' he said, holding up one of them.

I looked up from the papers. 'Are you fifty?'

'Come on, doesn't it take you back to your childhood? When your parents would sit and listen and you'd be doing a puzzle or reading a book. I love old Bollywood songs.'

'Were you happy as a child or something?'

'Weren't you?' he asked.

Mum peeked through the window and before I knew it she came shuffling in as Sakib stood up and said salaam.

'O-ho, you must join us for dinner,' said Mum once I told her who he was.

'You don't mind, do you?' he asked, looking at me.

Yes, I do bloody mind but that doesn't seem to matter much nowadays.

'The wife's away this weekend so it was just going to be me tonight anyway.'

I followed them into the conservatory and there was already a roar of laughter as Sakib and Conall were shaking hands. Note, Conall was not laughing.

'I'm serious,' said Sakib. 'This wedding's getting in the way of Sofia doing any work.'

I noticed Conall's eyebrows twitch. As he sat down, Sakib lifted his trousers, flashing a pair of rainbow socks.

'I was just telling Sofia: these songs bring back such memories,' he said.

'So, Betas,' said Auntie Scot, looking at me and Conall. 'After the wedding I hope we will hear happy news, hmm? Make sure you have three, four, in a row. Because leaving it late is very bad for you.'

'Hai nahin,' said Mum. 'Three, four! Soffoo still can't cook, how will she look after so many children?'

Conall's mum looked confused.

'*Babies*, Mary,' said Auntie Scot, so loudly that Sakib leaned back.

'Ah . . .' replied Mary, the colour rising to her cheeks.

'You must want lots of grandchildren, haina?' added Auntie Scot.

Everyone looked at Mary expectantly.

'Well, I . . . yes. But they're a big responsibility.'

She began talking about how hard it can be – one of those things couples should talk about before committing to it.

'Yes, yes, very good,' said Mum, looking at the ceiling where I could tell she'd noticed a crack. Maybe that was Malcolm's fault as well.

Silence.

'They are wicked fun, though,' Tahir said to Conall, bouncing Adam on his knee.

Sakib glanced at me before looking at the floor.

'You know . . .' added Maars after a few moments' silence. 'They should have a few years of fun before that, though.'

Why was my womb open for public discussion?? Conall stood up so abruptly everyone looked at him.

'Excuse me,' he said, leaving the room as Hamida watched him go.

When he came back he looked so out of his comfort zone, I almost told everyone to go home.

'Dinner's ready,' announced Mum. 'Groom's mother must be first,' she said, pulling Mary from the sofa and pushing her towards the dining room.

'Just keep thinking: it's all material for the book,' whispered Sakib to me as we got up and followed suit.

I had to laugh as I shook my head. 'Or for my suicide note.'

'Make a great posthumous story,' he replied, winking at me somehow without managing to look like a knob.

'You publishers – all about the bottom line.'

'Actually it's the Indian in me.'

'Soffoo, what a nice boss you have. And Pakistani!' whispered Mum as Sakib began talking to Uncle Scot. 'Why couldn't you have married him?'

Argh!

'Sakib,' she called out, 'you must come to the wedding with your wife, na?'

Conall was looking at Sakib as he graciously accepted the invite. Another guest to add to the list.

'He's Indian.'

'Acha? He doesn't look it. Chalo, at least he speaks Urdu.' Mum then continued. 'Which is better than your mother-in-law. I can't understand a word she's saying. Oh, and remind me to call Malcolm about the crack in the ceiling on Monday.'

Maybe he'll be able to fix the crack in my head.

I had to text Katie to let her know my dear mother had invited her boss to the wedding.

From Katie: Sweetu, that's hilarious! Please make sure you don't sit me at the same table, though. He's great, but I don't want to talk work on your bog day.

I couldn't help but think of Foz at the mention of guests, and looked at my phone to see if she'd messaged.

From Katie: Whoops. BIG day. Obviously xxx

It really does feel more bog than big.

As the evening thankfully came to an end it was time to pray. Mary watched Conall as he made his way with us back into the conservatory for joint prayers. I looked at her and for a minute I wanted to sit near her and, I don't know, console her. Sean engaged her in conversation, his eyes also flickering towards Conall.

'Does she mind?' I whispered to Conall as we walked out of the room, leaving Sean, Mary and Hamida behind.

He looked at me, giving me a sad kind of smile. 'Of course she minds.'

Saturday 23 March

7.20 a.m.

To Conall: Ever think of babies?

7.22 a.m.

> **From Conall:** Is there something else you want to tell me?

7.23 a.m.

> **To Conall:** Just wondering. Did your mum say anything about last night? Are you guys getting on OK?

7.24 a.m.

> **From Conall:** She was tired and went to bed.

The mad Pakistanis probably exhausted her.

7.28 a.m.

> **From Conall:** Do you think about babies? Sneak into my room. Best place to have this conversation.

If bloody only. Went downstairs and Auntie Reena, Auntie Scot and Mum were already downstairs – my very own three-woman birth-control system.

9.35 a.m. Ugh. As if by cosmic intervention, ClearBlue ads keep playing on my bloody YouTube. Is it time to start thinking about babies, I wonder?

I suppose there'll be plenty of time for that after the wedding. I checked my phone for any messages from Foz, but nothing. Babies and best friends will have to wait for another day.

Saturday/Sunday 30–31 March
The Easter Wedding Weekend

1.40 a.m. Diamantes shimmered in waves of magenta, oranges and reds that spilled into the room. Mum kept urging Suj to attack me with a blusher brush and eyeshadow. Hannah was looking after Adam as Katie walked in. The ad-lib mehndi was at home but of course no men were allowed.

'Sweetu! You look so beautiful,' Katie exclaimed. 'But not when you make that face,' she added.

She went across and helped Maria, darting from corner to corner re-taping the bunting. Everyone needs a Maria and Katie in their life.

How do brides get through weddings without a pocket of time in which to have a fag or something stronger? Thoughts of Dad punctuated the hours. I kept looking over at the girls, no Foz in sight, and wondered what she'd be saying – keeping things in order: perhaps bringing some Zen to my mother who ran around, frantic over the missing lids for the tubs of peanuts. I could see Mary observing her, semi-fascination and semi-consternation.

'Kathy –' said Mum.

'Mum, it's Katie.'

'O-ho, how many names can I remember? Conall and Sean and Mary and I don't know who else,' she said in Urdu as Katie waited for her instructions.

I had to apologise.

'To be fair, Sweetu – we do all sound the same.'

Poor Katie was coerced into looking after Mary. As aunties bent over to put oil in my hair and henna on my hands, my eyes kept flickering towards Katie and Mary, wondering what they were talking about when Hamida went and sat with them. She was all laughter with Mary, I tell you. Never seen her expose her teeth so much before.

'Come, Mary,' exclaimed Mum, lifting her off the cushioned floor. She led her towards me, making her dip her fingers in the oil and put it over my hair.

'What's this for?' she asked Mum.

'It's tradition,' Mum replied.

Mary took some henna and put it on the leaf on my hand. 'But what does it mean?' she asked.

'It means we put oil in the hair and henna on the hands.'

Mary looked none the wiser and Mum looked at me as if to say: *white people ask the funniest things.*

'Sorry, I must sound terribly ignorant, but why is everyone waving money around her head and putting it in her lap?' asked Mary.

'Oh,' Mum said, 'you don't worry about that. It's to keep away the *evil eye*. People see happiness and they don't like it; this money is for charity to keep bad things from happening.'

Mary went back to where she was sitting, got her purse and put a ten pound note in my lap. Mum took it, waved it over my head and put it down again.

'See?' said Mum. 'Now she is safe from all bad things.'

Mary gave a rather tight-lipped smile when I heard a kerfuffle at the door.

'Shut up!' I heard Suj exclaim from the passage. Just then, as Auntie number twenty-three was bending down to put oil in my hair I saw an image at the door. I had to squint to make sure I wasn't seeing things.

'Foz?'

Hannah, Maars and Katie turned towards the door as she beamed from the entrance.

'Well,' she said, 'that was a bloody long journey.'

I leaped off my seat to hug her, tears in my eyes. Mum told me to stop being so dramatic, but her presence somehow cushioned the absence of my dad. When the night was over, me and the girls sat in the living room; the first time I had been together with all of them in such a long time – it almost made the wedding worth it.

'When I got married I always thought I'd have a more distinct grown-up feel,' I said.

'I don't know. I think it's something you're born with,' said Hannah.

'Who wants to be a fucking grown-up, anyway?' Suj looked in the mirror and reapplied some lipstick.

'I think Hamida was born a grown-up,' I said.

Maria checked the baby monitor. 'Hamida was born a boring old cow.'

'Conall's definitely a born grown-up,' added Katie. 'As for Hamida. Awful woman.'

'Why? What did she do?' I asked, leaning forward, riveted by the information Katie was about to give.

'Nothing. But I can't abide by a person you don't like.' She pinched a tiny roll of her belly. 'All this food and no running is making me fat. My God, I forgot to tell you – your mother-in-law asked if I was Catholic.'

'What did you say?'

'I said yes.'

'But you're not,' I replied.

'I couldn't say, *actually I'm agnostic*,' said Katie. 'I just went with it, and you know, maybe I was a Catholic in a former life. Although, I did tell one of your aunties that I was spiritually a Muslim.'

'Is Conall's mum pissed off now he's a Muslim?' asked Suj.

'Do you think she hates me?' I said, looking at the girls.

'He's a grown man,' said Katie, reaching towards the table for more peanuts. 'It's *his* decision.'

Hannah shook her head. 'Mothers-in-law. Never underestimate their influence.'

'If they're not with you,' added Maars, 'they're against you.'

'Haw, Soffoo, you will never guess. Your Uncle Wasim is Hamida's father's best friend,' exclaimed Mum.

'What?' I said, adjusting my scarf in the mirror as Suj tried to put more blusher on me.

'I told you he was a colonel and of course he must know big people in Karachi.'

The look of pride shone on Mum's widowed face.

'Uncle Mou . . . I mean Wasim's *here*?'

'Of course.'

I could feel Suj's eyes on me.

'And I've told your Auntie and Uncle Scot I am engaged. Strangest thing, Soffoo. They were *happy*. They told me they thought I should get married again.'

'Oh. Great,' I said.

Who'd have thought that in the family dynamic I'd be the narrow-minded one.

Must not think about Mum's fiancé and why Hamida seems to leak into every part of my life. I took a deep breath. I couldn't understand the anxiety. Conall and I were married already – what could go wrong?

'Is the bride ready?'

Foz peered into the dressing room and looked at me for a good fifteen seconds.

'Are you crying?' I said.

'What? No,' she replied. 'OK, fine, but Suj was crying earlier.'

'Of course I cried,' said Suj, waving the brush around. 'I've been crying for a week.'

I laughed as Mum bustled round and then out of the door, rolling her eyes at us.

Foz looked at me again with so much pride I had to tell her to leave.

'OK, sorry. I'm going . . .' She turned round at the door. 'As if I wouldn't have crossed oceans for this day.'

'Suj, throw my eyeliner at her, please. I'd do it but I can't move my arms.'

But when I looked at Suj she was crying too and then Maars, Han and Katie barged in.

'It's my sister's wedding,' exclaimed Maars. 'Our mum's boyf's in there by the way and I've run out of ways to avoid him.'

'I thought we were being adults?' I said.

'Isn't avoiding each other what adults do?'

As I looked at the girls, I wondered why I've worried about anything, ignoring the anxiety in the pit of my stomach. What, after all, can an organ know?

Note for book: Count every lucky star you have – they will come in the shape of the friends you love.

It's difficult to know what kind of face to have on when there are three hundred people staring at you, while you're concentrating on not falling flat on your face. Especially when you're glancing at your mother-in-law, who's apparently wishing your prompt demise.

But there was Conall – wearing a sherwani. Imagine! I had no idea I was so partial to a sherwani. More importantly, I wonder how easy it is to unhook the buttons off one?

'Glitzy,' I said as I finally approached him, looking at the buttoned-up cream collar, decorated with green beads. 'A bit of cultural appropriation for the day,' I added.

He really is very handsome.

'Baji, baji,' said the cameraman. 'Look this way. Haan. Perfect. What a shot!'

I personally think it's fortuitous that Celtic and Pakistani colours are the same. Conall tugged at his collar. We both sat down, smiling at our crowd of admirers. I caught sight of Sakib with his wife.

'Congratulations,' said Sakib, coming on to the stage with her.

'So, you're the one who wrote the book he's obsessed with?' said his wife.

Up close I could tell how expensive her clothes were, her diamond earrings practically blinding me, a Chanel clutch in her hands. I was also rather transfixed by how clear and smooth her skin was. I didn't detect a smidgen of concealer or foundation, just this bright coral lipstick and mascara, elongating her full lashes. Sakib's smile seemed to falter.

'You both make a beautiful couple,' she said to us.

With which Sakib pursed his lips as they made their way off the stage.

'That was weird,' I said, leaning into Conall.

'What?' he said, seeming distracted. Then he looked at me so intensely I thought *maybe he wants to have sex*. I was figuring out ways I could hitch up my lengha without ruining my whole get-up (tricky, but not impossible), when Mum came up on stage and hushed us. 'What will people think with you two talking, talking, talking?'

I had to explain to Conall the concept of acting like a shy bride, which felt even more ridiculous given I'd already shagged the man I was sitting next to. Mum placed herself next to Conall – prime videography position – along with demonstrating her being a benevolent and accepting mother-in-law.

'When will this be over?' asked Conall.

'A couple of hours. Tops,' I replied, from the side of my mouth.

He shuffled in his seat. I'm assuming the cultural attire wasn't agreeing with him. Mum then waved over to Mary, who trotted on to the stage and sat next to me. I was getting jaw ache from smiling into the camera.

A queue had formed that went right to the back of the hall because if it's one thing 'Stanis like more than a song and dance, it's photos.

'Baji, bhai,' called the cameraman to me and Conall. 'Look here.'

'If this guy asks me to look at the camera one more time, I'm going to smear saag aaloo all over his lens,' I said, looking at Conall. But he was staring ahead. I followed his gaze that led to Hamida, clad in a deep purple outfit, her brown hair tied in a neat bun, highlighting her high cheekbones.

'Baji, baji!'

'O-ho, Soffoo,' Mum interjected. 'You have whole life to look at your husband. Look at the camera.'

The camera flashed, bringing us both back from our Hamida-filled vision, when Uncle Mouch came and sat next to Mum. He shouldn't be here. That should be Dad.

Mary glanced over at us as auntie number thirty-three was putting an envelope in Conall's hands before walking to me and asking the cameraman to take a photo.

'Congratulations, Beta,' she said. Then she looked over at Conall and said, 'Goray jism ka maza lena.'

What is *wrong* with aunties? Mum giggled as auntie number thirty-four walked up with her three children and husband.

'What'd she say?' asked Conall. 'White what?'

I was too perplexed at the look that passed between Hamida and him and at Uncle Mouch being in our family photo. And what's the point in different cultures if a person can't use language barriers as a way to hide auntie obscenities?

'Nothing,' I replied.

Mary looked increasingly uncomfortable. Foz was bent over with laughter in front of the stage, her shiny black hair tumbling forward as Katie stuck her thumb up at me. Conall rubbed his eyes. The camera flashed again, blurring my vision as Sean, Hamida, Suj and Hannah came on stage and Foz and Katie followed them. They squeezed in, Sean leaning in between Conall and me.

'This is great craic.' He laughed and put his arm round the auntie next to him, smiling into the camera. 'Isn't it, Ma?'

Mary looked over at him. 'Will you behave, Sean?'

Leaning in again, Sean said: 'Your friend, Suj . . . she single?' he asked.

I shook my head.

'Commitments are things everyone should pay heed to,' said Mary, unmoved and staring straight ahead.

What did that mean? For once, I'd like to not be perplexed by what someone says. Conall turned to me as there was a mass exodus off the stage to allow the next lot through.

'What did that auntie say?' he asked.

'Forget it.'

The next batch of photo-enthusiasts clambered on stage.

'More casual racism, no doubt,' he said.

'Oh, for God's sake.' I leaned in and whispered in Conall's ear, 'She said "enjoy his . . ." ' I paused. Fair enough that he's my husband but it was still embarrassing. ' "Enjoy his *white* body." '

He looked at me: first with confusion and then a small smile.

'Happy?'

Cameras flashed as people still queued, and he took my hand. 'Almost.'

That moment didn't last long. They never do. When we got home I went straight to the bedroom to get all the shit off my face and change into something that didn't weigh the size of a baby elephant. Hamida had gone to stay with Uncle Mouch and in a few days Conall and I would go away for a mini-break to finally get some time alone. I was walking down the stairs when I heard his mum speaking.

'It was a spectacle,' she said.

'Ma, don't –' Sean interrupted.

'This isn't to do with you.'

'Not today,' said Conall.

'You shirked your responsibility once, and you won't do it again.'

'I know, but I did try. I tried every day,' said Conall.

'Not hard enough,' Mary added.

There was quiet when someone closed the door. How am I meant to eavesdrop when people close the door? (Also, have realised, I spend a lot of time trying to overhear what Conall has to say.)

I leaned against the passage wall, listening to their muffled voices and then silence. Silence that I thought would break. After a few minutes, I decided to open the door and went in.

The blood had drained from Conall's face and Mary was wiping her eyes. Sean had his head in his hands. I looked at Conall for some kind of clue as to what had happened, but his expression scared me.

'Sofia,' said Mary. 'I'm sorry to have to tell you this.'

'Not like this,' interrupted Conall.

'Christ, Ma,' said Sean.

She raised her head and looked at me, her mouth firm, her manner no-nonsense.

'Who'll tell the poor girl?'

Poor girl?

The moment before your life changes can be a blur. It's a hodgepodge of confusion, ignorance and denial – looking to someone who might untangle it for you. Conall stood up and walked towards me.

'Listen to me, Sofe . . .'

'What is going on?'

He grabbed my hand, pressing it against his chest, as if I'd run away.

'I should've told you, I just never –'

Is he dying? Is he having an affair? Is he leaving me? What?

'I have a family,' he said.

I looked at Mary and Sean – their gaze averted from us. 'I know.'

He shook his head. Were those tears filling his eyes?

'Another family, Sofe.' His grip tightened, hurting my hand. 'I have a son.'

What? I didn't understand. What did he mean he *has a son?*

'Sofe. . .' His voice cracked. 'He has cancer.'

APRIL

For Better, or for Worse

Muslim Marriage Book

Most things are easier said than done: put the toilet lid down; pick up your wet towels; separate colours from the whites; don't say that about my mother. They all fit in with the general notion of forgiveness. (Incidentally – despite what you might've heard – Islam is big on forgiveness.) But what does forgiveness even mean? Is it forgetting? To forget is to set yourself up for the same fall, surely. (Some might call it stupidity.) Moving on? If that's what it means, then moving on towards what? Or does it mean to just get over it? Done with. Dusted. Finished.

And what if it's a bigger struggle? What if there's more to it than just putting a lid on it? How far does forgiveness stretch? The black and white of your single days – the certainty with which hypothetical questions were answered – don't feel so clear-cut any more.

Nothing will grey your moral codes more than the simple words 'I do'.

Easter Monday: 1 April

6.20 a.m. *When you love each other* are five of the stupidest words ever uttered. *When you are married* – that's another type of sentence. You can't do certain things as easily when you're married. Like run away. 'Marriage': the threading of two lives, from which you can't escape without doing some kind of damage.

I've heard the story in CliffsNotes version; in stops and starts, through fury and disbelief.

'I was young and stupid,' said Conall, me unable to imagine that version of him. Surely he came out, fully formed and principled in the manner of the man I married.

'I'd started drinking too much. My dad was . . . it's no excuse. When she told me she was having a baby I tried to do the right thing and married her. But it was all temporary, and one day I . . .' He paused, as if something was catching in his throat. 'I left. No note or explanation.'

Such characteristic silence.

'I fucked up, Sofe. Badly. I don't know why I couldn't tell you the truth earlier, and I'm not making excuses, but I barely wanted to tell it to myself. I was going to come clean, though. After the wedding. Because I knew it was time to make things right – the parents I'd ignored for so long because they were just a reminder of my own failing; my son; Claire – I just didn't know where to start.'

He ran his hand through his hair. I loved his hair.

'You think you can escape a thing. Or say sorry enough to make up for the huge fuck-up – God knows I tried with Claire . . . but it served me right for being so reckless in the first place.'

What was he talking about? He looked like Conall but why did I feel like this was happening to someone else? As if I was watching it all on a TV screen? I looked around the house, his voice drowned out by my own incomprehension. The home that's meant to be ours, but never has felt permanent. For some reason my dad came to mind. What would he have thought? The things I did and the shit I had to hear from everyone and it was nothing to me – I'd do it all again . . . until this moment. The light flickered. Conall looked at the floor again, placing his hand on his forehead. A shooting pain ran through my head.

'You lied?' I said.

A question, because none of it made sense and I had to ask him to make sure.

'I'm sorry,' he said.

'But you lied?'

It was no use having my voice crack, along with my heart, but it couldn't be helped. Everything in me felt like it had lost support, as if I was just made of blood and flesh. I took in his face, the broadness of his shoulders, the shades of tattoos on his arms, which I hate because I don't like tattoos, but thought I loved because they're his.

I have a son.
He has cancer.

There's a certain injustice in being told about another's misfortune while your own is unfolding. You've barely had time to absorb any pain before being asked to feel sorry for another's. Tragedy can quell anger – dispel the roots of rage and replace it with a detached kind of sympathy. I hugged him. It wasn't benevolence. He still gives me comfort: the person who unpicked the seams of our relationship in one confession.

When he left Claire he didn't go back for five years. He spent his time travelling – thought he was in some kind of Hollywood film, finding himself. My husband, the cliché. But when he went back, Claire wanted nothing to do with him. Last year, the days I spent in his home, writing my book, he was finalising his divorce.

'I was relieved,' he said.

I imagine it was cathartic, being able to let go of that guilt. But not to Mary. I can picture her, in her quiet, firm way: *come back home. Be a husband to your wife and a father to your child.*

'But that loss. Not being able to see my son . . . not wanting to ask because what would he think of me? What right did I have?'

He looked at me, while I couldn't meet his eye. Every feeling had bundled itself up and wedged itself in my throat. I don't know how breath made its way out. But here should've been the pleasing part. The redemption song. The happy conclusion to his laden story.

'When I converted, I thought it was the answer. That you were the answer.'

The note to the song felt all wrong. And he didn't even realise it. His conversion wasn't a testament to his affection for me – it was an attempt at absolution.

Conall's penance hasn't ended. It's only just begun.

Tuesday 2 April

9.45 p.m. Mum emptied the pilau in a dish, laughing at something Auntie Scot had said in the living room, as Uncle Mouch walked into the kitchen. In a low voice he said: 'See? Most people are happy for us. Forget about the ones who will gossip.'

'I don't forget anything,' she replied. 'But today I will try.'

I watched Mum with Uncle Mouch – this strange man bringing about a warmth in my mum that I can't remember ever witnessing. Auntie Reena stared into her teacup, her mouth bulging with paan masala, glancing over at Mum and Uncle Mouch now and then. I tried not to look at Conall, pushing him as far away from my visual periphery as possible. Even though he was all that was in my head.

'Maybe some people thought you could wait more than nine months before remarrying,' I said to Mum.

The words tumbled out and I didn't even realise until Mum just stared at me. Her colour rose as she stuck the spatula into the dish again, without taking her eyes off me.

'Forty years and nine months I waited.'

I looked at the ground and walked out of the kitchen, regretting the words as soon as they'd come out. Of course she waited. Life is context, isn't it? But no one lives in your head.

'You will come and visit us, haina?'

Uncle Mouch took his seat next to me. Everyone was chatting away and I only heard the vague sounds of Maars and Tahir discussing Adam not eating enough solids.

'Are you OK, Beta?' he asked.

I tried to smile.

'You'll come and see your mama and me in Karachi, haina?'

Once they're married they'll spend their winters in Karachi and summers in London: Mum's stitching her life together while mine is unravelling. I looked at Auntie Reena watching Mum, her eyes full of something like loss and I had to make sure I didn't look like that. *Judgement is better than pity.*

'Yes,' I said. 'Of course.'

'Your mother-in-law reached Ireland OK? Oh,' he said, looking at his phone. 'Hamida.'

She went to see her friends because she leaves for Karachi soon. All this time I was worried about her – why didn't I revel in the small dissatisfactions of life and be grateful there weren't huge ones? He read her message and then said: 'Beta, for reuniting me with her, I will keep our conversation on the plane a secret?'

I managed to muster a grateful smile.

'She is a good girl. A little stubborn; takes after her father. Why else doesn't he speak to his daughter? But . . . some things are too much for parents.'

I glanced over at Conall, talking to Uncle Scot.

'Soffoo – why aren't you eating anything?' said Auntie Reena, looking at my untouched plate of rice.

'She is keeping slim for her husband,' said Auntie Scot, laughing.

Tahir was playing with Adam and I noticed Conall stare at them. Uncle Scot slapped Conall on the leg and said, 'When you have your own, then you will know what it is to be a man. But let me tell you, doesn't matter how much you do. These wives will never be grateful.'

Conall's gaze rested on me. *I'm sorry*; it's what he said with every look. The worst part was that I couldn't even muster the courage to hate him. I thought I had rage in me. I wonder: were all those years of emotional celibacy worth the trauma of actually being in love if this is what you're reduced to? If I'd built my emotional immune system more before I married Conall, would this hurt less?

'What will you do now?' Auntie Scot asked Conall. 'Back to Pakistan or will you come and see us in Scotland?'

His hands were clutched together, his eyes tired. Ironic thing is he's shit at fake smiles or lies. Everyone waited for him to answer.

I waited for him to answer. The words weren't coming to him, though.

'My book's coming out this month,' I said. 'So, we're here for a little while.'

He looked at me again. *I'm so sorry.*

'Acha,' said Uncle Scot. 'But have you learned to cook? Your husband can't eat a book.'

My husband can eat shit.

Conall looked up. 'That's not why I married her.'

'Thanks to God,' replied Auntie Scot, laughing.

Mum stood up to serve the tea and I noticed a chain tucked into her kameez. As she bent forward it fell out and there it was; the engagement ring Dad had given her, dangling around her neck. I caught Maars' eye.

'Bhai,' said Mum, 'you don't think a woman wants anything else in life? Her baba would've preferred to read what she writes than taste what she cooks.'

Tahir cleared his throat as Adam began to whimper. 'I think I'll go and change his nappy.'

The room went quiet. I felt tears surface – *Dad isn't here; I've been horrible to Mum; she is still here; but she's marrying someone else.* Everything seemed to tumble around my head; a cacophony of fact and feeling I couldn't shake off. *Conall isn't who I think he is.*

'Shall we go home?' Conall asked me.

'You go. I'll come home later.'

When he looked at me I was torn between wanting to hurl something at him and hug him. He has a child and the child has cancer.

What a mess. What a God-awful mess.

11.10 p.m. When I came home he was sitting on the sofa. I put my purse on the table.

'You understand that I have to go,' he said. Unmoved. Resolute. Same old.

Forty-eight hours I went without tears and they weren't about to start now. I nodded.

'I'm not leaving, Sofe,' he added, as if to make clear that we were still husband and wife – that nothing had changed. What a joke.

I looked at him. 'As if I give a fuck.'

Cancer, mistakes, apologies – they have nothing on spite. He took a moment.

'OK,' he said, getting up. 'I'll go tomorrow.' He went to leave the room. 'I'll fix this, Sofe.' Just as he was about to close the door, he added, 'Just please . . . give me the chance.'

Wednesday 3 April

9.10 a.m. 'Sweetu!'

I was barely awake when Katie called.

'Hot Bikram Yoga, I tell you. It's the answer to life. Now, release date in two weeks – have you seen the publicity schedule? I haven't heard from you. I know the whole newlywed thing is very exciting – is Hamster out of your face now?'

'Hmm? Oh, yeah.'

'Praise God. Sorry, *Allah*. Anyway, you must *focus* now. Are you still in bed? Sex can wait. Also, we *have* to talk about Sakib and his wife. I mean talk about *tension*. Anyway, publicity schedule, Sweetu. Chop-chop.'

Katie had to go and I mumbled something incoherent. I sat up and saw bags packed by the door. My instinct was to grab my scarf, keys and leave until I could come home to an empty space. Life would be substantially easier if only I could learn to be more vindictive. But I thought about his son – even the thought jars in my mind, stumbling over the facts of my own life.

'Hi,' said Conall, walking in with two cups of coffee. He handed me one.

'Hi.'

'You didn't have to sleep here.'

I shrugged. 'Have you . . .' I watched the steam of the coffee swirl and rise in front of me. I concentrated on making sure it came out as fluidly as possible. 'Have you spoken to her?'

He paused.

'Mmm.'

'She's forgiven you?' I asked.

Another pause.

'I hope she will; one day,' he replied.

I took a sip of the coffee.

'I fucked up, Sofe.'

'You know . . .' I looked up at him.

'What?'

I felt the familiar lump in my throat. 'You're not who I thought you were.'

I couldn't help it. Tears streamed down my face. 'You were meant to be . . .'

He kneeled in front of me as I wiped the tears away.

'Doesn't matter,' I said as his phone buzzed. 'Your taxi's here.'

He didn't move until I forced myself to get up.

'Go,' I said, walking into the passage.

He followed me out and stood at the door.

'I hope he gets better,' I said. And I meant it.

'Be here when I get back,' he said.

I should leave, just to spite him. Maybe I will. And I won't leave a note either.

As he got in the car, Mum came out of her house, the recycling piled in her arms, before she threw it in the recycling box.

'Where is Conall going?' she asked as the car drove away.

I watched it turn the corner, the side of Conall's profile visible for a second before both disappeared from view.

Mum was assessing the state of the front gate. I watched her, so preoccupied with the fact that the gate had come off its hinge she didn't quite see her daughter coming off hers.

'Well?' she said.

'He's going home.'

It was only at that moment that I wondered whether he'd ever come back.

10.05 p.m. Conall called. I was going to ignore it, but every time I wanted to punish him I wondered if he was being punished enough.

'We've got a hospital appointment tomorrow,' he said. 'They'll give an update on what course of treatment we should take.'

'Sean's OK still staying at his friend's?' I asked. 'We'll have to give him money back on his rent.'

'Yeah, I know. He's fine.'

Quiet.

'You OK?' he asked.

'Yeah.'

Pause. I wanted to ask if she was there. If her partner was there – were they still together? What was it like for Conall – to see his child after so many years? What feelings were bubbling inside him?

'Well, I'd better go,' I said.

Another pause.

'Sure. I'll call you tomorrow.'

'Mhmm.'

When misery can't find company it finds nostalgia. I flicked through the girls' emails from years ago: paragraphs dotted with exclamation marks, question marks, sighs and LOLs.

That time when Foz accidentally fell on top of her date on the Tube.

The one where Suj went to the Cayman Islands for her second date.

That week Hannah decided to go into spiritual retreat because she was in a flux about whether she should keep going out with a married man.

That's how it used to be. Now each life's loose end has been tied up so neatly that I can't quite be the one to fray the edges.

Friday 5 April

12.05 p.m. Whatever else Claire might be, a pushover wasn't it – she never took him back. Had to admire her for that. I opened my laptop and went to Sean's Facebook page, scanning through his list of seven hundred-plus friends. None of the Claires were from

Kilkee, so I went through Mary's more modest list and found her. My arrow hovered over the name: a picture of her with a boy who looked about eight or nine years old. I clicked on the profile but it was set to private. The annoying thing was she looked kind. Her blonde wavy hair blowing in the wind. Her son's arms wrapped round her, squeezing her with one arm, the other arm waving in the air. I couldn't read any of the comments. I didn't need to. The picture was depressing enough.

I lay down on the sofa and stared at the ceiling: what was the need to lie? That's the real question. If he'd just told me before we got married, I might've been shocked – perhaps disappointed that he of all people had made such a huge mistake – but I'd have got over it.

Note for book: It's secrecy that breeds mistrust, not mistakes.

9.10 p.m. 'Sweetu! You can't spend the days following your wedding alone,' said Katie, marching into the house.

She'd messaged me and I'd told her that Conall had to visit his dad in Ireland because he was ill. I didn't have the energy to argue when she insisted on coming over to make supper.

'Are you OK?' she asked.

'Yeah. Fine.'

'So, I've organised an interview for you with *The Women*,' she began, putting the Waitrose bag on the kitchen counter. 'She lapped up the Muslim/Irish combo.'

'Right.'

I looked out into the garden, the acid churning in my stomach. I wanted to lie down again.

'Are you *sure* you're OK?'

Better get your acting up to scratch, Sofia Khan.

'Still hungover from the wedding,' I said.

'Imagine if you actually drank? Such a sensible Muslim. Anyway, she'll want to discuss the book and your relationship and, you know, the usual,' said Katie, pouring pea soup into a pan. 'Wooden spoon, please,' she said.

I took one out of the drawer and handed it to her.

'Oh, get the baguette – it's in my bag.'

I brought the baguette and got bowls out of the cupboard as Katie went through other interviews she'd lined up for me. When Conall found the vodka and had a go at Sean, was it because of all the lies? Was it the stress of keeping secrets? Why didn't I ask him more questions? Was I scared of what he'd say?

'What is *wrong* with you?'

I stared at her as I picked up the knife again.

'I mean, seriously,' she added.

Taking a deep breath, I said: 'Turns out my husband has another family in Ireland. Walked out on them. Including a son who, by the way, has cancer.' I turned round to slice the bread. Just then my phone rang.

'I want you to come over tomorrow for lunch.'

It was Mum.

'I'm not really feeling very well,' I replied.

'I don't want to hear anything. Maria is coming and Wasim will be there, so no excuses.'

'OK, Mum.'

As I hung up Katie was staring at me. 'I suppose we'd better sit down.'

It was all very soap opera-esque when I filled her in with the details.

'But he hasn't seen her all these years?' she asked. 'Or his son?'

I shook my head. 'She didn't want him to.'

'And the thing with his parents . . .'

'He and his dad never really got on, but I think it was more that they kept trying to get him to come back to Ireland. Reminded him of what he'd done.'

She munched on a piece of bread, deep in thought. 'It doesn't sound like Conall.'

'Tell me about it,' I replied.

'Is he . . .' She paused. 'Is he *staying* in Ireland?'

Pushing the bowl back, I replied that he wasn't. 'He said he'd be back in a few weeks once things were settled.'

She seemed to breathe a sigh of relief. 'OK. Good. He's not *leaving*.'

I looked at her. 'No. He said he'll be back; that he's sorry; that he'll fix this. God knows how.'

Katie leaned forward. 'Listen to me. Are you listening?'

I looked up at her.

'I know this is absolutely awful. He's lied to you and he's broken trust and all the things that he wasn't meant to. But . . .'

I put my hands out.

'*But*,' she continued. 'People fuck up. This is his thing that he has to mend. It can't be easy for him, but it's not meant to be. He did bad things: first he left his wife and child and then he lied to you about it.'

My eyes must have glazed over.

'You believe in God, right?' She took another deep breath. 'I wish I did in the same way. Or at all.'

'Thought you were a Catholic in your past life with the spirit of a Muslim?' I said.

'Oh, Sweetu – just because you wish something, doesn't mean it's true.'

Some pea soup dropped on her blouse, which she wiped as she added: 'This is how it was meant to be. It's not easy, but you always say that you shouldn't trust anything that's too easy.'

I felt tears well up. 'God, I can talk a load of bullshit.'

'This is your chance.'

'To what? Drive off a cliff? Push him off one?'

She tutted. 'To show what forgiveness looks like.'

Ugh. Fucking theory and fucking practice.

Saturday 6 April

3.50 p.m. 'I told your Auntie Reena to stay but she packed her bags and left. Tells me she feels she's in the way. Le, so what if Wasim comes to visit? But if you ask me it is good in case she gives me the evil eye.'

Maars was already sitting with Adam in the living room, Tahir flicking through TV channels.

'Acha, Tahir, you take Adam to the park for half an hour,' Mum said to him.

He looked round the room. 'Auntie, I'm kind of tired –'

'Young man like you is tired? I am fifty-seven and do I say I'm tired?'

Tahir sighed and left the room. Before Maars could ask why her husband had been kicked out, Mum sat down and glared at us. A bit like when we were younger and had broken something.

'What do I look like to you?' said Mum.

Maars and I glanced at each other.

'Am I a servant?' She looked at both of us expectantly.

'Er, no,' said Maars.

'A nanny?'

'No . . .' I replied.

'A fool?'

Perhaps Mum needs to be put on some kind of medication. I could steal some of her pills.

'Don't look at each other, look at *me*,' she said.

She took a deep breath. 'Wasim asked me how my daughters would take the news of me getting married. You know what I said? I said they are good girls – their minds are open and they will understand.'

Oh dear.

'Maria, at the wedding you didn't once ask if he was OK. You didn't sit to talk to him or tell Tahir to.'

'Mu—'

'Maria, you are married with a baby; Soffoo, you are now married and will have babies too, and what will my life be? Have you thought of that?'

How was I ever going to tell her what's happened with Conall? But maybe having a life that's not fully about us will soften the blow.

'I was expecting gossip from people, but it's my daughters who have surprised me, making me feel I am doing something haram. If Allah doesn't stop me, then why should anyone else?'

I looked at my wedding band, twisting it on my finger.

She hesitated. 'And if there is a problem then . . . then think twice before speaking to me.'

Pause.

'OK?' she said.

We both nodded.

As Mum got up to go to the kitchen, Maars said: 'Sorry, Mum.'

Mum nodded at her.

'Me too,' I said. And I think this time I meant it.

'Chalo, doesn't matter. Get the onions out.'

Well, at least I could cry and blame it on the onions.

When I opened the door to Uncle Mouch, Hamida was with him.

'Hi,' she said.

She knew. She knew everything.

'Show me the garden,' she said to me.

As we went out she didn't wait two seconds to say something.

'I love Con but God, he's frustrating.' She looked at me as if in disapproval. 'Listen, I know you don't like me, but you should know that he's made a mistake and I hope . . . I hope you can forgive him.'

'I don't think you should be telling me what to do.'

I went to go back into the house.

'You weren't meant to happen,' she said. 'But how much longer before he broke the veneer of being so *together*. Travelling around the world, trying to fix things, when he can't even fix himself.'

I paused at the patio door. 'Is that what you'd both talk about then?'

'He told me when we were in Afghanistan together – before he came to London for you. When he married you he said to me, "I've never felt so ashamed of my past as I do when I'm with Sofia. But she's the only thing that seems to make it better."'

I don't know why that brought tears to my eyes but it did.

'I should be the one he can say anything to.'

'I know. I told him that. I said she followed you all the way to Karachi, living a lifestyle she hates. You think she'll care. She will only care if you *don't* tell her. But he's Con, you know. That guy has serious issues.'

No shit.

'So all this time you were on my side?' I said.

She gave a wry smile. 'I was on his side. Still am. He drives me crazy but despite everything, he is still one of the best people I've ever met.'

'Best people don't leave their wife and child without a note.'

She stepped towards me, as if sizing me up. 'OK. Ya. I see why he didn't tell you.'

'Don't turn this on me,' I said.

The fucking audacity. She raised her hands in the air as if she wasn't here to pick a fight. 'You think you know him –'

'No. I don't,' I interrupted.

She paused.

'I bet you love this,' I said. 'Pretending to give a shit while my marriage falls apart, waiting for Conall to come to you instead of his wife, with all this sorrow.'

She laughed so hard it caught me off-guard. I mean, she went into hysterics. This is Hammy, who never laughs at anything. I looked at her in alarm.

'God,' she said, wiping her eyes. 'Every day Con makes me wonder *why* he chose you.' She laughed again. 'I mean, you're crazy.'

'Fuck you,' I said.

Here was the rage and everyone would know it as I whipped round to go back into the house and tell her to get the fuck out. But she grabbed my arm and looked me in the eye.

'Sofia,' she said, her expression implacable, 'I'm *gay*.'

It took a moment to register what she'd said. Was she joking? 'What?'

'No longer Mama and Papa's darling,' she added, that wry smile appearing again. 'You think it's because I don't care about their bullshit money and social status that they've disowned me? Please.'

'I . . . I'm . . .. what?'

'Yeah,' she said. 'So next time you want to make assumptions about me and Con, think again.'

'Conall knows?'

'Of course he knows.'

'He never –'

'No. I asked him not to. I didn't need speeches of morality from a hijabi.'

Speeches of morality?

'He saved my life in a hundred different ways last year,' she said. 'I wanted to do the same for him. In case he needed me.'

'Does Uncle Was—'

'I don't know. I think he's guessed it because he says he will look after me no matter what. I told him I'm a grown woman now. I don't need looking after.'

'I guess that's not the point,' I said.

'No.' She paused. 'This is it, Sofia. Con's going to have to deal with it all. I'm going to carry on with the documentary project without him while he finally faces up to his past.'

Who can tell the difference any more between passion and distraction? Before I could say anything else to her she'd already gone back into the house. Did I know anything at all? How much of what I see is just my own misinformation? I went back into the house too, while Hamida carried on as normal and I tried to hide my state of shock.

'Hamida's going back to Karachi next week,' said Uncle Mouch. 'I will miss her.'

When they left she gave me a final look before saying goodbye and I was left with the feeling that somehow I'd wronged her.

I watched Maars with Adam later and asked her: 'What's it like. Having a baby?'

'It's all right,' she replied. 'If you don't like sleep.' She picked Adam up, pressing her nose into the base of his neck.

'What would you do if something happened to him?' I asked Maars.

'Sofe, don't say stuff like that. It's bad luck.' Just then Adam waved a chubby hand at her face. 'Naughty! You do not hit Mama.' She wagged her finger at him. 'You hit the people Mama tells you to hit,' she whispered, glancing at Tahir.

A few minutes later she said: 'You don't understand it until you have one of your own.'

'What?'

'What it feels like to worry every second of every day. Constantly: *are they healthy, what's that rash, are they happy, will they be bullied* . . . on and on, like a washing machine.'

Is that why Conall rarely smiles? Because he's worrying about the son he'd hardly seen? And then the worst happened. All that worry combined with so much guilt and so much failure.

I felt it begin: the shedding of spite.

10.10 p.m. 'Hi,' I said as he picked up the phone.

'Hi. How are you?' he asked.

'Fine. How's . . .' And I realised I didn't even know his son's name.

'Eamonn,' he said. He paused for a while. 'It's extraordinary – kids don't give a shit about anything as long as they have an iPad or something.'

'What's he like?'

'Shy. A little geeky.' He lowered his voice. 'He doesn't quite understand where I've been. There's a lot of explaining to do.' He paused. 'He'll come out with something random. This morning we must've had some rotten mugs on us, because he looked at us and said: "Cheer up, everyone. It might never happen."'

And then his voice cracked.

'He'll be OK,' I said.

Quiet.

'God, I'm sorry, Sofe.'

I nodded. Not that he could see.

'I'm so, so sorry.'

Was he rubbing his eyes? Leaning against the wall? Sitting with his head in his hands?

'OK.'

Pause.

'Your parents OK?' I asked.

'The same. I'll come home soon.'

Another pause.

'Sofe?'

'Mmm?'

Pause.

'Pray for him, please.'

What else, after all, was there left to do?

Thursday 18 April

9.10 a.m.

From: Sakib Awaan
To: Sofia Khan
Subject: Congratulations

Happy publication day, Sofia.
I hope married life isn't overshadowing your new life as a published author. Lots of dinner parties, I'm sure. Sorry you're not able to have lunch but what about next week? Friday? Katie says you have an interview with *The Women*, so before that?
You should be really proud of yourself. I think I've mentioned that before.
Sakib

P.S. I'm still very disappointed at not being able to show my dance moves at your wedding.

9.12 a.m.

From: Sofia Khan
To: Sakib Awaan
Subject: Re: Congratulations

Thank you. Congrats to us both, I guess.

Friday is good.

P.S. Maybe you can show them at my next wedding. Failing that, there's always my mum's to look forward to.

Argh! Why did I say that?? I slammed my head on my desk.

Maybe I'll get a concussion and go into a coma. At least then I'd get some sleep.

10.10 a.m.

From Suj: What do you mean you're not having a launch party? We have to celebrate! We're coming over. Don't worry about food – Hannah and Foz are sorting that, and I'm bringing drinks. Make a salad or something. I'm so fat, but NOT AS FAT AS YOUR BRAIN! Love you xxxx

10.35 a.m. Went to answer the door and it was a delivery of flowers with a note:

Two flowers for each pair of pants I've bought you. You did good. Love, Conall

10.37 a.m.

To Conall: I'm about to mark this day in the diary. Thanks for the flowers.

3.50 p.m.

From Conall: Sorry for late reply, was at hospital. Today can be our new anniversary. We can decorate the house with pants and flowers.

3.52 p.m.

To Conall: How's Eamonn?

4.05 p.m.

From Conall: Responding well to treatment. It's stage one so they're able to prevent it from spreading. I'll call you tonight.

4.07 p.m.

From Conall: Thank you, Sofe.

11 p.m. 'There she is, published author extraordinaire!' Hannah and Foz were at the door throwing party poppers in the air (and almost in my face).

I laughed, taking bits of string out of my hair. 'Where's Suj?'

'Had to move some stuff into Charles's place,' said Han. 'She'll be over in a bit.'

'So where's this salad?' Foz scanned the table. 'It's OK,' she added, grabbing my arms. 'You don't need to make salads because you're an author!'

'I thought you guys had forgotten,' I said.

'Aren't you too busy shagging to think about us?' asked Han.

I heard Foz slam the microwave shut before she walked in with plates of food, when the doorbell rang.

'Toffeeeee. Sorry I'm late.' Suj turned round and locked her black BMW before she stepped in and took off her four-inch heels. 'Fucking traffic.'

She looked in the hallway mirror and seemed to remember something.

'Shit. The drinks,' she said. 'Right, I'll go out and get some.'

Foz said they'd already brought them because they knew she'd forget. She kissed the girls and looked at the table. The doorbell rang again. Maria stood at the doorstep, her face blocked by a huge hump of foil set on an oven tray.

'I've left Adam at Mum's. So, what are the odds that you actually made this salad?'

Once talk of the book had dwindled I couldn't quite believe how much talk there was of nappies and Tupperware.

'When did you all turn into middle-aged women?' I said.

Foz paused and stared at me. 'Have we become boring?'

'You just spent thirty-five minutes discussing Maria's roast recipe.'

'How's Conall's dad?' asked Suj.

This was the moment. It was time to come clean.

At first they seemed to think I was joking. Once it was clear I wasn't, the rage on my behalf ensued. I'd had enough of rage, though. Negative emotions are such a bore.

'How are you so calm?' said Suj. 'I want to rip someone's eyes out.'

Maria looked like she might be on board with that.

'Why didn't you say something?' said Han. 'My God, I'd have been on the radio within half an hour.'

'Goes to show you, doesn't it?' said Maars. 'You can't trust anyone.'

'Yes, thanks, that's very useful,' I said.

She looked round the room. 'Well, it's true.'

'Maybe we should concentrate on what she's going to *do*,' said Foz.

'She's going to kill him, that's what she's going to do,' said Suj.

I began clearing up the plates. 'No.' I stood up. 'I'm going to let him deal with the mistakes that he's made. In the meantime, I have to make sure I don't make any of my own.'

Friday 19 April

9.20 a.m. Maars called me.

'I might've reacted badly last night. Well, like a sister. Then I went in to check on Adam before I went to bed; his chubby face so peaceful that I thought I'd do anything to make sure he always had that look. I mean, I'd die for it. You know, without sounding dramatic.'

'What would you do if you were me?' I asked.

'I don't know, Sofe. I really don't know. But I do know that when it's a child; when it's *your* child – it'd be like living a daily nightmare. And for that you need people.'

'I thought you were mad at Conall.'

'I'm livid,' she exclaimed. 'But no one should have to go through that. No one.'

Friday 26 April

3.05 p.m. 'Are you nervous?'

'Hmm?' I looked up from my phone.

'About the interview? You seem distracted,' said Sakib, dumping a manuscript on the table as the waiters took our jackets.

I'd been checking for Conall's call. Maybe the next phone conversation he'd tell me when he's coming home. Maybe then I'd be able to muster the courage to tell Mum.

'No,' I replied. I looked up from my phone. We were at a Turkish restaurant in Shoreditch.

'I love this place. Getting my wife to come here isn't easy.'

'Doesn't she like it?'

He smiled and shook his head. 'Thinks it's too hippie. Can we get some sparkling water?' he asked the waiter.

Just as we were looking through our menus his phone rang.

'I'm really sorry but I have to take this. Order whatever you like. I'll be as quick as I can.'

He left the table as I looked around at the deep reds of the restaurant and its mahogany furniture. A few minutes passed as I turned the manuscript towards me: *Everything but the Other*. I started reading the first few pages – by the tenth page Sakib was sitting back down. 'That took an age.'

'Oh, sorry,' I said, pushing the manuscript towards him.

'Don't be,' he replied, looking round for the waiter. 'Why haven't they brought the drinks out yet?

'You're big on efficiency, aren't you?' I said.

He looked at his menu. 'Haven't got to where I am without it.'

He asked how the book was going, and as we spoke about it I realised how much I missed having this conversation with Conall: which chapter's a bit tricky, what parts he does and doesn't like. Maybe that's what relationships are about.

'What did you think then?' Sakib asked, glancing at the manuscript.

'That prologue needs to go,' I replied. 'They're handholding the reader and the first few pages are backstory.'

He got his phone out, tapping on his iPhone as my phone beeped. 'I've sent you the manuscript,' he said. 'If you fancy reading it.'

'Oh.' I mean, a bit random, isn't it?

'I agree with you. I'd give you the hard copy but . . .' He pointed to his glasses. I get migraines and I need to finish it this week.'

'Sure. OK.'

He smiled, and as he turned to call the waiter I caught the smell of Sakib's aftershave. Probably a good idea to stop smelling men who aren't my husband. We spent most of the lunch talking about our respective families and how we'd have to beg our parents to go to the library so we could get new books to read.

'Incredible, isn't it? Just how much can change in one generation,' he said.

I nodded, thinking about that moment Conall told me: *I have a son.*

'Or just in a day,' I said.

He gave me a curious look, taking a sip of his water. 'If you're worried about the interview, don't be.' Then he leaned forward. 'Think of this as just the beginning.'

'Beginning of what, exactly?' I asked.

He paused. 'Any kind of beginning is cause for celebration; no?'

'Are you an optimist or something?'

'With a happy childhood, don't forget,' he added.

I laughed as he raised his glass. 'To beginnings.'

I always thought my new beginning was when I got married, but maybe there are all types of new beginnings – you just haven't seen them yet. I raised my glass to his.

'To beginnings.'

MAY

He Said, She Said

The Women's *Kelly Bright Interviews . . .*

***Sofia Khan, author of* Lessons in Heartbreak and Laughter, *on dating as a modern Muslim woman and her happily ever after.* Out now, Ignite Press, priced £7.99**

Kelly: *First of all, I'm so pleased to have you with us to talk about your book. And can I just say I love your shoes.*

Sofia: *Oh, thank you.*

Kelly: *And congratulations on your happily ever after. (Pause)*

Sofia: *Thanks.*

Kelly: *So, just to begin, what are your thoughts on the recent bombings in Europe?*

Sofia: *Sorry?*

Kelly: *Do we need stricter border control? Revisiting foreign policy? Should parents and schools be paying better attention to children who might be prone to radicalisation? As a Muslim, are you worried?*

Sofia: *Well . . . (Pause) As a human being, I'm worried.*

Kelly: *Of course.*

Sofia: *Should we just, maybe, talk about the book? (Pause)*

Kelly: *Yes, yes, of course. It's really very wonderful. And what strikes me about it is your refusal to settle for what's expected – you're quite damning of Asian Muslim men.*

Sofia: *There are always exceptions to the rule, but I'd say they mostly walk around saying they want a fierce, independent woman, but at home they just want a younger version of their mother who they can shag.*
(Kelly clears her throat)

Kelly: *I loved the feminist thread throughout. Was it difficult growing up without any feminist role models?*

Sofia: *You haven't met my mother.*
(Kelly laughs)

Kelly: *That's very good. But didn't you wonder why she had to wear a hijab and yet your father didn't?*

Sofia: *He'd have looked very odd in a hijab. And anyway, my mum never wore one.*
(Pause)

Kelly: *Ah, how unusual.*

Sofia: *Is it?*
(Kelly clears throat)

Kelly: *Quite. OK. In a romantic twist of fate, your husband actually converted for you, didn't he?*
(Sofia nods)

Kelly: *Aside from the obvious romantic gesture, does the growing number of converts who are then radicalised concern you?*
(Pause)

Sofia: *Excuse me?*

Kelly: *I mean, on an objective level.*

Sofia: *So, you're not asking me whether I think my husband might become a terrorist?*

(Kelly laughs nervously)

Kelly: *Of course not. I mean, generally speaking.*

Sofia: *Is this linked to the book?*

(Pause)

Kelly: *I suppose I'm rather curious: would you have married him if he hadn't converted?*

(Pause)

Sofia: *My husband?*

Kelly: *Yes.*

(Long pause)

Sofia: *Would I have married him if he hadn't converted?*

Kelly: *Exactly.*

(Another long pause)

Sofia: *Well . . . I suppose . . . probably not. No. I wouldn't have.*

Kelly: *I think many women would find it extraordinary that you'd compromise your happily ever after because of your beliefs.*

(Long pause)

Sofia: *Come on. You and I both know that happily ever after doesn't exist.*

Wednesday 1 May

12.20 p.m. I sat at the table in the bookshop where I was signing books and slammed my hand on the published interview. Katie had just walked in.

'Hmm,' she said.

'*You and I both know happily ever after doesn't exist*. Why did I say that? What possessed me?' I said, scribbling my name for the twentieth time as I piled up another book.

I glanced at the door to see if Conall had walked in yet. He was coming back from Ireland and said he'd meet me here. Katie looked over at the clock on the wall behind me.

'It's just a glitch,' she said. 'You'll get it down next time.'

Next time?

'Will people hate me now they know I wouldn't have married him?' Never mind what my husband will think. 'It's just that I'd have been lying otherwise,' I continued.

Katie gave me a sympathetic look.

'But I can't go around telling lies just to be popular.' I put my head in my hands.

'I guess I should be used to being unpopular,' I added.

From Foz: Darling, have you seen your interview in *The Women* today? Was it meant to read like that? Also, which shoes is she talking about? Xx

From Hannah: Sorry been out of loop. Busy. Read your interview. Good! Interviewer came off as a twat. Although was that last line necessary? Call you later this week. X

'Ah, good, you're still here.'

I glanced up and saw Sakib looking down at me.

'She's worried about the interview,' Katie told him.

He paused. 'It was an . . . interesting piece,' he replied.

Oh my God, he thinks I think he wants to shag his mum. Though, to be fair, he probably does; he just hasn't realised it yet. Wonder what Freud would've made of the Asian man sub-group.

'Perhaps you need to be prepared to answer more uncomfortable questions. Ones that aren't to do with the book,' he added.

'Why?' I said.

'You wear a hijab. People want to know things,' he replied.

Katie cleared her throat.

'I didn't realise that *this*,' I said, pointing to my scarf, 'was the sum of all my parts.'

Wish I hadn't said 'my parts'. Wish I hadn't said a lot of bloody things!

Just then, as I glanced behind Sakib, I saw Conall, leaning against the wall, holding my book in his hands. God, isn't it pathetic how just the sight of someone can feel like you've been given a tranquilliser.

'Hello, wife. Any chance of a signature?' he said, handing over the book.

How can you be so relieved to see someone and at the same time not be able to meet their eye? I looked for signs of his annoyance about the interview, ready to counter it with, *you're not allowed to be annoyed. You lied to me.*

He and Sakib shook hands as Katie said she had to be back in the office for a digital meeting. She leaned in to hug me and said: 'Things are bound to go tits-up now and again. Don't worry about it. He's here. Remember that matters.'

Love Katie.

'Are you feeding her good sense?' Conall asked her.

'Always,' she replied.

'Say hello to Tom,' he added as Katie gave me a look and walked out of the shop.

'I was just saying to Sofia that she should expect to be asked questions that aren't to do with the book,' said Sakib.

Conall leaned his hand on the table. 'People ask stupid questions. Doesn't mean she has to answer them.'

He knows I wouldn't have married him if he didn't convert.

As a concept of course he'd have known this, but implicit understanding is so different from seeing it in print – from *everyone* seeing it in print. I looked at both of them and thought that this could be normal – this set-up. I could forget that he's only just returned from seeing his ex-wife and son. I could even fool myself into believing I don't think about this ex-wife: what she's thinking; whether she's missed him; if she wants him back. Loneliness can fog the hard-edged line of principle.

Sakib put a hand in his pocket. 'All the more reason to answer them.' He looked at me. 'It's not the first and it won't be the last time you have to do something you don't want to do.'

'Great, thanks,' I replied.

'Remember,' said Sakib, leaning forward, 'it's just the beginning.'

I glanced at Conall, his jaw clenched.

'Right, I'd better be going. Sofia, I'll wait for some new chapters from you.'

Sakib turned towards Conall. 'I think people will appreciate the honesty. No one who's married could possibly believe in happily ever after.'

I looked out of the car window at the double-decker buses as Conall drove us home. He beeped at a van that had pulled out in front of him.

'Feckin' indicate, would ya?'

The driver stuck his middle finger up at us. We both paid him the same compliment.

'Arsehole,' I said.

Conall manoeuvred the steering wheel with one hand as he turned into a side road.

'Interesting interview,' he said, stopping at a traffic light. 'Particularly the notion of Asian men wanting to "shag their mums",' he added. 'Your shining moment.'

I didn't want to smile or laugh. 'How's Eamonn?'

I noticed the veins pulse in his arms as he overtook three cars without looking in the mirror.

'He's fine. Ma begins to cry and he just says: "There she goes again."'

'And Claire?'

It took some effort to say her name. Beginning to accept something is all very well, but what about the subsequent small acceptances? The unexpected potholes you're meant to skip over every time you turn a corner.

'I'm sure she has lots to say,' he replied. 'But she doesn't. Not yet, anyway.'

A group of people walked past the zebra crossing, cheering and laughing. My mouth felt dry. Would she want him back? What was I missing when I was here and he was there? How am I going to slot into this new narrative of his?

'When will you go back?' I asked.

'Soon.'

He'll need to go back and forth for as long as everyone lives.

'Are you pissed off about the interview?' I asked.

I buoyed myself up for it – whatever he had to say, I'll say: *fuck you, you lied to me.*

'Lost any right to be angry with you a while ago,' he replied. 'Plus, I always knew what I had to do.'

If he could give me the wrong answer I could conjure up embers of anger and they could rage against his lies. We approached our road and he parked up.

'Listen, Sofe.' Pause. 'If you were half as sure about your beliefs, I'd have been half as sure about converting.'

He unbuckled his seat belt and looked at me.

I returned his gaze. 'Didn't you wonder: why should I do this if she can't accept me the way I am?' I asked.

Leaning his elbow on the steering wheel, he turned towards me. 'I did what I did because . . .' He searched for the words.

'I get it . . . What does it feel like, though?' I asked

'What?'

'I don't know any different from what I was brought up to believe. But I want to know what it feels like – praying, the whole shebang.'

He thought about it for a moment.

'I don't know. It's not like being around faith is new to me. But it's different this time. Perhaps I was just lazy with it before. Perhaps I needed it less then.'

'It shouldn't be a need. Nothing should.'

'No. It shouldn't.' He turned to look at me. 'Sofe . . . if you can forgive me – however long it takes . . .' He paused. 'I'll know that I must've done something right in my life.'

Why does he *always* say the right things? Just then Mum came out of the house and we got out of the car.

'Do me a favour,' he said. 'Go inside.'

'What –'

'This is my fault,' he said. 'Let me tell her.'

Thursday 2 May

10.20 a.m. Went over to Mum's this morning and Tahir was there, collecting new pans Mum had bought for Maria. He'd taken the day off work to help Maars reorganise the kitchen. If that isn't love, I don't know what is.

'There are times, Sofe, you've got to think of the lesser evil, isn't it? One day of reorganising the kitchen means I won't have to listen about not helping for the next two weeks.'

He tapped his head. Poor Tahir. But at least this shows that you can grow into your brains.

'These are the last straws,' Mum said to me as Tahir went up to use the bathroom. 'It is too much.'

'What did he say to you yesterday?' I asked.

'What does it matter how much he loves you or how sorry he is?' she replied. 'You know these goray with their love-shove. OK, he's divorced, doesn't matter.' She looked at me. 'I'm not that backward-thinking. But he also has a *child*.'

I did wonder what was so inhumane about a child – maybe she didn't want to be judged by Uncle Mouch. Bloody hell. I was beginning to see that the only way not to be judged was to be dead.

As Tahir walked into the room, he said: 'Maria told me, by the way.'

Mum gave me a disgruntled look: *see how people will find out*. My brother-in-law already thinks I'm this strange Muslim/modern London-girl hybrid. Not only did I marry a white guy, but now I'm sitting around while I watch him go back and forth to Ireland.

'I mean, what's the idea?' asked Tahir.

Nothing is as ominous to some people as ideas. But, in the end, I've realised that people are just obsessed with others living like they do. No matter who they are.

Note for book: Departure from the norm is akin to sin.

'Chalo,' said Mum. 'What can I say? You have made your decision and now you live with it.'

'Is that it?' Tahir asked Mum.

'Do you want her to lock me up?' I said to him.

'No, it's just . . .' He looked between Mum and me. 'Nothing.' With which he gave a bewildered shake of the head and left the house with his pan-filled box.

'Are you worried?' I asked her. 'About telling Uncle Mou— I mean, Uncle Wasim?'

She took a deep breath. 'I am too old to worry about these things now.'

Saturday 4 May

8.35 a.m. 'You need to give Sean money back on his rent,' I said without looking up from my laptop when Conall walked into the room.

'I'd forgotten about that.'

When I looked up he'd put tea and a plate of biscuits on the table.

'You could use the fuel before sending those chapters to your editor,' he said, getting his chequebook. 'He seems bossy.'

I picked up a biscuit. 'Thanks.'

It never ceases to amaze me how the small things make me love him.

'Listen,' he said when he'd come back. 'I forgot to ask – what does *soonthay* mean?'

Oh my bloody hell.

'Why?' I asked.

'Your mum mumbled something about me needing one when I spoke to her the other day.'

I put my head in my hands as I watched him.

'What?' he asked, looking up from his chequebook.

'It's . . . Oh God.'

'*What?*'

I paused. 'A circumcision.'

He looked at me, his face unmoved. 'A what?'

'You *know* . . . a circumcision,' I said, pretending my hands were scissors. 'She thinks you should have one.'

We stared at each other for a few seconds as he pursed his lips, not taking his eyes off me, the hint of a smile appearing.

'Don't, it's not funny. She's serious,' I replied, unable to hold back my laughter.

'*Is she high?*' he asked.

'I think she might be.'

He leaned back in his chair, shaking his head. 'Do you think we should pretend?'

'Knowing her she'll want photographic evidence.'

He laughed. 'Christ, your mum can be great craic.'

As I watched him sign his cheque I thought: *we have to be OK.*

'You're such a dinosaur – do an online transfer like normal people,' I said.

'Don't trust it. Speaking of,' he replied, looking up. 'Don't listen to your editor. You say what you want to say, not because you have to.'

I was about to respond when I noticed the cheque was for a lot more than I thought Sean paid. Conall paused.

'I send money. To Claire.'

Another pothole. I went back to looking at my computer. We both sat in silence for the rest of the morning and I had to wonder, what is the point of ever laughing with him when I just never know when the next pothole might appear?

8.50 p.m. I was writing about marital bliss while Conall booked tickets to Ireland to go and see his ex-wife and child.

Note for book: Do extensive search on partner's past in case of unknown family lurking somewhere in another country.

'You're still writing the book then?' Conall asked.

'Not much choice now.' I looked up at him. 'Don't say there's always a choice. Sometimes there isn't,' I added.

'Don't I know that,' he mumbled.

I'm not sure if he was referring to me writing the book or how life seems to have panned out.

'Listen . . .' He seemed bothered as I looked up at him again. 'If you want to come to Ireland, I can book two tickets.'

Did I want to know what happened when he went there? Who said what, and the way Claire might look at him? Yes. Did I want to witness it before my very own eyes; shifting and shuffling to try and fit into their foreign framework? No.

'Oh,' I replied.

'It's fine. You don't have to. I just . . .' He went back to looking at the laptop screen.

'I don't know,' I replied.

'No, it's fine,' he said. 'Of course. Only if you want.'

What do I want?

Sunday 5 May

8.10 a.m. Woke up thinking, *no man is an island.* It was all very philosophical for a Sunday morning with Conall's head stuck under his pillow. Despite past events, I still like having sex with my husband – the closeness of him; his breath on my neck; the way he'll stroke my hair afterwards and look at me so that it's impossible for me *not* to love him. It made me want to smother him with the pillow. I hate myself a little for all this dependency. Tried calling Suj last night (cinema with Charles), Foz (at an exhibition with a friend), Han (finishing medical article and then having dinner with Omar), Maria (date night with Tahir), Katie (spin class followed by drinks with Tom) and realised the further inconvenience of emotional dependency – and not just to do with husband. How independent can a person be when they constantly need to discuss the choice they should make?

Note for book: Who you think you are and who you are can sometimes end up being two very different things.

Tuesday 7 May

9.45 a.m.

From: Sofia Khan
To: Sakib Awaan
Subject: Everything but the Other

Hi, hope you're well. I've attached the MS with track changes. TBH, it's not really my cup of tea – bit on the navel-gazing side. Is the woman Asian? Big up to the BAME.
Sofia.

Probably a good idea *not* to say 'big up' to your editor, but as with many things in life, it can sometimes be too late.

4.15 p.m.

From: Sakib Awaan
To: Sofia Khan
Subject: Re: Everything but the Other

That was quick. Didn't expect so much detail. Look forward to reading your thighs.

Thighs??

From: Sakib Awaan
To: Sofia Khan
Subject: Re: Everything but the Other

Thoughts! God. Sorry. Damn autocorrect. I'd be grateful if you didn't sue me for sexual harassment.
Really sorry.
Sakib

It's good to know that even in the midst of semi-tragedy, I have the ability to laugh.

Wednesday 8 May

11.30 a.m.

From: Sakib Awaan
To: Sofia Khan
Subject: Thank you

Hi Sofia,
Finished reading your comments on the EBTO. Largely agreed with you.
I'm going to turn it down.
Appreciate your comments.
Best,
Sakib

11.35 a.m.

From: Sofia Khan
To: Sakib Awaan
Subject: Another MS?

Glad to be of use. Let me know if there's anything else you'd like me to read – and feel free to add me to your payroll.
Sofia

Thursday 9 May

11 a.m. Conall was leaving again. Haven't mentioned his offer to come to Ireland since that day. I think I can get used to the rhythm of this life, though, without having to be immersed in the other side of it.

'Call you when I get there,' he said.

And he always does. Like clockwork. He stared at me, as if he were about to say something, when my phone rang.

'Hello?'

'Hi, Sofia. Sakib here.'

Conall waited at the door.

Sakib was talking to someone else. 'Hi, yes, I'd like a decaf latte, large –'

'I was just –'

'No: *decaf*,' I heard Sakib say. 'Thanks.'

Conall rested his bag on the sofa.

'Actually, I think you'd make a great reader. If you're interested, that is. Honestly, the submissions I have are piling high. It's fine, keep the change.'

I was too busy glancing at Conall to really pay attention to what Sakib was saying and said I'd have to call him back.

'Of course. Sorry. I'm working till late, so whenever.'

And he hung up before I said goodbye.

'What was that?' asked Conall.

I must've been frowning. 'Oh. I don't know.' The words I'd just heard were beginning to sink in. 'I *think* Sakib was offering me a job.'

'Really?' he said. 'What kind of job?'

'I don't know yet. I said I'd call him back.'

He picked his bag up again. 'Would you be going in and out of the office?'

I shrugged. 'Why?'

He shook his head. 'Just wondering.'

I looked at the clock. 'You don't want to miss your flight.'

I walked him to the door as he said goodbye, kissing me on the forehead.

11.25 a.m. Spoke to Sakib again.

'Are you OK?' he asked.

'Yeah, why?'

'Your voice sounds a little a distant.'

'Oh, sorry.'

He paused and then told me about the job. 'You'll pass anything on to me you think is worth considering. You can work from home or come in – up to you. What do you think?'

Seemed like a win–win, really.

'Sofia?'

'Yes, OK.'

'Great. Good . . . You're sure you're OK?'

My husband's in Ireland with his other family. I am just great.

'Headache,' I replied.

'Well, drink some water, pop a pill and get to work.'

'Yes, sir.'

'Good woman.'

2.20 p.m. 'All this back and forth, back and forth,' said Mum. 'How expensive it is.'

'It's just Ireland,' I reasoned.

'Why doesn't he stay there until Eeman is better?'

'It's Eamon, Mum.'

She frowned, rubbing some kind of lotion on to her arms. Financial matters always have trumped emotional ones for Mum. Just then the doorbell rang and it was Uncle Mouch.

Complete with a basket of wedding presents . . . for Mum.

'We don't have our elders to do this for us any more,' he said. 'But why shouldn't your mama enjoy this part of getting married?'

I looked at the multiple outfits that shone with sequins, the gold that was taken out of its box to be appreciated by a mother flushed with . . . well, something.

'Acha, have we decided if we will have one function here and one in Karachi?' said Mum.

'Two functions, of course,' exclaimed Uncle Mouch. 'We can even have a third, just the two of us. But that will be our honeymoon, haina, Mehnaz?' He leaned forward and raised his eyebrows suggestively to Mum. Mum giggled. I think I was going to be sick.

I watched as she brought him tea and he asked how her day had been. What was truly grotesque was that Mum hadn't seemed to have outgrown blushing whenever he paid her a compliment. *Have you changed your hair? That suit looks nice on you. You look younger every day.* I had to keep reminding myself of Maria saying that we need to be adults.

'Beta, how is your . . . husband's son?' he asked. 'It is the worst thing,' he added. 'To watch your child go through this much pain.'

It made me wonder what Conall was doing and who was making sure he was OK.

5.15 p.m. Have prayed a lot. For various things, but mostly for contentment. Life never was meant to be easy; it's being OK with it – even at its shittiest – that's the real graft.

11.20 p.m.

To Conall: Next time you go to Ireland, fancy taking me with you?

11.25 p.m. He called.

'Yes, Sofe. I do.'

And apparently there was no time like the present. 'I'll book you a ticket for tomorrow.'

I started at the suddenness.

'Is that too soon?'

Something about Mum carrying on with life with such gusto made me ashamed I wasn't doing the same.

'No,' I said. 'I'll see you Friday.'

Friday 10 May

3.20 p.m. As a child of immigrant parents you'd think I'd appreciate frugality when it comes to things like flying. I chewed my £5 Pringles and rolled my eyes as a round of applause piped through the plane's speakers to congratulate itself on arriving on time. I told myself that as a person of spiritual matter it's better to be on a cheap flight to go and see husband than be in first class with someone you want to push out of the flight.

'So,' I said as he met me at the airport. 'This is home?'

He took my bag and looked at me. 'Didn't you think you'd stand out enough with a hijab – you had to wear red lipstick too?'

I'd have been annoyed if he hadn't looked amused. But when we got into the car Conall gripped the steering wheel with both hands, his knuckles becoming whiter than usual. A knot of anxiety expanded in my gut.

'Let's go then,' he said.

I watched the road open up to a cascade of rolling hills on one side, set against a bright blue sky. On the other side the expanse of a dark blue sea stretched out against jagged cliffs. It was like looking through Instagram's chrome filter. I wound down the window and breathed the fresh air.

Reconciling the Conall I knew to this serene setting felt odd – like trying to insert a piece that belonged to a different puzzle. But when I glanced at him I wondered whether he didn't fit in perfectly. I caught a glimpse of my hijabbed self in the side-mirror. Now *that* is out of place.

Conall slowed the car down as a flock of sheep blocked the road. They were being shepherded by a man with a brown hat and grizzly ginger beard, who waved at the car. Conall muttered something under his breath. The man approached the car and looked into it. Conall wound down the window and the noise of the bleating sheep flooded in.

'Conall?' said the man. 'Conall O'Flynn as I live and breathe?'

His eyes flickered towards me and it might sound like a cliché, but he really did tip his hat at me.

'Jack.' Conall shook the man's hand. 'How are you?'

And here, I'm afraid, I lost the conversational thread. I leaned in, I focused on the moving lips, the gesticulating hands, the furrow of the brow that was then replaced with a hearty laugh, that was then replaced with a more pensive look, but I could not, for the life of me understand a word of what Jack said. And forget Jack. Suddenly Conall was saying things that didn't make sense either. I understood 'Ma and Da . . .' and 'wife' (mostly because Jack then looked at me again and nodded with a benign smile), but other than that I was lost, and quite frankly, it was giving me a headache. I got out a bag of M&M's.

'Look after yourself, Jack.'

With which Jack tipped his hat at me again and the last of his sheep bumbled off the road.

'*What* was the conversation?' I said.

This must be how he feels when we're all talking Urdu. Conall looked at me, starting up the car.

'Welcome to Kilkee, Sofe.'

Detached houses stood with drystone walls and cobbled paths. The pebbles crunched under the tyres as we turned into a driveway and stopped outside a yellow house. A black-and-white collie came bounding up to us.

'Jessop! Down, Jessop, c'mere, boy,' said Conall.

Jessop panted, his tongue lolling around. The front door opened and Mary appeared in her slippers and green, knitted cardigan. Conall and I walked towards her, Jessop still jumping round us.

'Sofia,' she said, her arms still folded as I leaned in to give her a kiss.

The first thing I noticed was the quiet. The kind of quiet that makes you want to fill the silence with inane remarks like *what a lovely home* and *weather's nicer than expected*. We wandered into a dimly lit passage where Conall put my bag down, the faint smell of vanilla and dog lingering in the air. There was a table with a collection of photographs and I recognised Conall as a teenager in one of them. I watched real-time Conall telling Mary about bumping into Jack as we walked into the open-plan kitchen. Daylight flooded in through the patio windows.

'Put the kettle on, won't you, Conall. I'll show Sofia into the room.'

He'd already opened the fridge as Mary led me up the wooden spiral staircase.

'Here we are,' she said.

A vase with peonies stood in the middle of the windowsill – a huge pane that looked out into the garden downstairs. I looked round at the yellowed newspaper cuttings that were framed on the wall – all of Conall doing some kind of sporting . . . thing.

'He was a top hurler in school,' she said, looking at the pictures and smiling. 'Fierce focus,' she added.

'Not much has changed then,' I replied.

She patted down a crease on the bedspread. 'I think that quite a lot has changed.'

Did she mean Eamonn, or her son's religion, or just her son generally?

'He made mistakes,' she said, still patting down the bed. 'Don't think he hasn't been given a piece of my mind.' She paused. 'But I know he regrets what he's done – he just buries things. Still, he knows when he's done wrong – it's why he won't ask anything of you.'

What would he want to ask of me? Before she could say anything else the front door slammed shut as we heard: 'Christ, your son's been at it again.'

I looked at Mary.

'Colm! You'll be wise to know we have company,' she exclaimed, looking at me.

'Well, he's an eejit and everyone should know.'

'Now's not the time,' I heard Conall say.

We began making our way down the stairs.

'Oh, if the prodigal son says so then my lips are sealed.'

Mary walked into the dining area while I stood at the door with Conall's dad's back to me.

God, I hate tension. It gives me an ulcer.

'Well,' he said, turning to look at me. 'Let's see what my son married without so much as an invite to his parents.'

His eyes took in my scarf; his face red and rugged and the distinct smell of alcohol emanating from his mouth. He took me by the shoulders and I saw Conall step forward.

'Colm, best you sleep this off,' said Mary.

'Be good to sleep off this whole nightmare, don't you think?' he said, leaning towards me.

I glanced at Conall. 'A coma right now wouldn't be a bad thing,' I replied.

His grip loosened a little as his eyes bored into mine. A few seconds passed as he burst into laughter, putting his arm round me as we walked to the table. Mary's lips were pursed.

'So, Sofia,' he said. '*Sofia*. Isn't that Catholic?'

'Sit down, Colm, I'll make you some food,' said Mary.

Colm turned his gaze to Conall.

'Sofia, you know the problem with kids nowadays, don't you?' He paused, waiting for an answer. *Mad fathers?*

'No,' I replied.

'She's polite, I'll give you that,' he said to Conall. Colm leaned forward, squinting at me. 'They're too damn sensitive.'

Conall's hand rested on his forehead.

'Take our Sean, for example. Sitting on the phone, telling me about his job and promotions and I couldn't give a . . . well.' He lifted his hands. 'I won't swear in front of a lady. A Muslim one at that.' He looked at Conall. 'See, don't tell me I don't have respect for people.'

Oh dear.

'But you can't say anything to kids nowadays without them telling you you're being obnoxious. I'm being a parent, you eejit. And as a parent can't I expect that my kids stay in their home town to run the family business and not want to go and be bankers and photographers?' He looked at Mary. 'They're quick to say how disappointed they are but don't for a minute think about *our* disappointment.' He looked at Conall. 'The hypocrisy. Bet he's told you all about what an awful dad I was, hasn't he?'

If only, I wanted to say, as Conall glared at his father.

'Family business wasn't good enough for you?' he said. 'God forbid. Anything to do with family's not good enough for you.'

That's when I wanted to go and hug Conall because his dad clearly didn't see the side of him that built shelters and looked after people and always tried to do the right thing. Apart from lie to me. Obviously.

'For God's sake, Colm,' said Mary.

'She's their defence lawyer,' said Colm to me, sticking his thumb towards Mary. 'Always been soft. On the inside, anyway. They don't say it but they don't know why she didn't pack her bags and leave me years ago.'

'I must've had rocks in my head,' she said, watching him as if she was a teacher who'd caught a student smoking behind the shed.

'And then there's my grandson . . .' His eyes glazed over as he stared at the table, tears surfacing. 'Oh, he's grand. *Funny*. Answer for everything.' He looked up at me. 'Doesn't God have a funny way of showing he's merciful?'

Mary put a cheese toastie on a plate in front of him. 'Eat that.'

'What do I want with food?' he said, faltering as he stood up.

'Your son . . .' he added, looking and pointing at Conall, as if the sight of him gave Colm physical pain. He couldn't seem to find any more words, though. 'I'm going to bed.'

With which he walked out of the room.

'Well,' said Mary, sitting at the table and pouring tea into a cup. 'Your father always did like drama.'

4.10 p.m. 'Soffoo, they have linger-y here, fifty per cent off.'

'What?' I whispered as I came into the bedroom to answer Mum's third call.

'Linger-y.'

'You mean lingerie?'

Pause. 'Lounge-aray?'

'*Lingerie.*'

'This spelling is very weird.'

'It's French.'

'Le, are we living in France?'

'What are you doing in the lingerie department, Mum?'

'I'm buying some for myself, of course. Maria told me she doesn't want anything. Silly girl – so cheap these bras are.'

Oh my actual God. My mother wants us all to have matching marital underwear. *Vom.*

'I'm kind of busy here, Mum.'

'How are your in-laws? I hope you took Mary a present. Have you given the toy I put in your bag to Eemon? Oh, I have to go before this woman takes all the nice knickers.'

4.12 p.m.

> **From Maria:** If Mum calls *don't answer.* You'll never recover from the conversation. Trust me. How's Ireland? You OK? xx

9.35 p.m. 'So, that's your dad then?' I said that evening when Conall and I were finally alone.

Conall rested his hands on his hips as he stared out of the window. 'In all his glory.'

'Could've been worse,' I said. *Probably.*

'You know the worst thing? Whatever shit he used to say to us; however many ways he disappointed us . . . at least he stayed.'

He turned round, not quite looking me in the eye. 'It's depressing. Knowing he was more of a father to me than I've been to Eamonn. And it doesn't help me like him better for it.' He rubbed his eyes. 'At least now you know the other reason I don't drink.'

Just when I thought I'd peeled back a layer of Conall, he reveals ten more.

'Well, feelings can be complicated,' I said, playing with the corner of the bedspread.

'How do I fix this, Sofe? Tell me. With your characteristic logic.'

When I looked up he was already standing over me. I shrugged and took his hands.

'Don't make the same mistake twice.'

Saturday 11 May

3.55 a.m. Conall already awake and praying Tahajjud. People find it hard enough to pray the compulsory five times a day let alone the middle-of-the-night prayers. In the midst of thinking that I can't be the fat-arsed, lazy wife who missed morning prayers in the face of all this holiness, I also thought, *at least there's something that's giving him comfort*.

'Bloody hell,' I said to him, getting out of bed.

I stumbled out of the room and into the bathroom to do pre-prayer ablutions. Almost fell asleep on toilet seat. Got up and noticed the small cabinet above the sink. Being nosy is, apparently, a trait that defies sleep deprivation. I took a peek inside and, amongst other pills, there was a bottle of Diazepam prescribed for Mary. Is that why she always seems so calm? Pills? Poor Mary. I could've done with some of those pills myself. I'd just about managed to apply whatever contortionist skills I had to get my foot in the sink (it being higher than most sinks), when the door handle turned. Argh! I'd forgotten to lock the damn bathroom door. Before I could move, say, or do anything, the door was already open and Conall's dad stood there, watching me without a hijab, bare legs, and a foot in his sink. Seems the O'Flynn men all walk around in their boxers.

'Oh,' I said, averting my eyes from Colm's hairless chest and pot belly.

He didn't move. 'Why's your foot in the sink?' he asked, with a genuine look of curiosity.

'I'm doing ablutions. For praying.'

'Christ.' He took a deep breath. 'It's three in the morning, you know.'

I nodded. *Why was my foot still in the sink?*

'You finished then?' he added.

My senses had awakened as I took my foot out – my arms and face still wet. I made to move out of there as quickly as possible when he said, 'Don't you need a towel? You get athlete's foot, verrucas – all sorts otherwise.'

VOM. Why was the second conversation I was having with my father-in-law about *athlete's foot*??

'Take another towel.' He stepped into the bathroom and began looking in the side cupboard. My God, that bathroom felt small. He handed me a white towel.

'Oh. Thanks. Thank you very much,' I said, taking it and manoeuvring past him to get out of the door.

'Now you make sure you dry right between the toes.'

I nodded and dashed back into our room.

'My God,' I said.

Conall was staring out ahead, sitting on the floor, when he turned round.

'That was *gross*.'

When I mentioned his dad he stood up as if ready to go out and do or say who-knows-what. By the time I finished the story about the drying between the toes Conall's face had relaxed.

'He did that?' he asked.

I nodded. 'At least he didn't catch me with my pants down.'

I put my scarf on, pulling down my sleeves and getting ready to pray as Conall sat on the edge of the bed, seeming to contemplate something.

'What?' I asked.

'Nothing.' He looked up at me as he paused. 'I guess he must like you.'

I don't know how giving someone advice on foot hygiene is tantamount to liking them, but perhaps Conall wasn't the only O'Flynn man who defies understanding.

10.20 a.m. Getting ready to go to hospital after a breakfast of father-in-law asking if I had to pray again, and mother-in-law preparing lunch platters.

'You eaten?' Conall's dad barked at him.

'Coffee's fine,' Conall replied.

Mary and I both looked at them.

'Does no one any good if you don't eat anything.'

'I'm not hungry.'

'Well, of course you're not hungry. Your son's in hospital.'

Quiet.

'But praying's not going to fill that hole,' he added.

Conall looked up at him. 'I suppose drinking does that for you?'

'You should try it some time. Help you to crack a smile.'

'I think we should go now,' interjected Mary.

'Well, thanks to you, Dad, I tried it for a while and I can't say it did much good.'

I think I'd have preferred to have a conversation with Mum about matching lingerie. Colm scoffed as he wiped his mouth with his napkin and got up.

'You don't blame your parents for everything, do you, Sofia?'

He waited for me to answer. Mary was almost as still as Conall – I guess that's where he gets it from.

'Oh, I don't know . . . in the end we all mess each other up in one way or another.'

Mary looked unimpressed but Colm let out a laugh. 'You want to take a leaf out of her book,' he said to Conall.

Conall stood up, taking the plates, as he mumbled, 'In case you haven't noticed, I have.'

10.25 a.m. I realise this isn't about me but what do you wear to see your stepson and husband's ex-wife for the first time?

3.30 p.m. Conall spoke in monosyllables. Walking into the hospital, I grabbed his hand – practically cracked one of my knuckles. Mary and Colm walked behind us.

We turned a corner into a room splashed with reds, blues, oranges and greens. Claire was sitting with Eamonn, looking over his shoulder as he played with his iPad. I watched her, looking so calm and sad. This was the woman Conall had once loved, had a child with, married and left. She was betrayed by the man whose hand I held and it made me wonder how much a person can really change? The old Conall must still be there, inside, caged in the confines of his own principles that were perhaps waiting to burst under the weight of reality. Eamonn's hair was as curly and black as Claire's was straight and blonde. Conall let go of my hand.

'They've got a new reading area for children then,' commented Mary.

Claire stood up, tapping the iPad as Eamonn put it away. Her floral dress swayed as she stepped towards me.

'Hi,' she said, putting out her small hand.

'Hi,' I replied, shaking it.

We stared at each other for a fraction longer than seemed necessary. Conall was already kneeling in front of Eamonn. 'How're you doing, kid?'

'Got to level eight on *Clash of Clans*.'

Colm went and sat next to him. 'Get it out then. Let's see what you got.'

Eamonn glanced at his mum. She nodded as he picked up the iPad again.

'First say hello to the lady,' she said to him.

I smiled at him as he got up and shook my hand.

Mary cleared her throat. 'Isn't that a lovely jumper you're wearing,' she said, kissing him on his head.

What am I doing here? I caught Claire looking at me as I decided to join in the jumper-complimenting session.

But then Eamonn looked up at Conall, and with a familiar look of focus said, 'Dad –'

The word was a jolt. But even more so was Conall's response to it; slipping into a role after a nine-year absence. Claire folded her arms and watched them as Eamonn asked when Conall was going to teach him to box with his new boxing gloves. When did Conall get him boxing gloves? Eamonn glanced at Claire.

'Mam told me not to tell you, but she's already shown me. I could throw a right jab and knock Grandpa out right now.'

Mary and Colm laughed as Conall looked at Claire. 'I bet she did. Your ma always had a good right hook.'

'Tattle-tale,' she said, ruffling Eamonn's hair. Her hand rested on the back of his neck. 'It's always paid for me to know how to fight,' she added.

And there it was: a look between her and Conall that only two people with a shared history can have. It wasn't as if the ground had been taken from beneath my feet, but something was slipping away. If I knew what exactly, I'd have tried to hold on to it.

I waited with Mary, Colm and Eamonn as the doctor asked to speak to Conall and Claire. I watched Eamonn and thought of Dad – what if the worst happened? No wonder Conall was getting up to pray in the middle of the night. This isn't about comfort; it's about clutching on to a semblance of hope.

'Yes!' Eamonn exclaimed as he got to the next level. I noticed his dimpled cheek as he looked at the screen.

'I could do with some tea,' said Mary, looking at Colm.

'Right then. Tea allowed in your religion?' he asked me.

I semi-laughed, but to be honest, I don't know if he was serious or not. 'Thanks,' I replied.

'Young man, you come with me and tell me about your ma's right hook.'

Mary watched the two walk down the corridor; Eamonn reached his arm up, his hand just about resting on Colm's shoulder.

'Grandchildren bring out the best in you,' she said. 'You stumble through as a parent and make all sorts of mistakes – ones you don't realise until you pay for them later. But with a grandchild, there aren't any mistakes. It's just joy.'

Perhaps that was the reason Conall managed to be in the same room as his dad – all this love his dad has for his son.

'It was good of her to let you both see him still. Considering,' I said.

'Claire's not a spiteful girl.'

Which didn't feel entirely truthful given she hadn't let Conall see Eamonn when he'd finally wanted to correct his mistakes. It might've taken a while to forgive him but five years seemed rather harsh.

'Her dad passed away when she was young and her mother doesn't exactly do well for herself,' added Mary. 'And let's just say she wasn't the maternal type with Claire. Anyway, a single mother bringing up a child isn't cheap. We do what we can.' She rested her hand over her bag. 'It's not like Conall to push people and forgiveness has to be earned. My boy's always shown less than he feels. But he's realising that sometimes you have to be what other people need you to be, not what you are.'

I looked towards the door that Conall and Claire had walked through, wondering what he needs me to be, and what I need him to be – and who gets to win in the game of necessity. As Eamonn and Colm approached, I thought about Maria, Tahir and Adam – what if she found herself without Tahir and, God forbid, potentially without Adam?

'Claire seems tough,' I said to Mary.

'She's a woman, dear,' Mary replied. 'She's had to be.'

And it wasn't over for her yet. I knew it the second we saw the two of them come out of the room, her face drained of colour and her eyes red-rimmed; Conall's face taut and a heart – I knew, without him having to say – full of regret. Whatever was slipping away from me now, I couldn't grab on to it, even if I knew how.

9.15 p.m. Colm took a third beer from the fridge, slamming the door shut. Conall glanced at the bottle in his hand and looked away.

'I don't need your judgement,' said Colm, opening the bottle.

The most noise made at dinner was the clattering of cutlery, which was ironic given no one was really eating. The cancer'd reached stage two. They'd have to begin an aggressive course of chemotherapy to contain it. Eamonn had taken the news with a shrug and an 'OK.'

'Will I die?' he had asked so matter-of-factly it almost made *me* cry. Conall was on one side, Claire on the other. She looked at Conall as he put his arm round Eamonn.

'Everything turns out just as it's meant to,' he replied, pulling him closer. Claire's hand went to her face.

'Better tell Ma that,' Eamonn replied. 'She says nothing turns out the way it's meant to.'

Now Conall stood up from the table, just as Colm sat down. He went to leave the room. 'Tell him to give that shit a rest, Mum.'

'My son thinks it's OK to have abandoned his family, but not to have a drink,' he said, looking at me. 'What does your religion say about that, eh?'

'Leave her out of this.' Conall stopped at the door. 'Come on, Sofe.'

'You go, let her stay. We're having a chat.'

'Colm, that's enough,' said Mary.

'What did a girl like you see in him?' Colm asked. 'I asked Claire the same and she laughed and said *the folly of youth.*' He shook his head. 'To be honest, all he's ever needed is to loosen up.'

Oh God. What was I doing here? I glanced at Conall.

'This is the shit you put up with?' said Conall, looking at his mum.

Mary stood up, clearing the plates from the table. 'Don't speak about your father like that.'

I got up and began to help her.

'You can leave that,' she said to me. 'Both of you get some rest.'

As we were walking out, Mary added: 'We'll be going to Sunday Mass tomorrow.'

Conall turned round. 'No, Ma. Sorry. We don't do Mass. We'll meet you at Claire's.'

Mary paused.

'Christ,' said Colm.

'You'll have it your way then,' she said, and we walked out of the room.

We both sat on the edge of the bed. Conall rubbed his hand over his face. 'What have I done?' he said, looking at me.

I put my arm round him, bringing him into a hug, taking in his familiar scent. 'Your dad's just upset.'

'I mean all of it,' he replied.

Of all the many regrets that he has, when he looks at me, am I on the list? There was a knock on the door and when I opened it Colm was standing there with another towel. He handed it to me. How many towels did he think I needed? He glanced into the bedroom, but Conall's back was turned.

'Thank you,' I said.

He waited for a few moments before he said to me: 'You know, he made some mistakes but . . . it's not like I think I'm any better than him.' He paused again. 'You'd do well to know that,' he called out, watching Conall.

He didn't turn round.

'Anyway, I'm . . . Forgive me. It's not the easiest time,' he said.

I don't know if he was talking to me or Conall. I told him not to worry, wishing Conall would turn round. Colm waited, and just as he was about to leave Conall looked over his shoulder without meeting his dad's gaze.

'Goodnight, Dad.'

I closed the door and said to Conall: 'I think we should go with your parents tomorrow morning.'

'To Mass?'

I nodded.

'No. I've read up on it online and it's not right to take part.'

'I'm not saying we should start a Holy Trinity club. Sometimes you do things for the people you care about – not because it's right, but because you love them,' I added. 'Did you see your mum's face? And what websites have you been looking at?' I asked, stepping away and pushing back the duvet. 'There's some whacko stuff on some of those sites.'

He stood up too, lifting his side of the duvet.

'We'll just not sing parts of the hymns that mention Jesus being the son of God.'

He laughed, then seemed to remember he shouldn't be laughing. 'Fine,' he said. 'But if I go to hell because of it then you're coming with me.'

Oh, Conall. We're already bloody there.

Sunday 12 May

11.30 p.m. I thought it'd be a quaint cathedral with stone floors and intricate carvings set against stained-glass windows, but it was just a stone building with whitewashed panels, a small crucifix placed on top.

People looked at me and smiled – unsure, pleasant; proper. A man came and smacked Conall's dad on the shoulder with his thin, long hands. 'Mahoney's cousin's funeral tomorrow.'

'We'll be there, thank you, Ted,' said Conall's mum.

'Hello,' he said, looking at me.

'Hi,' I replied.

Everyone paused. He smiled. I smiled back.

'This is . . . Sofia,' said Mary, as if she had to physically dig into her throat and pluck my name that had lodged itself between her windpipe and throat.

The priest walked in and the congregation stood up, picking up the missalette laid out in front. I looked around and did the same. Conall stood there with his hands clasped in front of him. His mum glanced at his hymnless hands as I nudged him.

'You made me come here, but you can't make me sing,' he said.

'Why do you have a problem with the "City of God"?' I asked. 'There's no mention of Jesus being the son of God or anything,' I said, skimming through it.

Conall took a deep breath and closed his eyes as I looked round at the sea of white faces. I must've been an eyesore.

'Do you think I should've worn a less colourful hijab?'

'No, Sofe.' Conall sighed.

'If old Sarah in front of us can wear a hat that big you can wear a hijab that orange,' said Colm.

'He's trying to make an effort with you,' I whispered to Conall as the singing began.

When we finished the priest began his reading: '*O give thanks to the Lord, for his love endures forever . . .*'

'Now, is it just the son of God stuff you have a problem with?' Colm whispered to me.

I don't mind theological differences, but isn't it rude when you have them in a church? I looked over at Conall whose eyes were still closed. Maybe he was meditating.

'Sons and fathers . . .' added Colm. 'Is that why he's Muslim now?'

'Because of Jesus?' I asked.

I noticed Conall take a deep breath as the priest's eye flickered in our direction.

'If he took Confession he'd just be done with it, wouldn't he?' said Colm, his voice raised as people looked our way.

'. . . *Their soul melted away in their distress*,' spoke the priest.

'Ssh, Colm . . .' whispered Mary. 'You'll get us thrown out.'

'What psalm did he say this was?' I asked, flicking through the pamphlet, trying to change the subject.

'If you ask me, it's all guilt,' said Colm.

No shit. More faces turned towards us as I tried to give my most winning smile. I think I might've scared people.

'No new religion's going to help that.'

'Christ, Dad. Would you give it up?' said Conall – his voice outrising his father's as more heads turned our way. 'It's not because of Jesus.'

'So, it's Mohammed? Now, I'm a bit hazy on that. Tell me more about him.'

'Colm, honestly.'

'I'm trying to understand my son, Mary.'

'By asking about Mohammed?' she replied between pursed lips.

'Well, he seems to like him.'

Oh God. And I mean, *literally*, God.

The priest stopped his reading. 'Perhaps you'd like to take this conversation outside?'

Mary looked embarrassed and enraged in equal measure. I looked around, wondering what to do.

'Pardon us,' said Mary, giving a tight smile, hands joined firmly together.

The priest cleared his throat. '*They rejoiced because of the calm and he led them to the haven they desired. Let them thank the Lord for his love, the wonders he does for his people.*'

6.45 p.m. Colm had gone out with his friend and said he'd be over later. As the rest of us entered Claire's house there was a weird stillness to it; a quiet that needed to be broken for comfort before sitting in it. But nothing I said could take away from the reality that Claire was Conall's first, while he was my first, and the imbalance of it threw me off.

Mary had insisted on making lunch since Claire had enough to deal with. She handed the vegetable lasagne to her. 'Where is he?'

'Upstairs. His friend's come over,' said Claire, looking at Conall.

'You OK?' he asked her.

It was normal for him to show concern, but even as he did something snagged in me: I was caught in the tendrils of my own sprawling jealousy. Claire nodded, folding her arms, leading us into the white and bright living room. I suddenly wondered: doesn't she *mind* that I'm here? Would I mind if I were her? Except I don't know, in her place, what I'd do with any of this. It was the worst kind of jealousy because it wasn't just about their shared past, or even their shared present; it was her, with all her stoicism and good nature – the jealousy born of admiration. If it was any other circumstance, I would probably have wanted to be her friend.

'I'll go up and say hello,' said Conall, as Mary said she'd use the bathroom.

Claire nodded for me to follow her into the kitchen as she carried the lasagne through.

'Do you want me to help?' I offered.

'No, thanks.' She put the lasagne in the oven before she turned round and looked at me. I noticed she wasn't wearing any make-up. 'He's making up for lost time,' she said as we heard Conall's laughter from Eamonn's room.

I nodded.

'Good of you to come. Considering,' she added.

Saying 'no problem' sounded a bit feeble, but it was all I could muster.

'He almost seems like the man who I first met,' she said. 'Before he left.'

She gave a faint smile. I wanted to say he was always this man to me, just covered with those inevitable layers of confusion and self-loathing, that, let's face it, we've all had. I looked round the kitchen and noticed Eamonn's boxing gloves flung over one of the chairs.

'Conall taught me,' she said.

Another jolt.

'We met at university and I'd get trouble from guys when I'd come home late so he taught me how to defend myself.'

She smiled at the memory.

'He taught me too,' I said. 'Except it was to punch the next person that called me a terrorist.'

She laughed and it caught me off-guard. 'Typical Conall.'

I wanted to ask her; when did he begin to change? Why? How? But it wasn't the same as hearing it from him – he was so trapped inside his own head sometimes that he probably didn't even realise the impact of what he said or did.

'I'm sorry,' she said. 'I didn't congratulate you on your wedding.'

It seemed such a ridiculous thing to say, I was embarrassed just having to hear it.

'I have to say I was surprised how quickly it happened,' she added.

We heard more laughter come from upstairs as she began putting placemats on the table.

'When you know, you know,' I replied.

Her hair fell over her face so I couldn't read her expression. 'I thought I knew too.'

I folded my arms as she turned towards me.

'Sorry, I'm not being presumptive –'

'It was a leap of faith,' I interrupted.

She paused. 'And where has it got you?' Her voice was so low and soft I wasn't sure whether to be offended or not. 'Where has it got any of us?' she added.

She turned round as I saw her take a deep breath. Should I go and hug her? She didn't look like the type of person who was used to them. Just then Mary walked in. Claire went to get plates out of the cupboards as Mary looked into the garden.

'Those flowers have really grown,' she said. 'You always were good in the garden,' she added.

Mary turned round as Claire smiled at her and handed me the plates.

'Well,' she said, looking at me – sad, almost friendly. 'People never really change.'

12.20 a.m. When Conall fell asleep I went into the garden to have a fag. (I probably shouldn't have, but frankly it was a miracle I wasn't smoking a packet a day.) Colm sitting on the porch took me by surprise.

'Oh, sorry,' I said, hiding the cigarette and lighter behind my back.

He glanced at me before he looked back out into the garden.

'I'll leave you to it,' I said.

'Sit,' he said, so firmly that I practically leaped into the chair next to him. 'Smoke, I won't tell.'

I sheepishly lit my cigarette. I squinted and leaned back just so I could see the back of Colm's head – it could've been Dad sitting in that chair.

'God gives you grandkids to make up for the mistakes you made with your own children,' he said after a while. 'But then He can take them away. Just like that.

'My son Sean now, he left this place too – and he can be an eejit – but at least I can sit and have a conversation with the man. But his brother . . .' He paused. 'Chalk and cheese.'

The ash on my cigarette fell and I put it out, holding the butt in my hand.

'Well . . . we can't change the past, can we?' he said, still looking out into the garden.

'No,' I replied. 'But we can learn from it.'

He gave a wry laugh. 'Spoken like a woman with youth on her side.'

'He's grateful, you know. For the way you are with Eamonn.'

'I don't do it for him,' he said.

'No. He knows. But he's grateful anyway.'

'I've never given him an easy ride, but you have to be tough in life, don't you? How else do you survive? When he left – Christ, I could've killed him. A man doesn't just leave.' He paused. 'But what if I had tried harder when he came back to make amends with Claire and see Eamonn? When she said that she didn't trust he wouldn't abandon him again, Conall told Mary that what he wanted didn't matter any more. He had to do what Claire thought best.'

I could imagine it. Colm looked at me. 'He won't run away again, will he?'

What an absurd notion. 'Of course not,' I said as emphatically as possible.

He nodded thoughtfully. 'Good. Because, Sofia, I tell you – this time I might take some of the blame for it.'

I wanted to go into the room and tell Conall: see; regret lives inside everyone.

Monday 13 May

10.50 a.m. I'm back home, having left my husband behind with his ex-wife. I sat on the sofa as soon as I came in, the curtains still drawn. All I'd wanted was for him to come home with me, but even as the thought came into my head I knew how selfish it was. The phone rang.

'Hi, Mum,' I said.

'You're back?'

'Yes, Mum.'

'Why are your curtains still drawn?'

Because I want to shut out the world forever more. She began telling me about her lingerie as I lay down on the sofa and thought of the various looks that passed between Conall and Claire; Conall's face every time he looked at Eamonn; the ease with which he'd slipped into his past life as a reformed person. Of all his regrets, what was the biggest? Having left his family behind, or now being tied to me so he can't be the father he needs to be?

'Mum, I have to go. I'll call you in a bit.'

I hung up, instantly dialling Conall's number. I had to know the answer.

Claire picked up. 'We're on our way to the hospital,' she said. 'He's driving.'

'Can you ask him to call me back?'

She paused. 'Sure.'

11.20 a.m. He hasn't called. Can't move from sofa. If I don't open the curtains Mum will probably come over and do it for me.

11.45 a.m.

From: Sakib Awaan
To: Sofia Khan
Subject: The Happiness by Shahida Al-Fadhl

Hi Sofia,
Good weekend? I've attached a new MS for consideration.
Let me know what you think.
Sakib
P.S. How's the marriage masterpiece coming along?

11.48 a.m.

From: Sofia Khan

To: Sakib Awaan

Subject: Re: The Happiness by Shahida Al-Fadhl

Thanks for this. It's coming along *great*.

3.05 p.m. 'Hey,' Conall said.

They were still at the hospital. Some kind of delay with the chemo session.

'How long will it take?'

'Another hour. It's an aggressive session.'

My need to know about his regrets dissipated – a shameful badge of self-involvement in the face of radiation.

'Listen, I might not come home until the weekend,' he told me. 'I said I'd look after Eamonn for a few days. Give Claire a break.'

Be the person someone needs you to be.

'OK. She'll appreciate it.'

'If she'll let me. She's struggling but she won't admit it.'

It doesn't matter how complete you are before you're married; the person you're with pokes holes into you – one by one – and they replace these scooped-up holes with pieces of themselves. What happens if they leave? Do you walk around as a perforated human form?

'Sofe?'

'Hmm?'

'You OK?'

'Yeah. Sorry. Just got an email from Sakib. He's sent another manuscript.'

He paused.

'I'll leave you to it,' I said.

I lay back on the sofa and wondered, comparatively, how perforated Conall might be. Most importantly, who it was that filled in the scooped-up pieces.

Friday 17 May

8.50 a.m.

> **From Foz:** You're not on my recent call list. You know how nervous that makes me.

As an antidote to life's worries I've buried my head in the professional sand. My new job's proving a decent distraction from my empty bed and too-full brain.

Saturday 18 May

9.35 p.m. Conall went to see Sean before he came back home.

'Is he all right?' I asked.

'Grand. Going to Ireland tomorrow to see Eamonn. Said he needs a normal father-figure around him. The bastard.'

I smiled. He looked at me.

'You know what we haven't done in a long time?' he said.

I raised my eyebrows. He ran up the stairs and came back down five minutes later with a packet of cigarettes.

'No . . .' I said. 'We don't smoke any more. Heart attacks. Lung cancer. Clogged arteries . . .'

My gaze rested on the packet as Conall looked down at me. 'Sofe, you've always been a terrible liar.'

We both sat on the garden step as I glanced over the fence. 'Have to be careful of The Eyes next door,' I said.

Conall lit a cigarette and gave it to me. 'It's completely normal as an adult that you still can't tell your mum you smoke.'

I took a long drag of the cigarette. 'Some things are best left unsaid. It just feels so good, you know.'

'Filthy habits always do.'

I nudged him. 'Not all filthy habits.'

He began talking about taking some wedding photography jobs in Ireland since the freelancing wasn't paying the bills.

'Ireland?'

'Just when I'm there. Makes sense, doesn't it?'

Note for book: Just because something makes sense, doesn't mean you'll like it.

We heard a cat cry in the distance as Conall looked round the garden. 'It's a decent place this, isn't it?' he said.

I peered over the fence again, putting my cigarette out of view just in case Mum was spying on us. 'Locale is a little too close to home sometimes,' I said.

He took a puff of the cigarette and looked towards Mum's house. 'It was either this or she'd have packed her bags to come and live with us.'

'Now someone's going to live with *her*,' I said.

He nodded. 'Good for her. And us,' he said.

We both gazed up at the sky, barely a star in sight. Some calypso music started playing, which at least shut the cat up.

'Why didn't you tell me?' I said, unable to look at him. 'All those times you had the chance. Before we got married. After we got married.'

He paused. 'You never made mistakes.'

I turned to him, first of all thinking *of course I've made mistakes!* And then I thought, *so, it's* my *fault?*

'I don't mean it like that.' He rested his arm on his knee, the ash on the cigarette burning. 'I mean . . .' He looked away. 'Sofe, in a life full of disappointment – and I don't mean this so you feel sorry for me, but my dad wasn't the easiest man and with all of the shit from my past . . .' He rubbed his brow with the palm of his hand. 'The anger about my ma putting up with him and then my own drinking, I just . . .' He looked at his cigarette. 'Telling you was worse than having to tell anyone . . .'

He looked at me, hard. 'Do you get it?'

To be honest, I still didn't.

He took a puff of his cigarette, looking away. I looked at his side profile, his Adam's apple jutting out beneath the bristles of hair.

'The way you saw me,' he said, 'I thought maybe I could actually be that man – even though I knew I wasn't. You made me think I could be.'

I put my hand to his face and stroked his beard. 'We sat exactly here last year, having a cigarette,' I said.

He looked at me. 'You leading me astray with nicotine.'

'What was it that made you think, *of all the women, this is the one I want to be with*?'

He stared at me, a plume of smoke swirling out from the side of his mouth. 'Hmm.' He thought for a moment. 'You have a nice arse.'

'Shut up. It's *huge*.'

'One of the things I'm grateful for. It's a wonder I ever noticed,' he added, 'what with all the material you cover up with, but like you say . . . God has His plans.'

I rolled my eyes and turned away, but I could still feel his gaze on me.

'It was here. That's when I knew,' he said.

I flicked some ash on the ground.

'When I was in Afghanistan, sitting out here with you was the moment that played over and over in my head and made me get on that plane to come back.'

'Bloody hell. Who'd have thought so much could rest on a moment.'

He looked serious. 'I'd do it again.' He pulled me towards him, as if he wanted to say something but couldn't quite find the words.

'Well, long-haul flights are an arse, so let's try to avoid that,' I said.

When he wrapped his arms round me and looked back up at the night sky, I thought: isn't it incredible how the biggest decisions of your life can hinge on just a moment?

Tuesday 28 May

10.10 a.m. Coming back to Ireland together wasn't the plan, but Conall said a friend of his is travelling and he's able to stay in their home.

'We've not really had proper time – just us, have we? His conservatory overlooks the sea. You can go for walks and get lots of fresh air.'

'I hear that's good for you,' I replied.

'Hide the cigarette butts from me,' he added. 'The usual.'

So here we are. And, you know, at least it's not Karachi. Even though I bet Conall wishes it was.

2.50 p.m. Conall brought Eamonn back for lunch. I noticed how the circles under his eyes were that much darker against his pale skin. How long before he begins to lose his hair? Eamonn stared at the untouched food on his plate.

'Want to watch a film on Netflix?' I asked.

'Mum never lets me watch Netflix,' he said.

I looked at Conall.

'Oh, she won't mind,' he said.

So we sat and chose a film, drew the curtains in the living room and sat on the sofa with him. It was a bit odd – this kid who I'd known for about five minutes was now like a ready-made family. But am I allowed to just put my arm round him or give him a hug? What would he think? What would his mum think? And if I don't, then will Conall think I don't like his son? Half an hour in and Eamonn had fallen asleep on Conall's shoulder. He went to put him to bed when the doorbell rang.

'Sorry, I'm early,' said Claire, walking in and looking for Eamonn. I told her we'd been watching a film and he fell asleep.

'Which film?'

'One of the Marvel ones,' I replied. 'Would you like some tea?'

She paused. 'That stuff is full of violence.'

I turned round from getting two mugs out. 'Oh. Sorry. Conall –'

'Conall tends not to think about things.' She dropped her handbag on the table. 'I'm sorry. You're not to know.'

'Oh, it's fine.' I filled the kettle with water.

She took a seat and put her head in her hand, looking at the table. 'It's not something to be grateful for,' she said.

'Sorry?' I asked.

'After years of Conall's absence.' She looked up at me. 'But I am grateful that he's here now. Every time I think it'll get better, it doesn't and he's there and . . .'

I watched her as she tried to get the words out. She shook her head. 'I just wish as much as he does that he could stay.'

The kettle began to whistle as I looked at her, trying to grasp the full meaning of what she'd said. A look of desperation came over her, one that felt so incongruent with the Claire I'd seen. 'He won't say it to you. He loves you.' She paused here. 'But I just know he wants to stay. Wouldn't you? To make up for all those mistakes? You know him. You know he does.'

If I didn't know any better, I'd think she was begging me. The steam filled the air, shrouding Claire in a mist as Conall opened the door and walked in.

'Hey,' he said to her. 'You're early.'

He came and took another mug out as I poured the scalding water in it. She composed herself, shaking her desperation off. He gave her an odd look as she feigned a smile.

'All OK?' he asked, looking at me.

I nodded in the most persuasive way a person who's been bulldozed with words can.

He wants to stay.

'I know he's not going to be well,' she said to Conall, 'but I wanted to invite some of his friends for his birthday. Make a deal of it, like.

'This place is bigger so maybe we could have it here?' she continued. 'We won't know how he's feeling that day and so at least he can rest if he's home.'

''Course,' replied Conall. 'You don't mind, do you?' he asked, looking at me.

I shook my head.

'Thank you,' Claire said to me. And if ever there was a look of genuine gratitude, there it was.

I should've asked her to stay for dinner, but I couldn't quite bring myself to do it. I apologised to God for lack of open spirit, but I suspect it was one of those times that God felt I was apologising to the wrong person.

10.55 p.m. 'Do you want to stay here?'

I blurted it out. Just like that. In bed. Because if I had any more fucking thoughts in my head it'd explode and that's the last thing anyone needed. Plus, maybe this is the evolution of modern marriage: what happens between people who understand each other's wants and needs, etc.

'What?' He put his book down and looked at me.

'You've one foot in London and one here – isn't it a little much?'

He considered me for a while.

'Aren't you tired?' I asked.

He closed his book. 'Exhausted.'

'So stay here.'

'Without you?'

I nodded.

'Is that what you want?' he asked.

'Isn't it what you want?'

His silence told me the answer to that one.

'I'm not here to make someone be somewhere they don't want to be,' I said.

'Right.' He looked down at his book.

Why wasn't he saying more? Why wasn't he saying: *No, of course I don't want to stay here. I want to stay wherever you are.* Which, given his disposition and the fact that life isn't a Hollywood film is a little unrealistic. But sometimes you want the unrealistic.

'And you wouldn't stay with me?' he asked.

There are moments of truth that come along in life, except you only see them in hindsight. If I knew that he was truly sorry for all that he'd done, then I should've nodded and said: *I'll stay with you.* If I looked at him, I'd have wanted to reach out and touch the lines around his eyes, the contours of his face, and disappear into his arms. So I avoided his gaze, only glancing at him, before staring at the bedsheet. Even then, my head almost moved involuntarily to say I would stay, despite the fact that the words seemed to be locked in my mouth.

'I . . .'

'What, Sofe?'

Between Karachi and Kilkee, I had to wonder why I'm constantly moving from country to country for him.

Note for book: You'll probably think you're a much better person than you actually are; there will be times when the disappointment in others is nothing compared to the disappointment in what you turn out to be.

'If I don't want you to be in a place where you're unhappy, why would you want me to be?'

'You're my *wife*,' he whispered.

I nodded.

'Staying here'd just be temporary,' he added. 'Until Eamonn's better.'

'What about the documentary that was once so important?' I asked.

'Life has a way of showing you perspective,' he said.

'But where would we go afterwards?' I asked. 'London? Karachi?'

In the haze of flying back and forth, I'd almost forgotten the long-term picture: where exactly was home?

He shook his head, looking deflated. 'Sofe, I changed religion for you.'

The words came out from his mouth, but they seemed to belong to another person. I stared at him in disbelief, pulling off the bed covers and getting out of bed.

'Fuck you,' I said. 'You changed it for yourself because you couldn't live with having walked out on a wife and baby.'

He clenched his jaw. Why did he get to be the martyr? I walked out of the room, slamming the door behind me, managing to bang my foot on the kitchen chair on the way. Grabbing a glass, I filled it with water. *I changed religion for you.* The audacity.

'Listen.'

I started, spilling some water on the floor.

'Sorry,' said Conall. He got a cloth and cleaned it up. 'I didn't mean that. It just came out. I just meant that there are compromises to be made.'

This was not helping the anger that was bubbling somewhere in the pit of my being. I had to laugh at the sheer mettle of this man.

'You want to talk *compromise*? Are you actually fucking kidding me?'

'Yes, compromise. Putting up with shit you might not like.'

'Oh, don't go and bring my book into this. As if the two can compare,' I said.

'*I'm* not the one that brought it up.'

'But you were thinking it.'

'Sofe,' he said, grabbing my glass of water and practically throwing it in the sink as he stepped towards me. 'I *need* you.'

If I were a better woman, maybe I'd have put my hand on his face and said, *OK*.

I folded my arms. 'Well, I've been needing you for a while now and I've somehow managed to survive. I'm sure you can do the same.'

For a second, as he bore down on me, it looked like he might hit something. His body was too close to mine, but I wasn't going to budge – neither in thought nor form.

'Stay here,' I continued. 'And be a Muslim, atheist, Buddhist – whatever the hell you want.'

I thought he might step back, but he just came in closer. I glanced at his hands, clenched into fists.

'I *didn't* mean that,' he said.

The problem with feelings is when they start coming out they tumble forward – a tumult of words, gushing out of your mouth. His fists tightened, his knuckles white, his face a kind of rage.

'It's my fault,' he repeated. 'I should never have –'

'I know; lied –'

'Married you.'

We spoke at the same time. But I heard him: a lightning of words, searing through my own bitterness.

'I was selfish, Sofe. I had no right to bring you into all of this,' he said. 'I'm sorry.'

Perhaps I knew it all along: *he should never have married me.* Panic rose to my chest, swelling in my throat, pushing tears and my very own nightmares to the surface.

'Of course you are.'

In a second, his fist rose and hit the cupboard behind me. I started, unable to look away from him.

'Christ, Sofe. I'm *sorry*.'

'I know.' I glanced at his hand, his knuckle red from where he hit the cupboard. His eyes were brimming with tears as a pain in my head brought my own to the surface. 'So am I.'

Friday 31 May

11.55 p.m. It was dark when I arrived home and walked up the stairs, getting straight into bed. An hour or two must've passed when I heard footsteps in the passage. I opened my eyes as the handle on the door turned and I thought I was going to be killed in body as well as in spirit.

'Who is it?'

'Sofe?'

I turned round and switched my lamp on. It was Foz.

'Fuck. You gave me a heart attack.'

'Sorry,' she said. 'I got a message from Conall. He told me where he kept the spare key.'

I stared at her. It felt too much like a dream.

'Oh, Sofe. What happened?'

I looked at her face, concern etched in the knit of her brow. That's when the tears came.

'I don't know,' I said, a loud sob escaping me. 'I just don't know.'

She took me into her arms and all I remember is crying there for what seemed like forever. The tears just kept coming; every time I remembered his face; every time I thought of what I'd had; every time I thought of how easily I'd lost it.

I tried to catch my breath as she tucked me into bed. The vision of him leaving me at the airport flitted around my head, bringing a new wave of sorrow as I fell into a dreamless sleep.

JUNE

The Art of Losing isn't Hard to Master

Muslim Marriage Book

What are your partner's vices? Whatever they are, you'd better believe you can't change them. And don't think of the person you're marrying today; think of who they used to be – do your research, people, no one likes a blast from the unknown past. In fact, take each of their evils and multiply them by ten, because that's the ratio of vice (the ones you know of, anyway) you'll have to live with once you're married or living together. Because the one piece of advice people don't seem to give before you get married is: be prepared.

For the best of times, and the worst of times.

Saturday 1 June

11.20 a.m. They say that endings are hard, but no one ever says how easily they can come about. When I opened my eyes I forgot why they felt raw, why my head hurt, or why it felt like some kind of vital organ had been scooped out from inside me. Then I saw the empty side of Conall's bed and remembered. I tried to hold the tears back; but you can't pull back from falling. I clutched on to the bed covers because I'd forgotten how physical the pain could be. I thought of when Dad died – how one loss is always connected to another by virtue of it being loss. How sad it was to have accumulated so many in the space of one year.

'Sofe?'

Light came through the door as it opened.

'Are you OK?'

I couldn't open my mouth.

How was anything going to be OK ever again?

9.10 p.m. 'Sofe? Sofe, wake up.'

I turned round and squinted at Foz, who was standing over me. 'Darling, I'm sorry but your mum's banging at the door and I think she's seen me because I had the light on.'

It took a while to register what she said. 'Just . . . just tell her I'm not well.'

Moments later Mum came barging in and I felt a cold hand on my forehead. 'Fozia, get me a cold cloth. Why didn't you tell me you were ill?' demanded Mum. 'Where is Conall?'

My tears ducts were empty or I'd have cried again. 'I'll be fine, Mum. I just need some rest. He's still in Ireland.'

'Le, why doesn't he just live there? I was calling and calling you, wondering where you have died.'

On the inside, Mum. On the inside.

'Then I called Maria and she was calling you too, but you didn't pick up and Conall didn't pick up. We almost rang the police.'

The screen of Mum's phone lit her face up – like the ghost of my married present.

'Haan,' said Mum, speaking into her mobile as Foz came in with a cold towel. Mum slapped it on my forehead.

'She is here. She thinks she's so ill she couldn't pick up the phone.' Mum then put the phone against my ear as I heard Maars.

'Oh my God. Where the hell have you been? The woman was calling me *all* day. I have a baby to look after, you know? Anyway, what's wrong with you? Are you OK?'

'Yeah, just need some rest. Bad migraine.'

'Better get Mum out of the house then, because she's not going to help.'

Foz was looking down at me in concern and it turns out the tear ducts weren't so empty. Turning away from Mum and Foz, I had to wonder – how am I going to tell my family that my marriage is over?

Sunday 2 June

8.20 p.m. 'Your mum brought some food round.'

I had to shield my eyes from the sunlight streaming through the living room window. Foz stared at me.

'I know,' I said. 'I look like shit.' I sat on the sofa. 'You don't have to stay. You've got things to do.'

She got up and went into the kitchen, bringing back a bowl of chicken soup. I didn't even realise I had tears in my eyes until one fell into the soup. I put the bowl on the coffee table. This house was meant to be our home but it's never been more than transient. I put my hand over my eyes.

'How does this happen?' I said.

I felt her arm round my shoulder.

'I know.'

'I don't understand.'

You're meant to get married, then you're meant to just *be* together. No one ever mentioned that your wants and desires might not meld with your partner's. No one said that you might not be enough for each other – that each respective feeling could collide into a kaleidoscope of disaster; that someone could slice something out from inside you, and whatever's lost you know you'll never be able to find it again.

Note for book: The only thing that is ever certain, is uncertainty.

Friday 7 June

9 a.m.

> **From Hannah:** Did you know that having a job and having the hundred spare hours you need to fill out adoption papers are incompatible? Where are you, by the way? Xx

I had to forward the message to Foz, who was at work. She'd tell Hannah. Hannah would tell Suj and maybe she'll do me a favour and tell my mum and sister.

Every morning my hand instinctively flops to Conall's side. That moment that I open my eyes and it's dark, and there's no sound, my heart feels so heavy I wonder whether I can even lift myself out of bed. But I do. Mainly because using the bedroom as a toilet would be the peak of depression. Bodily functions are such a hindrance to fully embracing misery.

1.35 p.m. Suj came over. The speed with which she heard and then turned up at my doorstep had me sobbing in her arms.

'I can't fucking believe it,' she said.

We didn't talk much. Told her I was tired and went to bed again. When I woke up she was sitting on the floor in the bedroom, the light of her phone illuminating her face.

'Let's go away somewhere,' she said. 'Just us.'

I curled up, facing her. 'I don't want to go anywhere any more. I want to stay.'

She nodded. 'OK then. We'll stay.'

Why couldn't she just be here because we were having lunch, or a catch-up date? Why was the fog of reality clouding each moment that should be day-to-day life?

'We've been here before, Toffee,' she said.

'Where's that?'

'Bullshit hell.'

I almost smiled, but it hurt my head. 'What happened last time?' I asked.

'We got out of it, that's what.'

Saturday 8 June

7.10 p.m. I'm going to have to begin all over again. It's not even like two steps forward and three steps back; it's back to the drawing board of life. Things hadn't been ideal but dissatisfaction wasn't disaster.

What have I done?

'Well,' I said, putting my feet up on the cluttered coffee table, 'at least splitting up with my husband means we've managed to get together.'

Suj paced the room as Foz picked up the dirty plates and took a bite of my uneaten omelette. 'You made this, didn't you?' she said, spitting it out.

I nodded. 'Maybe I'll become a gourmet chef.'

'Keep the ambition alive, but let's not lose sight of reality, darling.'

I almost laughed, but it managed to quell itself before it reached my mouth. In all the years I've known Foz I've never quite appreciated the calmness of her; the things she says when she doesn't say anything. The aura of no-nonsense-ness.

Hannah crossed her legs at the ankle and leaned forward as if she was about to conduct a therapy session. 'Have you really thought this through?'

I didn't want to do this. I wanted him back, right beside me, complaining about something I'd done or said and then laughing at it in the same breath.

'I don't belong there,' I said. 'I can't slot into that life he has – and I don't want to be the reason he can't do what he needs to.'

'Which is?'

I looked at Han. 'Be a father to his son.'

The photos of the family that Sean had put up were still on the mantelpiece. There was only one of Conall and me in the passage. It's suitably cheesy: me looking at him and laughing, him with his hands out, looking at the ground also laughing. Laughter, laughter, laughter. Is this why Conall captures moments? Because he knows you just never get them again?

'So. You actually told him to move?' asked Han.

Suj stopped pacing and looked at me.

'Just telling him what he already wanted,' I replied.

'Oh, he's such a knob,' said Suj, looking at her phone.

'To be fair, *he* didn't suggest it.'

'No, sorry, Toffee; I meant Charles.'

She typed something on her phone as I fumbled around my dressing gown and got out a packet of cigarettes and lighter.

'You started smoking again?' exclaimed Suj. 'Toffee! After all that shit with your dad. What are you doing to yourself?'

'I'm not sure being alive right now is my best option.'

Foz took the packet from me and lit one up too. After all of this, people will begin to find out. A series of humiliations every time a new person's discovered what's happened. Sofia ran away with a white man who'd lied about having a son and now they're splitting up. It's a culmination of everyone's hedged bets, expectations and raised eyebrows that have been heaped upon my stupid optimism – and they will all see it. I thought of Auntie Reena: *I don't want people's pity.*

'Where are you planning to go?' said Han. 'I mean, you can't stay here, can you?'

'I don't know,' I replied, observing the plume of smoke swirl out of my mouth.

Deal with the physical matter. (Forget the emotions of heartbreak.) Where do you live? (Without the person you were meant to spend forever with.) What do you take with you? (Don't think of everything you have to leave behind.) How will you survive, financially? (Worry about spiritual survival after.)

I watched Suj look at her phone again. 'Why is Charles a knob?' I asked.

She flicked her hand in the air. 'Doesn't matter.'

'I bet it does,' I said, looking at Foz.

She nodded.

'We all have the capacity to be knobs,' said Han.

The four of us contemplated this and agreed that this was probably a profound truth.

'What about Conall?' added Han. 'Is he just going to live there forever? What about his work? I mean, hopefully Eamonn recovers, but then what will he do? Go back to Karachi?'

I took another drag of my cigarette. 'He can go to hell for all I care.'

Seeing as I'm there it only seems fair that he should be too. Just then I noticed Suj staring towards the door. When I turned round there was Conall, squinting through the smoke, with a bag in his hand.

'Already there, Sofe.'

12.05 a.m. What is it that makes you ache for a person? How does a feeling manifest itself as something so physical? If I could understand how, I could undo it; like an exorcism for feelings.

Conall coughed, looking at the ashtray that was full of cigarette butts.

'Well, it's not as if I can drink my sorrows away,' I said.

He paused. 'I want you to stay here.'

For a second I didn't understand what he meant. Then it dawned on me. 'No,' I said. 'I'm not living here any more. I'll get my things and leave.'

'Where will you go?'

I don't know. When there are so many broken pieces how do you even begin to put things back together? How do you create something new from the splintered fragments of something old?

'I don't know,' I said. 'I'll stay with Foz or something.'

'And then?'

'It's got nothing to do with you any more, has it?'

He was about to say something when there was banging at the door.

'Conall, where have you both been?' exclaimed Mum as he went to open it.

God, please, somehow transport me out of this place.

Mum came in, wincing at the smell of smoke. 'Uff, who has been smoking?'

Conall looked at me.

'Soffoo, what are you looking like in that dressing gown?'

Her eyes rested on the ashtray. Heartbreak's made me reckless.

'Haw hai,' she said, looking at us expectantly.

'It's me,' said Conall.

She tutted as she took the ashtray and emptied its contents into the bin. 'Disgusting habit. You know her baba used to smoke? Look where he ended up.'

'It's not Conall, Mum. It's me.' Maybe it *is* me. Maybe I'm just not wife material.

'Hain?'

'They're *my* cigarettes. I smoke.'

She paused.

'Maybe you should sit down,' Conall said to Mum.

'Soffoo . . .' She sat down in a daze then looked up at me. 'But –'

'Listen,' said Conall to Mum, sitting on the coffee table opposite her.

I went and sat next to him, my leg touching his and me missing the feel of it already.

'Mum –'

'You are smoking . . . *cigarettes*?'

'You were right, Mum. We're too different,' I said.

Here was me, picking up the first broken fragment of this relationship. She looked at both of us again. Conall looked at the ground; the one that seemed to be taken from under me every time I had to open my mouth.

'Conall's moving back to Ireland. To be with Eamonn, and I'm . . .' The words snagged in my throat. 'I'm staying in London.'

Mum kept looking between me and Conall. 'Soffoo . . . you are *smoking*? But you were so good in school.'

Who'd have thought that that was the tragedy here?

'Mum,' I said, leaning forward to make her understand. 'Conall and I . . . we're . . .' I couldn't get the words out, because as soon as they fell out so would my tears and I didn't want to cry in front of Mum. Certainly not Conall.

'We're going our separate ways,' said Conall.

It was like a pellet of truth, puncturing any hope there might've been. She looked at both of us; her expression changing from shock to defiance.

'You think I have rocks in my head?' she said.

My instinct was to glance at Conall, but it's better to try and kill that as soon as possible.

'What?'

'Soffoo, I am not born tomorrow. I was married for thirty-five years; you think I can't see when a husband and wife have problems? You think I don't see your red, red eyes?'

I felt Conall's gaze on me.

'No,' she said. 'You will make this work. Me and your baba gave you too easy life, this is the problem. You children walk away from everything as if it's nothing. Did you see me run away every time marriage got hard? Hmm? Conall,' she said, turning to him. 'You are sensible. What is this?'

Where was his *I should never have married you* now?

'It's my fault,' he finally said.

'I can't believe you let her smoke!' said Mum. 'You must call your mother and father.'

She began planning some kind of family intervention. Perhaps I should've told her that my mother-in-law was probably sending off for a marriage licence for Conall and Claire this very second.

'No, Mum. That's it.'

'And where will you live?'

'Here,' he said.

'No. Not here,' I replied.

Mum's fierce gaze rested on both of us. 'No,' she said. 'She will come live with me –'

'I can't,' I interrupted.

'Soffoo, you listen to your mama for once. You stay with me, and when you come home, Conall, you will both talk to each other and stop ruining everyone's life.'

Reality certainly has a way of pissing on your sentimental ideas of moving on.

'She'll stay here,' said Conall, looking Mum in the eye. 'But you need to understand,' he added, shifting forward, looking her in the eye. 'This is over.'

And here was Conall, taking the fragment from me, and crushing it to dust.

Sunday 9 June

8.20 a.m.

From: Sakib Awaan
To: Sofia Khan
Subject: And another one

Hi Sofia,
Sorry about the weekend email. Though you know it's a sort of rule of thumb for me. (Did you know that 'rule of thumb' comes from an old English law that stated you couldn't beat your wife with anything wider than your thumb?)

Anyway, how are you? Just wanted to send you another MS. Have you got any more chapters for your book to show me?

I looked towards my door, wondering if Conall was awake or not. He said he's going to leave tomorrow for Ireland. This time he won't be coming back. How can I possibly go through the farce of writing a book about marriage when my own is falling apart? I reread Sakib's email.

8.40 a.m.

To: Sakib Awaan
From: Sofia Khan
Subject: Muslim Marriage Book

Hi Sakib,
I think you should know that Conall and I have decided to separate. Given this, continuing with the book feels disingenuous.

I know this is inconvenient, unprofessional and without warning but I hope it doesn't affect my job as a reader. I'll send back the advance and sort out any paperwork you need.

I'm really very sorry.

8.48 a.m.

To: Sofia Khan
From: Sakib Awaan
Subject: Re: Muslim Marriage Book

Sofia, I'm very sorry to hear that.
Can you come into the office tomorrow?
Think we should talk this through, properly.
Sakib

I wish Sakib could understand that I can barely get out of bed. But there was no reason for me to sound more pathetic than I already feel.

9.45 a.m. Bumped into Conall on the way to the bathroom. Awkward dance of you-go-first. I'm getting out of this place because while he's here, all I want to do is crawl into bed with him and hold on to him forever.

12.15 p.m. 'Oh, Sofe.'

Maars hugged me as well as she could, balancing Adam on her hip as I entered her home. I took him from her and watched him drool as he grabbed my face.

'He's missed you,' she said.

We passed the kitchen and went up a few steps into the living room. 'Mum's going on about your cigarettes.'

I shrugged. She stood at the doorway, folding her arms as I made small talk with Adam. If only all small talk could be this easy.

'Are you sure you want to do this?' she asked.

Why does everyone make it feel like there's an option? No one *wants* to split from their husband. Watching Adam, I realised: Conall and I will never go through sleepless nights together because of a crying baby; we'll never play in the park with our son or daughter; watch them take part in a school play or be at their graduation. A whole future erased at the push of a verbal button. The sob seemed to come from nowhere. I wasn't going to cry today. But grief doesn't just swell inside you; it knocks you over when you least expect it. Before I knew it Maars was by my side and rocking me in her arms. I held on to Adam as if he was the thread in the seams of my sanity.

'Come on,' said Maars. 'Let's get you to lie down. I'll make your favourite; lasagne. And I'll get Tahir to bring muffins on his way home,' she added as we made our way to the guest bedroom.

'Last thing I need is to be divorced and fat,' I said, wiping the water dribbling from my nose.

Maars took Adam and put him in his cot as she tucked me into bed. All I remember is her stroking my hair until I fell asleep.

11.15 p.m. Maars dropped me home and I think Conall's in his bedroom. After tomorrow, I don't know when I'll see him again.

Monday 10 June

10.20 a.m. Katie cornered me before I went into Sakib's office.

'Sweetu.' She stared at my face. 'You have to start answering my calls.'

I nodded. 'Sorry.'

'Don't be silly. Listen, I've been reading up on different kinds of bereavement and . . . well, this is sort of like that.'

Why was the light in this office so bright?

'They say, when you've lost all hope you just have to understand that the people who love you the most carry it for you. Until you're ready to have it back again.'

I was going to cry.

'I'm holding on to it for now,' she said. 'Don't you worry.'

She kissed me, gave me a nod and headed back to her seat. Wish I could tell her I love her. I'm guessing she knows.

When I knocked on Sakib's door he wasn't there so I just went in, sat down and waited. About five minutes passed when I heard: 'How are you feeling?'

I looked up to see Sakib, smiling down at me.

'I'm just dandy,' I said. I lifted my head up which felt rather heavier than usual – on account of a headache rather than a sizeable brain.

'So . . .' he began. 'You're alone now?'

Doesn't mince his words, does he? The words were pellets hitting me like a machine gun. *Du-du-du-du-du-du-du.* Why is it such a taboo word, anyway? What's wrong with being alone? I mean, we're all alone in life – and death come to think of it. I spread out my hands.

'So it seems.'

He nodded. 'Your email . . .' he began.

'Sorry.'

He put his hand out as if to say, not to worry. 'It's a dilemma.'

No shit. My eyes settled on an MS on his table: *How to Build a Life*. Sakib opened his drawer and offered me a biscuit.

Which is when I burst into tears.

How was he to know that's exactly what Conall used to do when I had dating problems? Biscuits used to do the trick then. I need something a lot more hardcore now. Sakib looked so alarmed I wasn't sure what to do. *Stop crying, Sofia. STOP.*

'Ready?' he asked.

No, I'm not fucking *ready*. I nodded.

He leaned forward. 'I'm a very good agony aunt. Well, I like to think I offer good advice, anyway,' he added.

I tucked my hands between my knees.

'On a professional level this isn't great for you or me,' he said. As he leaned back, he added, 'But this is personal: I want to give you a few weeks to decide, and if you still don't want to go ahead, then I'll understand. If you ask me, though – it'd be a mistake. You have to think long-term.'

I can barely think about how I'm going to put one step in front of the other and he's asking me to consider the bigger picture. *Good advice* indeed. Then Mum's voice came into my head: *Soffoo, you didn't think when you married a gora. You just did what you wanted.* What would happen if I just quit now? What does the professional future hold?

'How can I write a book about marriage when I'm not in one?' I said.

He took his glasses off and nodded. 'I get it. But sometimes you have to think beyond the present. You don't want to decide on something now that might be a mistake. Feelings pass. Give it some time. If it helps, then think of the book as fiction.'

I looked at his gold watch glinting in the light.

'Forget everything that's happened for a moment, and everything that might happen. This is your opportunity,'

'For what?'

'To do and be something outside of your marriage. It's not just an escape for your readers. It's for you too. Isn't it?'

I told him I'd think about it. As I was about to walk out of the office he said: 'You know you're not really alone, don't you?'

I tried to give him a convincing smile.

'Katie's been coming in every day for the past week, asking me if I've spoken to you. Now I know why.'

This time my smile wasn't so forced. 'She's tenacity personified,' I said.

'She is.' He got some papers out of a file and added. 'Aside from that, if you do ever want to talk about things . . . anyway, I'm sure you have your people.'

'I do.' For the first time since Ireland the tears that came to the surface were ones of gratitude.

'It's just.' He paused, seeming to struggle with whether he should continue or not. 'I know what it's like to have a failed marriage.'

'Oh,' I said. 'I'm sorry, I thought you were both –'

'Incredibly different. After being married for eight years. Anyway. Just so you know.'

You'd never have guessed it to look at him. It was only a few months ago he and his wife were at my wedding. I glanced at his hand and noticed he was still wearing his wedding band. I turned mine around on my finger. It's time to take it off now and return it to the man who gave it to me. One of my last acts of closure.

'Thank you,' I said to him.

'No need to thank me, Ms Khan. Just write me a book.'

6.45 p.m. When I got home, I thought, *this is it: one last goodbye.* As I entered the house and put my bag down in the living room I noticed that everything was immaculate – an empty vase on the coffee table. There's nothing more depressing than an empty vase. Apart from an empty soul. Conall's old papers and magazines seemed to have been cleared out. I went into the kitchen and dishes were washed, counters spotless. I ran up the stairs, into the guest bedroom, and it was empty. No bag or sign that he'd slept in there. When I went into our bedroom and opened our wardrobe all his clothes were gone. I sat on the bed, staring at the empty side of the rail and shelves.

I went back downstairs – maybe he was in the garden. He wasn't. As I walked back into the living room I noticed that the picture of Conall and me in Karachi had gone. Looking on the floor, I wondered if it'd fallen off the hanging. I opened the cabinet drawer and saw the frame there; empty. Just like the last goodbye.

Saturday 22 June

11.55 a.m. 'Soffoo, *Soffoo*.'

Mum was chasing me, waving my red thong, crying out for me to stop as I sprinted towards a ferry.

'*Soffoooo*.'

I'm looking back and running faster, but she picks up speed and is only metres behind me, her face screwed up in rage, trying to hit me with my thong.

'Hai hai, Soffoo, is this a time to be asleep!'

I started awake and saw the curved figure of my mother looming over me. 'Huh? What?' I mumbled.

She'd already whipped the curtains open and I squinted against the bright light. Looking round the room she took a whiff and, thankfully, decided to ignore the stale smell of tobacco and the ashtray of cigarette butts on my bedroom floor.

'You should come and live with me,' she said.

Not sure what's worse, marital breakdown or living with Mum again. 'No, Mum.'

'You left the kitchen door unlocked.'

I asked where Foz was and she said she wasn't home because she'd already looked in her room.

'How did you get in?' I asked, rather alarmed.

'Conall gave me keys before he left.'

Amazing that Mum hadn't shared this piece of vital information earlier. What did he say? Did he mention me? Why did he leave without saying goodbye? This is what he does, though. Why should I be surprised?

'That was good of him,' I said, sticking my head back under the covers.

'Soffoo, shall I ask you a question?'

I grunted.

'How many days did I spend in bed when your baba died?'

I paused. Zero. It was straight from the hospital to organising the funeral, informing relatives, sorting paperwork – the paraphernalia of death.

'You think I didn't feel it? Haan, I know, he was difficult – but you think there was nothing there?'

I felt a tear pass over the bridge of my nose. 'Maybe I'm not as tough as you,' I said, peering over the covers.

'I am very strong, I know,' she replied.

'And modest.'

She stood and began clearing up the glasses, then she picked up the ashtray.

'After your baba, I would go in the garden when everyone was asleep, light one of his cigarettes and sit and listen to his favourite songs. You think you can afford to smoke?' she added, waving the ashtray at me. 'How expensive cigarettes are. And look at your face. You are young, Soffoo. Don't waste your youth in mourning.'

Sunday 23 June

1.15 p.m. Why are there no biscuits in the house?? My appetite seems to have reappeared and all I want is to stuff my gob with five chocolate digestives at a time.

'That's a lot of banging,' said Foz, appearing at the kitchen door.

It looks like she's moved in here permanently, but I'm not entirely sure.

'Is one fucking biscuit too much to fucking ask?' I exclaimed, opening the cupboard by the door for the tenth time.

'We could go out and get some.'

'Ugh.'

She'd turned round and gone back into the living room.

I opened the smallest cupboard with the spices and began taking them all out to search for anything that might be hidden in the back. And there was a packet. But sellotaped to the packet was a piece of paper. I took it out and it was an envelope with my name on it. In Conall's handwriting. I went into my bedroom and stared at it for I don't know how long before I conjured the courage to open it.

Sofe,

I'm not sure when you'll find this letter, but I'm guessing if you were rummaging through the cupboards long enough it means you're ready to read it. I never have met a woman with such perseverance when it comes to looking for biscuits. If you found it any sooner I'm pretty sure you'd have burnt the letter in a fit of rage. And I wouldn't have blamed you.

I'm sorry for many things, Sofe, but nothing more than not having told you the truth in the first place. Especially because you're the most honest person I know. I thought I was done with cowardice. I wasn't.

If I'd stayed to say goodbye I know you'd have given me that ring back and I can't have it. You can throw it in the bin or bury it in a pile of cigarette ash, but I hope you keep it because it's yours.

Always has been. Always will be.

Yours,

Conall.

P.S. Look in the cubbyhole, behind all the boxing gear.

I wiped my eyes and ran down the stairs, opened the cubby hole and took out the punching bag and mismatched old gloves. There, in a box, was what looked like a year's supply of biscuits.

JULY

With or Without You

Monday 1 July

8.40 a.m. I don't know whether having to tell people about the end of your marriage is exhausting or a distraction. Maybe when I say it out loud it'll still feel like someone else's narrative. It's only when I'm alone that I remember it's mine.

Which is shit, because I'm alone.

Thursday 4 July

10.15 a.m. 'Thanks for coming in,' said Sakib.

I sat down and looked at the piles of manuscripts, stacked against the glass wall. Each pile had a letter labelled above it.

'Are those in alphabetical order?' I asked.

Sakib sprang up from his chair when he saw one of the letters had fallen off. 'There's no such thing as organised chaos,' he said. 'You're either organised or chaotic.'

Conall was all organised chaos. Or perhaps he was just chaos. Even though he seemed to bring the opposite of that to my life. Until he told me about his secret family, of course. Sakib sat at his desk and leaned forward, clasping his hands together.

'So, have you thought about the book?'

I've not thought about anything for the past two weeks. But why do something you don't want to do? Something you barely have the energy for – that's so completely the opposite of what your life's become.

'I'll be honest,' he said. 'This is selfish. I want you to do it because I think it'll be great. Even if it's painful.'

'You don't mind inflicting pain on me?'

He gave me a smile. 'It's not optimum, but whatever doesn't kill you . . .'

'. . . slowly destroys your soul.'

'No. If I thought it'd do that . . . well, I'm not that selfish.'

I considered it for a moment. Apart from reading manuscripts for Sakib, what else will I do, except sit at home and wonder where it all went wrong? Plus, the last thing a person wants to do is appear feeble to their editor. But wasn't this like lying? How can I write it without being completely disingenuous?

'OK,' I said. 'But maybe . . .'

'What?'

'Maybe it can't be like the first one – all happy and light. It can't be a guide.'

He nodded thoughtfully. 'What are you thinking?'

'I don't know.' I shrugged. 'Perhaps something more honest than it has been so far.'

Sakib paused. 'Yes. Yes, I see what you mean. I think that's a good thing.'

'Honesty then,' I said.

He leaned back, giving me a big smile. 'Honesty. Good. I'm so pleased.'

'I'm glad someone is.'

'That's the spirit.'

I shook my head as I took out the manuscript I'd read for him.

'This was really good,' I said.

'You think we should publish it?' he asked.

I paused. 'Yes.'

'Why?'

'Oh. Because it's really good?'

'I'll need specifics,' he said.

'Do we have to disassemble everything?'

He clasped his hands together. 'If I'm giving someone money then I want to know why.'

I gave him all the reasons I loved the book. 'It's the universal struggle of trying to find happiness and then realising it's not what you have in life, but what you make of it that matters,' I added.

I'd made my choice – what was I going to make of it now that I was without Conall?

'Exactly.' He considered me for a while before speaking. 'We don't get to make many choices, though, when we're Asian.'

'Please. What decade are you living in? Things have changed.'

'Not enough,' he said. 'Change isn't just about what you can and can't do. It's about mindset.'

This was all rather philosophical territory to be honest. I just wanted a good book to be published.

'Thanks, Sofia,' he said, getting up.

'No worries.' I noticed a flash of hot pink socks. 'Socks say a lot about a person,' I added.

He laughed and picked up his trouser leg for a better look. 'What's that then?'

I picked up my bag. 'That you read all the fashion mags.'

'Is it that obvious?'

I considered him for a moment. 'Completely. Did you used to get all the girls? There's a certain brand of Asian girl for whom *you* are prime target.'

He rested his hand on the handle. 'What type's that?'

'She has very straight hair. And she's quite beautiful, naturally. But, you know, in that prosaic way.'

'That's good news. I think. I can take prosaic.'

'You know what Oscar Wilde said? *Let us leave pretty women to men with no imagination*.'

'That was Proust.'

'Was it?'

I got out my phone and googled to check. 'Oh, you're right.'

'I know. And thanks for telling me I've no imagination.'

I paused. 'You know sometimes I don't –'

'Think before you speak?'

'Sorry. I didn't mean it like that. Your wife's very pretty . . . I mean, was. Well, I'm sure she still is. And not in a prosaic way. Sorry.'

I waited for him to open the door. As he did I paused. 'I don't mean to be nosy – but what was it? You know, that changed things with your wife?'

He cleared his throat and seemed to be experiencing physical pain, searching for the words.

'Sorry, I shouldn't have asked.'

'No, it's fine. It's just – we grew apart. To be honest it was probably more me than it was her. Some people stay the same their whole life; consistent. And then some people just evolve a little later. I went from this weird, geeky kid to, I don't know. This.' He opened up his arms. 'And now that I'm here I think we both realised we didn't work any more.' He looked at the ground. 'She said she loved that geeky kid.'

That was it, wasn't it? Conall was still evolving. Perhaps I was too.

'Are you OK?' he asked.

I nodded. 'Fine. Grand.' I've never said grand in my life. As if speaking like Conall would make up for him not being here.

'Are you OK?' I asked.

'Oh, yeah. Yeah, fine.'

I think we both knew this wasn't true, no matter how much he seemed to want it to be.

'You know you can come into the office whenever you want. For your reading. Katie would love it.'

'But that would mean having to get out of my pyjamas.'

There it was. The one look I wanted never to see on anyone's face. Pity.

'I'm joking,' I added.

'Listen, some things are too late to salvage,' he said. 'But for you, this could only be temporary.'

'Nothing temporary about an ex-wife and child I never knew about.'

He looked a little taken aback.

'Bet you never had that problem with your wife.'

Sakib pressed his lips together and cleared his throat. 'Right. No. Anyway, thanks for your thoughts on the manuscript and oh . . . do you mind not mentioning it to anyone?'

For a moment I wanted to ask why, but who cared? 'Sure. Of course.'

'I'm glad you're going ahead with the book,' he added as he opened the office door. I noticed him glance at the wedding band still on my hand. 'I'd have been wrong about you otherwise.'

5.50 p.m. Walked across the Embankment today, looking out into the murky River Thames, set against the blue sky. What was Conall doing this very moment? Bought a Snickers at a newspaper stand and read the headline: *EDL Plan Protest March Against Islamisation of UK.*

I know what Conall would've said if he read that. A lot of swearing, actually. Thunderous face. Slamming things. So much rage, helping to diminish mine somewhat.

'Sad state of affairs, isn't it, love?' said the man at the stand as he handed me my change.

I nodded.

Isn't it just.

9.35 p.m. I had cheese on toast for dinner, which was only marginally depressing because I couldn't be bothered to switch the light on once I'd sat down. So, I ate in the dark, with nothing for company but the sound of my own munching.

Friday 5 July

7.25 a.m. Bills are never more depressing than when they come in the name of your husband who no longer lives with you. On top of which the bathroom tap wasn't working properly. The water's either freezing or boiling. Nothing and no one believes in moderation any more.

8.15 p.m. I'd gone into Sakib's office to read today and came home to find Mum with a feather duster in hand, cleaning the top of the blinds.

'Soffoo, when was the last time you cleaned your home?'

I was too distracted by the bathroom sink on the dining table. She told me she'd got someone called Uncle Salim to come and fix my tap for free and now she was fixing my entire house.

'There's so much to do. Ramadan is next week and I have to make koftay and spring rolls . . . Salim Bhai,' she exclaimed into her phone as it rang. 'Not the kitchen tap, the bathroom tap. Crack,' she said when she put the phone down.

'So, in the process of fixing the bathroom tap he broke the sink,' I said.

'You think about your broken marriage, Soffoo.'

I threw my bag on the sofa, trying my best to ignore my broken marriage, actually. 'When are you and Uncle Wasim booking your flight to Pakistan?'

Mum said they'd decided to cancel a wedding event in London even though I told her not to for my sake.

'And who will look after everything here? Uff, look at all this dust. I'll go after Eid. If your baba was here, what would he say? He spoiled you and then he died. Men only think of themselves. And what are these overdue bills? I didn't raise you and Maria to be so un-responsible.' She paused, which felt pretty remarkable. 'Don't worry. I'll give you money.'

'Mum, I don't need money, honestly. It's going to be fine.'

'Don't argue. Your baba and me didn't work so hard so you could struggle.'

I felt a lump form in my throat.

'Chalo, chalo. It will be OK.'

The doorbell rang and it was Maria, armed with food.

'Why's there a bathroom sink here?' she asked, putting the dish of biryani on the already over-occupied dining table.

'What do you girls think? Everything happens like magic?' exclaimed Mum, shaking her feather duster at us. She then stormed out of the room and into the kitchen.

'Bloody hell,' said Maars. 'That woman really needs to get married.'

Sunday 7 July

2.50 p.m. I was attempting to make a stir-fry as Foz was coming over to stay when my phone rang. I didn't recognise the number.

'Hey, Sofia?'

It was the voice – they sound so alike I don't know why my heart plummeted to my ankles.

'How are you?' asked Sean.

'Fine,' I said, sitting on the kitchen floor, urging my heart to get back to where it belonged.

'I'm sorry. The whole thing's just . . . well, you know.'

I reached up to switch the hob off before I was splattered with hot oil. I'd already got sweaty enough.

'Life,' I said. 'I guess your mum's happy.' I added.

'No . . .' he said, not very convincingly.

'How's Eamonn?'

'He was looking better yesterday.'

Why are there so many facets to missing someone? It's never just the person, it's everything around them that becomes important because it's linked to them. It's not about cutting a cord; it's discovering that the cord has roots and you need better shears.

'He's such a great kid.' Sean paused. 'Christ, I hope he gets better.'

'Me too,' I said.

'Have you spoken to Conall?'

'No.'

He paused. 'Think you might?'

'Why?' I asked.

'He's having a tough time. If he heard from you –'

'I can't.'

'No. Of course not.'

I waited for him to say something else.

'Is that it?' I asked.

'No, yeah, well . . . Yeah.'

'What?'

'How's . . . doesn't matter. Forget it. Do you need anything?'

Yes. Your brother. 'No, thanks. I'm really fine.'

I sounded rather more sprightly than I felt. I don't want Conall to think I'm fine. I am the opposite of fine. I heaved myself off the floor, switching the hob back on. The vegetables were looking very limp.

'Right.'

It was the first time Sean's voice had ever been curt. I wanted to explain that I was lying, actually, but by that time tears had sprouted from my eyes as if from nowhere, falling into the hot oil. My cooking is literally made of sweat and tears.

Wiping the tears from my face, steadying my voice, I said: 'Is there anything else?'

He paused again. 'No. I guess there isn't.'

10.10 p.m. Welcomed Foz home with my veggie stir-fry.

'I could get used to this,' she said.

'Well, why don't you just move in with me?'

She looked at me and hesitated. 'Really?'

'Of course,' I exclaimed.

Hurrah! My best friend's moving in with me!

'It'll be like old times,' she said. 'When you used to stay with me and we'd smoke out on the outside step.' Just then she looked into the dish. 'Although perhaps we should go to your mum's for dinner.'

Hmph. When we got there, Auntie Reena was around. She's come up with a life plan: budgies. Fozia glanced at me.

'Don't you worry about your husband leaving you,' Auntie said, smiling at me and grabbing my arm. 'When your mama leaves we will be single girls together.'

1.40 a.m. I shook Fozia awake. She turned over, peeling back her blindfold a fraction and taking an earplug out.

'Am I just a few budgies short of being Auntie Reena?' I said.

She lifted her duvet. I slipped into her bed as she handed me another pair of blindfolds.

'We're all only a few budgies short of being Auntie Reena.'

Tuesday 9 July

3 a.m. A month of fasting has begun. We all went to the mosque last night and the sermon followed by Taraweeh prayers was about perfecting the self – using the month to become a better version of yourself. Pfft. What if there's only one version and that's the one you've become? What if this is me in my entirety? I wondered what would Conall have thought of the sermon?

'It's a decent aim, isn't it, Sofe?' he might've said. Then he'd have smiled in that annoyingly amused way he has, looked at me, and added, 'You've done a pretty shoddy job all these years with yourself. Maybe this time you'll actually achieve it.'

First step towards separation recovery: stop having fictitious convos with the person you're separated from.

Perhaps Ramadan has come at the right time. It'll make me think of higher, spiritual things as opposed to the empty side of my bed.

God, I could do with his arms round me.

Friday 19 July

12.40 a.m. The girls came over for iftari – to break fast. Asked Suj and Katie to come over as well to partake in fast-breaking ritual of stuffing gob. We tried to keep the convo strictly spiritual in honour of the month, but apparently worldly relationships are too much at the forefront of everyone's thoughts.

'Being married's hard work, you know,' said Katie. She was putting the plates out with Suj while the rest of us came back from praying.

'You don't have to make me feel better,' I said.

'It's true,' Katie said, in a higher pitch than usual, which of course meant it wasn't true at all. Not for her anyway.

'How were you sure?' Foz asked Katie. She picked out a piece of limp lettuce from the salad I'd made.

Katie paused and thought for a moment. 'I wasn't.'

'Katie's such an unromantic twerp sometimes,' I said, cutting in. It's Ramadan, so I'm curbing my enthusiasm for swearing.

She replied: 'Fine. I was sure. But that's because he's basically my best friend – after you, obviously, Sweetu,' she said turning to me. 'Anyway, we spend too much time thinking about this kind of thing. There's life beyond marriage.'

There's life beyond everything – doesn't make it any less sad.

Foz picked out another piece of limp lettuce. 'The one thing we told this girl to make,' she said, contemplating the lettuce for rather a long time.

'Obviously you'd rather be with them than not,' I said. 'I mean, what other reason makes sense?'

Suj was checking her phone and Hannah snatched it from her, putting it on the table.

'Shrivelling ovaries,' offered Hannah.

'Not wanting to die alone,' said Foz.

'Being bored,' added Suj.

'If you're bored then take up a hobby,' I said.

Katie rolled her eyes. I looked at Hannah. 'Not much you can do about shrivelling ovaries, I'm afraid.'

'Shrivelled, more like,' she said. 'By the time the adoption agency's processed our paperwork, I'll be a shrivelled human being. But if my last relationship taught me anything, it's to be with someone who'll be enough. Babies or not. Rich or poor. That kind of thing.'

It's nice to know that good marriages do exist. That people can be content with one another, despite wider adversity. Suj looked agitated, not touching the food on her plate. And not just my salad.

I filled my glass with water. '"It might be that you love a thing which is bad for you, or hate a thing which is good for you."' I thought a quotation from the Qur'an was fitting for the occasion. Everyone seemed to be lost in their respective thoughts on this.

'Yeah,' said Suj, taking her phone back from Hannah. 'But how are you meant to work out which one is which?'

Thursday 25 July

10.05 a.m. Things I thought of when I woke up this morning: it's been forty-five days since Conall left; is he waking up in the middle of the night to keep fast? Why do I care? I need to do laundry.

I'm going back to sleep.

1.55 p.m. I went in to work to have lunch with Katie since I started my period (God is considerate and gives women a break from fasting and praying once a month). I asked that we go to the café round the corner from work in case Sakib sees me.

'Why?' she said.

'I don't need him to know my menstrual cycle,' I replied.

Outside the building I gulped my coffee before going to throw it in the bin, and sod's bloody law, Sakib walked past me.

'Worked from home this morning. Late-night Taraweeh prayers are taking their toll.' He rubbed his eyes and looked towards the bin. 'Don't worry, your secret's safe with me.'

Ugh.

We went in and got into the lift. When the doors closed I smelled his aftershave and feelings started going on in places they had no business to be. Bloody separation and bloody periods. Plus, *it's Ramadan.* Plus, *it's Sakib.* I observed his profile; the wavy hair, Romanesque nose, tan skin. I looked down at his shoes to divert my attention. *What is wrong with me??*

'No colourful socks?' I asked, noticing the black pair he was wearing.

He pointed a shoe upwards, but didn't reply. I tried not to breathe for the rest of the journey to the fifth floor.

'Are you OK?' he asked.

I pursed my lips. 'Mhmm.'

'Your face looks strained.'

I had to breathe. 'That's just my face.'

But he ignored me as we came out of the lift.

I walked up to Katie's desk as he was about to go into his office when he said, 'Don't go hiding away for lunch.' He looked at me and something seems to have changed about him. 'We're all adults here.'

6.55 p.m. The desk opposite Katie was vacant so I've ended up staying and reading. Most people have left (Katie had spin class), but Sakib's still in his office, his door ajar.

'You should go home,' I called out from my desk. 'Have a nap. God, I feel tired for you.'

Ah, Suj calling.

11.40 p.m. Bloody hell. Soon as I picked up, she said: 'I told my whole family about him. Dealt with all kinds of shit; people saying how Mum's looking down on me, disappointed – but I thought fuck 'em. She's going to be happy because I'm happy and now the man who's meant to be making me happy has fucked off somewhere.'

'What happened?' I asked.

Apparently he received a message from an ex.

'I swear if he's fucking around I'll go mental and slash his tyres.'

'Stay away from sharp objects, Suj. Do not slash another man's tyres. I mean it.'

When she said OK and put the phone down, I was pretty convinced she wasn't listening. Sakib, however, was listening. I turned round and he was standing there with his eyebrows raised.

'Just . . . offering some advice to a friend.' I put the phone in my pocket, observing his pallor and the rather grumpy edge to him. 'Are you getting enough nutrients? You should eat protein at suhur. Things like avocados.'

'Are you eating avocados?' he asked.

'I'm a hijabi. I'm meant to look sullen and severe. Hungry?' I asked.

He shrugged, pulling up a chair opposite me. Leaning his head back, he closed his eyes. I don't mean to sound prudish but why do men insist on spreading their legs as wide as humanly possible? Especially when some women are trying to keep certain feelings at bay. Stop flashing me your balls, for God's sake. It's Ramadan.

'Never really feel hungry,' he said. 'Just the lack of sleep.'

My pad really did need changing. I picked up my bag when he opened his eyes.

'You should come over for iftari one day,' he said.

I replied that that sounded lovely.

'Actually come over today.' He looked at his watch. 'I drove into the office. It's already almost seven o'clock.'

'Oh, I don't know, maybe a weekend would be better.'

'No, no. I'll drop you home, don't worry.'

I don't mean to be anti-people but the last thing I wanted was to spend an evening with my boss. Especially one who wears after-shave that smells so nice. *Ramadan is a time for community and kindness and blah blah bleugh.* All I wanted was to go home and scream into my pillow. Plus, I should call Suj back and get the full story. It's probably fine – I'm sure Charles hasn't pissed off any-where. He's mad about Suj.

Sakib was already standing up and waving his hand about. 'Come on. I could do with the company.'

He parked his Mercedes in the garage outside his detached house. I surveyed the wilted flowers that looked like they'd once been beau-tifully arranged in baskets.

'The wife took a flower-arranging class. Only she's no longer here to tend to them.'

'Ah.'

He opened the front door.

'Should I . . .' I pointed to my shoes, wondering whether I should take them off, the flooring was so pristine.

'Oh, great, if you don't mind.'

Sigh. This is why preparation is key. Feet are meant to be in socks or shoes, not flashed about in your boss's face.

Just then his phone rang and he answered. Turns out it was the flower-arranging wife.

'Hi. Fine. You?' He looked over at me, smiling apologetically as he led me through a rather grand passage, into an even grander liv-ing room. He closed the door behind him, through which I could hear muffled voices.

'How's Dubai?' I heard him ask. 'Not my choice. Yours. I asked you to stay.'

Oh Lord. Domestics. Who'd have 'em, eh? Not me. I stopped listening because a) it's rude and b) I was nosing about the room with its French windows overlooking a green lawn and what looked like a pond. There were pictures of Sakib and his wife, which I leaned in to inspect. They looked like such a good couple. Never can trust what's on the outside.

Sakib walked into the room and switched on the spotlights as he closed the blinds. 'Sorry about that.' He rubbed his forehead.

'She's in Dubai?' I asked.

He nodded. 'Her family has a home there and she decided to go for a break. Or I wouldn't be living in this house.'

He looked around at it, as if wondering what he was even doing here. 'Her parents bought this home for us,' he explained.

'Ah.' I mean, it was clear she was basically loaded. 'What will happen?' I asked.

He shrugged. 'All the small things – the windows, the flooring, the paint . . . we picked it out together. Built it to become what it is. I love it. I don't know what will happen. But she's not vindictive. And I hope I'm not either. I guess as with everything else we'll come to an agreement.'

'Gosh. How amicable.'

He gave a sad smile. 'Yes. Amicable.'

I wasn't sure what to say. The silence around us became louder than my big mouth. And I felt sorry for him – almost walked up to him and gave him a hug. It was all rather perturbing. 'If you want, we can make a plan for another day?'

'What? Nonsense. Stay put.'

The discomfort must've shown on my face. He raised his eyebrows. 'What would the aunties say, right? Plenty of wagging tongues if anyone found out.'

'I love that this month of forgiveness and reflection isn't lost on them.'

He looked thoughtful when he replied, 'Probably lost on all of us.'

Sakib took off his jacket and rolled up his shirtsleeves, revealing his tan arms. 'Let the tongues wag. I'm going to cook up an iftari you won't forget.'

Get your shit together, Sofia. You do not need to be close to a person. The further you are from things, the better. I shook my head vigorously as I followed him into the kitchen.

'Are you OK?' he asked.

'Hmm?'

'You were shaking your head.'

'Oh, nothing. Thought I was getting a headache.'

'You *thought* you were getting a headache?'

'It's gone. It's fine.'

I stopped short at the door and looked at the kitchen, which was basically the size of our living room. Or what used to be '*our*' living room . . . whose exactly is it now? Looking at the steel island in the middle of the kitchen, it rather felt like a place where you'd put an animal to slaughter.

'I like kitchen islands,' I said.

Sakib opened up a cupboard and asked, 'Do you cook a lot?'

I practically chortled on my own spit. 'Er, no,' I replied. 'But it'd be nice to pour cereal into a bowl on a kitchen island,' I added. 'I'm not about to go to Ikea and pick one up, though.'

He took out a jar of sauce and a few other bits and pieces, which looked rather foreign to me – item-wise that is.

'This kitchen definitely isn't Ikea,' he replied.

All right, mate, I wanted to say. I didn't, though, it being Ramadan and all.

'Chicken stir-fry?' he asked.

'Sure. Can I help?'

He went over to the humungous fridge and took out a bunch of vegetables. 'Put together a salad?' He handed me an onion.

I held it in my hand. 'What do you want me to do with this?' I asked.

He paused, his eyebrows contracting. 'Are . . . are you joking?'

I laughed, which could've meant either yes or no. He seemed to think it meant yes as he handed me a knife. 'Careful with that. State-of-the-art knife. One cut and it'll bleed you to death.'

I looked at its fine blade. 'Bloody hell.' I was going to retort with some witticism about money literally bleeding someone dry, but was rather engrossed in the mechanism of peeling the onion. So to speak. I realised Sakib was looking at me, concerned.

'Why don't you slice the top of the onion first?'

'Hmm? Oh. Yes, exactly.'

He tied on an apron, still looking concerned. Conall never tied on an apron when he cooked. His shirts were always splattered with some kind of ingredient.

'How has a Pakistani girl made it through life without peeling an onion?'

I rested the onion on the chopping board. 'Excuse me, I've *peeled* an onion before. Anyway, I didn't realise it was such an imperative.'

'It's just not very . . . usual,' he replied.

'Your point?'

He began chopping the mushrooms. 'Didn't Conall think it was odd?'

Past tense. Would this knife really bleed me to death?

'Sorry. I . . .' He cleared his throat.

'I can't say our conversations revolved round the kitchen.'

He pointed the knife at me. 'Don't get mad. It's Ramadan.'

I chopped the top off the onion and peeled the outer layers, thinking how I always did a shitty job at hiding my annoyance.

'How's the book coming along?' he asked.

'It's . . . I'll get there.'

He put the sliced mushrooms to one side. 'You're doing the right thing,' he said. 'By carrying on with it.'

I couldn't quite bring myself to look up. He was right because if I didn't have the book, what would I have? Where is the meaning? Is this why so many married people get stuck in a rut? The comfort of marriage diluting the need to do something *more*? Conall still has his passion for travel and photography. Apart from the obvious health, family and friends (for which I'm grateful, God – obviously), now I don't have a marriage, what else do I have to strive for? That feeling of non-direction I had in Karachi has only ballooned. When the onion stung my eyes it took a little bit of convincing that it was that, and not life, which was making me cry.

'You would say that,' I replied.

'Well, I guess I always do have some kind of agenda,' he said. 'You don't get far in life without one.' He chopped a red pepper in half. 'But aside from that, I genuinely think it's true.' He sliced the pepper into long strips. 'What's amazing,' he continued, 'is that your parents were OK with you marrying him. I mean, it's impressive.' Apparently, beneath the professional, educated demeanour, Sakib was as nosy as the next brown person.

'My mum didn't have a choice,' I said. 'And my dad certainly didn't. Being dead and all.'

Sakib flinched.

'Oh – did I make you uncomfortable?' I said.

'Sorry. None of my business.' He put the peppers in a colander with the mushrooms. 'It's just so different from my parents.'

'There,' I said, having mixed all the contents of my salad in a bowl. 'Are they hardcore?'

He let out a small laugh.

'Like, proper fundo types?' I added. 'The kind *Daily Mail* readers would go crazy for?'

'That's a little harsh,' he replied. 'They're just quite traditional. Kind and lovely, but traditional.' He peered into my bowl of salad as he said, 'An English degree was only allowed if I went on to study the law.'

'Hang on, you're a lawyer?'

'Lapsed. Books is all I wanted to do. Started out as a solicitor – no coincidence that I worked giving legal advice to publishers.'

I looked at him in wonder. 'How did you manage to make such a great and solid leap? Into publishing.'

He turned round and added sesame oil to the chicken sizzling in the pan. 'Told you. I always have an agenda.' He looked at his watch.

'Twelve minutes to go until fast opens, according to Googs,' I said.

'Drinks. Fridge.'

I opened it and looked at the organised shelves, taking out a bottle of elderflower juice and sparkling water.

Sitting at the table, he put on Sunrise Radio, which made me laugh.

'Old habits die hard,' he explained.

It just reminded me of Ramadan with Mum and Dad when they used to put the radio on, waiting for fast to break. Sakib looked towards his plate, while his lips moved in prayer. When the call to prayer broke out he exclaimed, 'The dates! I didn't get the dates.'

It was the first time I'd laughed, genuinely, in a while. I realised how odd it is that this man is my editor/boss. He rushed to get a tin, opened it, and put it in front of me.

When he returned from praying we ate, and as he went to put the dishes in the wash I got up to help.

'No, you've done enough work as a guest,' he said. 'Anyway, Husna only used the kitchen when she baked her complicated cakes or hosted a five-course meal. This is my arena on a day-to-day basis.'

'You're a bit of an anomaly as brown men go, aren't you?' I said. I contemplated him for a moment. 'Hm.'

'What?'

'Nothing. I just wondered: where were your types when I was looking for a husband?'

And I didn't mean it as *ooh, I wish I'd met you years ago*, but I realised it must've sounded like that. I felt my face flush and thought he might look alarmed, push me out of the house, that kind of thing. But in a rather disconcerting non-frazzled manner, he just smiled and said, 'Maybe you were looking in the wrong places?'

I thought I'd been in precisely the right place at the right time, which is how Conall came into my life. When I got home the house was so quiet that the only place that felt wrong at all, was that one, right now.

On the plus side, at least I no longer felt like screaming into my pillow.

Saturday 27 July

11.35 a.m.

From Maria: How are you doing? Will come over tonight to drop iftari off and bring Adam too. Won't ask if you've heard from Conall, but just so you know – I'm here. xx

Love Maars.

2.30 p.m. I'd been plodding along for almost a month without any communication from Conall. Then it hit me: what is the end result of separation? A vortex of some sort seemed to open up in my stomach. Hearing the TV on downstairs, I went and joined Foz on the sofa.

'Thought you were going to the mosque this afternoon?' she said.

I shrugged. 'Still on my period. Plus, it's too hot.' I slumped further down the sofa.

'Me too,' she replied.

Video footage of a bomb went off on the TV; a reporter came onscreen.

'Isn't life depressing enough?' I said.

In theory, Ramadan is meant to be a spiritual illumination, but there is no light in a vortex. Foz switched the channel.

'Oh *God*,' I said. 'Not bloody sports.'

'I wish you *would* go to the mosque.'

Just then the doorbell rang.

'Who the hell is that?' I said.

Foz balled up my scarf and threw it at me. 'Put that on.'

And then I heard the voice. This voice that I never thought I'd have to hear again: slightly high-pitched, uneven, smug; travelling through the passage and into my furry brain.

'Come in,' said Foz.

She reappeared in the room, the unexpected guest hidden behind the door.

'*What* is he doing here?' I mouthed just before Kam came into view. I think I might've scowled. There he was, with his oily hair and glaring, white teeth.

'Hi,' he said. His gaze flickered towards Foz when I didn't answer.

'Hi,' I said eventually.

I watched as my best friend pulled out a chair for her ex-boyfriend – the boyfriend who didn't have the balls to tell his parents about her when they were dating because she'd been divorced. *What* the hell was going on?

'How are your parents, Kam?' I asked.

'Good. Yours?' he asked.

'Well, one's dead but the other one's OK.'

He looked at Foz again. 'Oh yeah, God, I was really sorry to hear about that.' He cleared his throat.

'Do you want tea?' asked Foz.

'Can I have coffee, babe?' he asked.

Babe? And, of course, your royal bloody highness, don't worry about the fact that it's Ramadan. Have your coffee, have cake, but don't think you can have my friend.

He looked at me. 'I've kept a few fasts,' he said, as if reading my thoughts. 'Just hard, with the long hours and work and everything.'

Ugh. We heard clattering in the kitchen as Foz put the kettle on.

'God understands what's in your heart,' he added.

'Indeed. Which is maybe why you should be worried,' I replied with a smile.

He shifted in his seat. 'Still the same then, Sofe.'

'Just a little wiser.'

When Foz came in with the coffee, she turned to me and mouthed something that looked like '*Behave*'.

'How's the world of banking?' I asked him. And then I couldn't help myself. 'Still making money on the back of other people's poverty?'

His gnashers came out again as he laughed. I might've rolled my eyes. Even Foz looked at him, seeming to wonder why he was grinning.

'What's so funny?' she asked.

There's such genuine curiosity behind Foz's questions that it's impossible to be offended by her. Conall on the other hand used to say that even my questions sounded like accusations. I was too busy getting my phone to hear Kam's reply.

To Suj; Hannah: OMG. Get your sunglasses out. The gnashers are back. What the hell is going on??

When I glanced over at Foz and Kam, he seemed so engrossed in what she was saying that I wondered whether people could change.

He looked at me. 'You look tired, Sofe. Why don't you take a nap?'

Maybe not. I nodded and sighed. 'I know, some company can be quite exhausting.'

'Sofe . . .' said Foz.

'Oh, Foz, come on. Kam knows I'm just joking. It's Ramadan – I wouldn't dream of being a bitch.'

'Don't take this the wrong way, Sofe,' he said, reddening. 'But that's probably why Foz is here with you, instead of your husband.'

'*Kam*,' said Foz.

I clutched my hand to my chest. 'Heavens,' I exclaimed. 'How could I possibly take that the wrong way?'

From Suj: Toffee, WTF are you talking about? What is he doing there? Fucking extra UV protection for those teeth.

'I love Foz,' he said.

It came as a jolt. I'm assuming by the look on Foz's face, it came as one to her too.

'Congratulations,' I replied. 'That makes two of us.'

'People make mistakes,' he said. Then he looked at her. 'Sometimes you just need to be forgiven for them.'

What is up with all this talk of forgiveness? What if Conall begged for mine? What if I got on a plane and said: it's OK, we can work it out?

'Sofe. Do you mind?' she said.

There's nothing worse than watching your friend plunge into the murky darkness of unsatisfactory love, so I got off the sofa and dragged myself up the stairs. Staring at the bedroom walls, I looked at Conall's number on my phone before taking out a fag. I was hanging out of the window, puffing away, when my bedroom door opened.

'Dirty fag-head,' said Foz.

'*What* was he doing here? I mean, haven't you learned your lesson?'

She took a deep breath and came into the room.

'Sorry,' I said – not sounding very sorry. 'It's just that he's so *annoying* with his stupid teeth constantly on display. Close your mouth, man. And that *hair*. He's like some kind of immigrant, Euro-trash hybrid with his inability to tell his Vs from his Ws. Sorry.'

'Well, now he and I both know how you feel about him,' she said, walking over and taking a cigarette from my pack.

From Hannah: Excuse me? What do you mean Kam? Can you please clarify that this is the same Kam she broke up with last year and I haven't missed some vital piece of information in the midst of my adoption drama?

Foz looked over at me before I could hide the message. 'I knew you were texting the girls.'

'Again. Sorry.' It's a wonder I have any friends left, to be honest.

'I can't explain it. I know Kam can be annoying,' she said. 'I don't know what he puts in his hair. But he's also funny and sweet and well . . . he's already told me we're meeting his parents after Ramadan.'

This was just awful. I had to tell Conall. For a second I lost the thread of what Foz was saying and had to shake any Conall-related thought out of my head.

'And I love having a fag. But, darling, no one changes,' I said.

'We both love fags,' she said. 'Bloody expensive, though, aren't they?'

'Tell me about it.'

We both paused in thought. 'So, not only are you getting back together with Kam, but we're also turning into our mothers.'

She laughed. I looked at Foz's face. It's such a lovely one; the kind that makes you look twice, admire its shape and features. I've loved this face for over a decade, but never in all this time have I felt compelled to throw my phone at it. I told her as much, which just made her laugh again, though it wasn't a joke.

'We've just always said that one of us should be happy,' I said. 'And seeing as that's not going to be me, the duty falls upon you.'

'Is it me or were his teeth even whiter than usual?' she said.

I laughed as she rested her elbows against the window, overlooking the street. 'But honestly? I *am* happy.'

Bloody hell.

'Life, darling,' she said. 'You never know what feeling's going to come and hit you straight in the chest.'

Tuesday 30 July

2.20 p.m. Fasting again. Have spent past two hours trying to concentrate on reading the new manuscript that Sakib sent. Visions of doughnuts keep swimming in my head.

2.25 p.m. Doughnuts and biscuits.

2.28 p.m. Sod this. I'm going over to Mum's.

3.50 p.m. Not sure if Ramadan is taking its toll but Mum's being very grumpy. All I did was ask how Uncle Wasim is and when they're going to Pakistan, so Maars and I could book our tickets, and she practically shouted: 'When I get some peace in my life.'

Bloody hell; take an interest in your mother's love life and that's what you get. Didn't ask what exactly was so unpeaceful as had fear of onion bhajis, frying in the pan, being thrown at me.

4.10 p.m. Auntie Reena's come over. She keeps talking about her budgies, but she's also started taking computing lessons. She says you can't live in the world and not know technology. Mum looked quite proud of her.

5.05 p.m. Oh my God! Auntie Reena just told me she's very sad that Mum's broken off her engagement! (Though, truth be told, she didn't look very sad.) Went storming into garden where Mum was watering flowers and demanded to know what was happening.

'Soffoo, don't ask me ridicklus questions.'

I had to grab the watering can from her. She looked at me – same look of resolution I've seen on her when she's negotiating with our window cleaner – 'I won't be the mother who thinks of herself when her daughter's life is not settled.'

There, under the gathering clouds, Jesus, quite literally, wept.

'But, you can't do this,' I exclaimed as she pushed me into the conservatory and out of the rain. 'Not now. Mum, this is the best thing that's happened to you.'

She hesitated. A short nod as she paused. 'No. That was having my daughters.' Tears sprouted from my eyes.

'Chalo, chalo,' she said. 'It's done and it's the right thing. Now be quiet and let me get on with my work.'

I couldn't believe it and had to call Maars.

'Listen, she's doing what she feels is best,' she said.

'You knew.'

She paused.

'But, Maars,' I said, sitting in my old room, 'it's wrong. More wrong than it felt when she said she was getting married in the first place.'

'I tried telling her you're a grown-up, but you know what she's like when she gets an idea in her head. She said it'd be a distraction. "*My children come before any man.*"'

'But I'm a thirty-one-year-old woman.'

'Well,' said Maars, as I heard Adam gurgling in the background, 'we'll always be children to her.'

I couldn't believe it. I've been so absorbed in the state of my marital collapse that it didn't occur to me Mum's relationship was also collapsing.

'Maars,' I said, 'this isn't right. I know we hated the idea but he was actually quite nice.'

She paused. 'I know, Sofe. If I'm honest, I think it's made me sadder than . . . well, what happened with you.'

If I was honest, I think I'd say the same.

8.15 p.m. Between Mum's newfound single status, Auntie Reena's budgies and my friends' various relationship issues, I needed to speak to him. I looked at Conall's name on my phone. He'd tell me what to say to Mum to persuade her to change her mind. He'd understand why this is all wrong. I tapped on his name and hung up before it had the chance to ring. *You can't just go back to him every time you need to know his thoughts on a thing.* That's not how it works. But I can practically feel my bones twitch. Every inch of me feels restless and unsure.

Thank God – Katie calling.

9 p.m. I have the answer! I'll go into spiritual seclusion! Not forever, obviously. Just for the last ten, most holy, days of Ramadan. Told Katie what happened and about my restless limbs, and she suggested I take up yoga. I don't think stretching my limbs is going to help so I told her about the concept of seclusion (aka itikaf) – going into your room or mosque and shutting yourself off from the world, devoting each moment to prayer. It feels like there's a lot to pray for and I don't even know where to start.

Because I'm not busy distracting myself with food my mind's throwing all kinds of questions at me. What does it all mean? What, for example, was the purpose of ever meeting Conall? After the hundreds of dates with stupid men, it felt like such a stroke of divine luck to end up with him. As if he was the culmination of all those wrongs made right. Maybe it's a sign that there is no right to a wrong – that there are just happenings – some good, some shit. (Oops. Shouldn't swear when fasting.) What was the point of Mum meeting her childhood sweetheart forty years later, only for her to end it?

Maybe it's my fault for trusting one person so fully. All this time people had me believe that getting married was growing up. The subtext to this is simply that you come face-to-face with human fallibility. What's more – you have to live with it.

Except I'm not living with it. I'm living with the remnants of what it's left behind. And now, even though she doesn't have to, so is my mum.

AUGUST

Come, All Ye Faithful

Muslim Marriage Book

If there's one thing I've learned, it's that there are two choices in marriage: to stay or to leave. Because no one changes and so you need to change your expectations. And if you don't, then you need to take them elsewhere. The grass is always greener, but if yours is looking a little parched, rather than gaze longingly at the side you can't ever reach why not get off your arse and water it.

Thursday 1 August

3.35 p.m. Major phone withdrawal symptoms. Keep reaching for it, then stop self and reach for Qur'an instead. Hope recitation counts when eyes are constantly flickering towards mobile. Diary entries are surely allowed as record of spiritual progress.

8.25 p.m. Chucked phone out of room with note to Foz to let everyone know they can only contact me through her if there's an emergency. What is the point of seclusion if you can't mentally seclude yourself from social media/WhatsApp, etc.?

11.50 p.m. Am sitting on bed, staring into space wondering *why* I met Conall. Because it's never the what (well, not usually); it's the *why*. That question could put someone in a padded cell. Which I kind of am right now. Minus the padding.

Friday 2 August

12.35 p.m. Wonder if he thinks about why I came into his life? Why *did* I come into his life?

Saturday 3 August

11.10 p.m. Perhaps the purpose is not to search for the 'why' but just embrace the result of it.

1.55 a.m. Just spent past half an hour crying for God knows what. Missed Dad, missed Conall, then thought about Mum next door, alone, and cried about that. Then I cried because I thanked God for Maars and the girls, which then made me cry more because what if no one manages to be happy? I was never naive enough to think life was going to be blissful post-marriage, but I never knew it'd be harder. Apparently when you invest more, you feel more, and so I guess you end up losing more.

Sunday 4 August

1.20 p.m. Just watched YouTube video of a woman scholar (of which, btw, there aren't enough) and she was having a go at the men who don't support their wives who want to study further – who want to make something of themselves – you know, those women for whom marriage isn't the only thing in life. Conall doesn't fit into that misogynist boat – but it did make me think how sometimes one person's life begins to mean more than the other's and that you must bring your own meaning. Thank God I never really believed in the adage, *Love conquers all.* It can barely conquer itself.

6.45 p.m. Was having a nap (sleep is not just a sign of depression) when the doorbell rang, and I heard Sean's voice as Foz opened the door. I got up and leaned against the door.

'What's *itti-calf*?' he asked.

Foz explained, which was followed by a moment of silence.

'I tried calling her but it was going to voicemail,' he said.

He did sound rather distressed. I opened the door – one foot outside the room, so I could see his side profile from over the bannister.

'She's upstairs?' He peered up as I stepped back into the room and closed the door. 'I just need five minutes.'

What happened?? Was Conall OK? Was it Eamonn? I had half a mind to go downstairs and ask myself.

'She can't come out,' said Foz. 'You can write her a note if it's urgent, but this is her time, really. To think.'

The doorbell rang again. When Foz opened it I heard Mum's voice. 'Sean, tell me. Won't he come back? Won't he think of my Soffoo?' I don't think I've ever heard such desperation in my mum's voice.

'No,' said Sean. 'That's the thing. I need to speak with her.'

I wanted to rush down the stairs, grab Sean by the shoulders and shake him. But what was the point? Time to dedicate yourself to the moment, Sofia Khan. I closed the door to shut out everyone's noise and lay back in bed. Don't concentrate on what's outside, but what's *inside.*

7.25 p.m. Got a note through the door from Fozia:

Sofe,

I know you're not allowed to speak to anyone (does my tosser of a brother even know you're doing this?)

When you're out of seclusion, itikaf – whatever it's called – you have to call me. We need to talk.

Sean

I folded the letter up and put it in the bedside drawer, heaving myself off the bed and decided to do ablutions and pray.

Monday 5 August

10.55 a.m. Another note through my door from Foz.

> *Hannah asked for you to pray for her adoption situation. Also, Suj (are we sure she's not secretly a Muslim?) said can you pray that she finds out whether Charles is cheating or not. (I know, but I'm just the messenger.) Think you know better than anyone what to pray for your mum – who, by the way, wants to turn the kitchen and conservatory into one room. Maria says you should just pray for yourself.*
> *Don't forget me.*
> *Love you xxx*

1.50 p.m. Had a moment of pathetic behaviour where I looked through Conall's drawer, took out a T-shirt and held it for a while. It still smells of him. Then I folded it up again and put it back in the drawer. Seems there's no answer to why certain things happen, but if I carry on with all this wondering I'll drive myself (and others) to bloody insanity.

Wednesday 7 August

12.35 a.m. Have watched back-to-back YouTube clips of stories from the Prophet's (peace be upon him) life. I thought I had problems – it doesn't quite compare to being socially ostracised and exiled. Also, it's not what happens in life, but how a person reacts to it. The poem 'If' came to mind (because who says literature has no place in Islamic learning?): '*If you can meet with Triumph and Disaster and treat those two impostors just the same . . .*' But where am I meant to muster that much patience and dignity, hmm, Rudyard?

12.40 a.m. Thought of Mum – though not exactly dignified, and often not patient, there is something resilient about her. I can settle for resilience.

Thursday 8 August

2.20 p.m. It's Eid tomorrow, so preparing to come out of seclusion. Swear I've forgotten what people look like. Read Foz's note again, making sure I've done as everyone asked (and more, hopefully). Prayed for Dad. Obviously. And Eamonn. Now I get why people go on retreats. It's not to find answers. What you have now *is* the answer. You go away to accept it.

So, things I've established in past ten days . . . Actually, it's just the one thing: don't think about what you've lost. Think of the things you still have. And what, if you look for it, you might find.

Friday 9 August
Eid

Things to do: *Finish book. Find next bestseller and become editorial star. Sort out Mum's love life. Give up biscuits. Fill each second of each day with forward momentum. DON'T LOOK BACK.*

10 a.m. The best cure to stop obsessing about getting married (when you're single), I've discovered, is getting married and going through a soul-destroying break-up. It's like when you binge on pizza and end by throwing up – you'll never want to look at pizza ever again. All those years spent fretting over meeting someone – the things you'll *need* – and turns out all you need is Eno salt.

10.10 a.m. OK, Eno salt and sex.

And maybe someone to hold on to.

11.25 a.m.

> **From: Sakib Awaan**
> **To: Sofia Khan**
> **Subject: Eid**
>
> Happy Eid, Sofia. Hope it's a good one.
> I'll give you the weekend off but I expect a full update on the marriage book on Monday ;)
> Sakib

Isn't it amazing what spirituality can sometimes do for a person. The book! Yes, of course you'll have the book!

(Things spirituality doesn't affect: feelings about men who use winky faces.)

3 p.m. Came back from visiting Dad's grave. I wonder: would he have shaken his head in disappointment at me? Gathered me in his arms and let me cry? Would he have told me to let it go or try harder? *Marriage is no joke. You made the commitment – do what you have to. Think of what your mama and I went through. We stuck by it until the end.*

Perhaps I wouldn't have let it go if Conall hadn't thought it was a mistake. Perhaps I'd have stood by him and weathered the marital storm because, well, it's Conall. It would've made me pathetic and maybe weak, but I think I'd have borne the label. *There's no choice here, though, Baba*, I whispered, looking at his dark grey marble headstone.

Beta, one thing I have learned in life is that there is always a choice.

I don't know where the tears came from but they streamed down my cheeks. I didn't sob, I was looking at the grave, thinking of all the things you can lose in a lifetime. But you still get out of bed in the morning; I think that is choice enough.

11.20 p.m. 'Darling,' said Foz, having come back from dinner with her family and me having settled into a food coma after dinner with mine. 'We need to talk.'

'What's happened now?' I sat up and looked at her face.

'Nothing.' She sat next to me, tucking one leg under the other. 'Everything's fine.'

She paused. 'Itikaf did you good,' she said.

I nodded.

'You're feeling better?' she asked.

I nodded again.

'You look better,' she added. She stared at me. Then she took a deep breath and leaned forward. 'Listen . . .'

'Oh my God, can you please just come out with it,' I said.

She paused again. 'Kam and I are getting married.'

A vision of fluorescent teeth and greasy hair flashed before me. There it was sitting on a stage; there again, standing at the end of the aisle; and then walking away, getting into a car. *Boom, boom, boom.* And all the while it was next to my beautiful, lovely Foz.

'Sofe?'

There were a few moments where my mouth refused to open. My brain seemed to be a tumult of conflicting directions: *say something; don't say anything; shake her; get your shit together*; *tell her to get her shit together.* Why must everyone do everything based on feelings? Feelings are life's worst road blocks.

'Come on, Sofe. Say what you have to say.'

'I . . . OK.'

She looked at me. 'OK?'

'I mean, you're throwing your life away to an unworthy cause, but fine.' I paused. 'It's your choice.'

Smiling at me and picking her handbag from the floor, she said, 'It is.'

There's nothing you can do or say; people always will do what they want, but it was time for acceptance.

'I'm going to bed now,' she said, standing up, still looking at me. 'I'll need to move out soon.'

'Move out?'

She sat back down again. 'We're getting married next month.'

'*Next month*? Why so soon?' I wish a person could give another some time for acceptance.

'I don't want to wait any more. Listen . . .' She put her hand on my leg. 'It's all going to be fine because in the end it'll just be all of us, in our old people's home, literally washing each other's shit. But, in the meantime, we need to get some stories to tell when we're old and grey.'

'Like "remember that time you married the guy with the gnashers?"'

She laughed and nodded. 'What about that time you ran away with a white guy?'

'Remember how I found out about the ex-wife and son at my wedding?'

It didn't quite make us laugh. Give it forty years.

'I can't believe you're leaving me on my own,' I added.

'Oh, darling.' She took both my hands in hers. 'I will *never* leave you on your own.'

But I could see her driving away in that car, waving back at me as she headed towards a semi-detached and two-point-four children; parking up next to all the other semi-detacheds with Han and Suj.

'No,' I said. 'I know.' Because even though it wasn't true, at least she believed it when she said it.

Saturday 10 August

12.50 p.m. I was in my room, working, and trying not to think about what I'd do after Foz left when the doorbell rang. Foz answered and I heard Sean's voice. Suddenly remembered his note to me. It's all very well being in the mood to move onwards and upwards, but it still feels like you're running on a treadmill when people keep popping back into your life. I prayed Foz would pretend I wasn't at home.

'Sofe,' she called out.

Maybe not.

'Good to know how long it takes you to call when it's an emergency,' he said, looking at me as I came into the living room.

'Sorry,' I replied. 'Got busy.'

'Can we talk?' he asked, glancing at Foz. 'In private.'

Foz said she had a few errands to run and left the house. I didn't want to talk in private. I didn't want to talk at all. I wanted to just *do*: write the book, get Mum back with her fiancé, read manuscripts. Maybe even learn to cook.

I sat down. So did he.

'It's about Conall,' he said.

I shot up off the sofa. 'Do you fancy some tea?'

'No. Thanks.'

As I went into the kitchen he followed me.

'Orange juice?' I added. 'Apple juice? Sparkling water?'

'What? No, I don't want anything.'

'How've you been?' I asked.

'Sofe, I'm worried about him,' he said.

Getting a mug out, I put a teabag into it. 'I have to say it feels weird eating and drinking again now Ramadan's over.'

'Are you hearing me?' he said, stepping forward, looking at me as I watched the kettle boil. No words seemed to make their way out of my mouth – this must be some kind of post-Ramadan effect.

'Something's not right.'

I remembered the smell of Conall's T-shirt and made a mental note to throw it out; put all of his things in a bin bag and store it in the attic. Give it to charity. Just get rid of it.

'Don't take this personally,' he said. 'I'm not judging, but you go about your Muslim-ness normal, like.'

'Muslim-ness?'

'You know. Moderate.'

He watched me pour the water into my mug. I turned to him.

'Sean, I just spent ten days locked in my room, praying to a being that most people think is a fairy tale. And not the sweet, happy-ending type. A Grimms-type fairy tale.'

He scratched the back of his neck, screwing up his face.

'I pray five times a day. Fast *eighteen* hours in the summer. Wear this piece of material around my head in the scorching heat, knowing that it's not unlikely that someone might one day beat me up for it.' I picked up my mug of tea, raising it to the ceiling. 'All in the name of this fairy tale.'

He took a deep breath. 'Well, you *act* normal.'

'Yeah, cheers,' I said, walking past him and back into the living room.

'No. You know what I mean. I'm not judging. It's grand. Really.' He paused. 'Eighteen hours, though? Christ.'

I put the mug down and folded my arms.

'Anyway, that's not my point. He's acting odd.'

When I asked what this oddness entailed, Sean basically mentioned all of the things I'd just listed. Minus the hijab. Obviously.

'Can you imagine what my ma is thinking? I was there last weekend and Eamonn's chemo isn't working too well, and Conall just says: "It's all in God's hands".'

Sean looked at me expectantly, as if this information should be alarming.

'Calm as anything,' he added, sitting down. 'And he's distant like.' He paused. 'Somewhere else.'

All Sean was telling me was that Conall was still a Muslim. The idea of it was comforting; he *is* consistent; he can be solid.

'Listen, it's not like I read those shitty tabloids, but Sofe . . .' He leaned forward, resting his arms on his legs and clasping his hands, reminding me so much of Conall that a big bubble of something seemed to be floating up within me, threatening to burst and smear my insides with . . . *feelings*. 'You hear stories of . . .'

I raised my eyebrows in expectation. 'What, Sean?'

'You need to talk to him,' he said.

I considered Sean for a moment. 'No,' I said. 'I don't.'

'Aren't you worried about him?'

I should give up my need to move on and go to him and make sure he's OK. I shook my head. 'No.'

'But you lo—'

'No,' I repeated. 'What he does, thinks, says – it's got nothing to do with me any more.'

All six foot of Sean seemed to deflate a little, as if a shot of air had been taken out of him. 'You don't mean that.'

I nodded. Perhaps I didn't, but one day I would. I must.

'Bu—'

'He's not lost his marbles, Sean,' I interrupted. 'Been radicalised – whatever you're thinking.' I mean, honestly.

Sean blushed as he looked at the floor, then stood up. I told him to stay but he said he had to go. Opening the door, he said: 'How do you know?'

'Because I *know* him,' I replied.

'We thought we knew him too. Then he . . .' He paused. 'He's not the same.'

I shrugged. 'I don't think any of us are.'

He seemed to hesitate for a moment. 'You know . . .'

'What?'

'Who he is now – it's everything to do with you.'

Monday 12 August

8.10 a.m. Spent majority of weekend with Maars in an attempt to get Mum to reconcile with Uncle Mouch. All I hear in response is: 'Until you are settled, I will never be settled.'

3.15 p.m. I think this marriage book might very well be finished (like my actual marriage) in another week. Emailed Sakib to let him know. He responded with: '*Fantastic ;)*'

I don't understand this sudden need to send winky faces.

8.20 p.m. Have gathered up all of Conall's things and put them in the attic. Foz helped me as she'd also started sorting her things out. All this shifting and moving around – where am I meant to go from here? I almost fell through the attic ceiling thinking about it.

Wednesday 14 August

4.10 p.m. Knocked on Mum's door.

Me: Mum, why don't you email Uncle Wasim to wish him a Happy Pakistan Independence Day?

Mum: Get lost.

Me: If I do, will you marry him?

Mum shuts door in my face.

Tuesday 20 August

11.10 p.m. I have, in true professional form, finished the book. It's almost impossible to read a book you've written about marriage without thinking about your husband, no matter how many of his items you've hidden from sight. But it's the penultimate episode of this life series. It could only include one other thing.

To: Conall O'Flynn
From: Sofia Khan
Subject: House

Hi,
Wanted to let you know that I'll be moving out at the end of next month. Date tbc, but I'll let you know and you can organise tenants or whatever you need.

I looked at the email.

I hope Eamonn is doing better.
Sofia.

11. 35 p.m.

To: Sofia Khan
From: Conall O'Flynn
Subject: Re: House

Hi.

Thanks for letting me know. When you have the date, drop me a line.

Conall.

Hain?? Is that it? I charged into Foz's room. She was on the phone, changing into her pyjamas, as I shoved my phone's screen in her face. She looked at it.

'Let me call you back,' she told someone.

'Can you believe it?' I exclaimed.

She reread it. 'Right.'

'I mean can you *actually* believe it? As if he wasn't my husband, but some man I'd met on a date or something.'

'But isn't it a good thing?'

'How is this good?'

I looked at the email again as she took a seat on the edge of her bed. 'He's moving on.'

My gaze rested on her.

'Now you just need to read it over and over to do the same.'

Wednesday 21 August

11.20 a.m.

From: Sakib Awaan

To: Sofia Khan

Subject: Book

Thanks for sending this through. Read the first few pages and I think I love it already.

Well done.

Sakib

I don't know why but I wanted to print that email out and pin it on my wall. It can go alongside Conall's email from last night.

Monday 26 August

11.45 a.m. 'I think it's better than the dating book,' said Sakib, squinting because of the sun in his eyes. He moved his chair round, joining me in the shade.

'Why?' I said.

He shaded his eyes and I pushed my chair back a bit – close proximity and all that. 'It's just more insightful – more depth,' he replied.

'Oh.'

The waitress came with his lemonade and my milkshake. He reached into his briefcase and brought out a manuscript. 'Can you read this and report back tomorrow?'

'Tomorrow?'

He took a sip of his drink, lifting his little finger as he did so. Picking up the MS, I looked at the last page – four hundred and thirty-six.

'Might just need a few days.'

'I'm on a deadline with this, Sofia. I need to know you can work with me.'

'Right.' I put the MS in my bag and stood, picking up my milk-shake. 'Guess I should make a start on it.'

'Wait,' he said, following suit. 'Why don't you read it in my office?'

'Why?'

'Because I get lonely.'

The concern must've shown on my face as I put my sunglasses on.

'I'm joking,' he said, straight-faced.

His jokes are very hard to get sometimes.

'Oh.'

'You can tell me your thoughts as you go along. And anyway,' he added as we began to walk back to the offices, 'it'd be good to have a bit more structure to your working hours. Don't you think?'

Words like *structure* give me hives. 'Not sure if that's necessary,' I said.

We reached the front of the building and he opened the doors for me. 'I think it is.'

Friday 30 August

8.20 a.m. Oh my fucking days. If I believed in reincarnation, I'd think that Sakib was a fascist in his previous life. I've read four manuscripts since Monday and am in the office already, with number five. On top of which it's really difficult to get comfortable on the sofa in someone else's office. Every time I laugh, or say something, he throws me this withering look, to which I respond with: 'I can work from home.' And he just says, 'It's fine.'

Plus, I still don't have a house to live in, and living with Mum again would send me over the edge, even though she insists it's the right thing to do. Imagine: mother and daughter, living together and getting over their respective collapsed relationships. Shudder.

One more look from him and I'll throw the manuscript in his face.

9.45 a.m. He sighed. Really loudly.

'I don't think I get paid enough for this,' I said.

'Nor do I,' he replied, putting an elastic band around a bunch of papers. 'What are your thoughts so far?'

'Hard to form amidst all the sighing.'

'So you can't work like this?'

I looked up. 'Having my own desk might be nice. So I don't end up walking like a ninety-year-old before I'm thirty-five.'

'What else?'

I settled my hands on the manuscript. 'Coffee and a muffin if I'm expected to start work before nine thirty.'

'And?'

'My own office and a huge sign on the front that says *Queen of the World*.'

Sakib didn't look very impressed. Someone had obviously fallen off the wrong side of the bed. 'Queens don't put their shoes on someone else's sofa,' he said, looking at my pumps.

I made rather a point of shifting my feet off the sofa, standing up and brushing down the beige suede.

'OK, OK,' he said. 'I get the point.'

Amazing what happens within a week when you're practically locked in a room with someone eight hours a day.

'You can put your shoes back on the sofa,' he said.

I put my hands out. 'No, *no*. I wouldn't dream of dirtying your sofa with my scummy shoes.'

'*Please*,' he said, joining his hands as if in prayer.

I sat back on the sofa, picking up the manuscript again.

'Put your shoes up,' he repeated

'Nope,' I replied.

He shot up off his seat and grabbed my ankles.

'Oh my God, what the hell are you doing?' I exclaimed, laughter escaping as he swivelled my legs on to the sofa.

He held on to my ankles, pressing them against the sofa. I looked at him and realised that Sakib is, beneath it all, a little mad.

'Keep your shoes on the sofa, *please*. Or I won't hear the end of it.'

Just then there was a knock on the door as it opened. Katie's head popped through, seeing me splayed on the sofa and Sakib with his hands clasped around my ankles. He straightened up and cleared his throat.

'Oh. Sorry,' she said, throwing me a look.

'That's quite OK,' he replied.

I was still a little shocked by Sakib's display of madness.

'They're starting the digital meeting now,' she said.

'I'll just get my notepad and be with you.'

Katie gave me another look before turning round.

'I'll have a coffee on your way back,' I said.

He'd grabbed his notebook and pen. 'You don't ask for much, do you?'

'Got to take what you can,' I said.

When I looked up he was standing over me, one hand in his pocket. 'And that's exactly why, when I leave this place, I'm taking you with me.'

SEPTEMBER

Opportunity Knocks

Monday 2 September

10.45 a.m. 'I did things the wrong way round last week,' he said as soon as I walked into the office. He gestured for me to take a seat.

'The thing is, Sofia . . .' He looked at me. 'Since Husna left it's made me re-evaluate everything.'

I know how that feels.

'She used to be the only one I ever really wanted to be with.'

'"Ever" is a vast word for someone who's only in their thirties,' I replied.

He rubbed his wedding ring for a while as he nodded. 'I've played it too safe in life – studying law when I really wanted to be an editor. Ever regret a thing like that?'

'Not really,' I said.

'Never?'

I shook my head.

'You *never* regretted anything?'

'There's my marriage – but I'm beginning to get over it.' This wasn't particularly truthful. It just seemed like the right thing to feel, under the circumstances.

'Don't you say the most charming things?'

I gave the best smile I have – which, according to Conall, looks like I'm constipated.

'I don't want to leave the world without a mark,' he said.

I leaned forward. 'Are you dying?'

'No.' He looked over my shoulder at the office door and lowered his voice. 'I don't want to do this for the rest of my life – working for other people, always looking for the bottom line. They talk about bringing diversity but they're still the ones who get to choose what type.'

'It's the way the story goes,' I replied. 'Quite literally.'

He sat back. 'Don't you care?'

'Of course I care.'

'Don't you want to do something about it?'

'I want to do something about many things.'

He stood up and started pacing the room as he looked at me. 'I want to launch a publishing company.' He paused, as if waiting for my reaction.

'Oh. That's . . . that's great.'

'Specifically for authors from ethnic minorities. There'll be schemes which give opportunities that people like you and I never had when we were younger.'

He looked at me, eyes sparkling with excitememnt.

'Imagine: first-off, Muslim authors only. All of them – white, black, gay, lesbian, whatever. Then we introduce all ethnic minorities. And then,' he said, leaning his hands on the desk and looking into my eyes, 'we take over the world.'

'We?'

He nodded. 'At first I thought I'd move and take this idea to Dubai because Husna loves it there and she has her family home – and God knows they need a bit of culture . . .' He sat back down and looked at me rather intently. 'But then I realised: fix what you need to fix at home first. Don't get me wrong. London's not what it used to be – especially when you're Muslim.' He took off his glasses, tapping them on the table. 'All this social angst is just a prelude to something bigger. Probably worse.'

'Aren't you the harbinger of joy,' I replied.

He smiled and, don't take this the wrong way, but he had a twinkle in his eye. It suited him.

'That's why I want you to do it with me.'

I must've looked perturbed as he got flustered and said, 'I mean come and work with me. I wouldn't be able to pay you much to begin with, but if it's a risk you're willing to take . . .'

'Work?' I said, making sure I hadn't misheard anything. 'With you?'

It was so unexpected. I had a hundred questions: How would it be organised? Where would our office be? Where would we even begin? What would happen to my book?

'I've spoken in confidence to Dorothy – or, as you like to call her, Brammers –'

Sakib is a very disapproving person, isn't he?

'She'll handle things with that. Don't worry. I wouldn't do anything that might jeapordise things for you. But I will need you to be there from the beginning while I work my notice. I don't want to wait around. Can you handle it?'

I didn't know – I was still trying to grasp it all. What a risk he was taking! Funding this all by himself. There was something about the urgency in his voice that gave me a sense of urgency too. Who knew if I could do this? But wouldn't it be exciting to try? Not write about about *my* dating and *my* marriage but be a part of something new and different. Of all the questions one specific one came to mind. 'Why me?'

He adjusted his tie. 'I like you. In a strictly professional sense, of course,' he added rather quickly.

I mean, calm down, love. The feeling is mutual. So what if he has a nice face?

'How you work and the kind of books you love are different from mine.' He leaned forward. 'I think we'd make a good team. Don't you?'

Something fluttered in my stomach. I had the sudden urge to hug him and say *thank you* because you don't realise how deflating it can be when no one wants you until someone finally does (in whatever capacity, really). He looked away as he noticed my tears surface. I just nodded. 'Yes. I do.'

7.15 p.m. I looked at the room with Mum, Auntie Reena, Maars and Tahir in it.

'Le,' said Mum. 'You never listen to me. Women your age are making fifty, sixty, seventy thousand pounds and you will be earning like you have just started working. I told her,' added Mum, looking at Auntie Reena. 'People do banking – stock-breaking. O-ho, like that Sameena.'

'You must let children do what they want,' said Auntie Reena.

'She is, and now look,' said Mum.

'Are you sure you want to do this thing with Sakib?' asked Maars.

It's as if my marital mistake has made my family question all my decision-making abilities. My heart beat faster. What if they were right? Was I just being impulsive? Jumping head first? Whatever you do in life, be resolute. Whether that's leaving your husband or starting a new job.

'I mean, you've been a bit all over the place, haven't you?' Maars added. 'You need head space for this kind of thing, right?'

I wavered and then steeled myself. 'No. This is what I'm going to do,' I said, hoping I sounded more convinced than I felt.

Mum shook her head at me.

'Well then,' Maria said. 'What do you need? Shall we go office furniture shopping?'

'You'll need decent insurance,' said Tahir. 'Give me Sakib's number – my mate can give him a discount.'

Thanks to God for Maars and even Tahir.

Thursday 5 September

8.10 a.m. Bloody hell. I have manuscripts coming out of my ears. I thought being a reader for Sakib was bad – try being your own bloody boss. On top of which I don't know where I'm going to live!

7.50 p.m. We pulled up outside Sakib's house.

'Do you need to get something before we go to the new office?' I asked.

He took off his seat belt and with a huge smile said: 'What do you think starting out a company means?'

Turns out he wants to use his *home* as an office.

'What about your wife?' I asked.

He got out of the car. 'Are you going to stay in the car?'

'God, you're bossy.'

'Don't worry. I've spoken to her. She plans to stay in Dubai – starting out a fashion label. And I have enough saved to cover the mortgage for a while as we get started.'

He led me into the house, past the kitchen to another room that looked out into the garden.

'I'll get two desks here,' he said, squaring out his arms, eyes in deep concentration. 'We'll have plenty of light coming in.'

I looked round at the panels, light wooden flooring (real, naturally), flowers potted everywhere. He turned to me, resting his hands on his hips. It reminded me of Conall. It all felt so small and uncertain. The garden and panelling began to lose some of its sheen as the reality of what I was about to do began to set in. Something this serious can't just be a distraction from life; it has to be a part of it.

'This is about building something,' he said, looking at me earnestly. 'It'll be hard work, but God, it'll be fun.'

'What, with you constantly breathing loudly every time I say something?'

'OK, I'll stop doing that.'

But then . . . the idea of building something of your own – putting your heart and soul into something other than a bloody marriage.

'Oh, before I forget.'

He rushed out of the room and returned a few minutes later with a rectangle frame, handing it to me, a look of mischief on his face. I turned it over and laughed. I mean, really laughed. It was a sign: *Queen of the World.*

'Let's hope one day you pay me like a queen as well,' I said, looking at him. He was so excitable that it began to catch on. 'What will we call it?' I asked.

He paused. 'What do you think of *Avaaz*?'

'*Voice*?' I said.

'Too cheesy?' he asked.

'Totally.'

He looked into the garden, concentrating.

'But sod it,' I said. 'Let's use it.'

He turned round. 'Really?'

'Yes. Let's be brown and cheesy. Just once in our life.'

Then he did something entirely unexpected. He strode up to me and hugged me. I couldn't help but hug him back. As we let go I composed myself. 'Right. We're really doing this then?' I said.

He looked serious for a moment. 'If you're sure you want to. It's a big commitment.'

It occurred to me: if you do a thing, then do it well; put your all into it – just like Conall used to. I nodded, thinking about the money I'd received from the second book – how I could actually put it to good use. 'If this is something we're building, though,' I said, 'then I want it to be mine as well.'

That's when he went from being my boss, to being my business partner. Something lifted in my heart. A lightness. One without patches of dark. It was hope springing – right here, in what would be our office. My office. I looked at the sign and you know what it brought? Meaning.

I was about to be queen of my own world.

Saturday 7 September

2.45 p.m. Went to Mum's for lunch and Maars came over too.

'Soffoo,' said Mum. 'Now at least you must move back home? If you put all your money in a new business how will you survive?'

I looked at Mum, her rationality a blight on my freedom. 'But –'

'Listen,' interrupted Maars, 'if you want to do this – I mean, *really* want to do this, then you have to make some compromises. Right?'

I nodded. Mum tried to suppress her smile. Maybe she wanted me around more for herself than me? The thought hadn't occurred to me before.

'OK,' I said, looking at Mum. 'Time for me to move back home.'

I must focus on the bigger picture. It's just added ammunition to make the business venture work. This, after all, is my freedom at stake.

Sunday 15 September

11.15 p.m. The troops came to help me move my stuff into Mum's at the same time as Foz was moving hers into Kam's flat. We both have a lot of shit. Well, *had* a lot of shit. I've purged my life of extraneous items – in the physical sense. It's the step you take before purging yourself of extraneous emotional items. This is moving forward; leaving behind the house that was your husband's. Although moving back into your mother's feels a lot like regressing.

I watched Katie seal up a box, scrawling *Books* on to it with a marker pen. She looked at it for a moment before adding *Classics*. 'Genre is important,' she said. 'Moving and organising things is what I live for.'

She wasn't being ironic. Love Katie.

'Is your brother-in-law going to take the heavy things next door?' she asked.

'Yes, I guess he should. Is it very heavy?'

She put the lid on the marker and looked at me, her face flushed. 'Well, I'm sort of carrying a baby, so don't think I should carry anything else for a bit.'

I almost fell off the bed.

'Foetus, actually – more accurately speaking,' she added.

'You're *preggers*?'

She nodded, smiling, and looking at me in utter joy.

'Oh my God, you're having a baby!' I exclaimed, pushing myself – in a rather ungainly manner – off the bed and into her arms.

'Early days – it's only been seven weeks, but I had to tell you. Obviously.'

'Why are you here? Why aren't you resting? You shouldn't be *moving* things.'

She waved the marker at me. 'I'm pregnant, not an invalid.'

'I needed some good news. Is Tom over the moon?'

'He's not said one negative thing about general life since we found out.'

'That's quite something,' I said. 'Can I text him?'

'Yes, of course. He'll be thrilled. He's walking around with his chest puffed out as if *he's* going to push something the size of a melon out of his vagina.'

I got my phone out and composed a message to him, feeling, for the first time in a long time, as if there was some kind of hope. Apparently some of it can be found in one sperm and one egg coming together.

'Just one thing,' said Katie.

I looked up at her.

'Tom and I have been talking about this for the past week, and I wanted us to decide before I told you.'

I pressed 'send' as I nodded.

'And feel free to say no if it's too much – it's just that we feel that you'd be the best person for it.'

'What?' I asked.

'We'd love it if you could be the godmother.'

Hain?

'*Me?*'

'Yes. You.'

'Godmother?'

'Yes.'

'To your baby?'

'No, Sweetu – our dog.'

People talk of milestones in life – graduating from university, getting your first job, buying a house, getting married, etc. – but no one really thinks about the milestones that are offered to you. And how they can mean so much more when they're unprecedented.

'Sarcasm doesn't suit you,' I said, barely able to control my tears.

'Well?'

'You're really sure?'

'You don't realise how much we love you. Anyway, no one else would be quite the right fit.'

The question 'why' they did came to mind, but I am far too grateful to want to give myself the evil eye.

'Hang on,' I said. 'Can you have a Muslim godmother?'

She thought for a moment. 'Changing times, Sweetu. We're making new rules now.'

From Tom: Cheers, Tinker. Can you wear a properly bling Pakistani outfit at the christening? We're gonna show 'em how it's done. Tom xx

With a lot of rapture, a few tears and more gushing than is appropriate to record, I accepted the role of being another human being's spiritual and moral guide.

I closed the door to Conall's house, posting the keys through the letterbox and entering Mum's house once again. As I stood in the passage it was as if nothing had changed in two years since before I even knew Conall's name. Sitting on my bed, in my old bedroom, I wondered how you can be in the same place where you started yet with an entirely new path set out in front of you.

For the first time in a long time, I am going to sleep with a smile on my face.

Thanks to God.

Tuesday 17 September

8.25 a.m. I'd forgotten how much the damn house phone rings. Moving back home could be the thing that drives me to insanity.

8.40 a.m.

From Sakib: I hope you're awake. Get ready. I've taken holiday and we're going office supply shopping.

Oh my God, if it wasn't so inappropriate I might've kissed him if he were in front of me.

9.40 a.m. Maars is upset that I'm going office furniture shopping without her so I told her to come with us.

Sakib might as well get used to Khan family interference.

6.45 p.m. 'Your sister,' said Sakib. 'She sure can bargain-hunt.'

Maars went back home as Sakib and I went to his house and had to carry through two new desks. I accidentally hit the corner of the box on the bannister. I heard Sakib inhale rather dramatically.

'Oops. Sorry.'

'It's fine. Don't worry.'

I looked at the chip. 'You can just paint over it.'

'Sofia, it's *fine*.'

I walked backwards with the box in hand. 'OK, you need to stop pushing.'

He flinched as the box knocked against the kitchen door.

I put my end of the box down as he did the same.

'You're going to have to accept that sometimes in life things get chipped,' I said.

'That's a really expensive door,' he replied, walking up and rubbing the wood.

'Fucking hell.'

'Please don't swear.'

'Sakib,' I said, putting my hands on my hips. 'There are two things you need to come to terms with.'

He lifted an arm and rested his hand on the door.

'Things are going to get chipped and I'm going to swear.'

'It's just not very ladylike.'

I raised my eyebrows.

'Fine. But you'll have to come to terms with the fact that I care when things get chipped.'

I watched him for a while. 'Fine.'

We settled the box into the office and I watched as he opened it up. He ripped the tape and laid out the pieces of the desk on the floor. 'How good are you at fixing things?'

I looked at him, holding up two of the table legs in my hands. 'I'm about to learn.'

9.10 p.m. When I got home Mum was standing with Adam in her arms.

'Hey, monkey,' I said, taking him from her. 'What's he doing here?' I asked.

'What am I here for but to look after your children and do your work for you? People say when children get married you are free.'

'He's not *my* baby,' I said, then looked at Adam and whispered, 'Of course you're my baby.'

Mum was looking into the distance. 'All your life you work, work, work. Then you are old and almost dead.' She looked at me. 'Where is the time to enjoy?'

When I began the Uncle Mouch conversation she stopped me, as per.

'Then you can't complain,' I said. 'Don't blame me for the choices you make.'

'You don't understand what responsibilities are. When you have your own children, then you will know.'

I might've exhaled.

She shook her head. 'Every year you are starting your life over again. Sometimes a husband, sometimes a job, and here I am doing the same thing every day and who notices? What do I get?'

'Well, *we* notice,' I said as Adam started whining. I took the seat next to her and added, 'It's not too late. It's not like Uncle Wasim's going to marry someone else. Better get in there.'

'Life isn't like this, Soffoo. You can't break things and make things when you want. You think – if Conall came to you now and said sorry, you would listen?'

It only just began to dawn on me; Mum had broken off her engagement for my sake and now she regretted it.

'We tried forty years ago and we tried now and it wasn't in our kismet.'

I watched her, looking at the blank TV screen, as I squeezed Adam's hand in mine.

The thing is, sometimes, you make your own kismet.

Wednesday 18 September

7.30 a.m. And sometimes this kismet means swallowing a little bit of pride and making a phone call you never thought you'd have to make. Isn't it just the way life goes: the only person who can help me reverse my mum's regret is bloody Hamida. Or, it would be, if she ever answered her phone.

9.10 a.m. 'Sofia?' said Sakib, waving at me. 'I still have another job to go to so can you do that or not?'

'What?'

'Develop that spreadsheet?'

'Oh. Yes. Sure.'

'You'd probably better put your phone in the drawer.'

I pointed at him. 'You're not my boss so you can't tell me what to do any more.'

'I don't think I ever could,' he mumbled.

I glanced at my phone again.

'Is that Conall's call you're waiting for? It's no wonder he doesn't want to speak to you with your charming moods.'

'Where the hell are the staplers?' I said.

Sakib stood up. 'I'd tell you to organise your desk a little better, but I'm not your boss any more.'

I was looking under all my papers and found them before I shook them at him. He stood there while I put them in the stapler, only they weren't the right size.

'Bastard thing.' I slammed the stapler on the desk and went back to my emails. 'It's not Conall's call I'm expecting.'

He picked up his briefcase (what does he even have in there?). 'Moving on already?'

I looked up at him pretty fast. What was that supposed to mean?

'I'm still married.' As the words came out of my mouth I realised: I'd moved out of the house, Conall was now in Ireland and yet we were still married. This wasn't right.

'Ignore me,' he said, raising his hand and making his way out of the door. 'I just thought maybe you were going to . . . I don't know. Forget it.'

He left the house, but forgetting didn't exactly come very easily.

10.05 a.m. Why isn't bloody Hammy picking up her damn phone??

3.50 p.m. Have called her about ten times and also texted her, but nothing. Maybe will have to ask Sean if he's been in touch, but really, last thing I need is a conversation with him on how worried he is about Conall.

Friday 20 September

9.40 a.m.

> **To: Hannah; Foz; Suj:** My God, I need a fag. Working with Sakib could lead me to much worse, I tell you.

9.50 a.m.

> **From Hannah:** Ooh, is there sexual tension sizzling?
>
> **From Suj:** You dirty cow!
>
> **From Foz:** Is something actually going on here? Darling, maybe you should think about speaking to Conall . . . I mean, to be able to move on.

Honestly. These girls would have me marry a tree if they could.

6 p.m. Sakib came back and kept giving me weird looks over his computer screen. He smiled and looked at his empty plate before looking back at me.

'You know what I think sometimes?'

I waited for him to continue.

'Never mind.'

'No, what?' I said.

'I sometimes think you can be a little –'

Just then I received a message.

From Suj: I can't fucking believe it. It's true. He was cheating on me.

'Is everything OK?' he asked.

I said I had to go and make an important phone call and dashed out of the room.

'What the hell happened?' I said when Suj picked up the phone.

She'd been right. She said she got so mad she can't even remember what she said to him. Just that he left with a cut on his brow because she threw a picture frame at him.

'Everything OK?' asked Sakib when I walked back into the office.

I nodded, staring into the computer screen. Poor, poor Suj.

'You sure?' he added.

I looked up at him. 'Just a friend having a few problems.'

'Ah. Well, feel free to go make any calls you need.'

12.10 a.m. I went over to Foz's – we tried to get Suj to come over but she said she was going out with some girls from work. Then I got a call from her five minutes ago.

'Toffeeeeeee. I love you so much. Did you know that? Did you know how much I love you?'

'Where are you?' I asked.

'I *love* you. No-mie! Nay-oh-mi! I'm speaking to my *best* friend in the *world*.'

I mouthed to Foz that Suj was on the phone.

'Will you still make your salads in our old people's home?' said Suj.

'She's pissed,' I whispered to Foz.

'No, Toffee, I'm not! I just love you.'

Quiet.

'What are you looking at?' Suj shouted, presumably at a passer-by. 'Do you have a fucking problem with brown people?'

'Suj, listen to me. Where are you? Are you safe?'

'No one's safe in this world because it's full of wankers.'

Foz got up. 'Do we need to get her from somewhere?'

'Suj, tell me where you are and Foz and I will come and collect you.'

'Is Foz there? Oh, I *love* her. Give her the phone, Toffee. Did you know she says she's worried about you?'

Foz must've heard her and went to take the phone from me. I nudged her away.

'I told her, Toffee. I said, "Don't worry about our Soffee Toffee. She is always OK!" You are, aren't you? Because if you're not I'm going to fly to Ireland and drag Conall back because, Toffee, I swear you guys are meant to be. Oh, it's Hannah calling. Hannah! I love you!'

'It's still me, Suj.'

Then the phone beeped as she hung up. Foz was already messaging Hannah when I put the phone down. We both looked at each other.

'Right,' I said, getting up. 'I'll put my scarf on and you get the keys.'

Saturday 21 September

4.20 a.m. God Almighty. All this activity has given me a stomach ulcer. I picked up a KitKat from the kitchen drawer before Foz and I went looking for Suj. Foz looked at me and then at the KitKat.

'It's to line my stomach,' I said.

Hannah told us that she gleaned Suj was near a club in Mayfair. After much googling, driving around and calling Suj, she finally called us back. She was outside Charles's house.

We made our way back to the car. 'This is why no good comes from drinking,' I said.

Foz got in the driver's seat and started the engine. 'Don't tell me you couldn't do with one right about now.'

Suj sat in her parked car. I got into the passenger's side as Foz got into the back. Suj was staring out of the window at what I presumed was Charles's house

'What are we looking for?' asked Foz.

'Lights,' replied Suj.

I leaned over Suj to take in the view of the house. 'It's quite big, isn't it? The house, I mean.'

Suj looked at me, the rim of her eyes red, her eyeliner still immaculate. 'Is Hannah at home?'

I nodded.

Foz got out her phone and called her. 'Yeah, no, what? *No*, I'm not passing on that message.'

Suj turned round as Foz stared at her for a few moments. She sighed. 'Han says that you should put sugar in his petrol tank.'

'Hang on,' said Foz as she put Hannah on loudspeaker.

'What you want to do is get some superglue to glue his windscreen wipers to the screen. Sorry.' She lowered her voice. 'Omar's friends are over. And you can also superglue the locks. Don't forget the boot. But you'll need lots of glue for that. One per lock, I'd say.'

'It'd have to be strong,' said Suj.

'Of course,' replied Han.

I peered over at Foz, who was shaking her head.

'Or you could just actually slash the tyres?' I suggested.

'*Sofe*,' said Foz.

'I'm joking! Look at me, Suj. Look at me.'

She turned my way.

'Vandalism is *not* the answer.'

When I looked into her eyes, though, there was such hurt that anger surged into my veins. In that moment I wished I had a knife so I could slash his tyres for her.

'How could he do this to me?' she said, tears in her eyes. 'Why does he think he can get away with it?'

Foz reached out for Suj's arm. 'This isn't going to help anyone.'

It was the rational versus the passionate.

'Unfortunately, Foz's right,' came Han's voice. 'Plus, he has a restraining order against you so you should probably leave.'

'A restraining order?' exclaimed Foz.

'Was I not meant to say anything?' said Han.

Bloody hell. This was news to me. I told Suj to start the engine – one of us would stay with her and the other would follow her back home. But she just sat there. Foz looked at me nervously. Just then the lights of Charles's house came on, a figure appearing at the window. In an instant Suj was out of the car and strode towards his house in her four-inch heels, picking up a rock and throwing it at his window.

'Shit,' said Foz, as we both followed her out.

Charles appeared at his door. 'What the fuck are you doing? You're not meant to be here.'

A rather long argument ensued, Foz and I standing a few feet away like her entourage.

We heard sirens in the distance.

'That's the police,' he said. 'Leave now or you'll get arrested.'

Suj scoffed as Foz said she was getting the car. Even in my mode of panic I had a quiet but deep admiration for Suj's unflappability. It almost made me want to update my Facebook status. But there's a time and a place for everything and the sirens were getting louder.

'I'm telling you, Suj. Don't make it worse.'

'*Me*? I've made it worse. You fucking cu—'

Foz pulled up and rolled down her car window. 'Get in!'

'Suj, let's go,' I said, pulling her away from him, the sound of the sirens getting ever closer.

'I'm sorry,' he said, with such sincerity that I wondered what went wrong and why I wasn't here for her – in a proper way – to know?

I leaned into her ear: 'We'll come back. We'll slash his tyres. Whatever you want.'

She raised her head: defiant, proud. My Suj. 'Fuck this shit. Let's go.'

And we would have done too, if that hadn't been the moment when his new girlfriend appeared at the door.

Being in an actual prison – not just the prison of your mind – changes a person. Especially when your ex-boss/current business partner shows up. He was the only person I could call who'd be at all useful given his short stint in law.

'A restraining order against your friend?' he said as he sat next to me in the interview room. 'And you actually accused the police officer of arresting you because you're Muslim?'

I smiled at him, as emphatically as possible. 'Oops.'

'Have Foz and Suj given a statement?'

'I don't know. They were in a different cell and I don't have supersonic hearing.'

'Perhaps you can be sarcastic on Monday?' he said.

'Sorry. I know this isn't the time, but do you have any chocolate?'

'Are you joking?'

'Sorry. I left my KitKat in the car. It's for my stomach lining.'

'Have *you* said anything?'

'No. I thought I'd exercise my civil rights.'

'Well, common sense prevails.'

He shook his head. I was reminded of Conall.

'You're lucky he's not pressing charges against any of you. It didn't take much persuading, to be honest.'

I looked at my hands, shame personified. 'Thank you,' I mumbled.

He looked at me. 'You know, a criminal record will increase the business insurance.'

Sakib dropped me and Foz home (it apparently being easier to explain to my mum why I was coming home at four in the morning than to Foz's parents). We got out of the car when my phone rang. I picked it up.

'Hello?' I said.

'Hi.'

'Hi.' I sat back. It was Hammy! '*Hi.*'

Thanks to God!

'Is everything OK?' she asked. 'I was out of Karachi.'

'Next time maybe suggest therapy for your friend Suj,' said Sakib to Foz.

'Oh, are you busy?' she asked. 'Shit, sorry. I just realised it's four in the morning there.'

'How are you?' I said. For some unknown reason the familiarity of her voice made me feel *nice* towards her.

Then, as if he were talking to a child, Sakib exclaimed, 'Sofia, *who* is calling you at this time?'

'Hello?' she said.

'Sorry,' I replied.

'Who was . . . never mind,' she said.

I saw Mum's shadow lurk behind her bedroom blinds before I saw her face peek through them.

Sakib cleared his throat. 'Sofia – seriously?'

'This is important,' I said to him. Didn't he know my mum's happiness depended on it??

He looked at Foz and raised his arms to the sky. 'Is she always like this?'

'Listen, I need to speak to you, Hamida.'

'Yeah, sure. Have you spoken to Con?'

Even the moment I was feeling real gratitude towards Hamida, I wanted to hit something when she mentioned his name.

'No, it's not about him.'

'I think –'

But before she could finish Mum's front door opened and she appeared with rollers in her hair, bending down, looking at us all in the car.

'Shit,' I said. I opened the car door.

'Haw . . . what are you doing?' exclaimed Mum.

It felt very busy for four o'clock in the morning. Foz was in the process of explaining something or another to Mum and then Sakib walked over to them. Mum's frown eased. I wondered what utterly embarrassing comment she might be coming out with to Sakib.

'Hello?' said Hammy

'Soffoo,' Mum called out. 'At least shut the car door.'

Sakib looked over at me and adjusted his glasses. Foz made staccato head movements; I'm assuming to get me off the phone and join the so-called party.

'Sorry,' I said. 'Can I call you later?'

She paused. 'Fine.'

It didn't sound like she thought it was fine but when I said thank you, I really meant it.

11.35 a.m. I called Hamida back and told her that I needed to be in touch with Uncle Mouch. I could've got in touch with him via Facebook but it seemed better if Hammy spoke to him – ease him in before I contacted him directly – seeing as he seemed to care about her so much.

'I liked your mum,' she said.

Which really is a wonder, to be honest.

'She was kind to me,' she added.

'She regrets it, Hamida,' I said. 'It was because of me and, you know, what's happened with Conall.'

There was a crackling down the line.

'Listen, Uncle's been good to me. It's not my place to say anything to him which might upset him,' she said.

'I know, but when he spoke about you he seemed to really care and I thought maybe . . .'

More crackling and a longer pause.

'Sofia, I might say something now that you don't like, but I'll say it anyway.'

I paused. 'OK.'

'If you and Conall are over, then please just divorce him.'

'Excuse me?'

'He's been this great friend to me and hearing him the way he is . . . it's not good for him.'

'Hamida, he's the one who left *me*.'

'I know there are always two sides to a story, but to be honest, I'm not interested in your side.'

The bluntness somewhat disabled a response from me. Incredible, isn't it? Conall lies to me, turns round and tells me about a family he has, that he should never have married me and he *still* manages to be people's favourite. I sometimes wonder if people would be so forgiving towards him if he were brown.

'Do it and I'll speak to Uncle Wasim. As I said, I liked your mum.'

Was this *blackmail*?

'What are you gaining from staying married to him?' she said. 'You wouldn't talk to him when Sean asked you; you don't care, so what's stopping you?'

'If he wants a divorce, then he can pick up the phone and say it to me himself – three simple words and it's done.'

She gave a small laugh down the phone. 'You're something else, Sofia. He'll stay married to you for fifty years before he does that. Yaar, just do it. You'll be free and so will he.'

I paused.

'Anyway, I said what I needed to say,' she said.

'Will you speak to Uncle Wasim?'

The house phone rang and Mum picked it up. I heard her say, 'Haan, just very tired with the same, same work.'

'I have to go,' I said, with which I put the phone down.

12 p.m. Sod Hammy and her blackmail! I'm going to find Uncle Wasim myself.

12.40 p.m. Ugh. Have just trawled through Mum's Facebook account and can't find him. Then went through all Pakistan relatives' accounts in case there were mutual friends. Also did a search for him, but didn't know his surname and there are about a million Wasims.

1.15 p.m. 'A divorce?' said Katie when I called her.

'Yes.'

'He just has to say he divorces you three times and it's done?' she asked.

'Yes.'

'This sounds very efficient. And you can just do it over the phone?'

'Yep.'

'Incredible. It's good in so many ways. You don't have to talk to him and, you know, *feel* things.'

'Yes, but can you believe she asked that? I mean, in exchange for my mum's happiness?'

'It's very ballsy but she's his friend. I'd probably do the same if it was you.'

I really was expecting more energy from Katie's condemnation.

'But if it's what you want for your mum, then the only one standing in her way, Sweetu, is you. Sorry.'

'Has everyone taken a bluntness pill?'

'Oh, stop it. We get them from you.'

'Thanks, mother of my godchild.'

'Why do they call it morning sickness when it happens *all* the time? Anyway, I don't mean to be blunt, but don't you want to be free of it all?'

I'm beginning to realise that no one can ever be free of anything.

12.10 a.m. Foz's hen night was an evening at Hannah's, with the girls, feeding Suj nothing but platitudes: 'This is *good* for you.' 'It'll get better.' 'He wasn't right for you, anyway.' Even as the deluge of words came out of our mouths they felt hollow.

The light caught the glint of Foz's ring.

'That ring's almost as blinding as his teeth,' I said.

'Are we all getting sunglasses at the wedding?' asked Suj, stabbing at her drink.

Foz looked at both of us, too content, I suppose, to be offended. Hannah took Foz's hand and inspected it. 'The clarity is amazing.'

'He did OK, didn't he?' said Foz, observing the stone born of hard-earned cash and lasting affection. We all decided to agree, without quip, that he did. Idiot.

I didn't say anything about my phone conversation with Hammy – there already seemed to be enough going on. When Suj dropped Han and then me home, she said: 'Fuck, Sofe. Starting over again. I can't bear it.'

I put my arm round her, the handbrake in the car digging into my thigh. I couldn't bring myself to say that it'll all work out again. Because, really, what do I know? Then I gave her leg a squeeze and said, 'Hey, remember that time we got arrested?'

Monday 23 September

8.40 a.m. 'Hi,' I said as Sakib opened the door to his house. I handed him a bag with croissants. 'For breakfast,' I added.

'Oh. Thanks.'

I walked, with my head bowed, towards the office and took my seat.

'Recovered?' he asked.

'Yes. Thanks.' Switching my computer on I pretended to organise some papers, just for something to do as I felt his eyes on me. 'Thanks for your help on Saturday,' I added, without quite looking at him.

'It's fine,' he said. 'I see where you get your charming language from now.'

I raised my eyebrows at him.

He put his hands up. 'OK. None of my business.' Then he said, 'Foz invited me to her wedding, by the way.'

Hain? I looked up at him.

'Should be fun,' he added.

'Oh.'

'Maybe I should make a speech?' he said.

'Great. Give me a chance to throw eggs at you.'

He laughed, getting up, ready to leave for work for the day. 'I have a sudden appreciation for the calmness of my wife.'

Pffft. Clearly he's never heard about the storms that follow.

Sunday 29 September

8.20 a.m. Have spent entire week trying to figure out a way to get in touch with Uncle Mouch and have found nothing. There's no number in Mum's diary, nothing in her phone's contacts list, nothing online. Asked Maars and she's also tried to investigate when she's come to Mum's, though I've not told her about Hammy's ultimatum – which might sound dramatic, but that's exactly what it is.

And now must go and begin preps for Foz's wedding tonight.

11.40 p.m. 'Simple is the answer,' said Mum as we took our seat at the restaurant table. 'Anyway, it's her second wedding and why make a fuss for that.'

Foz and Kam were sitting at the table next to us, talking and laughing. Han waved at us as she walked over with Omar. Just then Sakib appeared and took a seat next to me. Suj nudged me, but I'm not sure why.

'Where's your sister?' he asked.

'Had another wedding to go to.'

'Your daughter,' he said, turning to Mum, 'is a very hard worker.'

I eyed him suspiciously.

'Is it?' she replied. 'Then you must give her a pay rise. She can't live with me forever.'

He looked at me and raised his eyebrows. Suj leaned in and whispered to me, 'He's flirting with you.'

'Drink your mango juice.'

A few seconds later I leaned into Suj's ear and added, 'He might very well get back with his wife. Plus, I'm still married.' Which only reminded me of my conversation with Hamida.

'We need to get our shit sorted,' she said, looking over at Foz and Kam.

Sakib was all affability, pouring drinks for everyone and speaking to Omar and, most disconcertingly, Mum. At one point I wanted to say to everyone that he's not always this nice, but perhaps it might've looked a bit petty. Anyway, he lightened the mood. He picked up another naan and put it on my plate.

'I think this is just what I needed,' he said.

'What? Naan?'

He paused and squinted at me. 'You know what you're like?'

'What?'

'You're like a fox. They look sweet and innocent, but really they're just . . .'

'Eating food out of your bin?'

'Destructive.'

'Harsh.'

Which it was, but it was also quite amusing. His eyes flickered towards Han, whose gaze rested on us every so often. She began filling her glass with juice as he looked away from me.

'A fox?' said Han, leaning over Suj.

'Sshh,' I said, in case he could hear. 'You both need to stop.' Honestly!

'Are they trying to set us up?' he said to me.

Oh God. I had to slowly turn round to him, while giving Han and Suj the evillest look I could manage.

'Come on,' he said. 'We're brown, we're both on the brink of divorce, we'd be an excellent match in anybody's eyes.'

I gave a weak smile, feeling the colour rise to my cheek.

'Don't worry,' he said. I was suddenly rather too aware of his close proximity and the way he held my gaze a little longer than necessary. 'We both know this would never happen.'

'Never,' I said.

When Foz drove away in her car with Kam I linked my arm with Suj's.

'Let's get you on Tinder,' I said.

'Might as well,' she replied. 'And then maybe you can join me.'

Not knowing where my heart is located most of the time nowadays, I managed to discover at this point that it had wedged itself in the pit of my stomach. Dating horror came flooding back to me and had me clinging on to the idea that maybe, just *maybe*, my marriage is salvageable.

That was until I saw Conall.

2.10 a.m. His voice. You can forget the intonation of a person's voice so quickly, and then you hear it again and it's like pouring liquid balm over the cracked, hardened parts of a ridiculously susceptible heart.

'Hi,' he said, pausing outside his front gate as Mum and I got out of Sakib's car.

Conall looked into the car, while Mum was captivated by his beard that had grown at least a fist's worth. He had a bag in either hand, the veins in his forearms protruding as he seemed to be clenching his muscles. I bent down and thanked Sakib.

'All OK?' he said.

I nodded, with which he drove away.

I glanced at Conall's jeans, folded up, revealing his ankles. If he'd been walking with a bunch of guys coming from the mosque, he wouldn't have looked out of place.

Was he an apparition? I'd have thought it, especially since Mum merely nodded at him and went into the house. My feet were made of lead.

'Hi,' I replied.

Then he looked at the ground and made to walk past me.

'Conall.'

He stopped just next to me as I looked at him. 'What are you doing here?'

'Needed some things. Tenants moving in tomorrow.'

'How's Eamonn?'

He didn't seem to want to meet my gaze; just nodded. For a moment I thought, *he's back; he's here to try and make it work.*

'I didn't think you'd be here,' he added. 'I'm sorry.'

Being well acquainted with myself, I thought anger would've been the predominant emotion. It begs the question whether we ever do know ourselves. Or maybe sometimes someone comes along and they bring out the unknown parts of who you are. And right then I felt such a cascade of disbelief I could hardly believe in myself.

'Right.'

Then he met my gaze and I wondered how you could want to turn away from the same thing you want to clutch on to for the rest of your life.

'Honestly,' he added. 'I'm sorry.'

He looked back down and walked away, the two bags in his hands. There was nothing I could say to him, other than to whisper, 'So am I.'

Monday 30 September

9.05 a.m. Not sure how I got into work since my body felt like it was in an iron cast. Mum asked what he wanted. When I told her I thought she'd ask more questions, but she just hugged me. So it is better to be home than alone.

'How'd it go?' asked Sakib as soon as he opened the door for me.

'Rather not talk about it.' I glanced over at him, rubbing his forehead as he answered an email. 'Doesn't look like you slept very well,' I said.

'That makes two of us.'

'What'd you think of the Saloni submission?' I asked.

He sighed again. 'Haven't finished it yet.' Then he stood up and opened a window, gazing out at the fir tree in his garden. 'I'm not used to being alone.'

I looked up. The sheer honesty of the statement unnerved me. You're not meant to say these things out *loud*.

'Your little encounter had me reaching for the phone to my wife.'

'And?'

He had his hands in his pockets as he looked at me. 'And . . . I realised I'm still the same geeky guy now as I was over fifteen years ago. Only not enough for my wife to be happy with me.'

I wanted to ask if he fancied a fag, but I suspect he's not the smoking type – there are the people who are frayed and there are people with neat, tailored lines.

'Can't help change.'

He smiled, as if to himself. 'I thought I'd grown out of longing – hankering after the popular girl.'

I looked out into the garden with him. 'The more I think about it, the more I realise we don't grow out of anything – we grow over it.'

The office phone rang. Sakib picked it up, answered the queries and put the phone down again.

'Well,' he said, about to leave for the day. 'Time to carry on growing over.'

I wouldn't admit it to him, but he was right. It was time to grow over.

OCTOBER

Big Girls Don't Cry

Tuesday 1 October

8.25 p.m. 'Oh meri bachi,' said Mum as she grabbed my face and kissed my cheek.

'Mum, really. It's fine.'

Maars and Tahir exchanged a look.

'Honestly, you guys. It's the sensible thing to do.'

It was hardly a surprise that I was officially going to get a divorce. Just then the doorbell rang, Mum answered it and we heard Auntie Reena howl: 'Hai hai!' She heaved into the living room like a wave and looked at me, Maars and Tahir. 'They've gone!' she said.

'What's gone?' Tahir and Maars asked in unison.

I was still slightly taken aback by Auntie's doughy form, blocking Mum from entering the room.

'*Meri chirdiyan*,' she said, clutching her chest. 'My budgies have flown away.'

'Reena, my daughter is losing her husband and you are worried about your budgies.'

Auntie Reena looked at me, aghast, and scurried up to me. 'Beta, are you sure?'

Despite her separation, her devotion to husbands doesn't seem to have waned. Anyway, this wasn't about me being sure, it was about there not exactly being any other choice.

'She is doing the right thing,' said Mum. 'Why the hell she should wait and wait her whole life?'

I glanced at Mum as Tahir shifted in his seat. Now I can tell Hammy and she can get in touch with Uncle Mouch. Katie was right; the only impediment to Mum's happiness has been me.

Maars nodded. 'Exactly, Auntie. Mum's right.'

Tahir flung his arms into the air. 'You're telling her to break up her own marriage?'

Auntie Reena shook her head.

'What marriage?' said Maria.

'Don't you think he deserves to know what you're planning?' he said. 'Don't you think you should give him a chance? Let him tell you what he's thinking?'

'Who is he to tell her anything?' replied Maria.

'God forbid anyone tell any of the Khan women what to do,' said Tahir.

My brain was beginning to hurt.

'Beta,' said Auntie Reena, 'marriage is about compromise and understanding. He made a mistake. He's a man.'

I guess the mistake wouldn't be quite so forgivable if he was a woman.

'Auntie,' said Tahir, laughing, 'as a man, even I don't think that's right. I mean, what he did was messed up – but two wrongs don't make a right.'

Tahir picked up Adam and stood. 'I'm taking him into the other room,' he whispered to Maars. 'I don't want my son to end up feeling emancipated with all this talk.'

'Do you mean emasculated?' I said.

'See?' he said. 'It's like men don't matter in this family.' With which he held Adam's head to his shoulder and marched out of the room.

'Le,' said Mum, looking at Tahir in the other room. 'What's happened to him?'

'Mawlvi at his mosque's started saying how the world's gone mad because women are man-controlling,' said Maars.

'That's just what we need,' I said, thinking of exactly how I'm going to ask Conall for a divorce. 'Mawlvis telling men how dangerous we are. Better get T out of that shit,' I added.

'Hid his car keys last night.'

'Good, because the kind of guy that can't tell between emancipated and emasculated is prime fundo material.'

And just then I thought of Sean's worried face when he came to my house, Conall's long beard and rolled-up jeans. I had to shake the stupid notion out of my head. Muslims are meant to be immune to this kind of propaganda.

To Hamida: Hi. Have you had a chance to speak to Uncle Wasim? It's time everyone moved on. I'm emailing Conall, to say as much.

I don't want to be someone who reconciles themselves to a future, I want to be someone who forges it.

Wednesday 2 October

10.10 a.m.

To: Conall O'Flynn
From: Sofia Khan
Subject: Us

Hi,
I don't think it'll come as much of a surprise that I think the right thing to do now is get a divorce. It's only an Islamic one so I just need you to get in touch with an imam and we can do it over the phone. No need to even speak – I could tell how little you wanted to do that last time I saw you. There are no legal complications so that's one less thing you need to worry about.

The sooner we can arrange this, the better for everyone.

S

That was it. The emotional finishing line in this marathon of a marriage. Me, coming in last and losing spectacularly.

Friday 4 October

7.15 a.m. Have been checking emails incessantly the past few days and nothing. From Conall or Hamida. Tried to call Hamida but her phone was switched off.

5.20 p.m.

To Sean: Hey. How are you? Listen, I need to speak with Conall, but he's not answering his email. Could you check if he's received it, please? Hope you're well. x

Saturday 5 October

2.50 p.m. Tried to call Sean but it went straight to voicemail. Why is no one answering their phones or emails??

Sunday 6 October

10.45 a.m.

> **To Sean:** Hi, don't mean to keep bugging you but I really do need to know whether Conall received this email. Get back to me ASAP please. Thanks Sx

Monday 7 October

8.30 p.m. I lunged for the phone as soon as it rang.

'Sean,' I said. 'Where have you been?'

'Do you know how much time we waste on phones and social media?' he said.

'Sean?' It was his voice but it didn't sound like him, if you know what I mean.

He sighed. 'Just trying to get some balance.'

'Oh.'

'Seeing your nephew go through that shit makes you think.'

'How is he?'

He paused. I think I must've held my breath.

'In remission.'

I raised my head to God and had to say a silent thanks.

'Beating me at chess too, the little bastard,' Sean added.

I counted that it was only ten days ago I'd seen Conall looking so . . . well, browbeaten.

'How long's it been?' I asked.

'A few weeks. Anyway, what can I do you for, Sofe?'

I told him I'd emailed Conall and hadn't heard back from him.

'What kind of email?' he asked, a tinge of suspicion in his voice.

'Think it's best I first hear from him.'

He paused again. 'Sofia, don't take this the wrong way, but when I asked you to contact him you didn't and now . . .'

'It's time to move things forward,' I said. 'For everyone.'

'Right. I get it.' He sighed again. 'Well, he's away for a few weeks. Gone to Kashmir with Hamida.'

Kashmir? I put my head in my hands. That man has a death wish.

'*What* is he doing there?' I said, perhaps in a rather higher-pitched voice than normal. 'Eamonn's barely made it into remission.'

'Claire's mum contacted her and they're going to stay with her for a while. Claire said she needed some space.'

I heard a shuffle in the background. 'Why does it matter to you?' he asked. There wasn't animosity in his voice, just perhaps the type of exasperation only a brother can feel.

'Well . . . I suppose it doesn't.'

'You'll have to wait to hear from him. Where do you think I got the idea for a phone and social media detox?'

I had to laugh. 'He was born in the wrong era, wasn't he?'

Sean paused again. 'He'll be back. I'll tell him you called.'

'Just the email,' I said. 'No call needed.'

'Right. Fine.'

'Thanks, Sean.'

'Sure.'

There was more I wanted to say to him, but I wasn't sure what. 'Sean?'

'Yeah?'

'Be a bit weird if we stayed friends, wouldn't it?'

I waited a few moments before he spoke. 'Yeah. It would be.'

Thursday 10 October

8.55 a.m. 'Congratulations, Ms Khan,' said Sakib as he opened the door to me.

For a moment I wondered whether he knew I was getting a divorce.

'I think we've found the first book we need to publish,' he added as I came in and he grabbed his keys. 'Manuscript's on your desk. Read it today. I'll try to come home early.'

6 p.m. 'Oh my God, you're right,' I exclaimed as he walked through the door. 'I love it.'

He smiled at me before he sneezed. 'Isn't it wonderful?'

I nodded eagerly as we both dived into all the reasons we loved it when he sneezed again. 'Think I'm getting a cold. Must be all the excitement.'

'We have a first book!' I exclaimed.

He sat in his chair, barely able to suppress his joy. 'We do, Sofia. We do.'

Friday 11 October

8.05 a.m. Came over early as so much to do. Sakib answered the door in his dressing gown, face pale as he blew his nose. He went straight to bed.

10.05 a.m. Crept up the stairs, with Lemsip and a big bottle of water in hand, to see if he was awake. I didn't actually know which was his bedroom, and there was another flight of stairs going up. Lightly knocked on each door on first floor when I heard a moan coming from the room at the end of the passage.

Opening the door slightly, I said hello. Then I took in the four-poster bed and almost laughed out loud. What kind of a person has a four-poster bed?? I waited for a few moments to compose myself.

'Made you some Lemsip,' I said.

The bed was a crumpled mass of covers and strewn pillows; the curtains drawn, a faint smell of vanilla and sweat.

'Husna?' he mumbled.

'Sofia.'

'Ogh,' he said. Putting his head under the duvet, coughing.

'It's man-flu then.' I stepped up to the bed and put the mug down. 'You should drink that.'

'I hate it,' he murmured from under the duvet.

I went and opened the window a bit, keeping the curtains drawn. 'Just drink it,' I said, and left the room.

1 p.m. Give someone soup and more Lemsip and all you get is tantrums. Honestly.

1.15 p.m. 'Really sorry, but what budget did we agree for book jackets?'

'Five hundred and fifty,' came the answer.

'Right. Sorry. Thanks.'

5 p.m. Went up again with more water and he hadn't touched the soup.

'Don't blame me if you get a stomach ulcer from all this medication and no food.'

'I'm cold.' His head peeped out from the covers as I went to close the window.

'What do you want for dinner apart from all this lovely fresh air?' I asked. When he didn't respond I added, 'I can get you soup? Dry toast?'

'*Khichri*.'

Khichri?? Where was I meant to get that type of rice from? I certainly wasn't going to cook it.

'Dry toast it is then,' I said.

9.15 p.m. Just got home after an evening of ensuring the toast was eaten, the water bottle was full, the medication was all to hand.

'Sofia,' he said, the dimmed lighting shading his face, 'these are the times you miss the person you were married to.'

'You have a temperature,' I said. 'Not a tumour.'

When I went to get up he held my wrist, his hands clammy, and I noticed that his fingers were tapered at the tips. So unlike Conall's. He let go and went back to sleep after I promised that I'd come and see him tomorrow.

Monday 14 October

6.20 p.m. Bloody, bloody hell. I was packing up to leave when Sakib came home, throwing his keys on the desk.

'Listen, I wanted to say thanks,' he said. 'For last week.'

Picking up my bag, I replied, 'Don't worry about it. Consider us even now.'

'I mean it,' he said.

I told him I'd have done the same if he were a dog so it was nothing.

'Are you equating me to a dog?'

'You share many dog-like qualities.' (Sometimes, it's too easy.)

But then he stepped towards me, partially blocking the doorway. I patted his arms and told him I'd see him tomorrow.

'Wait,' he said, putting both his hands on my arms. His nose was still red, and I noticed a small cut from when he must've shaved this morning. He took a deep breath.

'Do you need an asthma pump?' I asked, because his breathing sounded a little shallow.

Why were his hands still on my arms? He seemed to notice me fidget as he removed them, and I realised that actually the weight of a man's arms on my shoulders was something I'd missed.

No, no, no. This was *no* time to feel *those* things again. I muttered a prayer under my breath at the sheer impropriety of A) having those feelings when I'm still, technically, married and B) having them in the presence of a man who was also married, which became a lot more oppressive.

'I need to be honest, Sofia.'

Don't say it. Don't even *think it.*

'Oh shit,' I exclaimed. 'Is that the time? I really have to go,' I said, pushing past him while looking back, waving, and almost tripping over the kitchen step.

'Hang on, wait.'

'Can't,' I called out from the passage.

'Sofia,' he called, running into the passage, but I'd already closed the door behind me and, for the first time in a really long time, I ran towards the Tube station.

Oh God, I need a toilet bowl.

Tuesday 15 October

8.20 a.m. Couldn't face it. Texted in sick. Realise this is cowardly and I'm probably being paranoid, but what if I'm *not*? Between being horrified at a declaration of some kind of feeling and realising how long it's been since, you know, being *close* to someone, what would I *do*? I mean, I wouldn't *do* anything, but, you know.

8.25 a.m. Mum just came into my room and said: 'How will you run a business if you take the day off with such small, small illness?'

Sigh. What happened? When did my mum become right about things?

Wednesday 16 October

9.10 a.m. When he answered the door I smiled really widely. He looked at the floor and let me in. In fact, he looked at the floor, the ceiling, the windows, his tea; *anything* but me.

'Feeling better?' he asked, staring at his computer screen.

'Yes. Weird migraine thingy.'

He pushed his hair back, usually wavy and in place, a little dishevelled today. He tilted the computer screen back. 'About the other day –'

'Don't mention it,' I said. 'It's fine.'

'Right. Yes.'

To be honest, I don't know *what* he was going to say but better not to risk it.

I am done risking things.

Saturday 26 October

10.20 a.m. Sakib went out to get milk so I called Sean. He picked up after my third attempt. When I asked him whether Conall was back, he said he thought he was but hadn't heard from him.

'Well, is Hamida back?'

He paused. 'Listen, there's probably just a delay. You know how it is.'

'Even so. Why don't you ask . . .' It took some effort to heave the name 'Claire' out of my mouth. 'It's just . . . Sean, it's important. Or I wouldn't ask.'

Sakib appeared at the door as I waited for Sean's reply.

'Fine. Sure. I'll speak to her. And I'll try to call his Pakistan mobile again.'

'What's wrong?' asked Sakib.

'Nothing. Well, a lot of things, actually.'

He stopped and looked at me. 'That's certainly true.'

I shook my head. 'We are both two very sorry people, aren't we?'

'Misery loves company,' he replied.

Then he put his hand in the air and high-fived me. I know. Ridiculous; high-fiving a divorce – especially since I wanted to crawl under my desk and cry most of the time. But Sakib bobbed to the surface of my despair, dispelling it with the knowledge that someone knows how it feels.

9.50 p.m.

From Sean: Sorry, Sofe. Couldn't get through to him. He did say he'd be back weekend of nineteenth. I don't think he has access to emails and, I don't know, it was a different SIM card or something. Will let you know when I hear from him.

Tuesday 28 October

8.45 a.m. Just received weird phone call from Sean. He said he's not heard from Conall yet, but apparently he called Mary to tell her he'd be going to some retreat in Karachi.

'A retreat? In Karachi?' I asked incredulously.

'The weird thing is that I got through to Hamida and she thought he was going back to Ireland.'

'But he's not in Ireland?' I asked. 'Have you called Claire?'

'Yeah – she said last she spoke to him, she told him not to come back until he's sorted his head out.'

'What's wrong with his head?'

'It's Conall,' Sean replied.

'But Hamida said he was going back to Ireland?' I asked.

Sakib looked at me over the desk and started mouthing something.

'Hang on, Sean. *What*?'

'Sorry, you OK for agent meetings over the next week?'

'Yes, fine,' I said distractedly.

'Listen, let me just double-check a few things and call you back,' said Sean.

I put the phone down.

'All OK?' asked Sakib.

'Yeah. I'm sure. Just some kind of miscommunication, I think.'

6.20 p.m. When I didn't hear back from Sean I called him after work, but he didn't pick up. Then I decided to call Hamida.

'Listen,' she said, 'I've spoken to Uncle Wasim and he's pretty hurt. Actually, I don't think I've ever seen him like this. Was your mum *the* Auntie Mehnaz my mama told me about?'

'Huh?'

'*Years* ago Mama told me that Uncle Wasim was in love with a woman but she had to marry someone in London, or something like that. It didn't click until now.'

'Listen, Hamida – have you spoken to Sean?'

'Haan. I told Conall to at least text his brother so he knows where he is. But you know what he's like and he's been . . . well, a little distracted for a while.'

'He said he was going back to Ireland?'

She paused. 'Ya, that's what he told me.'

'But he told his mum he was staying in Karachi for a few more weeks on some kind of retreat. And his conversation with Claire didn't exactly sound amicable.'

I stood outside the Tube station, waiting for her answer.

'He never mentioned anything about that. And a retreat? In Karachi?'

'Exactly,' I said.

'He specifically told me he was going home.'

'Home or Ireland?'

'Well, home.'

This really wasn't helping me much.

'To be honest, I was glad. I thought going back to Eamonn would help.'

'He's not home, though.'

'But he left six days ago.'

I told her I had to go, and called the only person I could call.

'Hi, Mary. It's Sofia.'

'Oh.'

When I asked about Conall she said that he was still in Karachi. Honestly, I was going round in sodding circles as people rushed in and out of the station.

'But he's not,' I said.

I filled her in about my conversation with Hamida and Mary said she'd call Claire. Fifteen minutes later Mary called me back. I was still outside the Tube station.

'Well, she swears he's still in Karachi. I'll be honest and say he didn't leave here on the best of terms with Claire. He's my son but I won't hide his faults.'

I leaned against the wall. What the hell was going on? 'Right, OK. So, where did he say he was staying?' I asked.

She hesitated. 'Well, he didn't say.'

'How long would he be away?'

She paused. 'I don't know.'

'Who *does* know?' I realise I might've been getting a little irate here, but this really was getting ridiculous.

'*Colm*,' she called out. I heard her fill him in.

'That boy does what the hell he wants without letting people know. You'll be here fretting over him while he's gallivanting, thinking he's changing the world.' He took the phone from Mary.

'Sofia?' he said. 'He'll be back when he wants to come back.' Though he didn't sound very convinced. 'Don't you waste another minute,' he added.

'Colm,' I heard Mary say in the background.

'I have to go,' I said, putting my phone away. Without thinking I turned round, striding towards the only place it made sense to go.

'Oh, hi,' said Sakib, looking surprised. This look swiftly turned into an expression of concern. 'What's wrong?'

'My husband.'

'What?'

I stared at him, confused, the voices of Hamida, Mary and Colm spinning in my head. *He's in Ireland; he's in Karachi; don't you waste another minute.*

'No one knows where he is,' I said.

'What do you mean?'

'I mean no one knows where he is,' I replied. What was happening? If no one knew where he was, then what did that amount to? 'I mean, I think he's missing.'

NOVEMBER

Lost

Tuesday 5 November

9.25 p.m. I was sitting at my bedroom window, watching the Guy Fawkes fireworks burst into the night sky and explode in reds, oranges, greens and blues, when my phone beeped.

> **From Sakib:** Listen, I know it's been a weird week, but this is the manuscript I need you to look at that came in over the weekend. Are you coming to tomorrow's meeting? It's important you're there.

I put the phone face down. Sakib's worked his notice and now I have to deal with him glancing at me over the computer screen every so often. Sean keeps calling, telling me something's not right – going on about Conall being *radicalised* – at which point I'm ready to hang up on him. But then I think of Conall with the beard and rolled-up jeans and his refusal to look at me . . . Then there's Mum. She and Auntie Reena have managed to come up with a conspiracy theory involving an elaborate in-house kidnapping job in order to get money from us. Of course, no ransom has been demanded, which, for some reason, hasn't deterred them from their theory. Claire says that she's tried to call his number but can't get through.

It feels so long since I've seen Conall I don't know what to think. I picked up the phone and dialled Sean's number.

'Well?' I said.

He sighed. 'I just don't know what the hell's going on.'

'Hamida messaged yesterday and said she's asked around but everyone thought he was going back to Ireland, just as she did.' I looked out of the window again. 'Would he do it again? Leave like that?'

'No.' He sighed again. 'I don't know. All I know is I spoke to Claire and she said his . . .'

'What?'

'I've not said anything to my parents yet, and told her not to either, but . . . she said he started speaking to Eamonn about Islam.'

'Right.'

'Is it normal, Sofe?'

'Is it abnormal?'

We'd been here before. Everything Sean told me just felt like about ninety per cent of most Muslims' day-to-day life. Next thing I know he'll be saying "Conall's stopped shopping at M&S; it's a sign."'

'I just wonder . . .'

'What?'

'With everything that Claire's told me and, well, what happened with you – what would keep him here?'

Monday 11 November

10.10 a.m. 'So, what did you think of the manuscript?'

My brain has gone into autopilot. I only seem able to think about things that are relevant in immediate time and space.

'Oh . . .'

'Don't tell me you haven't read it yet.'

'No, I have,' I said – attempting to mentally grasp the synopsis of the book that surely my brain would've stored. 'Good concept . . .' And then, when I could grasp no longer for the synopsis, I clutched at straws. 'Figured out the plot twist halfway through. Not for us.'

'Really?'

I nodded, pressing on my phone to see if I'd missed any messages.

'Yeah. I agree with you.'

'You agree with me?'

He looked at me with what I'd call scepticism. 'What was the twist?' he asked, sitting back and folding his arms.

I *wanted* to think of feasible lies, but all I could think of were the lack of messages on my phone.

'Did you read the manuscript?'

I lowered my eyes and shook my head. This didn't seem to have quite the charming effect it used to have on Conall. 'I'm sorry,' I said.

'You have to think about what you want, Sofia. I know you've been distracted, but he's a grown man. And I'd like you to be able to tell me the truth. Like a grown woman. What he's doing or where he is isn't really your concern any more.'

'No,' I said. 'I know.'

Why was there so much anxiety there – stuck in the pit of my stomach, leaking into every bone and sinew?

'Start noticing things,' he added. 'Like my socks,' he said, lifting up his trousers and showing the rainbow-coloured item.

I tried to laugh.

'Now switch off your personal email account . . .'

'Is this *1984*?' I asked.

'Yes, and don't forget how that book ended. Focus on *now*.' He rested his elbows on the desk. 'I *need* you.'

It reminded me of the time Conall said the same thing to me. Any day now, we'll hear from him and I can shout at him down the phone before divorcing him.

Sunday 17 November

12.30 p.m. Tried to call Sean but it was going to voicemail. You'd have thought with a missing brother he'd have his phone on all the time. Texted him to call back when he could. But what was I going to say: explain every way how the thought of where Conall might be catches in my throat and leaves me short of breath?

1.50 p.m. 'Soffoo,' said Mum, coming into my room with a sandwich. I was poised on my bed, twenty-five pages into the new manuscript, which felt like quite an accomplishment.

'You'll be blind with all this reading,' she said, handing me the plate. She leaned in closer. 'Haw, look, you have grey hair.'

'Thanks, Mum.'

'You shouldn't stress. It is all in Allah's hands. Though sometimes I wonder what He is thinking.'

'OK, Mum.' There was no need for heresy today.

She sat on the edge of the bed. 'I know, Beta.' She was looking at me, perhaps as if she were seeing her own (relative) youth. 'After so many years, I know how hard it can be. To let go of something.'

I put the manuscript to one side, tears streaming down my cheeks, and, for the first time in my life, sobbed in my mum's arms.

'I'm sorry, Mum,' I said, wishing I could magic Uncle Mouch back to her. That I could magic Conall back home.

She patted my head. 'O-ho. You are my daughter. You never need to tell me you are sorry.'

I need to wise up; accept; embrace. Some things are beyond our control. The sooner I get that through my iron-clad skull, the better.

Wednesday 20 November

9.45 a.m. Why hasn't Sean called me back? I've called multiple times but it's still going to voicemail.

7.50 p.m. Came home and for some unknown reason, I felt compelled to look at my *Muslim Marriage Book*. Skimming through the pages, I came across: *How far does forgiveness stretch?*

Oh, bloody hell, didn't see missed call from Mary!

8.05 p.m. When I called Colm answered and there was an urgency in his voice that I hadn't heard before.

'It's Sofia,' I said.

Silence.

'Where are you?' he snapped.

'London.' Where else would I be?

'I see.' He sounded gruff, tired.

'I received a call from Mary. Is she there?'

The receiver was handed over to her.

'I got your call. Is everything OK?' I asked. Even as the words left my mouth I thought, *what a stupid thing to say.*

'It's been four weeks,' she replied.

There are some things you have no control over. 'I know. I tried to call Sean but kept getting his voicemail. Just to, you know, ask if you'd heard anything.'

She paused. 'Didn't he tell you?'

Lack of control can also mean a surge of anxiety that weighs on your very organs. I barely wanted to ask. 'What?'

My heartbeats seemed to have gained momentum.

'Sean's gone,' she said, her voice breaking.

'Gone where?'

Is Conall dead? There was some shuffling as Colm seemed to have taken the receiver. 'For God's sake; he's gone to Karachi. Where else? Conall was never meant to be gone this long.'

I breathed a sigh of relief before what he said really hit me.

Why the hell has Sean gone to Karachi?? As I sat on the bed, taking in the reality of what Mary just said, I wondered: why am I not there with him?

Thursday 21 November

9.35 a.m. When Sakib opened the door I walked into the house, but instead of going through to the office I turned into the living room.

'What's going on?' he asked.

'If I go into the office I might not be able to say this.'

He shook his head and laughed as if he knew exactly what I was going to say. 'So he's decided, sorry, but rather selfishly, to fall off the face of this earth, not caring about you or his child . . . again, and now you're going to what?'

'I'm going there to find him,' I said.

He paused. 'Where?'

It all sounded preposterous, I'm sure, to him. I didn't say anything.

'Why are you doing this, Sofia?'

Sakib is the only one who ever calls me by my full name. I don't know what this means, but it means something.

'Because if I don't, then I'll be thinking about it; worrying about where he is and what's happened to him. Every time I'm moving onwards there'll be a snag in my step because he'll be there, in the back of my mind. He's still my husband. I need to find him. Then I need to divorce him.'

I waited for him to respond.

'And what about all this?' he said, spreading out his arms.

Why did I always seem to be in the middle of having to choose one thing or another? Sacrifice one thing for something else? My throat felt like it was closing up.

'I can't believe you're doing this,' he said, looking out of the window. He paused before looking back at me. 'I'm not waiting around – if you leave, you leave this behind too. I didn't get to where I am, waiting for people. Just *think* about what you're giving up.'

On paper it sounded like a no-brainer – what was I thinking? But paper can be deceptive; it carries no nuance; it has no heart. And it certainly doesn't know Conall the way I do. Because if *our* roles were reversed, there's no doubt in my mind he'd come to find me.

'I'll make it work. I'll work from Karachi – read manuscripts.'

He seemed to hesitate.

'Listen, I held the fort while you worked your notice. We're a team, right?' I said.

'Yes, but you know it's really taking off now and –'

'Please,' I said, my voice breaking. 'I need to go and find him, but I can't leave this behind.'

He looked at me, brows knitting with something like concern. 'OK. Fine.' He shook his head as if he could hardly believe the words coming out of his mouth.

'Thank you,' I said. 'Thank you so, so much.'

'Like you said – we're a team.'

Conviction cemented itself somewhere in my gut.

'Sofia,' he said, his voice softening. 'There are things that happen that you have no control over. Sometimes, you have to learn to accept them.'

'But I don't accept this,' I said. 'I don't accept it at all.'

9.35 p.m. 'What are you *doing?*' said Maars, stuffing a little too much puréed food into Adam's mouth. He spluttered it out. 'And why didn't Sean tell you he was going to Karachi?'

I shrugged. 'He didn't think I cared enough.'

Maars scoffed. 'That's rich.'

'I don't know. I didn't exactly act like I cared.' I wiped Adam's chin with my hand, rubbing the food on my pyjamas and picking him up.

'I still think you're overreacting,' she said. 'Give it a few more weeks.'

I thought about it – but Sean was already there – he clearly didn't think it could wait a few more weeks.

'Well . . .' she began. 'Not like anything I say will change your mind, but I still don't think you should go.'

'I don't think anyone does.'

10.50 p.m. Certainly not Mum. The worrying thing is she didn't even shout. She looked at me like I was one of the horsemen of the apocalypse.

'Going like this as if you are a heroine in a film.' She shook her head. 'Are you mad? Soffoo, where will you begin? What will you do? What can a *woman* do?'

It went on for a while in the same vein until she stopped and got her diary out.

'Haan, Hussain? Haan, I need to book tickets to Karachi. Give me good discount. No, two.' She shot me a look. 'For me and my daughter.'

Dear Lord. Apparently if I'm going to Karachi, Mum is coming with me.

11.05 p.m. Make that Mum *and* Maars.

Friday 22 November

11.40 a.m. Called Mary to let her know that I'm going to Karachi. She sounded surprised and relieved at the same time.

'He'll be all right, won't he?' she asked. 'Karachi isn't as bad as all that, is it?'

'No. No, it's . . . I mean. People live there.'

She paused, sounding tired. 'I wish I could know what happens in his head.'

I sat down, looking at the wedding ring I still hadn't managed to take off. 'You and me both.'

Sunday 24 November

12.05 p.m. Next Saturday can't come quickly enough. I've stuffed what I need in a case and started a Facebook page for Conall, with his pictures, asking for anyone to contact me if they see someone who looks like him. I don't know why no one thought of this sooner. Now all I'm doing is pacing the room or house, watching the clock tick. Mum on the other hand has emptied out her cupboards for things to take to Pakistan because there's a wedding that she's going to attend. Honestly.

3.50 p.m. Girls came over today – all just as dubious about me going as Maars had been. Though she'd calmed down considerably now she'd be there to overlook everything.

'God,' said Suj. 'Why can't you just let Sean handle it?'

'Because she's Sofe,' said Han. 'Can't not know what's going on.'

I couldn't help but laugh.

'Do you have everything you need?' asked Katie. 'Will you come back safe? I mean, you have responsibilities now.' She pointed at her stomach.

'What will you do if you find him?' asked Han. 'It's all very docu-drama isn't it?'

'Put it all behind me, at last. Other than wanting him to be safe, I also want this divorce.'

'Don't you need a fag?' asked Foz.

'I need more than a fag, love.'

Just then, she reached into her purse and brought out a packet of cigarettes. I almost fell on top of her when I hugged her. Hannah and Suj looked at us both in disgust whereas Katie just patted me on the shoulder and said, 'Sometimes you have to do what you have to do.'

'My mum's out, we can smoke in the garden,' I said, already rushing down the stairs.

As we all congregated outside – Foz and I revelling in the nicotine perhaps too much – Foz looked at me, thoughtful.

'Hey,' she said. 'Remember that time you went to save your husband?'

Tuesday 26 November

8.55 p.m. My God. What the hell is going on? The doorbell rang and who was standing there but Mary! I looked at her and then the small case she had in her hand.

'Hello,' she said.

It took me a few moments before I asked what she was doing here.

'Who is it?' called Mum from inside.

'Can I come in?' she asked.

'Sorry. Yes, of course.'

She stood in the passage, putting her case down.

'What are you doing here?' I asked.

'O-ho,' shouted Mum again. 'Who's at the door?'

'I saw your Facebook page. Don't know why I didn't think of it.' She put her hands in front of her. 'But then there are lots of things I didn't think of.'

I noticed how tired she looked. Just then, Mum came into the passage, stopping short at seeing Mary.

'Oh.' It was apparently all that could come out of her mouth in that moment. 'What are you doing out here? Soffoo, bring our guest in.'

Mary walked in without really looking around, her eyes still focused on me.

'Are you really going to Pakistan?'

I nodded as Mum said, 'Haan. We are all going.' As if it was a family holiday!

'Well.' Mary paused, looking from me to Mum. She sat down, placing her hands over her knees. 'I've decided I'm coming with you.'

DECEMBER

Triumph and Disaster

Sunday 1 December

10.25 a.m. When I find Conall, before I divorce him, I'm going to kill him. And the method of death will be him trapped in a confined space with my mother and Mary, with Auntie Reena exclaiming: 'First my budgies flew away and now you are all leaving me.'

We'd had lasagne for dinner last night because the night before Mary hadn't quite got to grips with the amount of spice in the food.

'That's quite a lot of chilli for lasagne,' she said, after the first bite.

'We don't like bland food,' said Mum, who then looked at me and puffed out her cheeks while Mary wasn't looking.

'But lasagne shouldn't really have chilli.' Mary looked at me.

'What does Soffoo know, she can't cook,' replied Mum.

'Hai hai,' Mum said to me afterwards. 'How will she cope in Karachi with food? She is going to be a lie-bility.'

'It'll be fine, Mum.'

'Lekin, you must talk to her and let her know. She can't think the food will be bland, bland.'

'Fine, Mum. I'll speak to her.'

And so I had to explain this to Mary, who looked at me thoughtfully before she said: 'Perhaps I should get some things from Sainsbury's for myself?'

A man is missing in the world and all anyone's concerned about is spices.

'I hope it doesn't appear rude. Because the last thing I like is fussy guests.'

I told her that everyone would understand as I looked for any update on the Facebook page.

'I hope so. I've not been away for so many years and Colm is just beside himself that I've made this decision, but . . .' She stopped and put her hand on my arm. 'I can't sit and wait any more for my son to come back.' Tears surfaced in her eyes, but she blinked them back.

Then I went out and bought some tinned food for her.

And now we're on the plane, with Maria and Adam in front of us and me sat between Mum and Mary, and a strong need for a fag.

11.10 p.m. We arrived at my chachi and chachu's house and Hammy and Sean were already there, waiting for us. Mary looked at the marble-encased house as she wrapped her cardigan around her. The vast expanse of the place was so different from where Conall and I had lived, with the goats nearby, that you'd hardly believe it was the same city.

'Very pleasing to meet you,' said Chachi – who is quite possibly the loudest and largest woman in Karachi. She took Mary's hand and pulled her into a hug that lasted as long as the flight here.

Poor Mary looked so relieved to see one of her sons. He didn't look like the same Sean I'd seen only four months ago. He had a beard too now, which Mary couldn't stop looking at, presumably from fear of having another son who's converted to Islam – domino theory of religion.

'Sofe,' he said. 'Fucking hell, what a drama.'

'You should've told me,' I said.

He sat down, rubbing his eyes. 'I know. I just didn't think you cared. Sorry. I'm glad you're here now.'

'Le,' said Mum. 'You know how fat she was and now look at her.'

Mary looked at Mum in consternation as Maars comforted Adam, who'd started crying.

'My poor bachi,' said Mum, pulling me into an unprecedented hug. She looked over at Hamida and nodded. 'How is your uncle?'

'Fine,' she replied.

Then Sean grabbed my hand and led me into the living room. We sat down and he began telling me everything he's done so far, bringing out a list of places he's been, people he's talked to.

Hamida shook her head. She'd not yet quite met my eye. 'He told me. He said, "I'm going to Ireland." This lying makes no sense.'

Mary stared into space as Chachi put her arm round her. 'Don't worry. We will find him.' Though when she glanced at Mum neither of them looked very sure.

'This is different.' He took a deep breath. 'Sofe, I've said it before . . .' He glanced at his mum.

'Oh God, not this again,' I said.

'Sean,' Mary said, rather sharply. 'What are you saying?'

I was shaking my head.

'Ma – don't fret, it'll be OK, but . . .' He blew air out from his mouth as he took her hands. 'I think he's been radicalised.'

'Oh, Holy Mary.' Non-Holy Mary clutched her chest as Mum grabbed her and exclaimed, 'Hai Allah.'

'OK,' said Maars, looking at me as Adam pulled her hair. 'Everyone has to calm down.'

Hamida frowned as mass hysteria broke out.

'He was saying all this religious mumbo-jumbo,' said Sean. 'Sorry, but you know what I mean.'

'Don't say mumbo-jumbo,' said Mary, coming out of her shocked stupor. 'Word cannot get out, Sean,' she insisted. 'They'll put him in jail. They'll take him to Guantanamo.'

'Mary . . . Mary? *Mary.*' I tried to get her attention, because she seemed to have gone into a trance. 'Your son has *not* been radicalised. And who was going to radicalise him in Kilkee anyway?'

'But Soffoo, Beta,' said Mum, 'you know this does happen. People who convert become very extreme sometimes.'

'Mum, a week ago you thought he'd been kidnapped.'

Mary's head shot up.

Chachi began talking about involving the police and Sean said no way because of what they might do. Mary looked petrified, while Mum exclaimed about her daughter's poor kismet. Maria had to give Adam to Chachi at this point and comfort Mum because of my poor fate.

I looked at Hamida, who was staring at me. She nodded towards the door and walked out. Leaving the others to spout their conspiracy theories, I followed Hamida up to the roof.

She stood there, her arms folded.

'God knows where he is,' she said. 'But this is ridiculous. Sean won't go to the police because he thinks Conall's turned into some fundo.'

I couldn't help it. I flung my arms round her and hugged her so tight I might've broken one of her ribs. Her arms were flopped to the side, until they slowly reached round me too. She patted me on the shoulder until I let go.

'You don't mind hugging someone like me?' she said.

'Like you?' I asked, confused.

'Aren't you scared I might hit on you?'

I almost laughed. 'I wouldn't flatter myself.'

Poor Hammy. She never liked me because she thought once I knew about what she was hiding I'd judge her. The only thing that made me sad for her was that people had rejected her so spectacularly that she'd rejected her faith. People ask what answer she'll give to God. They should be worrying more about what answer they'll be giving Him.

'Hamida,' I said, holding on to her arms, 'you're all I have right now.'

She looked around and then at the ground as she nodded. 'Conall might be many things,' she said. 'But he's no fucking fundo.'

'We're going to the police station tomorrow. First thing.'

'Bring that red passport,' she said.

I took a deep breath. He was here somewhere and we'd find him. 'Does Uncle Wasim know we're here?'

She nodded. After a few moments she said, 'You know, I didn't think you'd come.'

I watched her and wanted to say: of course I was going to come. It's Conall. But I'd have been lying. 'I almost didn't,' I admitted.

'What happened?'

It was basic human error – only acting the way you think another person might. 'If our roles were reversed, there's nothing that would've stopped him from doing the same for me.'

Monday 2 December

10.10 a.m. Note to self: British passport holder with a hijab on head is like walking around with a halo. I radiated a postcolonial glow with my impressive use of English grammar and conviction of faith. It was all very enlightening.

'Bhai saab,' I said, reverting to Urdu, which was only more impressive because, look! She can talk like the Brits *and* like us. 'I need to find this man.'

I had to fill out some forms, state his occupation, that kind of thing. The police officer, in true Pakistani style, played with the ends of his moustache and adjusted his maroon beret.

'Photographer? What does he photograph?'

Hamida spoke: 'He's been working with me on a slums project.'

He looked at her muddy trousers and dishevelled hair, and back at the paper. 'And who are you?'

She gave her name.

'Your parents?'

'Uncle . . . sorry, bhai saab,' I said. 'What does it matter who her parents are? Can you help us?'

'Haaris!' he called out. 'Yaar, he's white. If we don't do something British government will eat our head and someone will lose their job.'

God bless the United Kingdom! Although, of course, I was indignant on principle at prioritising on basis of colour. Obviously. He picked up the phone and called someone. Within half an hour there was a call on all police officers to be on the lookout for a six-foot-one, white, Irish man, with a beard and a lost soul. (That last part was mine.)

2.45 p.m. Just told the family what I'd done – Sean started shouting at me.

'Sofe, if they find him and realise what he's been up to they'll arrest him and keep him without trial. You think the government won't send him on a one-way ticket to Guantanamo?'

He grabbed his head and kicked the table.

But he's worrying about nothing. Conall isn't in the hands of some nut jobs, he is just lost and I am going to find him.

12.05 a.m. Couldn't sleep. Woke Maars up.

'What if Sean's right? What if there's even a nought point nought, nought, nought, nought per cent chance of Sean being right?' I asked.

She looked worried for a moment. 'Sofe, you need to hold on to that feeling.'

'Which one?'

'The one that tells you what the right thing is. Your problem is you do something and then instantly doubt it.'

Maybe she was right. Must hold on to gut instinct. It's very important apparently.

Even so; what if I've just sentenced my own husband to a lifetime in prison?

Tuesday 3 December

10.40 a.m. There was a knock on my door before it opened and I heard, 'Chai, baji?'

It was Jawad. There wasn't the same derisive look he'd worn so often when we were in the flat. When I asked what he was doing here, he said that Hamida felt they'd need help here while we were looking for Conall.

'Baji. I am sorry what's happened. He was a good man.'

'Is,' I said.

He nodded as he walked into the room. 'I didn't think he'd be one to already have a family and then lie, but then people make mistakes. My wife heard your mama was engaged and it was broken off?'

I busied myself with checking up on Conall's Facebook page.

'You know, some people gossiped, but we were both very happy for her.'

I looked up at him. 'Why?' I asked.

'My wife said that so many women don't get the chance to be happy when they're young. Why shouldn't they be happy when they're old?'

Friday 6 December

3.55 p.m. No word from the police. Hamida and I have been driving around distributing leaflets with Conall's picture all morning. Tired. Worried. Mary hasn't eaten anything. Sean hasn't told a joke since I got here. All this drama brings out the pessimism in everyone.

Sunday 8 December

10.20 a.m. Went to the police station for an update today with Hamida, while Sean handed out more leaflets. They said they've found nothing. *Nothing*. How is that even possible?

'He's a six-foot-one white man,' I shouted. 'You can't miss him. He has tattoos and a beard and looks like he'll throw you into a ditch if you cross him.'

Except when he smiles. Then he looks like the type of person who'll take you out of a ditch. I was going to yank on that police officer's moustache so hard I'd rip it off. What happened to my halo? Why was no one falling over themselves to help me?

'Your friend didn't tell us who her parents were,' he said, glancing at Hammy.

Her face went a shade of red. He put his feet up on the table and tapped his baton on the desk. Ah. Of course.

'How can I go against the wishes of a general?'

'Forget who I am,' she said in Urdu. 'She needs to find her husband.'

'Listen,' he said, ignoring her and looking at me, 'you go to your government and file a missing report. Maybe something will be done. But I do anything and I say goodbye to my job, and who will feed my wife and children?'

'Fuck this, Sofia.' Hamida glared at the police officer. 'And we wonder what's wrong with our country.'

As we got back into the car I looked at her, pausing before she put the car into gear. 'Are you OK?' I asked.

She barely nodded.

'Luckily,' I said, 'for every one of those police officers there are ten more people like you.'

Came home and Sean was with Mary. He said there's no way we're appealing to the government because of course my husband is now radicalised. Every time I want to tell Sean to get over it and pick up the phone to call the embassy, something stops me – this latent fear that there might be truth in it. How many risks is a person meant to take in life?

Thursday 12 December

8.10 p.m. 'Look how skinny she is,' said Chachi to me in Urdu, glancing at Mary. 'She will think this is how we treat our guests, letting them bring tinned food. Soffoo, you must think of these things – she's your mother-in-law.'

Just as I was about to respond that my priorities were more Conall than cuisine-related, guess who walked in – Uncle Mouch! Maars and I both froze in our respective seats, eyes darting between him and Mum.

'Salamalaikum,' he said, standing at the door in his white shalwar kameez, long leather jacket and Afghan hat. Hamida was standing with him.

'Uncle!' exclaimed Maars. 'Look, Adam. It's Uncle. Isn't it nice to see him?'

Mum straightened up in her chair as he glanced at her, nodding, probably quite perturbed at Maars' enthusiasm. He and Hamida came in and sat down.

He leaned forward. 'Beta, Hamida has told me all about Conall.'

Just then Mary came into the room and looked a bit taken aback by Uncle Mouch. Maybe it was the hat.

'Oh, come, come,' said Chachi. 'Wasim, this is *Mary*. Soffoo's mother-in-law.'

He stood up, taking her hand. 'Of course – I remember her from the wedding.'

Mum cleared her throat, looking flushed. Mary sat down.

'I hope they find your son very soon,' he said to her. 'Can you explain everything to me again?'

We went through the story as he looked on, nodding, knitting his brow, leaning forward, taking in every word. 'Hmm,' he said.

We waited for more but he'd fallen silent and was looking at the floor. I tried to catch Hamida's eye but she was also looking rather distant. Had they heard bad news? Were they hiding something from me? The clock ticked. Tick, tock, tick, tock. Uncle Mouch took off his hat. I'd never seen Mum so quiet – it was almost as if she'd been the jilted one.

'OK,' he said, getting up and taking his leave. Mum was looking at him but he left the room without a backward glance, Hamida in tow.

'What was the point in that?' I said, looking at everyone.

'You tell the story a million times you tire of hearing it yourself,' said Mary. 'But he seems like a nice man.'

'He is a very good man,' said Mum, her face reddening. 'And you know . . .' She looked at Mary, her breathing seeming to have got heavy. 'If your son hadn't left my daughter I'd be married to him now.'

Mary looked at Mum and then at me. Oh God.

'OK, well, let's not get into this now,' I said.

Just then my phone beeped.

From Sakib: Sofia, I didn't want to disturb you with everything going on, but I really need you to proof the attached material. I've had back-to-back meetings and won't have time. Needs to be sent back by the end of the day. Really sorry. How's the search going?

Bloody, bloody hell.

'What kind of a man doesn't tell his wife-to-be that he has a son, hmm?'

It was Mary's turn to go red this time. I opened the attachment as I heard Maars ask Mum to go and check on Adam.

'Well – we all make mistakes. Whatever happened to forgiveness?' Mary looked at me as I glanced up from my phone. 'For all your religion, you didn't think he might need you? Do you know what it's been like seeing my grandson go through chemotherapy and my son sit by his side, alone – no one to comfort him?'

Sean walked in.

'Why doesn't he go to his first wife for comfort?' said Mum, ignoring Sean's hello.

Mary's indignation came out in: 'Jesus. What a thing to say.'

Chachi looked disapproving and said in Urdu, 'Haw, is this how you call Jesus's name?'

'What's going on?' Sean asked, looking at me.

Where are you, Conall? Where the hell are you?

'His wife should've been there,' said Mary.

'Hang on,' said Maars. 'She *was* there.'

'Well, dear; yes, she was. And then she wasn't,' she said.

'Come on, Ma. It's not like you wanted her there anyway.'

'*Sean*.'

He lifted his arms up as if to say, *it's the truth, isn't it?*

'Uff,' said Mum. 'So many lies.'

'OK, Mum, thanks, we know.'

'Soffoo, you married him without thinking things through, telling your family or knowing who he is. This is what happens. On top of that, he's gora.'

'*Mum*,' I said, not even being able to look at Mary and Sean, who aren't so stupid they don't know by now what *gora* means. 'You have *got* to let go of that. You and your *you can't trust him, you can't trust him*. Yes, you were right! I know he lied, but maybe things just aren't that simple. I'm not saying what he did was right – I'm just saying that maybe things aren't always black and white. And for someone who says they don't mind I married a gora, you certainly mention it a lot.'

'Hain?' said Mum. 'Simple? It looks very simple to me.'

'He made a mistake,' I said. 'He lied. I know. But his mistake isn't the sum of who he is.'

Mum leaned back and raised her eyebrows. 'I said to you that you should stay with him. I never told you, *leave* him. After all,' she said, looking at Mary, 'marriage isn't this thing you can just throw away like that.'

Oh my God.

'Quite right,' added Mary.

'Anyway,' said Mum, 'I beg to pardon but I don't think Wasim's children would want their dad to marry a woman whose son-in-law is white anyway. Sorry to say.'

Mary's cheeks went bright pink. 'I see,' she said.

'To hell with them,' I said.

Mary took a deep breath. 'Well. I can't say people in Kilkee weren't talking about Conall marrying a Muslim.' And then she murmured. 'Let alone becoming one.'

Sean and Maars looked at each other.

'But he *had* to become Muslim,' said Mum.

'Isn't it time for dinner?' I said, glancing at the attachment that needed to be proofed.

'I think you're right, Sofe,' replied Sean. 'Dinner that these lovely people are making for us while we're here,' he said, looking pointedly at his mum.

'Astaghfirullah,' muttered Chachi.

'And why couldn't she become Catholic?' said Mary.

'Because Islam is right,' said Mum.

'I think we're all still quite jet-lagged, aren't we?' I looked at Sean, appealing for him to do something.

'And what makes you think it's more right than Catholicism?' said Mary.

I stood up. 'To be fair, how much do any of us know about the other's religion? Non-spicy tandoori chicken?' I said, looking at Mary.

Mary stood up. 'No, thank you, Sofia. I've lost my appetite. I'll go to my room now.' With which she turned round and walked out, Sean looking back at me with a sorry stare as he went with her.

'Mum, what is *wrong* with you? "Islam is right?" I mean, honestly.'

'Soffoo, you have spent too much time in London. She said you should become Catholic,' said Chachi.

'No. No, she didn't,' I replied. 'She just made a very valid point, which we can discuss *when my husband is found*.'

'Haw hai, Soffoo, are you becoming Christian?' said Mum. 'This is the day I needed to live and see: the man I was going to marry walk away and my daughter becoming a Christian.'

Friday 13 December

3.50 p.m. I got a message from Hamida to come to the slums and had to get Jawad to drive me. It was so windy my hijab kept flying this way and that. I stepped up on to a mound, littered with bottles and rubbish, but it was quite foggy so I couldn't see too far ahead. I noticed a new wooden shack a few metres away from us.

'Conall helped to build that,' I said.

Jawad looked at me with a wry smile. 'Conall was a good man, but it is funny that these goray help us to build things, when they are the ones who created so much of our mess.'

'Is,' I said in semi-hysteria. 'Is, is, *is* a good man.'

He looked at me as if I'd gone mad. I walked further into the slum as Jawad followed me.

Several children were outdoors playing cricket, and they ran up to me as soon as they saw us. I got my purse out and gave them some money. This just brought out another bunch of kids who asked for more cash. I'd run out of money when Hammy came out of one of the slums, telling them off.

'We have to stop this dependency of theirs,' she explained to me.

There were the same old tin roofs and crooked doors, crammed together. I looked around and took in the mass of homelessness hazed in fog.

Hamida gave me a sorry look, holding something in her hands. *What's happened?* Then she handed it to me. It was a photograph of me and Conall – the one that had gone missing from the house.

'I don't . . . what does this mean?'

She rested a Doc Martinned foot on one of the mounds. 'Anything really. I found it on the ground. I guess most likely that he came here, someone stole his wallet, took his money and left anything they couldn't sell.' She glanced at the picture.

'So he has no money?'

'Potentially.'

'If he was mugged, then they would've taken his passport too?'

'Mugged, dropped his wallet, who knows? But it means he was here.'

I looked at the mass of tin roofs and litter, no closer to knowing where Conall was, just a picture in my hand of what used to be.

7.10 p.m. I'd just prayed when there was a knock at my door. It was Mary.

'Am I disturbing you?' she asked.

'No. Come in.' I got off the prayer mat as she took a seat on the chair in the corner.

'Perhaps things got slightly heated the other day,' she said.

'I'm sorry.'

She looked so small in that chair as she locked her fingers together.

'I know he always felt like a black sheep,' she said. 'Even when he was a boy. Sean now, he has an easier nature. Goes with the flow. But Conall . . . When he met Claire I thought she'd be good for him. A strong girl. I could tell she was able to put him in his place, but his father . . . God love him, but he's not the easiest of men – Conall and he never saw eye to eye. What I'm trying to say is, what we gave him wasn't enough. Then he came to London and found you, and . . . well, I'm not surprised Conall converted. He was always looking for peace.'

I felt my eyes fill with tears because I knew this. Maybe I should've tried harder to forgive him. 'I know,' I said.

'Oh, Sofia,' she said, her voice faltering. 'I pray he finds it.'

I looked at her, admiring her ability to stop her tears from falling, even though I could see her eyes were filled with them.

'Me too.'

Tuesday 17 December

8.45 a.m. Jawad came in early this morning to ask what I wanted for breakfast. I went into the kitchen with him and it was almost like old times. When I told him what everyone was saying about Conall being radicalised, Jawad, for perhaps the first time I'd seen, laughed. Actually laughed.

'Bhai saab?' He filled his glass with water from the cooler and took a sip. 'He always talked to me about Islam.'

'Did he?'

'He used to ask me why I didn't pray regularly, like my wife. She'd tell me because I'm lazy.'

Turns out Jawad and his wife do banter. Who'd have thought it? God, maybe I am elitist?

'I told him I didn't have my wife's faith. I tell her He knows what is in my heart so how can I hide it?'

Rather abruptly, he left the kitchen. I was left wondering what I was meant to have got out of that conversation when he came back and handed me a book. It was in Urdu, and my Urdu reading skills are rusty at best, so it took me a while to decipher what it said.

'*Allah-walay*.' I squinted at the print. '*Sufi eh* . . . what? Ah, *Karam*?'

He nodded.

I smiled, rather pleased with myself but at a loss as to where this was headed. To be honest, I didn't think now was the time to start exchanging literary tastes, you know. And then it came back to me.

'He gave you this,' I said. 'I remember.'

Jawad nodded.

I looked at the book again and flicked through the fine pages. Closing it and feeling the curves of the printed title, I handed it back to him.

'I started reading this. I still don't pray like my wife. I still don't pray very often, but something happens to my heart when I read it. It is moved.'

I took the book back and looked at the title again. *Sufi*. Sufi, Sufi, Sufi. I closed my eyes and thought of the conversations we used to have about Islam. How much of it he couldn't get his head round, the parts that made him question things, and the parts that moved him too. Just like Jawad had been moved. And then it hit me. I ran out of the kitchen and into Maars' bedroom.

'Wake up,' I exclaimed, shaking her. 'Maars, you have to wake up.'

'Sofe, man. I was up most of the night with Adam. Sorry, I missed fajr but I'll make it up tomorrow.'

'No, listen – I know where I have to go.'

She turned over, squinting at me. 'Where?'

'To *all* the Sufi mosques in Karachi.'

11.10 p.m. Everyone thinks I've gone mad. Mary looked very confused.

'*We* aren't Sufi,' explained Chachi, looking sniffy.

I had to tell Mary about this rather mystical offshoot of Islam. My family thinks it's a whim, because some of these places can seem ungodly, but as Hammy and I drove around I realised there's something else in these places too. There's calm and serenity. And I just know that it will be here that I find him.

Wednesday 18 December

10.50 p.m. Sean and I got into an argument in the middle of the street. As if we aren't conspicuous enough. He said I'm wasting my time and I said he's wasting his.

'Sofe, your problem is you won't face up to the fact that my brother's lost his head. Even now, after all you know about him and his past, you still think he's looking for some kind of absolution.'

I wasn't going to stand around and waste time with this bullshit. Hammy and I got into the car and drove round the city again, visiting shrine after shrine, because this is where he had to be. Except he wasn't. But I won't stop trying.

Thursday 19 December

5.40 p.m. Just as Hammy and I were about to leave Mary asked if she could come with us.

'I don't know who's right here,' she said. 'But I know there's good in my boy.'

I looked at her. 'You'll have to cover your legs and head.'

She nodded and we were on our way.

After visiting the same shrines, driving past the shop with pink and green writing that always seems to catch my eye, Mary asked if we could sit down and observe people in them. We went back to the shrine next to the shop.

'I've never seen anything like it,' she said, sitting cross-legged on the drab red carpet. She stared at a white-bearded man, draped in green clothes and a red and orange hat. He was hunched over, sipping tea, muttering prayers.

'Are there any churches here?' she asked.

Hammy gave me a look. Churches here are for local Christians, who are generally from poor households.

We got to the Holy Trinity Cathedral and drove through the black gates that opened up for us. Mary looked a little out of her comfort zone since, unfortunately, the Holy Communion taking place at that time was in Urdu. But she prayed while we sat in the back and waited for her. Everyone stared as she walked back towards us; they extended their hands and smiled and hugged her. She came out looking flushed and happy.

'That was quite an experience,' she said. 'What's it like during Christmas?'

'I guess we'll be coming back here then,' said Hammy under her breath.

Sunday 22 December

10.05 a.m. Nothing. Nothing at all. We go to the same places every day, ask the same questions to the same people and we still have nothing. Maybe I'm wrong. Maybe I should be helping Sean with whatever hunt he's on. Mary doesn't seem to know anything any more. She makes the most of things and comes with us. Mum is getting ready for a bloody wedding, which we're all being forced to attend tonight. Just because you're looking for a missing person in Pakistan, it's no excuse to not attend the wedding to which you've been invited.

Every so often, though, Mum will spread the prayer mat out and at the end of each prayer say a supplication for Conall. Mary caught her one day saying it out loud, but didn't understand the Urdu, which is just as well because Conall's name was cushioned between a prayer that Mary gets out of Mum's hair as soon as possible.

8 p.m. I hate weddings. I am overdressed and unimpressed.

11.30 p.m. We were all sitting in our chairs, with our respective plates of biryani, when none other than Uncle Mouch came over to say hello.

'Sit with us,' said Maars, handing Adam to him.

He hesitated as he stared at Mum and held on to the baby he couldn't exactly reject. The looks between Mum and Uncle Mouch were all a little PDA for my liking, but it was progress. Mary made room for him as she choked on the tandoori chicken. I got some crackers out of my bag for her.

Monday 23 December

1 p.m. Sakib called to ask how the search was going, sounding stressed out.

'Is it manic?' I asked.

He filled me in on what was happening and told me he'd emailed me the addresses of some suppliers to chase today at some point.

'Sorry, it's just got very busy, but it's fine. Just – I am looking forward to you coming back.'

Is this how Conall would feel about his work? Despite the chaos everywhere, this anchor holding it all together, preventing him and everything else from falling apart.

'Me too,' I said.

9.10 p.m. Failure of a day. Nothing. Again.

Tuesday 24 December

3.20 p.m. Mum, Maars and I felt bad that Mary and Sean were spending Christmas in Karachi of all places, so Maars managed to source a tree! Chachi thinks it's great because, well, it involves fairy lights and decorations. Adam is also rather partial to these lights. We even managed to get some presents together. We surprised both of them and Mary cried. But it's nice to see someone other than me cry, to be quite honest. Then we lit the tree and it was all very nice except for the gnawing feeling in my gut that something had happened to Conall. That so many days of searching have amounted to nothing might mean something terrible is in the offing.

10.30 p.m. Oh my actual God. Uncle Mouch came over today while Mum was out with Chachi. He said he wanted to speak to me. He's spoken to some officials and put out a search for Conall!

'I've spoken to Hamida's father but he is a stubborn man. I know people in the police and army and I've done what I can.' Then he frowned. 'But you must stop visiting these shrines and churches, Beta,' he said. 'A lot of troubles in Karachi, and shrines are a big target as well as churches. These people don't care who they kill.'

'I can't stay at home and do nothing,' I said.

'Beta, I am doing everything now. You don't worry. And please, don't tell your mama,' he said. 'How is she?'

'She's fine,' I said.

He nodded and made me promise I'd stay in the house.

When I went to bed, I couldn't help feeling that something just wasn't right. That there was something round the corner, except I didn't know what.

Wednesday 25 December

9.35 a.m. I've been sitting in front of the lit Christmas tree for an hour and a half now. Jawad came in and asked if I was converting to Christianity, and warned me about the pain it'd cause my mother. Sigh.

Police are out patrolling the streets because they say a riot's going to break out. Apparently nobody cares that it's Christmas.

10.40 a.m. Mary came and sat next to me, handing me a small box. 'I know you don't celebrate Christmas, but, I just thought. Well: see for yourself.'

When I opened it, it was a necklace – the type that you open up and there's a picture in it. I used to love these when I was a child. To be honest, I'm a bit old for that kind of sentimentality, but when I opened it there was no picture. It was a calligraphy of Allah's name in Arabic. I looked at her.

'Well, now.' She patted me on the hand.

I got up and gave her a gift Mum and I had wrapped a few nights ago. She opened it, looking at the black needlework on the emerald green shawl.

'That's a beautiful colour,' she said.

I looked at it for a moment. 'Maybe we should've got something that looked less like a Christmas tree?'

She shook her head and looked at the tree again. 'What will you do? When we find him?' she asked.

I wondered whether to correct her 'when' to 'if', but it is Christmas and I thought I'd not be too Grinch-like.

I was going to divorce him, that's what. But something in me wavered – unable to bring the words out. I shrugged. Maybe I'm still waiting for that gut feeling Maars was telling me about. This time, when it comes, I'll not follow it with doubt – I'll simply follow it through.

12 p.m. Oh my God. Uncle Mouch just called saying that someone apparently saw a white man fitting Conall's description at the shrine in the Abdullah Shah Ghazi shrine. He said I have to stay home because there are police everywhere as a riot's broken out. But I couldn't just sit there and do nothing! I looked for Jawad to drive me but couldn't find him, so I grabbed the car keys. I'm going to this place, come hell, high water or riot.

1.10 p.m. Fuck. Stuck in car. People in streets, throwing stones at police. Police with batons, hitting people. Why the hell did I come out here??

5.55 p.m. Thanks to God for GPS, but not so much for Pakistani driving. I managed to get out of the traffic as people surged in the opposite direction. The road leading to the shrine was blocked, so I got out of the car, except my crappy sense of direction meant I couldn't quite recall which way to go. It wasn't exactly the stop-to-ask-directions type of atmosphere. People were shouting, hurling things at each other. One car caught fire and I prayed that Chachi's car wouldn't meet the same fate because I really didn't need to deal with that on top of everything else.

At that moment I realised that I should've perhaps left a note to someone. The rest happened so suddenly, all thoughts of telling someone where I was went out of the proverbial window. I was pushed on to the floor and couldn't get up. For a minute I thought, *this is how I'm going to die.* People lunged over me, stepping on me, until someone grabbed my hand and helped me up. By the time I looked up they were already gone. It was shove-or-be-shoved as I elbowed past the stampede. Then I saw the shop with the pink and green sign. I was close to the shrine. I followed the road and turned right on to the pathway. There it was. Except people were being evacuated from it.

I asked a police officer what was happening and he said there was a bomb blast in another shrine just fifteen minutes away from here, so they're evacuating all religious buildings. In the foray all I could do was look for anyone that looked like Conall.

'Have you seen a white man here?' I asked the officer. But he ignored me as he led a line of people out of the vicinity.

I had to push past people, like salmon in a stream of chaos, forcing my way towards the shrine. I squinted into the distance, seeing a figure emerge; he had a beard and was dressed all in white. Someone bumped into my shoulder as I stumbled towards the entrance. It *had* to be him. His back was now turned and he was bending over. Was he praying? Whoever it was, was clearly bloody mad. I got to the steps, the face hidden from view.

'Madam, you can't go in there,' said one of the police officers.

'Let me through,' I said, angling my head, trying to see his face – he looked a lot slimmer than Conall. 'There's someone in there.'

'*Get back,*' he said.

'I'm *British*,' I exclaimed, wishing I could wave my passport in his face. (Arrogance at its peak, but this was no time for niceties.)

'Conall,' I shouted. Again and again, over the din of the masses. Until the man finally turned round. His eyes settled on me, as if he didn't know who I was. Then he looked confused.

'What the hell are you doing?' I shouted. 'Get out from there.' I grabbed the police officer's arm. 'Why aren't you getting him out of there?'

He shouted out across to his colleague about a group of boys who were smashing the windows of a car. With which he and some others blocking the way ran towards them. I ran into the shrine.

'Sofe, what are you doing here?'

'What are *you* doing here? They're blowing up places left, right and centre. We have to go.'

'I'm not leaving this man.'

I looked down to see an old man who'd fallen over, unable to get up.

'OK, OK. I have a car not too far from here. We can both help him.'

We picked him up. Well, Conall picked him up and I tried to help.

'Wait here,' I said as I ran towards the car, got in, revved the engine and shot down towards the shrine. Conall put him in the back, got in the front, and I sped my way to the nearest hospital.

He held on to the dashboard because, let's face it, my driving isn't perhaps the smoothest.

'Are you OK, Uncle?' I asked the man in the back. He was clutching his stomach.

'Maybe I should take the wheel,' said Conall.

I couldn't speak. In all the chaos there was no time to think about anything but finding him. Now, he was next to me and I was so angry I could've pushed him out of the car.

We got to the hospital and sat in the waiting area in silence for the most part. I texted Sean to let him know I'd found Conall and that we'd be home soon.

After a while, Conall leaned forward, his head drooping so low I thought maybe he'd fallen asleep, when he asked: 'What were you doing there?'

I had my head in my hands. All the day's activities had made me nauseous and I thought I might throw up.

'Half the time you don't know where first gear is,' he said. 'Something could've happened to you.'

I looked at him in disbelief. '*You*,' I said, pushing him, forcing him to look up at me. '*You* happened to me. You and your fucking running-away act.'

He watched me, leaning back.

'I could just fucking kill you right now.'

'Madam, please keep your voice down,' said a nurse who'd walked up to us.

'Do you know what it's been like? Do you know what it's like, emailing your husband for a divorce, waiting for him and then finding out he's decided to do a runner – *again*.'

'Divorce?'

Then I ran out of energy. 'I didn't think you were someone who ran. Who *would* run. Again. I mean, what the hell were you thinking?'

He looked away, resting the palm of his hands on his eyes, and I wanted to pull him into a hug. I will never understand this urge I have to hold him, even when I'm angry at him. Even when I'm *right* to be angry with him.

'I wasn't,' he said. 'I know, Sofe. I didn't think of anyone.' He looked around the hospital. 'I've gone about everything the wrong way . . . I just didn't know what I was doing any more, you know? What was the point, like? Claire – she'd already done such a great job bringing up Eamonn that I wondered what I was even doing there? Wasn't I just ruining things?'

He turned towards me and I looked into his eyes, trying to catch him out in a lie. But they are the same eyes – and they'll always end up settling something within me, no matter how bloody angry I am.

'Right.' I stared at my hands, dirty and scratched. I realised I must look a mess. I noticed people's calves and shoes, walking past in different directions.

'You didn't think to tell someone where you were.' I shook my head.

I could feel his eyes still on me. 'Sometimes I think it's easier for people when I'm not around.'

'That's not for you to decide.'

We both sat, watching the chaos of the hospital unfolding before our eyes.

'I'm not like you, Sofe. I've searched for contentment my whole life and never found it. It's like you're watching the piece of this puzzle, floating over your head, and you know it's the piece to make the puzzle complete, but you can't quite grasp it.'

'And now you've grasped it?'

He leaned forward, clasping his hands. 'All I know is that I can't fail my son again.'

I don't know why tears surfaced my eyes.

'I have so many wrongs to right.'

'Sir, madam?'

The doctor stood in front of us and said the man was stable and that they'd found an ID card, so his family were on the way.

'Suppose we should go,' I said.

He nodded as we walked towards the car again, got in and drove back to Chachi's. As we reached the gate, I said, 'Oh, by the way. Sean thinks you're a fundo now.'

Before he could say anything the gate had opened and the whole posse was waiting there: Maars, smiling in relief as she held Adam, Mum already running towards the car as Mary clutched Sean's arm.

9.10 p.m. Sean has been speaking to Conall for the past two hours asking him various questions, most prominent of which being whether Conall thinks the West is evil. Conall slapped the side of his head. Every time I looked at him, a deep kind of sadness settled in me and I wasn't sure why. Maybe it was still that so much felt unsettled.

'Your beti didn't listen to me, Mehnaz.' Uncle Mouch came striding through the door, looking rather angry. That's when Mum discovered that he'd been helping to find Conall these past few days. She made room for him to sit down on the sofa.

'You boys. You'll be the death of me,' said Mary, holding on to Conall's face. I love that face. 'You'll never believe it but I think I might be getting used to spicy food,' she added.

Mum looked at me and mouthed, 'Thanks to God.'

Mary's phone rang and she handed it to Conall. 'It's your father.'

Conall looked over at me and smiled. You can't depend on your gut when your heart feels this way.

Thursday 26 December

12.35 p.m. Ha! My mum's engaged again! Apparently it takes a brave girl to do what I did and Uncle Mouch's daughter could stand to learn a few things from her new stepsister. I decided not to point out that bravery and stupidity are not the same thing because let's take the compliments when we can.

'We are not living life for our children any more,' said Mum.

I thought of Dad and felt a pang for him. I always believed she was the woman he loved and wanted to marry, and to see Mum like this with someone else felt like losing something. But she looked happy. I'd gladly lose a thousand things to see her that happy.

So, they're to be married in Tooba Mosque this Saturday with little ceremony. Maars Skyped Auntie Reena to tell her the news.

'Reena,' said Mum, leaning into the screen, 'if I can get another husband, you can get more budgies.'

Auntie Reena said she didn't need budgies because she'd moved on to taking driving lessons. 'Mehnaz. We will have a wedding party for you when you come back.'

And I'd been so sure the following year would be one of no more wedding parties.

6.20 p.m. I was on the rooftop when Conall came and joined me.

'I like it here just before the sun sets,' I said.

He looked out on to the horizon.

'What did your dad say?' I asked.

He looked at the ground. 'We only spoke for a few minutes. He wanted to know if Ma was OK and said me and Sean better get her back to Kilkee safely.'

He turned to face me.

'You know I didn't mean it,' he said. 'That I shouldn't have married you. What I meant was that I shouldn't have hurt you – in my head, marrying you caused you pain.' He held my face, brushing away a strand of my hair, lowering his voice. 'If I could do it all again I'd . . . Well, you know what I'd do differently. And I know, if I hadn't married you I wouldn't be here now.'

'Where's that?'

He looked into my eyes, and I think for the first time I could read his look – it was gratitude.

'So what? Are you Sufi now?' I asked when he didn't answer.

He smiled. 'Bet you didn't think you'd marry a cliché?'

I laughed.

'It's very . . .'

'Peaceful?' I offered.

He nodded. It's all I wanted for him, but even so, I couldn't help the dull pain that settled itself in my chest. He pulled me closer. I really do love his arms.

'I don't have any right to ask anything of you, Sofe. But you know I want you to come back to Ireland with me.'

I looked away and thought of everything that waited for me in London; namely Avaaz. Whatever choice you make in life, you will always have to give something up. But there it was: the gut. Nudging me towards what I should do.

'Thank you,' he said, kissing me on the forehead.

'For?'

'Getting on that plane.'

11.25 p.m. I watched him sleep – his chest rising and falling – listening to the familiar beat of his heart.

'You know I'm awake,' he said.

I laughed as he smiled, his eyes still closed. I tightened my arms round his waist, because you hold on to the things you love for as long as possible.

Saturday 28 December

3.25 p.m. Maars was changing Adam's nappy as Mum sat on the chair and I applied blusher on her cheeks, finally getting her ready for her wedding. She closed her eyes, as I put mascara on her lashes. I saw Maars wipe something from her eye.

'How do you make the right choice?' I asked.

'Have you prayed Istikhara?' asked Maars.

I nodded.

'Beta,' said Mum. 'Life without a husband I think can be very bore sometimes. But what if he dies?'

'Thanks, Mum.'

'O-ho,' she said, opening her eyes. 'How do you know what might happen? We all might die tomorrow.'

'Isn't your gran a cheerful one on her wedding day?' said Maars to Adam.

Mum simply sighed, closing her eyes, ready for the mascara again. 'All I'm saying is you have to think: if we all die tomorrow, what will we leave behind.'

Maars picked Adam up and put him on the bed with his toy giraffe. She walked over with red lipstick in her hands and applied some to Mum's lips.

'What did Baba leave behind?' she asked, her voice low.

Mum paused. 'You two.'

I wish I could stop crying at everything.

'One year ago, Soffoo, I probably would have told you to go with Conall – he is your husband, na. Forgiveness is best. Even some weeks ago I would have said the same.'

'I think I have forgiven him,' I said.

'Of course you have. Nice girl you are, really. Just a very big mouth you have.'

'What's your point, Mum?' asked Maars.

'Tst, o-ho.' Mum opened her eyes. 'I don't have a point. Flip a coin.'

'I'm not flipping a coin for my future, Mum,' I replied.

But before she could say anything Maars had already got a ten pence piece out from her purse. 'Tails you go to Ireland with Conall; heads your publishing company.'

'What, no –'

But she'd already flipped it and there she was: my sister with the answer to my future, clasped in her hands.

'Well,' I said, my heart beating rather fast. 'What is it?'

She lifted her hand. 'Tails.'

'Oh.'

'See?' said Mum, standing up and putting her hands on my face. 'You already know what you want.'

9.20 p.m. 'Sofe,' said Sean as we sat in a restaurant after Mum and Uncle Mouch's nikkah ceremony. 'I think you're right. I don't think Conall's radicalised.'

'No shit, Sean.'

Hamida laughed for perhaps the third time I've known her.

'I was just so sure,' he added, wagging a kebab in the air as he thought about it, which was a little distracting.

'It's very odd, though,' he added.

'What? Going on about religion?'

'Yeah,' he said.

A group of transvestites started singing and clapping at the bride and groom. Uncle Mouch got out some money and gave it to them.

'Hai hai,' said one, coming over to Sean and me, 'goray rang ka zamana kabhi hoga na purana –'

I started laughing.

'What's he . . . she saying?'

'They're regaling about the fact that you're white. You've pulled.'

Sean nodded at them in satisfaction. I got up and walked over to the mosque while everyone carried on with their food. Conall was already there, waiting for me.

'Are you sure?' he said, holding my hands.

I wanted to cry because of all the memories we wouldn't make in London. So many of them would remain here, static in a place that was never home. We stood outside Tooba Mosque, about to go in to get a divorce, just as my mum celebrated her marriage.

'You know what it'll mean, getting divorced?' he said.

'What?'

'No chance of you and me getting married again until you marry someone else.'

I looked at him, confused. What was he talking about? And then it dawned on me . . .

'Oh shit. You're right.'

I'd completely forgotten about that rule – once you've divorced someone you can't marry them again unless you've married someone else in between. He looked at me, seriously, my heart feeling like there was a two-tonne truck weighing on it.

'Speaking of,' he added. 'You'll never guess who Sean told me he'd come across on Tinder?'

'Who?' I asked, wondering if one of the girls had decided to set up a profile for me. It sounded so much like something I'd do, you have to wonder.

'Suj.'

Hain? 'Shut the hell up.'

He smiled and I looked into the distance, thinking of all of life's bloody ironies.

'I suppose we'd better get on with life then,' I said.

He clenched his jaw, his grip tightening around my hand.

'Sofe?'

'Yes?'

He looked at me. 'Nothing.'

'What?'

'It could be a long life, you know.'

'It could.' I stepped closer him. 'So?'

'So,' he said, putting his arm round me for perhaps the last time. 'I promise you – it's not over yet.'

I never know what those words really mean – whether they're just there to comfort a person, make them think that there is more than this, that you will return to the people who matter the most – doesn't matter if it's true or not. Or whether it's prophetic. I thought of Mum's life with Dad and now the life she'll make with Uncle Mouch. *You will always be with the people you are meant to be with.* The heaviness lifted a little. I don't know whether it makes me a fool or not, but it certainly gives me hope.

9.30 p.m.

From Sakib: Hi. Really glad you've found Conall. What happens now?

To Sakib: I'm coming home.

Acknowledgements

As my agent said: *every author hates writing their second book*, so I have many people to thank for making it easier.

Firstly, my agent, Nelle Andrew, who is always ready on the phone to talk through my latest panic about wanting to make a huge plot overhaul, and her husband, Jack Davy, who has become such a trusted reader. My unflappable editor, Joel Richardson, whose dedication to SOFIA KHAN has been unwavering and who even managed to stay calm when I accidentally sent him the first draft of the book. Cheers for not tearing up our contract after that.

Thank you to everyone at Bonnier for their hard work, including Claire Johnson-Creek, Emily Burns and Bec Farrell. Particularly Alex Allden for the beautiful cover design.

Also, team Midas for the work they did on the first book, especially Eve Wersocki.

Thank you, as always, to my Cornerstones family, even though I've now left them: Helen Bryant, Dionne Pemberton, Alex Hammond and Nicola Doherty for her editorial input. Special thanks to Helen who never bores of our Skype meetings and is always on hand to help me be a better writer. I'm also very grateful to Nafeesa Yousuf for her love and support.

Huge gratitude to Team Twenty7 authors whose secret thread on Twitter keeps me sane, entertained and makes me feel incredibly lucky to be in the company of such talented, wonderful human beings.

Also, thanks to my brown-writer team: Alex Caan, Abir Mukherjee, Vaseem Khan and Amit Dhand for helping me to keep it real by discussing things like the price of fish cakes.

And of course, thank you to the usual suspects: Mum, Nadia Malik, Clara Nelson, Sadaf Sethi, Jas Kundi, Amber Ahmed, Shai Chishty and Kristel Pous. I don't know if I can properly express how much love there is for all of you in my rather compact heart but I have in mind to dedicate one book to each of you, so let's hope I don't run out of ideas. Or that you don't run out on me.

I feel I should mention Zayyan and Saffah – my nephew and niece – even though they don't help me write so much as hinder it. But they are the light of my life and so I am grateful for that.

A huge and warm thank you to all readers of the first SOFIA KHAN book, whose excitement rubbed off on me when I needed it most. You have no idea how important it's been.

Lastly, of course, thanks to God for all of the above.

Read on for an exclusive letter from Ayisha Malik and a chance to join her Readers Club . . .

Dear Reader,

The character, Sofia Khan, came to me in what seemed to be, at the time, a stroke of literary lightning. This was it – I was going to write a Muslim *Bridget Jones*. Of course, it only seemed like lightning because when I really thought about it, my own dating life – and those of my friends – read like a Helen Fielding novel with a religious twist. Sofia Khan was the embodiment of the Muslim women I know and admire, whose travails of balancing professionalism, love, family and faith were both absurd and painfully real. Emphasis on the painfully.

Truth be told, it didn't feel like the most imaginative idea. But I played a safe game and I wrote what I knew; but what I knew, I realised, many people didn't. The book didn't begin with an agenda to educate people on the lives of modern Muslim women, and nor did it end with that, but you can't live in the world and not think about the unique opportunity you're being given when telling your side of the story. And what better way to temper hard-hitting subjects like racism and identity than in a novel where, essentially, everyone is a target for comedy?

As Sofia developed, along with the rather large cast of characters, things happened in the real world – as they inevitably do – only one of which was that we saw the rise of Isis. You'd think that this fact and writing would be quite unrelated, but as an author who also happens to be Muslim you can't divorce these things, because the need to be understood grows. We are each fighting for our place in the world, but I feel that the likes of Sofia have to fight that little bit harder. You could say that if there was any agenda – apart from telling a story – it was to normalise being Muslim.

So, while *Sofia Khan is Not Obliged* was dubbed a rom-com, to me it was really a story of a struggle; the internal one, pitted against the external one, which is why I knew, from the beginning, who Sofia would end up with (and it was always going to be a happy ending, because there is enough misery in the world, thank you). But the struggle never ends, and although I felt I needed a break from Sofia, I also knew that I wanted to tackle the idea of a happily ever after (because happy endings are all good and well, but let's have a bit of reality too.) Her story became less about her place in the world, but her place in a marriage. Because how well do you really know a person? And what does love, after all, have to do with it?

After two books – and quite a lot of novel-based drama – I'm ready to move on from Sofia Khan for now. I'm very excited about my next book with Bonnier Zaffre about a Muslim couple, living in the English Village, Babbel's End. The husband, Bilal Hasham, is left with a life – and village – altering bequest from his dying mother: to build a mosque in Babbel's End. After eight years of living in the community and being an integral part of their daily goings-on, how is he going to reveal his plan to his friends in the village? And, more importantly, how will a minaret look wedged between the local church and Life Art gallery? This is a story that's been in my head for over a year and a half and I can't wait to share it with my readers.

If you would like to hear more from me about Sofia Khan and my future books, you can email me at ayisha.malik@myreadersclub.co.uk where you can join the Ayisha Malik Readers Club. It only takes a moment, there is no catch and new members will automatically receive an exclusive short story. Your data is private and confidential and will never be passed on to a third party and I promise that I will only be in touch now and again with news about my books. If you want to unsubscribe, you can of course do that at any time.

In addition, if you would like to be involved and spread the word about my books, you can review *Sofia Khan is Not Obliged* and *The Other Half of Happiness* on Amazon, GoodReads, any other e-store, on your own blogs and social media accounts, or, of course, by dropping Sofia Khan casually into conversation if you liked the book. You'll help other readers if you share your thoughts and you will help me too: you have no idea how much authors can learn from well thought out reviews.

But for now, thanks again for reading and for your interest in Sofia Khan and her tumultuous world. I'm incredibly lucky to have such dedicated and intelligent readers.

With my best wishes,
Ayisha

Reading Group Questions

- How important do you think it is to learn everything about your partner before marriage?
- How do you feel about the title? What do you think *The Other Half of Happiness* means?
- How important do you think it is to share your religious beliefs with your partner?
- To what extent does the support from in-laws and family members affect a marriage? In what ways is this relevant to Sofia and Conall's marriage?
- What do you make of the ending? Do you think Sofia made the right choice?
- Could you have forgiven Conall for keeping that secret?
- If you've read *Sofia Khan is Not Obliged,* how did you feel about the way Sofia and Conall ended up?
- In what ways do the themes in *The Other Half of Happiness* differ to those in *Sofia Khan is Not Obliged.* Why do you think that is?

Want to join the conversation? Let us know what you thought of the book on Twitter using #SofiaKhan

Find out where it all began . . .

SOFIA KHAN IS NOT OBLIGED

'Brilliant idea! Excellent! Muslim dating? Well, I had no idea you were allowed to date.' He heaved towards me and looked at me sympathetically.
'Are your parents disappointed?'

When her sort-of-boyfriend/possible-marriage-partner-to-be proves a little too close to his parents, Sofia Khan is ready to renounce men for good. Or at least she was, until her boss persuades her to write a tell-all exposé on the Muslim dating scene.

As her woes become her work, Sofia must lean on the support of her brilliant friends, baffled colleagues and baffling parents as she seeks stories for her book.

But in the marriage-crazy relatives, racist tube passengers and polygamy-inclined friends, could there be a lingering possibility that she might just be falling in love . . . ?

Available in paperback, ebook and audiobook now.